THE MOONSTONERS

Also by
Barbara J. Dzikowski
Searching for Lincoln's Ghost

THE MOONSTONERS

Barbara J. Dzikowski

WIARA BOOKS

ISBN: 978-0-9840305-3-8 (print)
ISBN: 978-0-9840305-4-5 (ebook)
Library of Congress Control Number: 2019901159

To my family,

always, all ways,

and the One who blessed me with them

These three remain:
faith, hope, and love.
But the greatest of these is love.

1 Corinthians 13:13

THE
MOONSTONERS

PART ONE:

THE SHADES OF MOONSTONE

NOVEMBER 1972
NOËL

THERE it stood on the horizon of the Lake Michigan shore, a dusty gem called the Moonstone Inn. As soon as Noël Trudeau caught sight of it from the car window, she thought of the perfect name for them: she would call them *moonstoners*.

She and her youngest brother, Adam, were moonstoners. And Leon and Rick Ziemny. The Chavises, too.

To become a moonstoner was a complicated process, both a cosmic and personal one. It took a transformation, and the transformation was neither easy nor evident. Moonstoners were born in the shadow of a restless moon, not the light of the sun, during complicated, unsettling times. From there, they were flushed into stormy childhood waters, where they were pummeled and polished into various opalescent shades.

After stopping at the office of the Moonstone Inn, he drove her away to the Shell station in town, where a handwritten sign had directed them to register. Noël remained in the car, hugging her coat around her as she watched him through the filthy glass of the gas station. The chill of impending winter was in the air, the season of her deepest reflections. Despite the anticipation of what lie ahead for the two of them, she was distracted by the thought of her brother. What had led him to do it? How far back had it started?

She already knew the answers full well. The pummeling that had shaped both her and Adam into moonstoners had begun with a family secret back in Hyssop, Louisiana, when she was seven and Adam only five—a secret so immense that it couldn't help but set off the chain of tragedies that had followed, like the finger that struck the first domino.

She leaned back against the seat, remembering.

She had no idea where they were heading in the middle of that hot August night back in 1953. She only knew that they were running away from Hyssop, as far and fast as they could. Their daddy, Jack Trudeau, was crazed behind the wheel, their mama, Lily, vacant-eyed beside him. Nine-year-old Bo, six-year-old Steve, and Noël crouched terrified in the backseat, while Adam in the wayback of the station wagon pretended he was a doctor on a TV Western. Their clothes, some essentials, and just one of her mother's oil paintings (the best one) were heaped in the back with Adam or tied haphazardly on the roof, thumping and bumping overhead as they raced down unknown roads hour after hour in the pitch-blackness. Everything else—including Amelia Rosalie, the dolly she ached for—was left behind. One thing was clear: They were never going back to Hyssop.

It was midafternoon when they had stumbled into a quiet town called Willow, Ohio. Noël had sat up in enchantment as she peered out the window from the backseat; never before had she seen so many weeping willow trees, one right after another, sashaying in the breeze like the hand of God in motion. Her father had stopped the car suddenly in front of a robin's-egg-blue-shingled house with white wicker furniture on the porch and a sign out front that read: HARLEY WHARTON, MD. "We can trust a doctor, don't you think?" her father asked. When the kindly old doctor came out to the car and saw how many of them there were, he must've taken pity, for he helped them find a home to rent.

Four months later, on a bone-chilling Christmas Eve, Dr. Wharton had delivered her mama's last baby while Noël and her brothers hovered near the open bedroom door, standing in a row in ascending heights like little human stair-steps, the shadows bobbing on their faces as Doc maneuvered in front of the lone lamp at the bedside. Their father ushered them into the living room with him to wait it out, but Noël managed to sneak back into the bedroom just in time to see the emergence of a frightening, bloody blob.

Doc tried to make it cry, yet all Noël heard was the *tick-tick-tick* of the clock on the wall, and then her mother's unforgettable howl, the sound a wild animal might make as it's eaten alive.

Noël watched Doc disappear with the dead baby into the bathroom, and when he came out, it was dressed in white satin, transformed into something angelic. He rested it gently against her mother's chest, where she'd christened it with a name before passing out into permanent oblivion. *Monroe.* Another brother. It was the last word Noël would ever hear her speak.

"Can I hold Monroe?" Noël whispered.

She feared he'd be furious to see her there, but he merely raised his index finger to his lips to shush her, confirming that her presence was their secret.

He needn't worry; she knew how to keep secrets. Noël knew all kinds of them that her brothers didn't have one clue about; secrets she had told herself she would take to her grave, even if she lived to be two hundred.

Surrendering Monroe back to Doc, she had watched as he folded him inside a blanket, head and all, and carried him right past her grief-stricken father and the boys, directly to Green's Funeral Parlor.

≈≈

He returned to the car, holding up the room key—room number 4—and informed her they were going to be the only guests at the Moonstone Inn. It was late November, too far off-season for company. Sitting alone on a high plain surrounded by acres of woods and sand, the motel was completely isolated, no one or nothing around except the icy waters of Lake Michigan across the narrow street, rippling against the jagged rocks on the shoreline.

Noël felt as if they had fallen through some ineffable portal, a portal into a place where lost dreams were scattered along the deserted beach like seashells. Among them were the dreams of the 1960s, since an inordinate number of her generation—the ones born between World War II and the 1950s—were also moonstoners, spawned during a contradictory time when the righteous fight to stamp out Hitler's evil had drifted into dangerous slumber. Raised to be seen and not heard, their collective voice grew into a roar that had nearly, but not quite, changed the world.

Moonstoners were the discontents, the dreamers, the seekers of a newer world. Moonstoners were the ones who were broken by love, yet still they loved too much.

ONE

NOVEMBER 22, 1963
NOËL

THE year 1963 started out badly for Noël and her family; the unraveling of their secrets had begun. In the springtime, Aunt Clarissa put a gun to her own head, becoming the only suicide in Willow's history. And now there was this—Noël's second doctor's appointment in less than a week.

She tried to quell her anxious thoughts as she watched her father pour Rice Krispies haphazardly across five bowls, much of the cereal falling to the kitchen counter, a strand of his Clark Gable–like hair falling over one eye. Her brothers sat around the table. Bo was dressed in his Texaco uniform with the red star patch, exchanging playful barbs with Steve, while Adam's nose was stuck in a book, as usual. Noël glanced at the cover: *To Kill a Mockingbird*; his latest assignment for English class.

This time, she wouldn't have to undress or sit up high on the cold examining table because Dr. Wharton had already taken all the tests he needed. Today was the time for results. Of course, she'd have to skip school again in order to make the appointment, which meant leaving the house along with Steve and Adam, carrying an armload of books as they trekked to Woodrow Wilson High, then coming up with some excuse to turn around again, like forgetting her homework.

Was lying the same thing as keeping a secret? She tried to convince herself that it was.

"Take this to your mother and help her with it." Dad shoved a bowl across the counter toward her.

Leaving her cereal untouched, she got up from the table and headed into the living room where her mother sat on the sofa, a blanket over her knees, her mouth opening and closing soundlessly like a fish. Noël bent down to kiss her on the cheek, knowing there'd be no response, before retrieving the black TV tray with the big gold flowers on it, folded in the corner beside Aunt Clarry's identical tray.

Auntie used to dote on their mother every morning before breakfast—poufing her black hair up to perfection, clasping a strand of pearls around her neck, applying berry-red lipstick—anything she could to restore Mama's former dignity. Noël tried her best to continue the meticulous care, but it was difficult to manage during the school week, and Mrs. Neal, the neighbor lady her father employed to watch their mother during the day, made it clear she wasn't a nursemaid. So there Mama sat, still dressed in stained pajamas, her stringy hair flat against her pale cheeks. Not one glimmer of life left in her eyes. Even Aunt Clarry couldn't do anything to fix that.

"I'm sorry, Mama," she said, spooning the first mouthful between her mother's flapping lips. "Tomorrow morning, I'll do your hair."

≈≈

As Noël waited in Dr. Wharton's basement office, she twisted a coil of her raven hair round and round her index finger. Finally, Doc opened the door, his face clouded in distress.

Bracing for the blow she knew he was about to deliver, she fixated on the Currier & Ives calendar depicting a sleigh full of happy people being pulled through falling snow by a majestic horse. She loved snow. Snow covered up ugly things and made the world feel fresh and new again.

But there was no snow today. The unseasonably hot sun streamed through the lone window near the ceiling.

"I'm afraid I have some bad news, sweetie." His eyes softened as he perched on a rolling stool and wheeled closer. "You're pregnant."

She flinched, though it came as no surprise. She'd already missed two periods and threw up breakfast five days in a row. Still, the sound of it—cold, harsh, and certain amid the sanitized smells of the examining room—stung like a slap across the face. Dr. Wharton reached into the pocket of his white coat and handed her a handkerchief, a careworn smile deepening the lines around his eyes.

His nonjudgmental demeanor was a shot of blessed relief. As far as she knew, she held the distinct dishonor of being the only teenager in Willow to ever get pregnant. She squeezed his handkerchief between her fingers. "What do I do now?" Her voice came out like a little squeak from a deep, dark well.

Doc rubbed his fingers over his chin. "Well, for starters, tell your young man. I assume it's David Ketchfield?"

Now the tears came—flooding her eyes, blurring the room as she flashed back to that first night in the Oldsmobile: David's brutal, invasive hands. The torn pink dress she wore. Her own blood soaking the back seat of his father's car, and David rifling through the trunk to find something to sop it up. "It's a good thing they're vinyl," he kept repeating as he wiped the seats clean with a rag that smelled of turpentine.

"The Ketchfields are a fine family," Doc said. "I'm sure David will do the right thing."

She didn't respond. It's not like she hadn't already turned it over and over again in her head. Marriage seemed to be the only way out, she knew that, and yet it was a solution she abhorred.

"There are other options, Noël."

She gazed at him without focus. She knew her other options all right. Like manipulating a coat hanger or shooting drain cleaner into her vagina. But she couldn't do it. Her baby was a defenseless victim, a part of own heartbeat now, and the two of them were in this mess together.

"It might seem like the end of the world, but it's not. You're only seventeen. You're a beautiful young lady with your whole life ahead of you."

Beautiful? Why was that the only thing anyone ever said about her? Noël hated that she was beautiful in the same way her mother had been—commanding attention when all she really wanted was to be invisible. The boys in school had noticed her long ago. It petrified her when they stared at her as if she was worth something. If they got to know her on the inside, they would run for the hills. So, she kept her distance. Thankfully, her brothers were a wall around her when she needed them to be.

David Ketchfield had been different. Big and buoyant like an Old English sheepdog, he was the star football player, who would not take no for an answer, and he'd worn her down. He had big dreams, mostly about starting his own plumbing company after graduation, insistent that she'd be a part of them. After Auntie Clarry shot herself, Noël clung to him like a life raft. He kept her insulated, even from her friends. David had become her wall.

"There's always adoption. I can arrange a place for you to go." Doc's words sounded hazy, far away.

The night in the Oldsmobile had come without warning. Afterward, she couldn't stand to look at David, but it was too late. In a blink, he'd shifted from Jekyll to Hyde. She was damaged goods now, he told her, ruined for any other boy. Nearly every time he'd taken her out since then, regardless of the innocent start at the movies or the soda fountain in the back of Rose's Drugstore where he acted the perfect gentleman, it ended the same way—despite her protests, despite her cries, despite even stabbing into his flesh one night with the sharp end of her keychain. The mornings after in math class, she would catch him mooning at Janie Sutton, still sweet and unsullied in her cashmere sweaters.

No, she hadn't told her father, her brothers, or any living soul what was going on. When she returned from her dates, she would lock herself in the bathroom, running her hairdryer at full blast so they couldn't hear her sobbing, convinced that the whole thing was somehow her own fault. She already knew what her father would say: *People get what they deserve.*

"Noël? Are you listening?"

She nodded, though she hadn't heard a word.

"Bring your dad in here, and we'll have a long talk," Dr. Wharton said, probably repeated. "Together, I promise you, we'll figure this thing out."

Shutting the office door behind her in a fog, Noël stepped outside. The bright sun made her squint; it mocked her, shined a light on her shame. It was only ten-thirty, and though she'd intended to go back to school, how could she now? She couldn't go back home either. She supposed she could tell Mrs. Neal that she was feeling sick, which was half-true, but she wasn't up to enduring her endless chatter all day long.

Dried leaves crackled, brittle beneath her saddle shoes, as she passed the familiar row of downtown businesses—the Turning

Point Tavern, Kolby's Market, Harvey's Five and Dime. Bertha Olmstead passed her by on the street, her eyes narrowing at the sight of Noël skipping school. Thank heavens, Mrs. Olmstead was alone; not a soul nearby. Ever since Aunt Clarry's funeral, whenever she caught sight of a Trudeau, she'd start whispering behind their backs to anyone within earshot, sometimes in hushed tones, sometimes intentionally loud enough for them to overhear. "That woman should have been buried off by herself, where a suicide ought to be," she'd said during one of her louder outbursts. "Not among decent, God-fearing people."

Noël kept on walking, calculating. Dr. Wharton told her she was just over two months pregnant. That meant the baby would arrive in late May or early June, right around graduation. She and David were seniors, so close to finishing, but now she'd have to drop out before she started showing. No graduation. No prom dress. She would miss English class the most. Miss Perkins kept telling her that she had a real knack for creative writing and encouraged her to cultivate her talent.

Now all of that was gone in a poof. How was she supposed to hide her condition in a town the size of Willow? What would her brothers say? Her father's reaction scared her most of all. There was no way she could muster up the nerve to tell him, with or without Dr. Wharton by her side. But if she and David got married right away, maybe she wouldn't have to tell him at all.

Her feet swished through the dead leaves that had accumulated on the concrete sidewalk. By that time, she was far beyond the row of businesses that dotted Center Street and was walking through her favorite neighborhood of mostly brick homes.

Forced by Aunt Clarry's suicide to leave his traveling position, her father had accepted a job in personnel at the Luffkin Factory, a few blocks from the other side of downtown. For the past ten years before that, he'd been a salesman, traveling to New York, Boston, and Philadelphia, the same triangle of cities three weeks out of every month. He'd applied for that glamorous position immediately after Aunt Clarry had arrived in Willow to take care of them. Being apart from his children for such long stretches over the years, he was trying hard to reconnect with his sons, especially Bo, his golden boy. But not with her. Never with her.

A few blocks more and she reached the outskirts of Willow, where the sidewalks ended. Now she walked on the side of the road, passed open fields of harvested farmland, groves of weeping willows, their hanging branches dried and yellowed by winter, making the landscape appear excessively dreary.

Nearing noon, the sun was high. Her mind flitted from one thought to the next. Grief had grown her and her brothers up prematurely. Grief was a big black hole in your heart where someone precious had once been, and the wind howled through it, cold and empty. Grief was Auntie's untouched TV tray, her lingering scent in the attic bedroom, the empty chair at their kitchen table. Grief was their lost childhood.

After watching their mother topple and shatter into irreparable pieces, Noël thought their family had grown used to grieving. But when Auntie died, they were back to square one again, each loss reopening the one before. The most terrible thing about grieving, or maybe it was the best thing, was that it was inseparable from love. Grief was love's agonizing underside, the ransom you paid.

The next thing she knew, she was entering the oval archway to the Garden of Resurrection. A little more than a mile from town, it was the spot Noël loved most in all the world, a place where she could think things through. She found comfort in spending time among the tombstones, reading the epitaphs. There was history here, and history gave life connection, meaning.

For generations, families had made the effort to venerate the lives of their dead with poetic statements on their tombstones, making the Garden of Resurrection seem more like a place of life than death, or maybe somewhere in between the two. Some of the white markers were so old—dating back to the Civil War and earlier—that the inscriptions had nearly been erased, but most of the etched drawings remained visible. Noël looked from left to right as she walked, scouring the stones for her favorite images: an index finger pointing upward toward heaven, two hands clasped together in mourning, an anchor, a descending dove.

Drifting off the curving road, she cut through the dried grass on her way to her family's plot, pausing in front of an etched quote that Adam once informed her had come from Tennyson:

"I am a part of all that I have met."

Aunt Clarry had been here for seven months already. The caretaker had called to inform them that her new headstone had finally been installed, and this was Noël's first chance to see it. Halfway there, she paused to read the founder of the town's large stone. *Millard K. Baker, died 1841, age 49 years, 10 months, and 12 days*, followed by:

Remember me, as you pass by,
As you are now, so once was I,
As I am now, so soon you'll be.
So prepare for death, and follow me.

Maybe that was the answer. To kill herself, the same way Auntie had done with their father's shiny pistol, locked away again in his steel safe. In his *safe*. What an odd word for something that hid the deadliest of weapons. She tried to picture herself and her baby nestled together peacefully under the cold ground beside Auntie and Monroe, watching this unkind world float by.

Auntie had been a mother figure to all of them, especially Adam.

The second she'd learned that Monroe's stillbirth had rendered their own mother unable to care for them, Auntie had rushed from New Orleans to rescue them, to raise them, to love them as tenderly as her own.

Grief was a big, black hole, alright, and Noël had watched each of her brothers fall through it. Back in Hyssop, they had idolized the fearless, unconquerable boy that Bo used to be. But grief had paralyzed him. It made him stop trying, made his shoulders slump at the age of nineteen, made him waste his days pumping gas for a living and fritter his nights away. Steve, on the other hand, was a wild card. Grief had built a fortress around his emotions, making him a bit of a puzzle. And as for Adam, the brother to whom she was the closest, he had somehow managed to emerge as the strongest. Since the youngest always seemed to absorb the trickle-down fears of the entire family, she wondered how he'd been able to manage that.

Another epitaph snagged her attention:

Good night, beloved ones, do not weep.

I'm weary of earth. I long to sleep.

I shall awake with the dawning light of eternal day.

Good night, good night.

But she already knew how Adam had managed it; it was because he didn't know the full truth. How right she'd been to keep the secrets from him.

Adam himself had told her that his saving grace—his calling to become a surgeon—had occurred to him that awful night they left Hyssop. As they'd sped through the dark streets in the station wagon, Adam all the way in the back, he'd been playing a game of make-believe. (His childhood, thank God, was intact enough that he still could play.) And what he had pretended was that he was a doctor on *The Lone Ranger*, digging around inside Pastor Ray's chest with giant tweezers, pulling out a silver bullet, and dropping it into a metal tray—*clink!*—the thrill of it, the utter joy beyond his comprehension. "What could be better than bringing a person back from the brink of death?" he'd said.

He had shared all of that with her much later, including his own philosophy about grieving, which was: you could let the fires of grief destroy you or let them forge you. He urged her to do the same—to make definite plans, to keep moving forward. Though only fifteen, Adam already had his entire life mapped out: Marry Cynthia Andrews—his first and forever girlfriend, leave Willow, become a heart surgeon.

So, what was her plan?

Adoption was unthinkable and marriage to David a death sentence.

At last, she'd reached the family plot. Noël was the one who had chosen Monroe's inscription ten years ago, a common one for infants. Under the teddy bear-shaped marker was etched:

Budded on earth to bloom in heaven.

Auntie's new headstone, a large slab of swirling marble, paid for by their grandfather back in New Orleans, stood beside Monroe's. Noël's heart sank as her fingers stroked a series of voodoo Xs that vandals had already scratched into the marble surface. The kids from school had been conjuring up wild ghost stories about Aunt Clarry being some kind of voodoo witch to have committed such an unthinkable act.

"Why are people so hateful?" she said to herself, maybe to Auntie.

Suicide wasn't the answer; Noël knew that. Though she had nothing but sorrow for the depth of her poor Auntie's despair, she would never dream of leaving her brothers with that kind of heartache; not a second time.

And then, she suddenly noticed it—she'd been so distracted by the voodoo Xs that she just now saw the epitaph she had chosen. Noël had spent days on end combing through all kinds of poetry and inspirational books from the library for just the right words, and after all that effort, she'd ended up choosing this one. This old, familiar one.

But she loved the quote like none other. It was emblazoned in her memory because Pastor Ray back in Hyssop used to end his sermons with it all the time, his signature line, from the French philosopher, Blaise Pascal.

To say Pastor Ray was unforgettable would have been an understatement. She could still picture him—his white shirt flapping against his back in the wind like wings as they sat under the cypress tree listening to him preach. Pastor Ray made them feel like love was enough to save the world, even them, the grimy, forgotten ones in a run-down pit like Hyssop.

She stared at the inscription:

When one does not love too much, one does not love enough.

The Studebaker screeched to a halt, and Noël's father stormed out, heading straight toward her. "For Christ's sake, what are you doing out here?" he screamed. Adam followed behind him, his eyes worried as much as relieved.

Noël had lost track of time. And now she noticed that the sky had become a dark gray, soon to blacken into full night. The days were so short this time of year.

"I just wanted to—"

"I don't care what you wanted! I've been searching all over hell's half-acre for you! Do you have sawdust for brains?" Dad grabbed her arm and yanked her like a rag doll toward the car.

Adam took a defiant step toward him, then stopped, immobilized, as Dad continued his rant. "Why in the hell are you roaming around a graveyard in the middle of a crisis?"

Noël panicked at the word *crisis*. Did he know about the baby? Had Dr. Wharton betrayed her confidence?

"Maybe she hasn't heard about President Kennedy yet," Adam said softly.

President Kennedy? Noël's thoughts scrambled. Aunt Clarry used to rush to the television and turn up the volume whenever his face came on the screen, dazzled by his New Frontier dreams of equal opportunities for all, the end of segregation, putting a man on the moon, his contagious hope. "What about him?"

Dad shoved her into the backseat. "He was shot this afternoon, that's what!"

"Oh, my God! Is he okay?"

"No, he's not okay." Her father blinked several times to stop the trace of actual tears; a shocking sight. "He's dead."

Early the next morning, Noël and her family gathered again around the black-and-white television screen in various poses of stunned disbelief. The nightmare was real. In Washington, DC, a steady rain fell as the young president's body lay in state in the East Room.

It was difficult for Noël to absorb how somber the world had become in the blink of an eye. Even right there in Willow, nearly every downtown business had been draped in heavy black bunting, like a solid brick funeral cortege. But what struck her more than that was the expression on everyone's faces, whether on TV or their own neighbors, a collective draining of spirit. No one seemed innocent or untarnished anymore, as if every eye had been opened to the darkness this world was capable of housing.

If an individual grieved in steps, in stages, what would become of an entire nation suffering such a swift, simultaneous blow?

She knew how Pastor Ray would've answered that question. Grief teaches us what's important, he'd have said; it's love, and even if that love has been lost, it transfigures itself into different forms and goes on.

She ran her fingertips across her belly where her unborn baby waited.

DECEMBER 14, 1966
RICKY

RICKY Ziemny took a whiff of cold night air before sliding into his Camaro. Even under the heavy snowfall, Langston, Indiana, stunk. Discharge from the mammoth steel mills on the north side captured the city under a layer of soot that hung year-round like a mosquito net. Ricky had lived in Langston for twenty-one years, his whole life, yet he still chuckled when strangers rolled up their car windows as they passed through. His dad said it smelled like everyone in the city farted at the same time.

Tonight was Ricky's fourth art class in a series of ten, all of them his secret, prompting him to slip out of the neighborhood the past four Thursday nights in a row, telling his parents that he was working overtime at the mill. His father always seemed to have a doubting look on his face, but Leon, his faithful big brother, covered for him, explaining that it was some kind of special project that needed to be completed before the Christmas holiday. Ma didn't encourage Ricky's artistic tendencies, but Leon did. Occasionally he would wander into Ricky's room late at night just to see his latest painting.

Ricky's high school art teacher thought he was good enough to try for a scholarship to college, but why bother? After graduation, Ricky went straight to work at the steel mills, like every other man in his Polish neighborhood did, and had been doing, since the first wave of immigrants arrived around the turn of the century. Art school just didn't fit into their kind of world.

Ricky glanced up at the night sky. The dense, falling snow looked like powdered sugar flowing from a giant sifter, as thick as when Ma made *chrusciki*. As the mesmerizing snow swirled into his car's headlights, he considered the techniques he could use to capture those thick, iridescent flakes on canvas.

The class was held in the old community center building, just south of the main downtown. Not a great section of town either—it sat in the middle of the poor, rundown colored neighborhood that dragged on for miles. The only reason Ricky had even considered taking this class was the reputation of the instructor, Dan Ross, a bit of a celebrity in the local art community. Ricky had found out about it from a brochure that was tacked on the bulletin board at the art shop where he bought paint, and he'd stuffed it into his back pocket, debating for weeks whether or not to enroll. Late one night after the vodka put the courage in his veins, he'd slapped a stamp on the registration form and tossed it into the mailbox on the corner of their block.

Quite an eclectic little group had also heeded the call of the yellow brochure—a silver-haired grandmother who'd been painting fruit for more years than Ricky had been alive; Milo, an elementary school teacher who painted well, despite his severely arthritic hands; a couple of smug, braless high school girls who were planning to be art majors in college and were taking the class for extra credit; and a solemn, black-attired orthodox Jew, who seldom said a word.

Under the studio's greenish fluorescent lighting, they had painted fruit the first session, much to the grandmother's delight. The next session, they'd done another still life with multiple objects, including books, wine, and cheese. But lifeless objects held little interest for Ricky. His heart was in painting figures and scenes—and he found himself thinking more about drinking the wine than capturing its vessel on canvas. The third night, they'd copied a Monet painting; each student could choose a work from either his cathedral or his haystack series, and Ricky chose the cathedral. Monet used to paint the same subject repeatedly to capture subtle changes, an ingenious method to learn about color, light, and shadow. Someday—when Ricky found the right subject—he hoped to emulate the concept.

"Tonight," Ross instructed, "we're going to paint the human face. As Vincent van Gogh once said"—he paused long enough to light a cigarette—"'I prefer painting people's eyes to cathedrals. A human soul is more interesting to me.'"

Van Gogh's words, along with the opportunity to do portrait work, intrigued Ricky. Portraiture was an area he knew little about. Except for his first painting of his father's craggy face long ago, most of his work was abstract, depicting emotion rather than clarity of features. Van Gogh was right about the cathedral thing. As spectacular as even their own St. Stan's church was, it couldn't rival the intricacies of his dad's care-carved face. His eyes reminded Ricky of an old chihuahua's, watery and sad.

After taking a few more puffs on his cigarette, Ross briefed them on the plans for the evening. Tonight they were going to have a live model. "Don't get excited, men." He grinned. "This will be above the neck only."

When the door to a side room opened, a thunderbolt cracked against Ricky's ribs. He stared open-mouthed at what had to be the most beautiful human ever created—luminous eyes, straight-edged nose, perfect, full lips, and milky pink-white skin. She was a study in contrasts, her light flesh against the blackness of her hair reminded him of a John Singer Sargent painting. Looking no one in the eyes, she took her place on a folding chair in front of the room.

"Destiny smiled upon us tonight," Dan Ross said. "I was going to have you paint a face from a picture. But then I ran into this young woman, and she consented to be our model. Notice her distinct cheekbones and the delicate contours of her heart-shaped face."

"Yeah, she looks good even under these cheesy lights," Milo said.

When the model lifted her chin at Dan's request, Ricky got his first full look at her dramatic eyes—an indescribable shade of bluish green—not aqua like pool water, not turquoise like southwestern gemstones, not green like a rain forest. His artistic re-creation of her face was doomed; there were no colors on the palette that could be mixed to capture the indefinable hue of her irises.

"With that," Ross said, "I will leave you artists to your work."

The room hushed, only the barely audible sounds of paint-brushes on canvas could be heard. The model didn't focus on any one of the students; she stared straight ahead.

As Ricky formed the first brushstrokes, much to his surprise and horror, his hands were beginning to shake. *Oh, shit. Why now?* One of his nervous fits was coming on, and coming fast. He tried inhaling a deliberate breath into his lungs, which sometimes helped. A few seconds passed, but deep breathing wasn't working. The dreaded tingling in his body was numbing his fingers, searing his skin, inflaming his stomach. He knew the next phase would be red welts. Hot, itchy, and repulsive.

When he looked up, the model was gazing at him, her eyes growing wider, more intense; a look that told him the welts were already there. His cheeks on fire, he excused himself, informing Milo, who stood at the easel beside his own, that he was leaving for the men's room.

"Have fun," Milo said without glancing up.

Inside the bathroom, Ricky gazed as his reflection in the mirror, horrified by the sight of dozens of red, bumpy welts across his face, one of the worst attacks he'd had since high school. His hands struggled to find the flask in his inner jacket pocket. He unscrewed the cap and gulped down the vodka.

There was nothing to do now but wait—wait until the alcohol swirled through his bloodstream and calmed his nerves; wait until the welts disappeared. He inhaled another breath and sat on the bathroom floor, knees against his chin, trying to figure out what had caused the explosion of nerves this time.

It had something to do with that model. But what? It couldn't be simply because she was beautiful; he'd seen dozens of Leon's girlfriends up close. Though he got tongue-tied around them, he didn't go into nervous fits. Leon's girls were off-limits, under glass, like the women who sat inside the ticket booth at the movie theater.

It was different with the model. For whatever reason, he felt a connection to her. A strong connection. Maybe it was the sadness in her eyes.

He took another purposeful breath, another, and then another, until the strength began returning to his fingers and the heat slowly left his face. After about ten more minutes of contemplative deliberation there on the men's room floor, he touched the back of his hand to his cheek, and it felt cool and flat again. He glanced at the mirror. The welts had receded into that dark place where they disappeared until the next attack.

Only one person noticed his reentry into the classroom: the model. Her expression seemed to be one of relief, but it was probably his mind playing tricks on him. Or maybe it was the vodka.

Having moved back behind his easel, he picked up a brush and held it up to her face for perspective. Her eyes were still on his. Dabbing his brush into the palette with a steady hand, he started mixing the blues and the greens in pursuit of the elusive color.

And before he knew it, the two hours were spent. The model rose from her chair and vanished.

≈≈

A profound sense of loss seized Ricky as he slid into his cold car. Ross told them she wouldn't be back; her appearance was a one-time gift. He glanced across the street toward the community center building, hoping for a final glimpse of her. The street was deserted.

He turned the key in the ignition, but his car wouldn't start. Again and again he twisted it, hearing the *zzh-zzh-zzh* sound of the engine struggling to turn over, then a small click. Ricky didn't have a clue what to look for under the hood, but felt obligated to try. He peered into the machinery long enough to assume it was a dead battery and slammed the hood shut.

Returning to the driver's seat, he banged on the steering wheel. "Shit! Shit! Shit!" Now he had to try to find a pay phone in this crummy neighborhood and call Leon, who was probably still out with Stella, fogging up car windows somewhere. If Leon wasn't home, he didn't know what he'd do. He couldn't ask Ma or Dad to come get him, because they thought he was at the steel mill doing overtime. *Oh, what a tangled web we weave …*

Someone tapped on his window, and when Ricky turned to look up, the model was standing there. Adrenalin pumped through him as he fumbled to find the door handle.

"Looks like you're having car problems."

He was surprised by the sound of her voice, more childlike than he'd imagined. It was snowing harder now, the temperature dropping fast, yet his face felt hot. He knew the welts were there again, but she didn't act like she saw them. Maybe it was too dark, though he could see her face just fine beneath the glow of the streetlight.

"Would you like to use my phone to call someone for help?"

Her phone? Was she offering to drive him to her house? His tongue felt thick, like a wad of cotton. "Sure—do you live far from here?"

"Not too far." She pointed to the community center. "Just up two flights up from the art studio. Follow me."

He got out of the car, trying to calm himself. Their footsteps made soft crunching sounds in the fresh snow. As he trailed behind her in the dark blue of the silent night, the moment seemed increasingly unreal. The vodka had already worn off, but his mounting euphoria felt stronger than alcohol.

She opened a side door into a steep, dark stairwell, and he noticed two small mailboxes hanging just outside the entrance, one with a label that read, *F. Chavis, #2*, and the other, *N. Trudeau, #3*.

"My apartment's on the third floor," she said as they embarked through the narrow, winding stairwell, more treacherous than it might actually been because his eyes hadn't yet adjusted to the pitch-blackness. "Watch your step," she warned. "There's one stair near the top that's kind of wobbly."

Stumbling on it, he wondered what the N. in N. Trudeau stood for: Ned, or Nick, or Nelson—her big, strapping husband who would be waiting inside? It was too much to ask that she was the N. on the mailbox—she and she alone.

She reached for the round knob on the wooden door and pulled it open. "It's not the nicest place in the world. But it's ours."

The "ours" stung him.

The apartment smelled like a combination of mildew and deep-fried food. Candles were burning everywhere he looked. A fraying braided rug covered the hardwood floor of the small room, sparsely furnished with mismatched pieces. From the doorway of the kitchen emerged, not her hulking husband, but an old colored woman.

"Thank you for watching Adam tonight." The model smiled at her.

Ricky looked around the room. There was no dog. Adam must be her child. His hopes were dashed.

"You're welcome, baby. He was no trouble at all."

Ricky couldn't miss the way the woman, whoever she was, looked him over, as if trying to make certain he was trustworthy enough to be left alone with her. "So, you're the one whose car went dead on this nasty night?" she said. "We were watching you out there." She pointed to the large window facing the street. "And she insisted on going out there to help you."

"Mrs. Chavis is my downstairs neighbor," the model explained.

Ricky tried to take it all in. It was alarming to discover she was sharing the same building with *darkies*, as Ma called them. He didn't realize that people were actually living in the upper floors of the deteriorating storefronts lining Jackson Street. He could understand darkies being here, but her? What kind of husband would let his wife and child stay in a place like this?

The woman closed the door behind her, leaving the model and him alone in the dark room, lit only by the candles and the streetlight outside the window. "The phone's in the kitchen." She gestured toward the arched doorway joining the living room to a small kitchen, barely large enough for a stove, refrigerator, and a card table apparently being used as a dining table.

"I'm gonna go out on a limb here, but let me take a wild guess. You kind of like candles, right?"

She laughed. A lulling sound, like wind chimes. He'd never made a girl laugh before, at least not one older than ten and younger than fifty, let alone a girl like her. His heart sped up. "Is your husband working tonight?" He forced himself to sound as disinterested as possible as he moved toward the phone.

"It's just me and my son."

The news warmed him. "And how old is your son?"

"Two."

His exhilaration was momentarily dashed by his reluctance to pick up the receiver on the wall-mounted phone. He had no idea what he would say if Leon wasn't home yet, and he doubted that he would be. He looked as his watch. Eleven p.m. He could hear the sounds of N. Trudeau (or so he now assumed) moving around in the living room as he dialed the number. His mother answered after about six rings, an edge to her voice.

"What's wrong, Ma?"

"Your brother postponed the wedding."

"Oh. 'Til when?" Relieved, he feigned interest. If Ma knew Leon had postponed the wedding, then he must have gotten home to tell her so.

"Now he's decided he wants a winter wedding."

"What's the big deal if they get married next winter or next summer? At least he didn't call it off." He watched N. Trudeau walk into the kitchen and open up the refrigerator. (Was her name *Nancy*? He couldn't think of any other female names that started with an *N*.) She held up a bottle of pop, gesturing to see if he wanted one. He smiled, nodded.

"I wouldn't be surprised if that's the next thing he does." Ma paused. "Are you still at work, Ricky? Are you okay?"

"I'm fine. Is Leon there? I need to talk to him."

N. Trudeau handed him the pop bottle, then returned to the living room with one for herself. After a few seconds of the muffled sounds of Ma giving Leon more grief from the other end of the line, he finally heard his brother's voice. "Yeah, Ricky?" Leon drew out an exasperated breath. "What's up? Where are you?"

"Hey, my car battery is dead, and I'm stranded outside the art studio. Actually, I'm not really stranded. A young lady was kind enough to let me come into her apartment to use the phone."

"Wooo," Leon replied. Ricky could visualize his expression, the raised eyebrows, not one hint of a smile. Leon rarely smiled. "Are you sure you want me to come and get you?"

"Unfortunately." Ricky reveled in sharing this with his big brother, the original Casanova. "How long do you think it'll take?"

"How long do you *want* it to take?" Leon teased. He lowered his voice to almost a whisper. "Actually, I'm itching to get out of here. What's the address?"

"It's that old brick building on Jackson Street, the one that used to be a town hall when we were kids. I'll wait for you outside."

"On *Jackson* Street? Shit, Ricky, I had no idea that's where your class—" Leon's abrupt silence must have meant that Ma had come back into the kitchen. Ricky heard her angry voice in the background.

"You can't wait outside in the cold," N. Trudeau said from the living room. "Tell him to come up here to get you."

"Leon? She says to come up here to her apart—"

"Shush, Mom. I can't hear what Ricky's saying."

"I said come up to the third floor. You enter through the side door." Ricky paused. "So, you think it'll take a *really long time* to get here, huh?" In his desire to prolong his stay with N. Trudeau for as long as possible, he was hoping Leon would catch his drift.

"How about I give you an hour?" Leon said. "It might even take that long, since some of the main roads are closing."

"*An hour?*" Ricky again emphasized the words to ensure she heard them. "Well, if that's the best you can do …" He returned to the living room. "Are you sure you don't want me to wait outside?"

"Oh, come on. Do you really think I'd let you freeze to death?" She laughed; wind chimes. "You don't have to keep standing there, you know. Have a seat." She curled her legs beneath her body on the sofa.

Ricky plunked himself down on an adjacent chair. "How come you're so trusting? For all you know, I could be a masher or something."

She scrutinized him. "Well, it's not exactly like I don't know anything about you. I know you're an artist. I know you don't know much about cars. And I know your specialty is painting Holocaust images."

"How do you know that?"

"Dan Ross told me your first names and a little about each of you before I agreed to model." She sipped her cola, her eyes on the falling snow outside. "That was a weird experience that I'll never do again. But at least it brought in a little extra money."

He could hardly imagine that he was really sitting here with her. "And what do you do when you're not modeling?"

"I'm a waitress."

The flickering candlelight danced softly on her face. It seemed to him that her eyes were changing color in the dim room. "And what's your name?"

"Noël. Noël Trudeau."

The sound floated. "Noël," he repeated. "It figures that you would have a name like that."

"Like what?" Her eyes narrowed.

"A beautiful name."

Avoiding his gaze, she took another sip. "What's your last name?"

"Ziemny."

"Zhyem-knee?" She pronounced it slowly, the exact way he'd said it. "Well, it's nice to know you, Rick Ziemny. What nationality is that?"

"Polish."

"I never met anyone Polish before. Is there something special I should know about Polish people?"

He couldn't tell if she was joking. "Well, we like beer and kielbasa."

She nodded, puzzled.

Ricky stopped grinning, ashamed of his answer. "And we know about suffering. Poles share a long, brave history."

"Really?" She raised her eyebrows. "How so?"

"Poland was crushed time and time again. Even subdivided to foreign countries and wiped off the map a few times. But the Poles always rebounded. We're survivors."

"And how does the Holocaust fit into all that?"

"Poland was the first country to be invaded by Hitler, and millions of Poles were slaughtered in the Holocaust, including my own grandmother."

Her eyes widened. Uncurling her legs, she leaned in closer. Her interest surged through him, pushing him to continue.

"My father was part of the American troops that liberated the prisoners at Buchenwald. He wears that experience—the horrors he saw firsthand—permanently on his face. He doesn't talk about it much. So I went to the library when I was just a kid, pored over the pictures I found of survivors, and I couldn't get them out of my head. Those people suffered every single kind of loss and indignity you can imagine. But there was something in their eyes that the Nazis couldn't take from them. They couldn't kill their spirits."

Her lips parted, her eyes teared.

"And so, I paint them. I paint them because they inspire me. I paint them because they're testimony to the best of humanity contrasted against the worst. I think to myself, if they can survive what they did, I can surely survive my own little bumps in the road.

Painting them helps me feel closer to my dad, to my grandmother … closer to who I really am."

She stared at him for several seconds, transfixed.

Ricky could see how strongly his story had resonated with her, and he wasn't sure why. But he didn't care. He knew he was already in love with her. Inside this warm room, he had the growing sensation that he was outside of his own body watching this—watching *her*—happen to him, increasingly certain that the two of them were linked somehow.

When she finally took her eyes off of his, it felt physically painful. "How about you?" he asked. "Where did you come from?"

"From nowhere." Her voice was nearly inaudible.

"Everyone comes from somewhere."

"Maybe so, but I wish my mother had your Polish strength."

"*Had?* Is she still alive?"

"In body. But her spirit has been … wiped off the map."

He saw the sorrow in her face deepening. "I'm sorry. What happened to her?"

"It's a long story. A long story with a very unhappy ending." Her expression enlivened. "It sounded like someone put off a wedding at your house. Or am I being too nosy?"

"Not at all. It was my brother who postponed his wedding. Ma's lifelong project, to date, has been trying to get him married."

"And what about getting *you* married?"

He shrugged. Her eyes drifted to the candle's bouncing flame.

Was this really happening? Ricky savored the dreamlike quality of the moment—the falling snow outside, the shimmering candles inside, the luminosity of her face.

"War is a terrible thing, isn't it?" Her eyes were lost in whatever reverie the firelight was evoking. "All three of my brothers are soldiers now."

"All of them! Wow, that's rough."

"Bo enlisted just after the Gulf of Tonkin Resolution. He couldn't wait to go. It was like Vietnam flicked a switch inside of him or something. And Steve enlisted in the Navy as soon as he graduated. But Adam, my youngest brother, was forced to go."

"You mean, he got drafted?"

"Sort of. He lost his college scholarship and didn't have much choice. He's always wanted to be a doctor, so he's training to be a combat medic now. He's the one I worry about the most."

"How come he lost his scholarship?"

She put her drink down on the coffee table, looked him over as if debating whether or not to continue. "One of his friends was being bullied by a teacher, and Adam, inspired by Atticus Finch, felt it was his duty to stick up for him."

"Who's Atticus Finch?"

"A character in *To Kill a Mockingbird*. Didn't you see the movie with Gregory Peck?

"Guess I missed that one."

"Anyway, he got expelled for a few weeks after that, but that horrible teacher made sure it was enough to lose his scholarship." She lowered her eyes. "He thinks he's going over there to save lives, but ..."

"But what?"

"That's not the way war works, is it?"

Ricky took a long, slow swig from his bottle. "Vietnam is hard to understand. But sometimes I wish I could go."

"You do?" She looked surprised. "Why?"

"To stop the Communists."

"Oh, that." She turned away.

"Maybe other reasons too."

"Like what?"

"Well … like getting away from my neighborhood and seeing another kind of world. Doing something big and heroic, the way my dad did in the Second World War. Sometimes I get tired of living each day exactly the same—go to the steel mill, work like a dog, smell like one by the end of the day, and then do it all over again. Maybe that's the same way your brother Bo feels."

"Maybe. But you can be a hero right here, can't you? Learning how to live with people is a lot more heroic than learning how to kill them. At least, I think it is. Besides, the Second World War had Hitler. Who's the enemy now?"

He finished his pop. "Sometimes war is the only answer."

Her fingertips played with one of the candle flames, casting a carousel of shadow and light to spin across the ceiling. "I used to know a preacher back in Louisiana, where we grew up, and do you know what he used to tell us? 'Love is the answer.' And when we'd ask him, 'What's the question?', he'd say, 'It doesn't matter.'"

Ricky watched her get up from the sofa to bring him another cold, uncapped bottle of cola from the kitchen. "You only have the one brother?"

He nodded. "Leon is in the National Guard. But I can't even get into that because of my—" He stopped himself.

"Because of what?"

He decided to continue, trusting her as she seemed to trust him, particularly since she'd seen the welts earlier anyway. "I have this nerve condition that flares up without notice. It started back in kindergarten." He wanted to change the subject, before she could ask any questions. "Aren't you afraid to be living in the same building with darkies?"

"Darkies?" Her face scrunched.

"You know, coloreds."

"They prefer to be called 'black' now."

"Colored, black, Negro—what difference does it make what they call themselves? They're still too dark." He expected her to laugh, or at least smile. But she didn't. Instead the light vanished from her eyes, the muscles tensing in her face, and the cord that united them seemed suddenly severed.

"You don't know any black people, do you?" she asked.

"Sure—lots of 'em work at the steel mills."

"That's not the same as knowing someone." She looked away again, winding a strand of her long black hair around her index finger. "How can you have so much heart for Holocaust survivors and still use a word like *darkies*? I don't understand that."

He'd offended her. But how? It was just a way to describe Negroes, that's all.

Together they watched the falling snow in silence. He stole a glance at her profile in the candlelight. "I'm sorry," he said.

She took a sip of her cola. "If only all of white America was sorry."

Ricky was confused for reasons he couldn't comprehend. Didn't she understand the way the world worked? "Tell me about your son," he said.

Her face brightened. "Adam is the joy of my life."

"Same name as your brother?"

"Brothers," she corrected. "His full name is Adam Stephen Beauregard."

"Beauregard? Bo's full name, huh?" Ricky smiled. "And what about Mr. Trudeau, his father?"

"Mr. Trudeau is *not* his father!" Her eyes flashed with emotion. Fear or anger? She seemed embarrassed by her overreaction. "I didn't want his father's last name, so I took my own back."

"You're divorced?"

"Our marriage was a mistake right from the start."

"Then your husband must be a damned fool."

"You know what?" She didn't seem to hear his ardent defense of her, or maybe she was just pretending not to. "The best things come out of the worst sometimes, don't they? Like my son. And your paintings. My mother was an artist too. She painted her best work when she was in pain. I learned more about her from her artwork than from anything she ever said to me. I wish I knew more about art. Maybe I'd feel closer to my mother, the way it brings you closer to your dad."

Such a sad life she seemed to have led. She reminded him of the tiny wild rabbit with the smashed paw that he found in their backyard the previous winter, shivering alone in the wet grass. He'd had to earn that rabbit's trust slowly, but once he did, he'd nursed it back to health. He had the same sense about her, that he needed to move toward her slowly, with an open palm. Otherwise he'd frighten her away.

A knock at the door broke his thoughts. A quick glance at his watch revealed that the precious hour, more than an hour, was gone. How could he bear to leave this room and never see her again? As she got up from the sofa to answer the door, his mind raced. He needed a plan, and quickly. "Wait just a second." He reached for her arm to slow her; she startled at the sudden gesture.

Move slowly, you idiot, remember? "I'm sorry," he said. "I just got excited about an idea I had. Since you're so interested in art, would you, and Adam, like to go the Art Institute in Chicago with me on Saturday? We could see paintings by some of the greatest masters of all time."

"The Art Institute of Chicago?" Her eyes glistened in the candlelight. "I've never been to Chicago before."

"Then, it's a date."

"Please don't think of it as a date," she said."

His heart sunk.

Leon knocked again. This time, much harder. Patience was never one of his virtues.

"Don't get me wrong—I'd be lucky to date you," she said. "It's just that I'm not looking for a boyfriend. Adam and I are flying solo from now on. You have to understand that."

"I do. But maybe you're in the market for a friend?"

Smiling at him, she pulled the door open.

Leon was standing there dressed in a black peacoat, with shimmers of snow in his damp, dark hair and mustache, his hands stuffed into his pockets, his intense eyes immediately blazing into hers.

"This is Noël Trudeau," Ricky said.

Other than the searing look, Leon's only gesture of greeting was a quick nod.

"And this is my brother, Leon."

Her face flushed.

Leon's gaze shifted to Ricky. "Let's go." Turning around in the dark landing, he headed back down the stairs.

"Well," she said, a bewildered look on her face. She was obviously taken aback by his brusqueness, as was Ricky. "Your brother is a man of few words, isn't he?"

He shrugged, embarrassed. "He's probably just sore because he had to come out in a blizzard to get me. It looks pretty bad out there."

She glanced toward the window. "Yes, it does."

Every instinct inside of him wanted to kiss her before he left, just on the cheek or something, but he settled for her hand. He raised it gently and pressed it to his lips. "'Til Saturday."

≈≈

For the next several minutes in the falling snow, Leon jumped Ricky's car with the cables attached under their hoods. He didn't say a word, and neither did Ricky. Though Ricky was annoyed with him for his impoliteness to Noël, it seemed pretty low to blast him for it in the midst of his rescue efforts. He saw her watching them through her window, and he waved. After that, she disappeared.

Finally, Leon got the car started. "Follow me to Jake's," he said. "We'll leave your car in the parking lot of his garage, so he can put in a new battery."

It took over an hour to get there on the bad roads. Ricky tossed his keys through the slot in Jake Karkiewicz's garage door with a note and climbed into the passenger seat of the warm Dodge Charger beside Leon.

After a few minutes, Leon said, "So?"

Ricky knew it was his brother's way of inviting him to tell him all about his evening, everything about her, and Leon listened without interrupting. They were nearing their own street when Ricky concluded that he'd made a date with her for Saturday night.

"Break it," Leon said.

"What? Why in the world would I do that?"

Leon stared straight ahead.

"Talk to me!—this is no time to clam up. And, by the way, why were you so rude to her?"

Leon rolled the car to a stop in front of their house, but neither got out. He kept the motor running. "Look, I'll just say this flat out. Are you sure she's not a hooker?"

"A *hooker*?" Ricky could hardly believe his ears. Then it dawned on him. "Oh, I know why you're saying that. You're thinking that a girl like her would never give a butt-ugly goon like me a second look unless she was expecting to get something out of it."

"Come on, Ricky. That's not what I was thinking. It's just that she looks like a goddamned beauty queen or something."

"So what? From what I gather, she's had a pretty hard life. On the inside, she's a wounded spirit who's down on her luck. Kind of like Marilyn Monroe."

"*Marilyn Monroe?*" He stared at Ricky in the dark car as if he was delusional. "All I know is, one look at her, and I heard warning bells. And then you tell me that she's divorced, has a kid, and they're living all alone in a dump with coloreds."

The sound of a snowplow was grinding in the distance. "I'm not trying to rain on your parade." Leon's expression and tone of voice softened. "I'm really not, Ricky. If she was on the up and up, I'd be turning cartwheels for you. I just don't want to see you get mixed up in any trouble, that's all."

"So, that's why you came off tonight like one of The Avengers," Ricky said. "Save it for the comic books, and cool your jets. I told you, she's had a hard life. And you, my brother, are dead wrong about her."

THREE

1966
THECKLA

BACK in 1919, when Theckla Chavis was seventeen years old, she got married, left Mobile, Alabama, and became part of the Great Migration to the north. Before that, she'd been Theckla Bingham, the only daughter in a family of nine. Her daddy thought it a waste of time for a girl to get educated, but her mama snuck in plenty of books for her to read. Theckla loved those books, loved the way they smelled, loved to run her index finger under the words as she read them. But learning took a back seat the day she met the boy with the biggest smile, the brightest eyes, in all of Mobile. Freddie Alvin Chavis was full of sass, keen to take on the world. A saxophone player by night, he had crazy pipedreams of pitching in the Major Leagues one day. Theckla knew he was good enough to make it alright, but that didn't change the fact that he was a Negro.

And then came that day, that God-awful day, when life caved in on them.

After that, they headed north, where Freddie eventually landed a maintenance job in the Langston steel mills, and he and Theckla settled into the second-floor apartment of the community center building. She forced herself not to dwell too much on leaving her family behind in Mobile, or the horrific thing that had happened

49

to them there. Through the grace of God, both she and Freddie learned to live with it.

Two years ago, he retired, and in the spring of 1966, Theckla decided to quit her job as a cleaning lady at the Marriott hotel downtown, mostly because her back wasn't as strong as it used to be. Without a job to distract her, she found herself musing a lot more about what might have been, a pointless pastime, to be sure.

Oh, the changes they'd seen since they'd first moved into that old brown-brick building. Built in 1875, the sturdy, three-story structure was originally a millinery shop, where fancy white ladies went to buy their hats. But as the downtown area receded, it had gone through other identities. By the time Freddie and Theckla had moved in, it was a town hall in a still mixed neighborhood. Then a five and dime. Two years ago, it evolved into its current purpose, a community center building, home to various activities—GED and other adult education courses, art classes, free vaccinations for indigent babies, and a COGIC-sponsored congregate meal program serving hot lunches to the old and poor during the week.

She and Freddie could have afforded to move to a better place, but by then they'd remodeled to make it comfortably their own, and were surrounded by faithful friends. Besides that, they were hoping to return to Mobile one of these days, so why bother moving? Over the years, Theckla witnessed a steady stream of drifters take up residence in the upstairs apartment, coming and going like birds in the trees, here one minute, gone the next.

It was during the scorching days of August 1966 when Theckla first laid eyes on her, a scrawny white girl with a movie-star face, skinny as a rail and pale as the moon. As Theckla peeked out her front window, she watched the girl opening and closing her trunk dozens of times over the course of an hour to take out one brown paper bag full of belongings after the next from her beat-up car before hauling the makeshift luggage up the staircase. The girl appeared to be all by herself, except for a little blonde toddler with a Beatles haircut.

"Get away from that window, woman," Freddie said, but she paid him no mind. Understandably so, he harbored huge mistrust and little use for white people. After a while, he was spying on the newcomer right alongside her. "What's a white girl doing in this neighborhood anyway?" he asked. "Ain't she got no man?"

"Not unless he's hiding under the car seat. Maybe he's coming later."

"Don't make no sense."

"We should go up there and introduce ourselves," Theckla said.

"You keep away, you hear me?"

Freddie had learned to get along with the white people at the mill by keeping his distance from them, by leaving it at three phrases: "good morning," "good night," and "yes, sir." Saying anything more was asking for problems. But Christian charity always came first to Theckla, and she'd worked hard at overcoming her fears. Fear was the starting point for all hatred; she knew that better than most.

"Something's not right with a girl like that living here all by herself," he said.

"Maybe so, but welcoming her is the neighborly thing to do."

An hour later, Freddie was helping Theckla assemble cookies, still warm from their oven, on her mother's old silver platter. "Well, let's just stay a minute," he said. "Just long enough to be neighborly, like you say. We're bound to run into her sooner or later, so we might as well get it over with."

They knocked several times without a response.

"Who is it?" Finally, they heard the girl's wispy voice on the other side.

When they told her who they were, she opened right up, wearing a little white top with spaghetti straps, the bones sticking out all around her neck and shoulders, and she invited them inside. After being unoccupied for three years, the apartment had a stale, wicked smell that came hurtling into their nostrils. The place came furnished, so it already looked lived-in, to some extent, aided by the grocery-bag luggage cluttering the front room and kitchen. She told them her name and that she'd seen the "for rent" sign when she and her son came for one of the congregate meals.

For some reason, the child had taken an immediate shine to Freddie, even though Theckla was the one holding the tray of cookies. He stared up at Freddie, his floppy hair falling away from his face in the process, revealing a pair of round, close-set brown eyes. "I'm Adam!"

"You are, huh?" Freddie tried hard not to smile; he had some missing teeth and felt self-conscious when he opened his mouth too wide. "Take yourself a cookie, boy," he said, and Theckla lowered the platter. Adam and his mother devoured those cookies as if it was the first thing they'd eaten that day.

"Is your man going to be coming soon?" Theckla asked.

"No!" You couldn't have missed the alarm in her voice. She caught herself, then smiled. "It's just Adam and me."

Freddie shot his wife one of his looks, the one that tried to warn her to keep her mouth shut for her own sake, but Theckla's curiosity got the better of her. "You from Langston?"

"No."

Despite Freddie's silent protests, she tried a few more times to get the girl to open up, but nothing less than a crowbar would pry her open. Something about that bony girl instinctively tore at Theckla's heart. She had a gut feeling that Noël was hiding a load of secrets. Theckla understood secrets—she and Freddie had a mountain of their own—and she knew that some secrets had to be held inside in order to keep your pride, your sanity. She was betting that Noël's secrets were that kind.

"It'll be nice to have some neighbors again," Theckla told her. "Won't it, Freddie?"

Begrudgingly, he nodded, his eyes half-panicked, half-dancing. By then, he had problems of his own. Adam was stuck to him like a postage stamp, melted-chocolate all over their fingers as he clung to Freddie's hand.

"We don't have any children," Theckla said. "There's just the two of us. That's the way it's always been."

On a cold, snowy Saturday morning in mid-December, two days after that young artist's car had broken down in front of their building, Theckla and Noël were folding clothes together at Lucky's Launder-O-Matic down the street. They did their best talking while doing laundry. Something about watching their clothes, including their intimates, go round and round through the windows of the dryers made them feel a little hypnotized, a little more exposed and familiar in that warm room, heated by dozens of churning washers and lazy dryers. At first, the others at Lucky's would gawk at Noël—a white girl doing her weekly washing along with the rest of them—but they were used to her by now. She was one of them, poorer than she was white.

It was during previous Saturday morning laundry sessions that Noël had finally confessed, bit by bit, about the battering husband she'd left behind in some small town in Ohio, and it all began to make more sense. For her child's sake, she told Theckla, she would've stayed with him, but he was beginning to be abusive to Adam too. She'd been on the run ever since.

That particular Saturday, Noël's worries were focused on a topic much more humdrum—she was all in a tizzy because of that young artist with the dead battery. Apparently, he had asked her to go with him to Chicago, but she'd called him to back out, lying to him that Adam had caught a bug. "He insisted on bringing a book about the Art Institute over instead," Noël said.

Theckla placed a neat stack of clean towels into her plastic basket. "You mean you have a date with him?"

"It's not a date," she insisted. "I made that clear to him."

"Um-hm." Theckla nodded. "You can say whatever you want, but actions speak louder than words. All I had to do was take one look at that boy to know he's totally gone on you, smitten as a puppy dog."

Noël stopped sorting Adam's socks, her brows furrowing. "You really think so?"

"I know so. You're a very pretty girl."

She hung her head as if Theckla had insulted her.

"Well, you *are* pretty. Surely, you know that by now."

"Sometimes I think that's all I am." Noël threw down a sock in self-vexation. "Yippee for my parents, but I had nothing to do with it."

"You bring plenty to the table with your big, pretty heart, and don't you ever doubt it. … You like him back?"

"I don't know. I guess so. He's really easy to talk to. And he's a sensitive soul—for the most part. He's kind of a sad person."

"Like you, you mean?"

"I'm not sad!"

"And I'm not black." Theckla chuckled. "Does he know you're still married?"

"There's no need for him to know." She tossed the errant sock into her laundry basket unmated. "You're right, Mrs. Chavis. I need to nip this thing."

"Don't go putting words in my mouth. I didn't say one thing about nipping. I'm just asking you how you feel."

"That's just it, I don't know. Sometimes I get a little lonely, I'll admit, and it's nice to have someone to talk to. But I don't want another relationship. Could you come up and stay while he's there?"

"I'm no chaperone." Theckla shook her head at the odd request. "Besides, Freddie and me have dinner plans." She eyed her troubled face. "You afraid of him?"

"Of course not. He's gentle as a lamb." Noël's expression strengthened to one of resolve. "I'll let him come over tonight, show me his book, and that'll be it. Afterward, I'll tell him I can't see him again."

Later that night, Theckla talked it over with Freddie in bed. "Maybe it'll be good for her to have a man around here, watching out for her. I wish I had a nickel for every time she's told me she's afraid her husband's gonna track her down. I tell her not to fret about it—that he'll have to deal with us if he ever shows his face around here."

"Stop talking like that!" Freddie said. "We don't need no more problems with white men. You're getting too involved."

"*Me* too involved?" She shook her head. "Don't think I don't see you slipping that little boy of hers lemon drops or shiny new pennies from your sweater pocket whenever I turn my back." She and Freddie had gotten into the habit of looking after Adam when Noël went to her job at the diner downtown. She sometimes worked two shifts straight and still made next to zero—except when some good-for-nothing dropped a big tip in hopes of getting next to her.

"That's different," he said.

"It is, huh? And who's the one who insists we invite them over for supper every Sunday?"

"Well, someone has to fatten up their skinny asses."

She planted a big kiss on his cheek. "You know something? I love you, you sweet, old man."

"I love you too, baby." Freddie scrunched his pillow just-so before stretching out his legs underneath the warm blanket.

Leaning over toward the framed photograph of Jackie Robinson in his Brooklyn Dodgers uniform, she clicked off the small lamp on the nightstand. Earlier that day, she'd watched her husband get down on the floor on his hands and knees to play some silly game with Adam, laughing like she hadn't seen him do for years, without one thought about showing his missing teeth. He would've made a good daddy, her Freddie, if only they'd had the chance.

As she lay there in the darkness, her mind was working over-time. The truth was, in little more than four months' time, Noël and that little boy had breathed new life into them, given them a sense of purpose. She repeated that thought out loud to Freddie, but he didn't say a word. He must've already fallen asleep.

"Old folks like us taking a white girl and her child under our wings," he finally said. "Um-mm-mm. Ain't that just the damnedest thing?"

FOUR

APRIL 1964
NOËL

NOËL awakened in a cold sweat, the sun streaming through the small basement window into her eyes, stabbing pains shooting through her abdomen. Her baby wasn't due for another month. *Oh, dear God!* She clutched her belly. Something was horribly wrong.

The other side of the bed was empty. David had left hours earlier, before sunrise, for a hunting trip with his buddies. His parents, who lived upstairs, were gone to a First Methodist Church social. Doubled over in agony, she managed to make it up the stairs and over to the living room phone. Her brother, Adam, answered the second call she made.

"The baby's coming, but something's not right!"

"I'll call Doc Wharton," he said.

"I already did. He's doing rounds at the hospital. Can Steve get me there?"

Within five minutes, both Adam and Steve appeared at the Ketchfields' door to whisk her to the only nearby hospital, in Bedlington, over twenty miles away. Steve drove like a race-car daredevil while Adam, in the backseat with her, belted out the Beatles' current hit, "Can't Buy Me Love" to sidetrack her from the pain.

After they reached the emergency room, the last thing Noël

remembered was hearing the words "Cesarean section." Everything went dark after that.

She woke up in a different world, confused and disoriented. How long had she been here? Was it hours later? Days? Where was she? Glancing around the unfamiliar white room, she saw Steve sitting to her left, Adam on her right, thumbing through a *TV Guide*; David was nowhere in sight. Everything seemed soft around the edges, moving in slow motion, as if she was lying in a basket of clouds. She couldn't feel her own body.

"Hey, she's awake," Steve said. Both brothers leaned over her. "Welcome back to the world, sis. You had a baby boy."

Now she remembered where she was and why. "Is he okay?"

"He's better than okay." Adam smiled. "He's really, really small, but he's just fine."

"Are you sure?"

"Positive." Adam was still grinning, a smile she knew well enough to believe it was the God's honest truth. "He pees and squawks just like a baby should."

Even so, she had to see for herself to make certain he wasn't stillborn. Through hazy lids, she tried to get up, her arms thrashing, her mind unwinding backward. When she looked down, Monroe was sleeping in her arms. Dr. Wharton had just cleaned him off in the bathroom sink and dressed him in white satin. No longer the bloody dead blob who'd come out of her mother, he was miraculously transformed, more beautiful than any doll she'd ever seen, even Amelia Rosalie. His lashes were long and straight, his mouth forever frozen in a little "O" of astonishment, his tiny eyes glazed shut, never meant to be opened to this world. "Mama," Noël said, "you made even better than a baby. You made an angel."

From the corner of her eye, she saw Doc approaching. "No, don't take him away!" she cried. "I want him to stay."

"That's the best thing about angels. They're always nearby." Doc's voice sounded far away, as if coming from nowhere. Only it wasn't Doc. It was Steve.

"What on earth is she talking about?" Steve said to Adam. "What's wrong with her?" They were both gawking at her as if she'd gone stark raving mad.

"I think she's having some kind of a hallucination," Adam replied.

Noël blinked, the room swirled around her. Monroe was no longer in her arms. He wasn't nearby like Doc had promised. Neither was Doc or Mama. Where was she?

"Hallucination?" Steve looked petrified.

Struggling again to get out of bed, Noël felt too woozy, and she slipped back down like a noodle into her cloud basket. "I can't move." Her words were slurred.

"They shot you up with painkillers," Adam said.

Painkillers, huh? She wanted to tell them that they really worked, that she didn't have a pinch of pain anywhere—inside or out—but she couldn't open her mouth; her thoughts were floating away like monarch butterflies over the bed, translucent orange and black swirls, and before she knew it, they took her away on their wings. This must be what dying felt like.

She met her son for the first time later that Saturday night, a miraculous little bundle of rosy perfection, with wiggly toes and fingers too small to be believable. She clutched his warm, living body against her own, his tiny breaths saturating her with an overpowering gratitude. His eyes opened, closed again, his mouth moved, his little nose twitched. All parts were working as they should. He was a real baby, not an angel. She wondered how she'd ever lived without him.

By that time, others were in the room—Adam and his ever-faithful Cynthia, Steve and his latest girlfriend, Bo in his Texaco uniform with the red star patch on his breast, her mother sitting in a chair in the corner of the room staring into the overhead fluorescent light, her father glancing at his gold wristwatch, the Ketchfields standing like statues near the window. David hadn't surfaced yet; he was unreachable, they told her, still off hunting.

She caught a glimpse of herself in the mirror by the door, mortified. Several months ago, she'd tried to make herself ugly so that David wouldn't want to touch her, and she'd grabbed the pinking shears, chopping off her hair, handful after handful, with no rhyme or reason. Now that it was growing back, she looked even more like a freak.

After all the parents left, the nurse wondered if she had selected the baby's name yet for the birth certificate. David had insisted that he be named after him, but since he wasn't around and her brothers were, Noël boldly told her, "Yes, his name is Adam Stephen Beauregard." The nurse wrote it down and walked away.

When David finally appeared the next morning and heard the baby's name, his face turned bloodred, the sure sign he was livid, but he didn't say anything. Instead, he funneled his energy into charming the nurses when they came into the room, told the prettiest one that she was a dead ringer for Brigitte Bardot. Her eyelashes fluttered as she wrapped the blood-pressure cuff around Noël's upper arm and squeezed the little bulb, pumping air into the cuff until it hurt. "One-sixty over ninety," she said with a grin, too busy making goo-goo eyes at David to care that it was sky-high.

Dr. Wharton arrived, and David shook his hand, thanked him for taking such good care of her. When Noël saw the way David acted around other people, she wondered what was wrong with her. She wished she could turn back time. Undo it. Undo him. Return them back to the teenagers who never got into an Oldsmobile together on a dark night. But then she wouldn't have her baby, her perfect son. Adam Stephen Beauregard was worth living through any square inch of hell that David put her through back then, now, and whatever else was to come.

Five days later, David's parents were out having an early dinner at the Seashell Supper House. Noël was glad to be living with them, not solitary newlyweds in their own home. They were alone for the first time since the birth. No pretty nurses, no brothers, no buffers. After she put the baby down in his crib, she headed for the kitchen to make them something to eat.

"Adam Stephen Beauregard, huh?" he said. "You must think you're pretty clever, don't you?"

"What do you mean?" She faked ignorance as she gathered fresh veggies from the fridge, wondering what in the world had possessed her to snub him that way. She saw the glint of rising rage in his eyes. Her heartbeat escalated as she chopped celery at the counter.

"I'll tell you what I mean. You promised to *obey* me, remember that?" Grabbing both of her arms, he twisted her toward him. "You ruined my life." Shaking herself free, she walked away into the living room; he followed. "I'm still in high school, but I'm living like an old man in my parents' basement."

She was in the corner now, trapped.

"And you don't even appreciate the sacrifices I've made for you." He pinned her against the wall. "How dare you name my son after your brothers! How dare you humiliate me like that!"

"I'm sorry. I was doped up, I didn't know—"

"You're sorry alright. You're the sorriest thing I ever met. But sorry or not, you're going to get our marriage vows straight, right here and right now." He slapped her across the face; it stung like fire.

She tried to get away from him, but he slammed her against the wall and thrust his fist into her stomach hard enough to tear the stitches. She dropped to her knees. The amount of blood must have scared him.

"Come fast, Doc!" He yelled into the phone. "Noël fell down the stairs!"

Her world went black.

≈≈

When she woke up, Dr. Wharton was bending over her with his kind, sympathetic eyes, and she thought she might really be dead this time, just like Monroe, and that Doc had come to bundle her in this soft blanket of painlessness to carry her away to Green's Funeral Parlor.

"It's okay, sweetie," he said.

The sun beamed through the window. She squinted hard, tented her hand over her eyes as she looked around and realized she was back in the hospital.

"But you sustained some permanent damage. I'm afraid that you'll never be able to conceive another child."

"Is my baby all right?" she asked.

"He's perfectly fine."

"Yes, he's perfect. I don't need another baby."

FIVE

DECEMBER 16, 1966
RICKY

FINALLY, a parking spot appeared on the street, three full blocks down from the community center building. Even in the chill of a frigid Saturday night, Ricky's hands were sweaty and shaky from nerves; the heavy art book he was carrying, along with the portfolio tucked under his armpit, helped weight them as he walked toward her door.

A shuffling noise from behind made him twist around on the icy sidewalk, nearly losing his balance. Nothing there. Just his imagination. Walking alone in this neighborhood after dark made him skittish. Too much dissention was going on between the races nowadays, stirred up by Martin Luther King Jr. and his marches. Ma told him she couldn't understand why the Negroes were becoming so militant lately. Back in her day, she said, the darkies never caused a peep of trouble, and everyone got along just fine.

But getting mugged was the lesser of his worries. Noël had nixed their outing to the Art Institute, claiming her son wasn't feeling well, and he wondered if it was the truth. He feared that this would be his first and last chance with her.

She opened the door as soon as he knocked, even more lovely than he remembered, her coal-black hair framing that goddess face.

A little boy stood in the corner, glaring at Ricky as if he'd come to steal his candy.

"Adam, this is Mr. Ziemny."

"Ricky," he corrected.

"Rick-*ey*?" She smiled quizzically. "Okay, then. Call him Ricky."

"How're you feeling, Adam?" The little boy turned away from him, facing the wall. "Better, I hope."

"He can be shy sometimes," she said. "Please sit down and make yourself comfortable. Would you like a cola?"

What he'd really like was a giant sip from the flask in his glove box. "Yeah, that sounds good."

Just like the other night, she brought him a cold bottle of Coca-Cola from the fridge, but the vibration in the room wasn't the same. It felt less enchanting, more intimidating. The lamp was on and the fluorescent overhead kitchen light too; no candles were burning this time. Outside, the wintry night loomed pitch-black, except for the street light glaring through her window.

He took a seat on the sofa, hoping she'd sit beside him, but she didn't. She stood for a while before landing on the adjacent chair, the same one he'd sat in two nights ago. "So, Adam is two years old?" he asked.

"He'll be three in April."

"Three? You were pretty young then, when you had him."

"I'd just turned eighteen."

Ricky mulled over the numbers in his brain. She must've gotten pregnant while still in high school; a disconcerting thought. "Hey, Adam," he said, pushing Leon's dire warnings out of his mind. "I've got something a heck of a lot more interesting to look at than that old wall." Without moving his head, the child shifted his eyes to the side, his interest piqued. "Come over here and take a look at this book." Resting the portfolio on the braided rug, Ricky opened up the smaller book he'd brought along.

"Oh, honey, he brought a copy of *The Little Prince*," she said. Thumbing through it, she seemed captivated by the vivid pen-and-watercolor drawings. "How sweet. How very sweet. You should see these, Adam." She met Ricky's eyes for the first time. "How thoughtful of you."

The book had pleased her. Finally, he could breathe again.

As she kept oohing and aahing over the illustrations, Adam slowly crept out of the corner and, by the time she finished reading the first page aloud, he was standing beside her. She handed Ricky the book. "You take over."

Adam scrambled onto the sofa beside him. "When I was a few years older than you, this was my favorite book in the world," Ricky said. "I liked to draw pictures too, just like the little prince does, and the adults didn't understand mine either." He pointed to the little prince's first drawing of a boa constrictor digesting the elephant that the grown-ups mistook for a hat. "That's not a hat at all, is it?"

"No." Adam giggled.

As Ricky began reading from the place Noël had left off, he used funny voices and exaggerated expression to hold Adam's interest. He delighted in seeing the child's eyes grow wider and more fasci-nated, even though most of the book was beyond his grasp. Even better, Noël was mesmerized by the story. Long after Adam's atten-tion waned and he was nestled in her arms, Ricky kept on reading, solely for her benefit. When he reached the ending where the little prince leaves the earth to return to the stars, he saw tears in her eyes.

She cleared her throat. "I think it's bedtime for you." Against Adam's protests, (he liked Ricky now, begged him to come back), the two of them disappeared into one of the back rooms. Ricky could hear him saying his prayers out loud, blessing him right along with his uncles and a whole host of names he didn't recognize.

When she came back out, Noël gave Ricky a lingering gaze. "Thank you for that."

"For what?"

"For paying attention to him." She started lighting her candles one by one. "You made a real hit."

He swallowed hard, hoping he could win her over too (maybe he already had). But he brought out the big guns anyway, opening the heavy art book and patting the cushion beside him on the sofa. She took a seat on the far side, farther away than he was hoping, near the arm, where her fingers played with a loose thread.

For the next hour or so, he went through the book page by page, showing her the master artworks in the Art Institute of Chicago and telling her what he knew about them—the European paintings, the American artists, the way the various masters used color and light to create different moods. A particular painting, *The Coast of Labrador* by William Bradford, caught her interest and seemed to stir something inside of her. "Look at that lonely little boat," she said, "and all those sharp cliffs."

"What is this painting saying to you?"

"Saying? I don't know. It just makes me sad, for some reason, if that makes sense."

"It makes complete sense."

Though she might not have realized it, as the evening wore on, she had repositioned herself closer and closer to him, maybe just to see the paintings better. But every single time she shifted position, he noticed the way the candle flames danced with the movement. When he could feel her thigh nearly touching his, his heart raced. He turned to her, gazed into her eyes.

Quickly, she looked away, pointing to another painting and asking about the technique.

"It's called chiaroscuro. First attributed to none other than Leonardo da Vinci. It means using light and dark in the same work, for dramatic effect." Ricky seized the opportunity to try to learn more about her. "What kind of paintings does your mom like to do?"

"My mom?" Her face exploded in anxiety. "Oh, she doesn't paint anymore."

"What did she used to paint?"

She hesitated, still jumpy. "She used colors, sharp colors."

"Like this?" He flipped to a page showing an abstract composition by Wassily Kandinsky.

She stared at it. "A little."

"Do you have any of her paintings?"

"No." She stood up. "Well, just one. My father has it somewhere."

"Why just one?" It was obvious he'd struck a nerve.

"We left the rest of them back in Hyssop." She clawed at her hair.

Ricky kept his voice as gentle as possible. "What's it a painting of?"

"A red rose ... on fire."

"Whoa." He tried to imagine it. "Sounds dramatic. Why didn't you bring her other paintings from Hyssop?"

"We had to—leave quickly."

Escaping into the kitchen, she brought their conversation to a halt. When she returned a good five minutes later, she was carrying a plate of cheese and crackers which she put down on the coffee table, then sat on the far end of the sofa again.

"You know what?" he said. "You're the perfect model for a

chiaroscuro painting. You *are* chiaroscuro. You're light and dark together in the same package."

She sprung up and headed back toward the refrigerator, ostensibly to grab two more bottles of pop. This time when she came back, she settled on the chair, not the sofa. For reasons Ricky couldn't guess, their bond was broken again.

He glanced at his watch. It was past eleven. The shifting sands of the hourglass were nearly at the bottom, and this was his last, desperate shot. "I should probably go soon, but I wanted to show you one more thing. Would you like to see some of my paintings?"

"Your own paintings, you mean? Well, sure I would."

"I only brought two of them." He lifted his portfolio from the floor, opened it, and held up a painting of three Holocaust survivors being liberated by an American soldier.

"Oh, Rick." She rose from her seat, moving in closer to examine it. "You have an incredible eye." She stared at it. "Really, I mean it. This is powerful. It should be hanging in the Chicago museum."

He was relieved, ecstatic, to see how his work had affected her. "I've got a long way to go before that happens."

"No, you don't. I'm not trying to compliment you to be polite. I'm telling you the truth. You're an amazing artist. Let me see the other one." This time, he showed her a portrait. "Someone you know?"

"Very well. He's my dad."

Taking it from him, she examined it from top to bottom. "Your father has suffered."

"Yes, he has." Ricky absorbed her introspective expression. "When my dad was only six years old, his mother put him on a ship for America, along with her best friends. His father was really ill, TB or something, and Poland was in a bad way. They were poor peasants, but his mother somehow scraped up enough money to get him a ticket. Her greatest wish was that her only child would grow up safe, on free soil. She planned to join him one day. But, as it turned out, he never saw either of his parents again."

"How hard that must have been for him! And she was the one killed in the Holocaust?"

He nodded.

"What happened to your grandfather?"

"We never really knew. Sick as he was, he probably died long before the war started."

Sorrow drained her face—his sorrow—his family's sorrow. Wildly in love with her, he grasped her hand. "Noël, I want to see you again. And again and again. Can I take you and Adam to dinner next Saturday?"

Her expression went blank. "Oh, I—I don't know about that," she stammered. "It's like I told you before. I don't date anymore."

"Never? At your age?"

"My son is my whole life now. That's the way I want it."

Ricky stared down at the flames.

"Please don't be offended. Any other girl would jump at the chance to go out with you. You're a wonderful man, too good for me."

"Why would you say something like that? You're a very nice person."

She twisted a strand of her hair. "There're all kinds of things you don't know about me."

"Such as?"

"Such as … I'm not even divorced."

"You mean, you're still married?" Another gut punch. Once again, Leon's caution lights flashed in his brain.

"Sort of. At least, in name. But I left him a while ago."

"Wow." He turned away; tried to wrap his mind around this latest revelation. "Why did you leave him?"

She was pacing the room now, back and forth, forth and back, the candle flames bouncing with every movement, casting weird shadows on the ceiling and walls. "We got married too young. It was a mistake from the start."

"Where is he now?"

"Does it matter?"

All these riddles she was throwing at him. When he saw the fear in her face, his heart split open. He didn't give a flying fig if she was still married, or that she'd gotten pregnant in high school, or who her neighbors were. She was injured, and he would be the one to rescue her from all of it. "Please, let me do a painting of you. One portrait."

"Of *me*?" She seemed incredulous. "I don't think so. Why in the world would you want to—?"

Paint you?" He finished her sentence. "See, that's what I don't understand. You don't like yourself very much. And I can't figure out why, because I like everything about you. I like being with you. I like talking to you. And I don't see any harm in the two of us getting together, just friends, talking to each other."

She sat down, diverting her eyes as if she knew he was lying.

"And I think you like me too. A little, anyway. Don't you?"

"Well, sure I do."

"Let me do a portrait of you. And when it's done, I'll go away. If that's what you still want."

"I don't know, Rick." She pulled at a strand of her hair again. "I hate the thought of it. I like feeling invisible."

He had to keep trying; this was it. "Give me one chance to show you—*you*—through my eyes."

SIX

JANUARY 1967
NOËL

*It was a sizzling summer night; the humidity clinging to her skin like crawling insects, not one ounce of breeze stirring the Spanish moss that hung from the limbs of the cypress tree. As Noël rocked on her backyard swing, she noticed something laying in the grass just beyond. Could it really be? She slid off the swing and tiptoed closer. It **was** her—her long-lost dolly. Swooping Amelia Rosalie up in her arms, she saw her eyelids roll open, her glass eyes staring at her as if in warning. And then she heard them thrashing through the trees, and soon she saw them—a band of angry men, including Jack Ruby in a fedora hat, carrying torches in the black night as they marched toward their appointed murderous act. Amelia Rosalie shriveled to dust.*

NOËL woke up sideways in bed, the sheet knotted around her waist, her chest pounding. Another nightmare. It was no use even trying to fall back asleep. Pandora's box had already been jarred open for the night, the shards of Hyssop's memories flying around the room.

As she lay there wide-eyed, she longed for the mother's comfort that had been stolen from her. Oddly, it helped to hear the sounds of plumbing, of life, coming through the floorboards; a reminder that the Chavises were one flight below, nearby. Sometimes mundane sounds were the most soothing.

In many ways, Mrs. Chavis had become a mother figure to

her—a nurturing and stable presence, a truth-teller. Her long-suffering eyes honed in on what others missed, seeing only what mattered and leaving the rest alone. Best of all, her hands were a mother's hands: hardworking, earthy, and warm, the way a mother's hands ought to be, not smelling of perfume like her own mother's during the Hyssop days, or of medicinal hand lotion, like now.

And yet, Noël was sadly aware of the huge price Mrs. Chavis had to pay for her enduring faith and forbearance; they had been woven into her genes through generations of injustice. Why couldn't Mrs. Chavis have gone to school? Why couldn't Freddie have been a world-class pitcher when he still curved a baseball like a master? Because they were born black. And too many black people still got murdered, one way or another, for having dreams. Hyssop had taught Noël that bitter lesson.

She tossed in her bed, her thoughts shifting to Rick. Why on earth had she agreed to let him do her portrait?

She loved his conversation; she was interested in the things he had to say. And though her knee-jerk reaction to his compliments was discomfort and shame, she was inexplicably drawn to the melancholy in his eyes, his silly, crooked grin. She loved him without desire, like another brother, not the way he wanted. Was it right to keep company with him when his passion could not be reciprocated?

Freddie kept warning her not to let him go ("You gonna need a good man to raise up that little boy."). Maybe Freddie knew better, knew how the world turned without regard to our wishes, and that her feelings, or lack of them, were better ignored for the sake of her son.

She got up and stepped into Adam's bedroom. He was clutching Malcolm, his stuffed bear, dreaming contentedly, one foot dangling out from the skewed blanket. She gently slid his little leg back under the covers and brushed his forehead with a kiss before heading for the living room, where she turned on the television.

The familiar Indian-chief test pattern stared back at her. It was three a.m. on a snowy Friday in late January. Cynthia Andrew's latest letter lay on the coffee table in front of her. She reached for it, then leaned back into the cushions.

Getting Cynthia's address hadn't been easy. Or Bo's, Steve's and Adam's, for that matter. A month before Christmas, Noël had called home for the first time since escaping Willow. After her father said hello, he started in on her for running off and deserting David.

"What the hell were you thinking? It's time to get back to your husband where you belong."

Relieved, she had let him rant—if he couldn't think of anything else to say, she knew her brothers must still be alive.

"If you're not coming back, why the hell did you call?"

She called, she told him, because she wanted their addresses. She didn't elaborate. She didn't tell him that she was yearning for the sound of her brothers' voices, if only on paper; that being cut off from them was making her crazy with loneliness and fear, fueling her nightmares.

At first, he'd refused to share their contact information unless Noël confessed where she was hiding. "I'll come and get you myself if I have to," he said. "Your son belongs to him too, you know."

She got so scared, she almost hung up. Finally, who knows why, he stopped his tirade and gave her the addresses.

"Adam's not at Fort Campbell anymore?"

"Nope, he's all done with basic training," her father had replied. "He's in Fort Sam Houston, Texas, getting his A.I.T. to become a combat medic. Don't you even want to know how your mother's doing? You used to be her shadow. Now she could be dead, for all you care."

Noël's heart squeezed. He was right; she had abandoned her mother for the safety of her son. "Is Mama okay?"

"Depends on your definition."

That call had been nearly two months ago. As soon as Noël hung up, she'd written all four of them long letters. Since then, she'd received one letter back from Adam, not one word yet from either Steve or Bo, and three from Cynthia, including the letter that had arrived that morning, where she'd shared her plans to come visit Noël this coming weekend.

When Noël had first seen Adam's spindly handwriting on an envelope, she had burst into sobs. In his letter, he'd described the medical training he was receiving in Texas, and he'd underlined the words: "I'm more certain than ever that being a surgeon is my calling." Then he added, "When I get back home, the first thing I'm doing is pursuing my education. The government will help me. This will all work out for the good."

Cynthia had responded almost immediately. In her first letter, she began by saying that her family had moved away from Willow to New Junction just after Adam left for boot camp. Ensconced in Ohio State for her freshman year, she wrote in her flowery, loopy script: "Adam would love the college experience as much as I do. His life wasn't supposed to be derailed by Vietnam."

Noël took Cynthia's latest letter back to her bedroom, sat up against the headboard, and read it one more time. Cynthia's father used to be co-owner of the Luffkin factory, but he sold his share when they'd moved away. Her family had never wanted for money or opportunities.

"I've made so many new friends," Cynthia wrote. "I can't wait to tell you about them. A bunch of us flew out to San Francisco last week to the Be-In at Golden Gate Park. Did you see it on the news? It was beyond words. Over twenty thousand people came, including Timothy Leary and Allen Ginsberg. My mind was blown! I only wish Adam could've been there too. We don't have to be bound by the crap we've been handed down—the bigotry, materialism, oppression, hatred, and war. My poor, sweet Adam and all the other soldiers are being used so shamelessly. But a new world is brewing. I truly believe that our generation has the power to transform this planet. Out there in Golden Gate Park, love reigned supreme."

Noël had seen the event on the news, sensing just a spark of what Cynthia was describing as the camera panned the sea of euphoric, young faces. They seemed beyond idealistic, on the cusp of some radical shift. Was it congregate hope? Was it the kind of brotherly love Pastor Ray spoke of in his sermons back in the 1950s?

She glanced at the clock again, and it was nearly four-thirty a.m. She was going to look like an old hen tomorrow if she didn't get some sleep. Cynthia would probably find her dowdy after all her own exotic new experiences. Only two years younger than Noël, she seemed part of the future, a bonafide member of the Pepsi generation who "came alive" on the TV commercials; revolutionaries wearing flower garlands. But it was a revolution from which Noël was excluded.

She put the letter on the nightstand and curled up in bed, shut her eyes. The men were carrying torches again, along with Jack Ruby in his fedora hat. Her lids opened. She lay there, staring at the ceiling.

Where did dreams come from anyway? They were crazy fragments of the bits and pieces floating around inside our heads, and they came together like bizarre theater. She knew full well where the band of angry men had come from—and the object of their pursuit. Hyssop was never far away from her thoughts. But how in Sam Hill did *Jack Ruby* get into her dreams?

Earlier that month, she'd read in the newspaper that Ruby had died of cancer in a Dallas hospital, just after the Texas Court of

Appeals granted him a new trial. Somewhere in her subconscious, that irony must have been lurking.

An hour later, she was still tossing and turning.

Cynthia arrived around one in the afternoon, looking as Noël had expected: fresh as a marigold—frosted pale lipstick; a white turtle neck sweater and blue jeans; straighter, blonder hair; and long bangs that hung over her sky-blue eyes like Pattie Boyd Harrison. "College is agreeing with you," Noël said.

Cynthia gave her a glance that seemed to say she'd not fared as well.

"You got so big," she told Adam.

He brought out his baseball as she settled cross-legged on the fraying carpet. She politely accepted a glass of cheap red wine, screw-capped Mogen David, the best Noël could afford. "Uncle Freddie plays ball," Adam said.

Tell me more about this Uncle Freddie of yours." She grinned up at Noël, insinuating a romance.

"For gosh sakes, Cynthia. He's my sixty-eight-year-old neighbor who lives downstairs with his wife."

Cynthia's disappointment quickly dissolved. "He must be black then, too? I think it's so cool that you live in this neighborhood. It's good for little Adam to grow up around all kinds of people. I wish I had. But I'm sort of doing it now, at Ohio State, though there aren't many black kids there." Tossing the ball in Adam's direction, she watched him fumble it. He was still too young to manage a baseball catch with much precision.

"Bring out your bigger ball," Noël suggested. "The blue one."

"I want *this* one!" Hurling the baseball in the air with one jerking movement, he laughed joyously.

After Adam went to bed for the night, the two of them had time for intimate conversation and a lot more wine. Cynthia was going to stay the night, and Noël planned to take the sofa so that Cynthia could be well rested before the long drive back to Ohio State the next morning.

Noël lit her candles. By that time, they were comfortably reacquainted, like two old chums sharing confidences over a campfire. Still, Noël felt the slightest bit uptight in comparison as she settled on the sofa, shoulders hunched forward, while Cynthia opted for her lotus-style pose again on the braided carpet. She told Noël that she'd received numerous letters from Adam since he'd left, but none since he had gone to Vietnam.

"He's in Vietnam already. I thought he was still in Texas."

"He left there two weeks ago." Cynthia's eyes dimmed. "This whole Vietnam thing wouldn't have happened if he didn't lose that scholarship. I'm so scared for him, Noël. He's not cut out for what's in store—not for war. Adam is pure conscience, you know that. And this war is so unjust."

Noël took a gulp of wine, a big one.

"He lost that scholarship on principle," Cynthia mused, her fingertips stroking the lip of her glass. "Old man Curtis was such a bully. He'd pick on Arthur Conley in history class 'til he was a stuttering mess. And we'd all just sit back and watch it happen. But not Adam. No one else had the courage to stand up to him."

Noël knew the story well, the one that had broken all their hearts, but she listened as if it was the first time.

"So, what does he get for his good deed?" Cynthia moved her arm in rising anger, spilling some of her wine on the sofa cushions, but too incensed to notice. "Curtis bullies him right out of his scholarship, that's what. It's so unfair! The same way our government is unfair—shipping our boys off to a bogus war." She let the Mogen David hang on her tongue before she swallowed. "Adam keeps expecting life to be fair, but it's not. He doesn't know how to compromise. Or lie. Or go to war."

Noël nodded thoughtfully, pouring herself another drink and refreshing Cynthia's. They would both probably have a devil of a headache tomorrow. "He's been that way since he was a little boy," Noël said. "If it wasn't for Adam, I'd still be trapped with David."

"What do you mean?"

"The night Adam left for boot camp, he handed me an envelope with the money he'd been saving up for college, along with the keys to his car. He told me, 'Leave that son of a bitch. This is your only chance. Run fast and run far.'" Noël stared into one of the candle flames. "It was enough to rent this apartment and keep us from living in the car until I found a job. He saved us."

Cynthia uncrossed her legs and set her glass down on the coffee table. "I was wondering how you managed to get away. I knew you had his car, but—" Her voice trailed off; her eyes filled with tears. "My wonderful, big-hearted Adam. I had no idea he did that."

After Cynthia reclaimed her glass, they sipped on, drifting into their own thoughts. "That's not the only thing he did that night. "Can I tell you a secret, Noël?"

God, no. Not another secret. "Sure." Noël braced herself. "I'm good at keeping secrets."

A thin smile played at Cynthia's lips. "Adam and I got married that night."

"What? You're *married*?"

Cynthia held her left hand out flat in front of Noël. A plain gold band gleamed on her finger. Noël had noticed it before but thought it might be Cynthia's way of letting the boys back in college know she was off limits. "We got our rings at a pawn shop in Bedlington the week before."

Noël took in the happy news in the midst of her angst over Adam's well-being. "So, we're sisters now?"

Nodding, Cynthia drew her ring finger close to her heart, stroking it with her right hand. "The night before he left, he met me on the altar of the First Methodist Church. I was in a long white dress, the one I wore for my graduation party, and I helped him knot one of your father's swankiest ties. He looked so handsome." Her smile was full now, her eyes glistening. "We wrote our own vows. He told me he felt like the first Adam; like life was just beginning."

"My brother, the poet. Pastor Martin wasn't there?"

"Of course not! We couldn't take that chance. We thought it all through, and we didn't need those bourgeois rules. The only license we needed was the one on our hearts. God was on that altar with us."

Noël's thoughts were mixed. She could see that Cynthia truly believed it was a real marriage, but was it? Maybe it didn't matter; they could do it right when he got back. More importantly, she was grateful to Cynthia beyond measure for giving her brother the ultimate incentive to return safely from war. "It must be so hard for you to be without him," she said.

"It is." Cynthia grabbed a Kleenex from the folds of her pocket, dabbed at her eyes. "It's absolutely horrible to be without him."

"But why keep it a secret?"

"Are you kidding? My father would've cut me off if he knew I married before college." Tears streamed down her cheeks. "It was so amazing, Noël. After we left the church, Adam and I went to that abandoned shed off Route Five. We cleaned it up, made it real cozy with incense and a braided rug, kind of like this one, and hung curtains that I sewed myself with tassels on the hem. It was our idyllic honeymoon suite. And it was, *he* was, idyllic."

Noël thought of the bruises she had sustained on her own honeymoon night and felt a surge of envy. She knew that sex was supposed to be blissful, yet she'd never experienced that, nothing even remotely close. Yet loving her brother and Cynthia as much as she did, she didn't begrudge them a single moment of happiness. Smiling at Cynthia, she refilled their glasses once more, killing the bottle.

≈≈

The next day, Sunday, Noël felt a little depressed to see her go. During breakfast, Cynthia told Adam stories about the old days in Willow, reliving her memories of meeting Adam and their courtship. He'd written her scads of love poems, she told them—she'd saved them in a shoebox that she took with her to Ohio State—and she reread them each night before bed. "Thank God for school," she said. "It helps me keep my mind off being separated from him."

"There's this wild guy named Nathan." She grinned as she went on, "He's kind of our ringleader. An activist, full of ideas about how we can start a peace revolution and stop the war. It makes me feel like I'm doing something to help Adam." She leaned closer, assuring her voice was low enough for Noël's child not to overhear. "I've even tried a little pot."

Around noon, they said their final goodbyes. "Don't ever forget," Cynthia bent down in front of Adam, "you're named after the most magnificent man in the world." After that, she put on her strawberry-red woolen jacket and matching beret, and picked up her floral luggage, no longer the grieving war bride but a picture-perfect college student, bright-eyed and full of hope.

SEVEN

FEBRUARY 1967
RICKY

NEARLY midnight on a Saturday night, Ricky was putting the finishing touches on his sandwich when Leon returned home from another stint with the National Guard. Ricky watched as he tossed his car keys on the kitchen counter, not the hook on the wall like he was supposed to do. Their parents had been asleep for hours.

"Welcome home," Ricky said. "How was it?"

Uncommunicative, the way he always got when he got back from one of these weekends, Leon slumped into a chair at the table as Ricky hung his keys on the hook. Ma would be on Leon's case if she found them cluttering her breakfast prep space first thing in the morning. "Tired?" Though the answer was obvious, Ricky asked anyway.

"Positively beat."

"Can I make you a sandwich?"

Leon nodded. "Thanks."

Handing over his original masterpiece, Ricky regathered the ingredients out of the fridge—the mayo, turkey, Polish pickles, the freshly baked pumpernickel bread Ma had bought earlier that day at the Polonia Bakery. When he was done, he sat down beside him. "You want some milk to go with that?"

"No, Beaver." Leon got up to retrieve a bottle of vodka from the top cabinet near the sink. He poured two tumblers straight-up, and handed one to Ricky.

"Gee, thanks, Wally." He decided to try again. "How was your weekend?"

"Nothing to write home about."

He waited for more, but Leon munched on in silence. He held so much inside, and sometimes Ricky felt responsible for being the cause of his reticence. When they were kids, Ma wasn't much interested in anything Leon had to say. Overcompensating for Ricky's nerve condition, she gave him the lion's share of her attention, and there wasn't much left for Leon after that. "Ma is starting to get worried about this National Guard thing of yours, you know."

"Why now—in my last year? There's no way we'll get deployed to Vietnam."

"It's not that. She's all worked up because some coloreds were causing trouble uptown yesterday."

"So? What's that got to do with me?"

"You know Ma," Ricky said. "After Johnson sent the National Guard to Selma and Watts, she got it in her head that it's gonna happen here too. She says things are getting more dangerous in America than Vietnam."

"Mom has all kinds of screwy ideas. Langston, Indiana, is *not* Selma, Alabama." Leon shook his head. "So, what's the news around here? Tell me what I missed."

"Not much." As he stared into his glass, Ricky saw a wavy reflection of the light fixture overhead. "Stella came over today to do more wedding planning with Ma."

"That's nothing new."

"Except for the date, thanks to you. But not to worry. They're both excited now that you pushed it off until New Year's Eve."

Leon took a long sip.

"They're planning to turn the Pulaski Hall into a winter wonderland. And St. Stan's too. White orchids, white candles, white glitter, white everything."

"Pure and sanitized, like a wedding ought to be." Leon wiped the mayonnaise dribble from his chin. "Actually, I've been thinking we should move it back to next summer."

"You want to change the date again? Good luck with that one, Kemosabe." Ricky felt suddenly lightheaded, that joyous jolt he always got when the vodka was kicking in. "If Noël ever said yes to me, I couldn't marry her fast enough."

"Well, see, that's where you and I are different." Leon rubbed his greasy fingers on his National Guard fatigues as he rose from the table. Switching on the Magnavox radio near the telephone, he changed their mother's favorite station over to WLS in Chicago, where "Don't Let Me Be Misunderstood" was playing. Eric Burdon's gritty voice filled the kitchen.

Ricky watched as Leon shut his eyes and as good as disappeared into the bluesy sound. Music could do that to him. It was fascinating to observe; it transported him, enlivened him, like his own covert language.

"You know," Leon said, clicking the radio off after the song was finished, "that could be my theme song."

"Poor, misunderstood boy." Ricky laughed.

His brother was nearly out of the kitchen before Ricky had the nerve to blurt it out, the preamble to the gist of what had been bothering him all weekend long. "Hey, hold on a sec. Can I talk to you about something?"

Leon stopped in the doorway, turned around. "You want to go out to the porch?"

He nodded. His brother always made time to listen to him, and their front porch, the largest in the neighborhood, was the place to go whenever they needed a serious conversation. They grabbed their jackets, trailed out into the cool night air, and settled themselves on the front stoop. Come warmer weather, they'd haul the old porch swing out from the garage, but, for now, the steps would do.

Not surprisingly, Leon immediately reached into his pocket and pulled out a cigarette, lit it, snapped the lighter shut. "Well? What's on your mind?"

"You know how you told me a while back that there's something not quite right about Noël?"

"Yeah?" He sat up straighter.

"Here it is, plain and simple—you were right. She's still married."

"Holy shit, Ricky." Leon took a quick puff. "You better not let Mom know."

"It's not like she's still with him. She left her husband nearly a year ago." He shifted his skinny butt on the hard concrete.

"So, why isn't she divorced yet?"

"She's afraid, I guess."

"Of what?"

"That he's going to take her son away from her."

"I wonder why that is." Leon's eyes were hard. "Courts always rule on the mother's side … unless she's unfit." Though Ricky resented the implication, he dared not admit the same thought had crossed his mind. "How long is she intending to hide?"

"I don't know." Ricky shrugged.

"A few months? Years? Forever?"

"I said I don't know!"

The starry night was still, the narrow street quiet; it was too late to hear one peep from the neighbors. "I love her, Leon. I love her a lot. She's all I think about."

"Hold on there, Romeo. Start thinking with your head, not your wonky-donky. This could get ugly." Leon blew the smoke out from his nostrils. "I suppose dumping her is out of the question?"

"Completely out of the question. I'd never do that. So, what *should* I do?"

He stared straight ahead, took another drag. "Hell if I know."

"It's eating me up."

"I warned you."

"Spare me." He'd been hoping Leon had mellowed out about Noël, but he guessed he'd only been holding back to keep the peace. "This isn't the time for gloating."

"I'm not gloating." He threw his arm across Ricky's shoulder and left it there for half a second before withdrawing it to take another pull of nicotine. "I guess you'll just have to bide your time then, that's all. Wait and see what happens."

Ricky felt the need to confess before he burst. Though Leon was no Father Chet, he was the next best choice. He could count on Leon to be square with him, even when he detested his advice. "Do you know what I'm hoping for? I'm hoping Noël falls in love with me. And when she does, I'm hoping that gives her the motivation to ask him for a divorce. I'll be there to protect her, of course, when that happens. I'm hoping she'll marry me one day."

Leon's eyes fixated on the street light.

"Say something. What do you think?"

"Lots of hoping in there."

"Yeah. What's wrong with hope?"

"Nothing. It just never worked out much for me." He slung his arm around Ricky again. "But I—*hope*—it works out for you."

"Very funny."

"I'm not trying to be funny. I really do hope it works out for you."

The vodka was surging full force through Ricky's bloodstream. "Thanks for letting me vent. I feel better."

"I don't know why. I didn't have any answers."

"Yeah, you did. You said to bide my time."

"I'm good at that. Biding my time, I mean. Just ask Stella."

In the glare of the porchlight, Ricky cast a sideways glance at him. Leon looked spent. He seldom mentioned Stella, or any of his prior girlfriends, for that matter. He compartmentalized his love life, probably because it had become a continual tug of war between him and Ma. Ever since Leon had graduated from high school, she'd been pushing him toward marriage; and anytime he seemed close, he sabotaged the relationship to exert control over his own life, or maybe just to irritate her. But when Stella came along, Ma's pushing turned to shoving.

Like Ma, Ricky believed that Stella Minczewski was the one who had finally cracked his brother's enigmatic code. A secretary in the steel mills by day and a neighbor eight blocks away by night, she'd blazed a new trail in Leon's mysterious world. Stella was the first to get him to the point of actually booking churches and halls.

As the chill of the night sunk into Ricky's bones, he pictured his future sister-in-law's face—her curly honey-blonde hair, her ready, throaty laughter. "You really got lucky, you know that? She reminds me of a young Lauren Bacall."

"Who does?"

"Stella."

"I want what *you're* drinking."

"C'mon, Leon. You know she's pretty."

"Yeah, she's pretty enough, but—" His face was awash in gloom.

"But what? You love her, that's all that matters."

Leon smoked on, silent as a dead man.

"You *do* love her, right?"

"Love." Leon tossed his cigarette to the ground. "Who knows if there's really such a thing? Maybe there's just sex, then marriage. The end."

"There really is such a thing." Ricky eyed his brother sadly. "Trust me."

Within minutes, little Adam was off Ricky's lap, running after his ball. Now they were playing catch across the living room. Every time Adam caught it, he giggled in surprise, little crinkles forming around his eyes.

"You better stop smiling so much or you're gonna get laugh lines before you're five," Ricky teased. "Or else you'll get—tickle lines!" As he swung the squealing little boy around in the air, he watched Noël get a bottle of pop out of the refrigerator for when the rigorous game was finished and place it on the coffee table, no coaster or anything. Ma would have a conniption over that.

Later, after she tucked Adam into bed and returned to the living room, she began lighting her menagerie of candles, a ritual he'd come to relish. "You're so good with Adam," she said.

"I love playing with him."

She sat down beside him on the couch, her eyes reflective. "I think he gets lonesome sometimes."

"We all do."

"A child shouldn't."

Ricky wished he could capture her melancholy expression on canvas. In the corner of the room stood his easel with the half-finished portrait, his ongoing pretense to return every Saturday night.

"It's getting late," she said.

"Then I better get started."

Stepping over to the easel, he pulled out his palette. She didn't love him yet, but she would. He knew what unrequited love was, he'd had plenty of experience with it, of loving some girl from afar who couldn't even remember his name. But this time was different. There was a part of Noël that cared for him, he was certain of that, and that was the part he was fighting for.

He dipped his brush into the peachy, white-colored mixture that would become the lace fabric over her breasts. Her eyes were glazed on one of the candles, her thoughts seemed miles away. If she wasn't so detached from these portrait sessions, they might be wildly sensual. Even without her, they were erotic enough for him.

It was time to test the waters. He set his brush down and joined her on the sofa. Leaning closer, he dared to kiss her on the lips.

Noël jerked backward as if he'd splashed her with cold water, bumping his chin in the process. "I'm sorry!" She seemed mortified by her overreaction. "It's not you. It's *me*."

His heart was punctured. So were any delusions of himself as a desirable man. "Forget about it." He turned away before she could see the onslaught. The welts, bursting out like a spreading wildfire.

"Oh, no!" she said, when he finally turned to face her. "I'm *so* sorry!"

"Don't be." His embarrassment stung worse than her rejection. "It's not your fault."

She rushed into the kitchen to soak a washcloth with icy cold water. After returning to his side, she pressed it against his flaming forehead. Though it felt cool to the touch, it was insult to injury; his fantasy lover demoted to nurse. Without a word, they sat there until his face cleared.

"It's just that I'm not free to have a relationship." Her voice was kind, overly so. She was trying too hard.

"For the last time, Noël, it's okay. I get it."

"I don't want to hurt you. Maybe we should stop seeing each other."

"You're not hurting me! It was my mistake. I just got caught up in the moment, that's all. We're just friends. I'm good with that." He tossed the washcloth to the floor. "Let's watch TV or something."

Dutifully, she got up from the sofa, clicked the set on, and they both stared at it without paying attention. He glanced at her; she still looked tortured.

"I told you," he said, "this nerve thing isn't your fault. I've been dealing with it since kindergarten."

"Kindergarten?" she said softly. "What caused it back then?"

He debated if he should go on. Locked deep in his memory, it was a story he'd never shared. But love took risks, didn't it?

"Well … I was sitting in a circle on the tile floor with the other kids. And our teacher, a nun named Sister Thomas Moore, pointed at me to be the first one to demonstrate how to tie my shoelaces." He paused. "I tried to bring the two ends together. But the harder I tried, the more I fumbled it. And the kids started to laugh at me. The next thing I knew, I had what looked like giant mosquito bites all over."

"That must've been very scary to have it start that way, when you were so little."

"Not half as scary as recess was. That's when Billy Maciejewski, the toughest boy in our class, ambushed me outside. He poked me in the chest, the kids gathering around, and asked me if I had chicken pox or something. He said I must've gotten them because I was a big, fat chicken. The kids all started laughing again. And out came the welts, even worse than before."

Tears filled her eyes. "What did you do?"

"I stood there like a frozen jerk, that's what. But out of the corner of my eye, from the far side of the blacktop, I saw my brother drop his softball bat and start coming toward me. He was a second grader, a big kid to me at the time. Anyway, he stopped in front of Billy, hands on his hips, and told him he had a nose like an anteater. He offered to shorten it for Billy right there and then." Ricky laughed, a forced one. "And little, old Billy dissolved like a snowflake. Unfortunately, this nerve thing didn't. Or whatever it is. It comes out at other times too, like when I eat the wrong foods or stay in the sun too long."

She looked down at her lap. "We're lucky to have brothers like that, aren't we?"

"Yup, we are. My condition hasn't been so easy for him either." Another stowed-away, untold story. "Once he gave me a piece of his Bit-O-Honey bar, neither of us knowing I was allergic to it, and the welts popped out like crazy. Ma throttled him for it. … Ma blamed Leon a lot. Even if he was just standing there being the 'well' son."

She gazed at him in the candlelight, wiped the tears from her cheeks. "You know what? You're more of a friend than I deserve."

"Why do you say things like that?"

"Like what?"

"Like you aren't worthy of having a—friend."

She began propping up the couch pillow, one of her familiar mannerisms when she was trying to dodge a topic. Here he'd just gone and bared his soul, and she was propping pillows. "You never talk about yourself," he said. "I've known you for two months already. Don't you trust me yet?"

"Of course, I trust you." She was twisting her hair now; the crowning gesture in her vast avoidance repertoire. "There's just nothing to talk about."

≈≈

The following Saturday, he took Noël and Adam for a long drive east to Amish country. As he steered the car through the flat, still-brown countryside, they passed miles of pristine white farmhouses sitting far back from the road, white cotton shirts and identical dowdy dresses flapping on every clothesline.

After he parked the car, the unbelievable happened. For the first time, she started treating him like a boyfriend—whispering into his ear and smiling into his eyes as they strolled along together through the quaint Amish shops. It dawned on him that she must be trying to atone for rebuffing him the week before. When his hand searched for hers, her fingers tightened around it.

He didn't care what caused the change in her, even if it was remorse.

Some people gave them a second look when they passed, as if they were Beauty and the Beast. A couple of young girls in the shop were actually flirting with him, sneaking him secret, doe-eyed glances, wondering what the Beauty saw in a goon like him and curious to figure it out for themselves.

At one point, Noël found a miniature wooden cottage with paned windows sitting on a shelf, and she rushed over to it. Turning it this way and that, she scrutinized it from every possible angle. "Sometimes I dream about living in a cottage like this one, by the sea."

"Let me buy it for you."

"Oh, no, no." She set it down, hurried out of the shop.

For some reason, his offer broke the spell. After that, she was back to treating him like a brother.

By the time they got back to Langston and parted at her door, she surprised him with another sudden mood change. Moving near enough for him to feel her breath on his face, she closed her eyes, inviting him to kiss her.

"Really?" This time, he needed to be sure.

She nodded.

Tilting forward, he tentatively touched his lips against hers before actually puckering into the shape of a kiss. When she responded, his heart surged. The thrill of her was unimaginable; her lips felt soft as flower petals. He pulled her closer.

She backed out of his arms. "Let's just take it slow, okay?"

Finally, she'd given him permission to ascend to a new level in their relationship, yet the undisputable misery in her eyes robbed the moment of its joy. Ricky felt like he'd been dropped from a mountain top.

Back home, he grabbed a half-full bottle of Stolichnaya from the kitchen cupboard and hurried downstairs to the unfinished room of the basement, over to his easel where he feverishly continued his latest portrait of her face. With a heavy hand, he painted out her wistfulness, capturing the other Noël on canvas—the piercing one, the one who stared out at the world, him included, as if it was a predator to be kept at bay; the one who had the power to destroy him. He painted and guzzled until it was done: the best likeness of her yet.

As he stepped back to examine it, he was startled by a noise behind him.

"She's gorgeous," his mother said.

"I didn't hear you come down the stairs."

"I know. You wouldn't have heard a tornado; you were so focused. When did you start painting down here in the basement?"

A few days prior, Ricky had moved his art stuff into a corner near the washing machine. "I thought I'd spread out a little. Noël thinks I'm a pretty good artist."

She flinched, as if the sound of her name was a dirty word. "A French girl. Hmph. I always thought you'd find a nice Polish girl. Someone like Filena Domkowski."

"Filena Domkowski? C'mon, Ma …"

She looked at the portrait again. "You've been seeing this woman for a while now, every single weekend. Why haven't you brought her over to meet us yet?"

"There's plenty of time for that." He was eager to change the subject. "What time is it?"

"It's two in the morning. I couldn't sleep." She stepped closer to the easel. "Your French girl is right. You're a very good artist, Ricky." Without make-up, especially her penciled eyebrows with the exaggerated arch, Ma seemed softer, almost vulnerable. "Does she really look like that?"

"Close enough."

"My goodness." Ma sat down on an old crate near the dryer. Though she wasn't a heavy woman, Ricky wasn't certain the crate was sturdy enough to hold her. "She's pretty enough to be on the cover of *McCall's.*"

"I know what you're thinking."

"What am I thinking?"

"You're thinking just like Leon, and everyone else, including me. 'What's a beautiful girl like her doing with my ugly son?'"

"You're not ugly!"

"Compared to her I am."

"Compared to her, Princess Grace is ugly."

Ricky smiled. So did she. He settled down beside her on his father's case of Drewrys beer. "What's wrong, Ma? You seem to be at loose ends lately."

"My sensitive son." She leaned over, pecked him on the cheek. "Things are just changing so fast, honey. Too fast for me, anyway."

"How do you mean?"

"The Bartkowiaks want to sell their house."

"You don't say." He was flabbergasted—the Bartkowiaks had been their next-door neighbors since forever. "Wow. That *is* a lot to take in."

"Your father is heartsick, of course. Though you know how he is—he tries not to show it. I don't know what he'll do without Stanley nearby. They've been joined at the hip since they came over on the ship together. He's like a brother to him."

Ricky tried to assimilate the news. "They'll still see each other at the mills. It's not like they're leaving the country."

"Leaving the neighborhood *is* like leaving the country. The Jaworskis put their house on the market too. And the Cebelskis, of course. They're the ones who started the stampede."

"They just want to move to the suburbs. It's a status thing. You know, keep up with the Jones-skis. You can't really blame them for wanting cleaner air."

"Cleaner air? This is their home!" She repositioned her weight on the crate, and Ricky held his breath. "Everything seems to be changing lately. What's so different about now? I just don't understand it."

He tried to think of something to say that might give her comfort.

"This neighborhood has been a fortress to me." Her voice sounded heavy with grief. "Everything and everyone we want, need, and love is here, surrounding us, day after day, for as long as I can remember. Now suddenly, it's not good enough anymore. A nice, new neighborhood, with clean air and strangers, can't compare to all the history we have right here. Can it?"

"Things change." Ricky shrugged. "It's part of life."

"For over two generations, we've shopped together, worshipped at church together, gone to school together, married and had our babies together. Died together."

Her face switched from agony to anger. "Some darkies came to look at the Cebelskis' house today. What if *they* move in? At least Stanley and Helen know better than to sell their house to *that* kind, but the Cebelskis are desperate to sell. Next thing you know, we'll be having riots right here on our front lawns."

Her face was pale, drawn, chiseled deep with worry lines that no longer disappeared the way they used to when she changed expression. Ma looked old; even older than yesterday. She struggled to get up from the crate, finally successful after a few shaky tries.

Standing up beside her, Ricky gave her a long hug. "Things will get better. Just wait and see. Leon will get married to Stella, and you'll have that wedding of your dreams. By this time next year, you might even have a grandchild on the way."

A thin smile raised her lips.

"Who knows? Maybe even two of them."

"*Two* of them?"

"Maybe me and Noël."

Her mouth snapped flat. "She's not pregnant, is she?"

Ricky laughed regretfully, their failed kiss replaying in his mind. "Definitely not."

"Thank God." She patted his cheek. "I know my boys will be gone soon too. You're all grown up. And I know I haven't been very good at encouraging you to be an artist like *she's* doing. But it's just because you paint such sad things all the time, all those Holocaust scenes. You never paint flowers or sunrises. You only paint things that are breaking your heart." She walked over to the easel, fixed her gaze on it. "Tell me more about this woman."

"I love her, Ma."

"I know you do." She turned around. "But something isn't right. I'm your mother, and I sense it. Why are you keeping her such a secret from us?"

"I'm not."

"Yes, you are. She's the first girl you ever loved, and you're hiding her away."

"No, no. It's just that—"

"What?"

"She's got … some issues … she still needs to work out. That's all."

"What kind of issues?" She stared at him. "Go on, tell me. What issues?"

"Well … it's just that she and her little boy are trying to make it on their own since—"

"Little boy?" she interrupted. "She has a child?"

His wheels were grinding slower than his mouth was flapping. *Damn that vodka*, loosening him up like that.

His mother stared, waiting for more. "It's bad enough that we don't know her. And that she's not Polish or Catholic. And now you're telling me she has a son? You know how the church feels about divorce. If you end up getting married, she'll have to—"

"Whoa, slow down, Ma! We've got a long way to go before that happens. She's not even div—" He stopped himself.

Her jaw dropped.

Holy shit. He was in way over his head now.

"What were you going to say?" Her foot was tapping fiercely.

"Nothing."

"Dear God," she said. "Please don't tell me you were going to say she's not even divorced."

Ricky froze. He didn't have the foggiest idea what to say or do next.

"Well is she, or isn't she?"

He hung his head.

"You mean you're running around with a *married* woman?" Her palms sprang to her cheeks.

"It's not like that! She has no intention of going back to him."

"I'll bet she doesn't! Now that she's found a sugar daddy to raise her child, why should she? I'm sure she knows you make a good living at the steel mill. A married woman! *O mój Boże!*"

Now Ma was breaking into Polish, the sure sign she was over-wrought. Ricky's eyes rolled upward toward the ceiling.

"Don't make that face with me! … It's late now. Too late for this. But first thing tomorrow, we're talking about it alright." She blew out a deep breath, trying to calm herself. "At least I know why you've been acting this way, like she's ripped your heart out of your chest." She turned around and glared into the painted eyes of Noël Trudeau. "Now she's doing the same thing to me."

True to her word, the next morning Ma was waiting in ambush for him in the kitchen when he came in for breakfast. And all hell broke loose.

EIGHT

MARCH 1967
NOËL

A S Walter Cronkite gave the latest Vietnam update on the evening news, Noël turned off the television. Instantly, she put it back on. As much as the images distressed her, she knew her brothers didn't have the luxury of switching a TV dial to make them all go away, so she forced herself to watch them every night. The never-ending fire fights. The burning fields. The bloody maimed and wounded being lifted into choppers. The sea of flag-draped coffins.

The next news story was a clip of Bobby Kennedy on the Senate floor proposing a plan to end the war—the first time, Cronkite said, that Kennedy had broken publicly with President Johnson on Vietnam.

Hallelujah, Bobby. She closed her eyes. *Please bring them home.*

A letter from Adam had arrived earlier that day. Unlike the eight pages she received from Bo the week before, it was sparse in vocabulary. Vietnam had flipped their personalities. Bo was filled with passion ("I hate the gooks! They have to be stopped at all costs."), while Adam seemed strangely disoriented. In painstaking detail, Bo wrote about the Vietnamese culture, his philosophy on America's presence over there, including a two-page diatribe on the evils of communism. In contrast, Adam's sentences were terse, simple, more like a log than a letter: "It's hotter than hell here. But wetter and muddier than hot. My boot has a hole in it. To look more like a grunt, I carry my medical supplies in a Claymore mine bag. Medics are prime targets." Not one word about where his head was, just miserable observations. Only the first line was vintage Adam: "Greetings from the valley of the shadow of death."

Around eight-thirty p.m., after she'd tucked Adam into bed for the night, she opened a bottle of soda pop, root beer for a change, and settled again in front of the television, snug in her heaviest robe and flannel nightgown. Her candles burning, she turned the sound of the TV down to a faint mumble in the background. Except for the tinkly sound of Samantha's twitching nose every now and then on *Bewitched*, the apartment was quiet. She leaned back against the cushion.

A sudden sound of footsteps on the stairs startled her, followed by a series of short, rapid taps against her door. It couldn't be Mrs. Chavis; the footsteps were much too agile. After a pause, the knocks came again. *Rap-rap-rap-rap-rap.*

Who would be out there at this time of evening? Rick visited only on Saturdays, and never without notice.

Full-blown panic struck her. *Please don't let it be David!* Should she run to Adam's room, lock his door, and take cover? She flashed back to the old days in Hyssop when she and her brothers used to hide from the Jehovah's Witnesses.

Rap-rap-rap. Rap-rap.

"It's Leon Ziemny, Ricky's brother. Are you in there?"

Relief coursed through her veins, enough to make her shaky after the assault of adrenalin She shifted gears. What on earth was Leon Ziemny doing here?

His appearance from the one and only time she'd seen him flashed through her mind: standing out there in the dark stairwell with his hair dripping wet from snow, his piercing eyes. Tightening the sash of her robe, she inched closer to the sound of his voice. "What do you want?"

"I just want to talk with you."

Pulling the door ajar just a crack, she saw that he looked nearly the same, glaring at her in a way that made his dislike crystal-clear. His near-black hair wasn't soggy now; it was neat, well-groomed, his mustache punctuating his face with a disturbing handsomeness. Ruined as she was, she'd thought herself impervious to such girlish observations. She shored up her walls. "Rick's not here, you know."

"I know."

"Is he all right?"

"Oh, he's better than all right." His voice took on a caustic tone. "He's higher than Picasso. As we speak, he's creating another masterpiece of you, the *Mona Lisa* of 1967."

Another portrait? Rick had told her it took months to complete a painting. A storm of recriminating emotions for being Ricky's muse zinged through her, not the least of which was embarrassment. She glanced at the draped easel in the corner of the room. "Then why are you here?"

"Okay, then." He lifted one hand high on the doorframe. "If that's the way you want it, we'll have this conversation out here. Why are you dating my brother while you're still married?"

So, that was it, the reason he'd come here so smug and self-righteous. He was on some sort of chivalrous mission, a knight jousting for his younger brother's honor. She probably deserved this. Another wave of self-reproach surged through her. Time and time again, she'd asked herself the same thing.

"Well, then, say what you have to say." She opened the door wide enough for him to enter. "But, please, keep your voice down. My son is sleeping in the other room."

He stood with his back to the TV, arms folded. As he glanced in the direction of the hallway, she noticed that a muscle in his cheek was twitching, presumbably from nerves. A mortal chink in his knightly breastplate. She watched his eyes taking in the living room before perching himself on the edge of the sofa.

"I don't remember asking you to sit down." Her heart was hammering, from anger, no doubt, at his intrusion into her home (why had she let him in?), not to mention his reason for showing up in the first place—to shed light on her transgressions like one of Dickens' Christmas ghosts. She tugged her bulky robe tighter around her. "And why do I owe *you* any explanations?"

"Because I'm my brother's keeper. That's why."

What a pompous response. Yet, having brothers of her own whom she'd do anything to protect, she couldn't help but appreciate it. "And is that the way Rick sees it too—that you're his keeper?"

"Probably not." His eyes left hers. "Okay, definitely not. He'd be mad as hell if he knew I was here. ... Do you mind if I smoke?" He was already pulling his package of Marlboros out of his pocket.

"Yes, I do mind, as a matter of fact."

"You do?" He left his cigarettes alone, focusing on the soundless TV screen, giving her the freedom to observe him more closely for a few seconds. To his credit, he carried himself with complete indifference to his own good looks. She studied his face in the candlelight. There was a black-and-white quality about it, tinged with the muted color of his eyes, reminding her of a sepia photograph of a Civil War soldier. Or of smoke. Whatever stoked his inner fire burned beneath the surface.

"Okay, then, Mona Lisa, let's cut to the chase," he said. "What are you trying to pull with Ricky?"

"I'm not trying to pull anything." She sat down in the chair opposite him. "But I guess I can understand why you think I'm so—horrible."

Without disputing her choice of word, he gave her his full attention.

"The truth is that I'm separated. I left my husband eight months ago, and I'm not going back. I'm just as good as divorced."

"Only you're not. … So, why are you still married?"

"I ran away."

"You mean you're hiding from your husband?"

She lowered her eyes. "Sort of."

"What is he, Jack the Ripper or something?"

An awkward silence lingered as he appeared to absorb the new information. She'd been too quick to divulge it, and she was annoyed with herself. What if he found a way to use it against her?

"That's your side of the story," he said. "I bet your husband has his own version. After all, you're the one who took his kid and ran off on him." He looked away for a second, toward the hallway. "Is your son an infant?"

"No, he's almost three."

His fingers brushed the pocket where he kept his cigarettes. He seemed in dire need of one. "And how old are you?"

"Pardon me? What difference does that make?"

"It's just a question."

"How old are *you*?"

"Nearly twenty-four." He leaned back. "See? That wasn't so hard." He examined her quickly, from head to toe. "I bet you're barely twenty."

"For your information, I turned twenty-one last month." There she went again—the queen of keeping secrets—answering his nosy questions as if he had any right to know. What was the matter with her?

"Look, I know your marriage is none of my business, but—"

"That's one thing we agree on."

"But Ricky is. And that's why I'm here. You've turned our house upside down. My mother is a devout Catholic, and this whole business with you still being married is giving her Hail Mary fits."

It rattled her to learn that she was a contested topic in the Ziemny household, but she dared not show it. "So, your mother sent you?"

He redirected his eyes for a second. "She doesn't even know I'm here," he mumbled sheepishly. "Just tell me what you want from Ricky."

"What do you mean?"

"Another simple question."

"Look, as difficult as this might be for you to understand, Rick and I are friends. That's all."

"Bullshit. He's in love with you, and you know it."

Her face flushed—from more guilt, more shame, from who knew what else? Mrs. Chavis had told her the same thing from the get-go. When it came to Rick, whatever choice she made was the wrong one. Refuse to see him, and she'd break his heart. Keep seeing him, and she was leading him on. She was stuck. And now she was cornered by his bulldog of a big brother.

But he was right. And Mrs. Chavis was right. And Pastor Ray was right too—when you didn't love too much, you didn't love enough. And not loving Rick enough was worse than not loving him at all.

Close to tears, she feigned bravado "You're acting as if he's a child. Rick isn't some naïve imbecile, you know."

"I didn't say he was."

"But you implied it. He's a deep-thinking artist with a sensitive heart. He's kind and gentle and loving." Leon looked down at the floor, but she kept on going. "The truth is, I enjoy his company. And his friendship. Is there a crime in that?"

"No crime." He lifted his head. "Ricky is my brother, so you don't have to spout off his virtues to me. I know how trusting he is. That's why I'm here. And I won't let you hurt him." He scanned the room until he honed in on the covered easel. "I suppose that's a painting he's doing of you under there?"

Flustered by the mention of it, she remained quiet.

"Do you mind if I take a look?" He was already halfway across the room.

Though it was just an unfinished portrait, nothing indecent about it, she loathed its unveiling. She hated everything about that painting. Still, she couldn't help but admire Leon's confidence, his fearless aggression on behalf of his brother. He lifted the white sheet, her cheeks burning bright red as his eyes absorbed the canvas.

"Only half a face after all these months? It's a good thing he's not immortalizing you in the Sistine Chapel or we'd all be dead before it's finished." He returned to the sofa and leaned toward her chair, near enough for her to inhale the scent of his Old Spice aftershave. "But I can see why he chose you as a subject." His voice changed in tone and tenor. "You are beautiful."

For whatever reason, hearing that word this time sent her pulse racing. No, it wasn't because she was attracted to him, whatever that meant. It was because he was some kind of con man. He had to be, to be doing this to her, throwing her off-balance like this. Her cheeks were hot again, unbearably hot. Her mother also used to be a blusher when her emotions, good or bad, were stirred beyond comfort; a mutinous trait.

"Who are you really, Noël Trudeau?" He stared at her as if trying to decode her soul. Reaching inside his pocket, he pulled out a fifty-dollar bill and waved it. "I'm no artist, but how far will this get me?"

Stunned, her heart splintered. "You think I'm a—*prostitute*? How dare you!" She sprang up from her chair. "Where did you get an idea like that?"

"From you! Look at you. Look at this neighborhood you're living in." He glanced around the room. "It sure looks like a brothel in here with all these candles. Not to mention that you're dating, if that's what you call it, when you're still married to the father of your kid. And I did the math too, by the way. You weren't even out of high school when you got knocked up. So, stop pretending you're some kind of shrinking violet. Ricky might buy it, but I don't."

"How dare you!" she said again, then struggled to keep her voice down so she didn't wake her child. This cruel, despicable stranger was now pushing her most painful buttons. "You don't know anything about me!"

"I know enough. And I know how a girl gets pregnant."

"You think you're so smart, don't you?" She choked back tears. "You think you've got it all figured out. But you're arrogant and ignorant. For your information, I had no choice. I had to get married. He *forced* me!"

"He forced you to marry him?"

"No! He forced me to—" She couldn't say it.

His face blanched. "You mean, he *raped* you?"

"Call it what you want!" The floodgates were torn open. "Men like you don't care, do you? You just take whatever you want, no matter who it hurts. Never mind that he treats his own child like a nuisance—an orphan—a stain on his precious name. Never mind that he beat me up so badly that I can't have any more children. Never mind that he—" She stopped herself, but it was far too late. Her shameful confession tremored in the air like the aftermath of a violent explosion. Humiliated by her own candor—with him of all people—she wept uncontrollably. "Get out!" She flung the door wide open.

"Please—stop crying!" Pulling out his handkerchief from his pants pocket, he thrust it in front of her with remorseful eyes. "I'm the idiot of the century. I guess I had it—you—figured out all wrong."

"Just get out, okay?" She whimpered.

"I can't leave like this." He looked befuddled. "I'll stand outside the door if you want me to, but don't shut me out just yet." He stuck his toe in the doorway as she tried to slam it. It must have hurt, but he didn't even wince. "I have an idea that might help you."

"Does Rick think I'm a prostitute too?" Her thoughts were gnarled like thorny vines. "Do I look like a prostitute?"

"No. Hell, no. You're beautiful—I already told you that. Ricky thinks you're an angel. I'm the asshole who thought you were a hooker." His cheek muscle throbbed erratically. "I'm sorry. I'm a total moron."

His self-effacing apologies mixed her up even more. "Yes, you are." She dried her eyes with his hanky. "But you made your point loud and clear. I'll break it off with Rick first thing tomorrow."

"No, don't do that! Jesus, that would kill him!"

"Then what *do* you want me do?" A new wave of frustrated tears flooded her eyes.

"Baby?" Mrs. Chavis called out from the floor below. "Are you okay up there?" Noël heard the sound of her feet ascending the stairs, and so she stepped outside into the stairwell.

"What are you doing here?" Mrs. Chavis glowered at him when she reached the top.

"Don't worry, I'm okay," Noël said. "This is just Rick's brother."

"*Rick's brother?*" She leaned against the wall, trying to catch her breath. "Good Lord, I thought he was your—" She stopped herself.

"You thought he was my husband, didn't you? I'm so sorry."

Noël put her arms around her. "He's only here because he thinks I'm mistreating Rick."

"A tiny little slip of a thing like you?" Mrs. Chavis raised her eyebrows, though she avoided looking directly at him.

"He should know." Noël blew her nose into his handkerchief. "He's his brother's keeper."

Mrs. Chavis looked confused. Leon looked embarrassed.

"Just give me one more minute," he said. "And then I'll go. I promise."

"You gonna be all right up here with him?"

Noël nodded as she stared into his face. She couldn't figure him out. When she looked away, she saw Mrs. Chavis' eyes darting between the two of them, back and forth.

"Um-hm." Mrs. Chavis shook her head knowingly at the end of her inspection, keeping whatever she was thinking to herself. "I suspect you will be. ... But you just holler out if you need me."

As soon as her apartment door closed again, he resumed their conversation. "I just have one more question. Do you want to be divorced?" His voice was soft now, his eyes earnest.

"Are you kidding?" Noël handed him back his handkerchief. "Getting David out of our lives would feel like being born again."

"Then here's my idea." Glancing at the wet hanky, he stuffed it back into his pocket anyway. "What if I pretend that *I'm* your boyfriend, and go and have a talk with this guy—man to man? I'll tell him I'm madly in love with you and desperate to marry you. If he thinks there's a very determined guy in the picture, he'll back off and let you go. Won't he?"

His gallant offer, and the way he'd phrased it, without one mention of doing it for Rick, induced another flurry of unsettling emotions. He was a con man, alright, and he was making her jittery, confused. She fought the distraction of his eyes up close as she played out the ramifications in her head. "But I'm afraid he might try to take my son away, just to get back at me. Nothing is worth that risk. Nothing."

"What a predicament." His brows knotted. "You can't go on living in limbo like this forever."

"I appreciate the offer. I really do. But this way is safest."

He kicked the toe of his shoe against the floor. "Then, I guess it is what it is … but I sure feel bad that you have to live this way."

She shrugged.

"And I'm sorry for being such a jerk."

"You're not a jerk." Maybe she'd said it too quickly.

"I'm not?"

Their eyes locked. "No," she said.

"Then, what am I? Because I don't know right now."

Neither did she. He seemed a different man from the one who'd come to her door. In the flash of an evening, he'd gone from her persecutor, to her protector, to—maybe—a fellow pilgrim, trying to navigate a world strewn with land mines. Like this moment. This terrible, blurring moment when she could not force her eyes off of him.

"But you were wrong about one thing," he said. "Jerk or no jerk, I'm not like him. Your husband, I mean."

"I know. You just love your brother, that's all."

"Yup. I do."

They were out of words. It was time for him to leave—she knew that—but she stood there anyway. After putting her through the gamut of emotions tonight, she felt raw and vulnerable. His eyes seemed a kaleidoscope of changing, deepening hues. Something she didn't recognize was intensifying his face, triggering an equally unfamiliar reaction in herself. Was he aware of it too, or was she only imagining that he was? It was terrifying to lose her bearings this way.

She lowered her head to try to break the spell, but he lifted her chin back up with his fingertips, a touch light enough to be barely felt, yet she felt it everywhere—it ricocheted, vibrated, as if a wall inside of her was crumbling down. When he leaned even closer, she did not move away.

A car screeched suddenly against the pavement outside, jolting her—them—back to reality. Leon took a step backward. "Holy shit, what am I doing?" he whispered to himself.

The car skid away. Silence covered them like a shroud.

He cleared his throat, his expression reclaiming its original harshness. "Keep on seeing Ricky. It's none of my business. And I never came here tonight, you got that?"

She was the enemy again.

Her emotions sharp as stiletto blades, she listened to the sound of his footsteps descending the staircase, and then the door—as he slammed it shut between them.

NINE

APRIL 4, 1967
THECKLA

T HECKLA was busy preparing dinner, while Freddie and Adam played Fiddlesticks in front of the TV. "We need some ketchup," she called out to her husband. "That child won't even look at this meatloaf if it's not smothered in it."

Grabbing his cap off the rack, Freddie left for the Food Stop across the alley. When he got back home, he headed straight for the kitchen. "Trouble's brewing out there." He spoke in low tones so that Adam didn't overhear. "Henry Jones was shot dead by the police outside of Ruby's."

"Good Lord!" Theckla took the paper bag from his arms. "Why? What was he doing?"

"Nothin'. Just liquored up and acting the fool, the way he always does. Now a mob's out there, getting more worked up by the minute."

She glanced at the clock; it was close to time for Noël to be heading back home from her job, a seven-block walk that led straight past Ruby's Bar. "You better go out to the diner," she said. "Make sure she gets home safe."

With a weary nod, Freddie retrieved his cap.

≈≈

No more than five minutes later, Theckla heard the wail of a lone siren down the street, and another, then a third, until a whole brigade of police cars was screeching outside the window, some close, some farther away.

Adam looked up wide-eyed from his Bugs Bunny cartoon. "It's okay, baby." Theckla smiled at him. "You and me are snug as a bug in a rug." A pot was boiling over on the stove, and she hurried to sop up the mess. As long as she was down on her knees below the kitchen counter, she took a moment; she pressed her hands together and mouthed a silent prayer.

By the time Freddie and Noël finally stepped through the doorway a good hour later, Theckla was limp with relief. "Sit down here," she said as she helped Noël, stunned and chalk-white, over to Freddie's softest chair. Adam climbed on his mama's lap, but she didn't even notice him. "What's a matter with her?" Theckla asked Freddie.

"She'll be okay. She's just scared shitless, that's all. It's a riot out there. The police're cracking their skulls with clubs."

As the sirens kept coming, Theckla could smell the ashy scent of smoke through the open kitchen window, and she shut it tight.

Interrupting Bugs Bunny, the local newsman broke in with unblinking eyes, informing his viewing audience that buildings were being set on fire up and down Jackson Street, including Lucky's Launder-O-Matic. Giving Freddie a fitful glance, Theckla turned off the set.

"Just keep these lights on, woman," he said. "Nobody's gonna burn us up if they see we're in here."

She struggled to keep things as close to routine as possible. She went ahead and served dinner, insisting they hold hands while Freddie said grace, but all the while, Noël was like a bucking bronco, bolting from the table to check outside the front window again and again. "They're going to kill him!" she said.

"Kill who?" Freddie asked.

Without answering, Noël turned the TV back on. Walter Cronkite was reporting the national news. "This morning at New York's Riverside Church, Dr. Martin Luther King Jr. delivered a controversial speech called 'A Time to Break Silence'," Cronkite said. "A harsh criticism of U.S. government foreign policy, this was Dr. King's first anti-Vietnam statement."

"That's all King needs—to go out and speak against the war now too." Freddie shook his head. "If you ask me, that man just signed his own death warrant."

Freddie's comment, for some reason, was the final straw for Noël. She tugged at her hair, her eyes glassy and strange. Theckla knew it wasn't right for Adam to see his mother that way. "Noël, honey," she said, "why don't you and me go upstairs to your apartment, while Uncle Freddie and Adam raid my special cookie jar? What do you say?"

Freddie dangled a cookie in front of the frightened child. "See here, boy? It's your favorite—big old chocolate chips." Clutching Freddie's legs, he hid his face between his knees.

Theckla reached out for Noël's hand, but she startled as if she didn't know who she was. "No need to be afraid," Theckla said softly.

"Where's Amelia Rosalie?"

"Who?"

"My dolly!"

Theckla gave Freddie another worried glance. "Your dolly must be upstairs. Let's go see if we can find her."

Steadying Noël with both arms, she tackled the short trip up the steps to her apartment as best she could, a horrible trembling rocking Noël's body all the way up. Once inside, Noël stood in the doorway of her own home without a scrap of recognition in her eyes.

"It doesn't look like the same place without candles burning, does it?" Theckla said. "Why don't you and I light some for all those troubled folks out there?" As more sirens roared by, Noël's eyes darted around the room. "Yes sirree," Theckla continued without missing a beat. "Let's light up those candles. That'll make us both feel better, don't you think?"

As Theckla ignited the flames one by one, Noël perched tentatively on the sofa, watching her. Remembering Freddie's advice about keeping the lights on, she switched on a lamp, but Noël squinted and covered her eyes, and so she settled for placing a row of lit candles in the front window instead.

For the next half-hour or so, she played Noël's music on the record player, turning the volume up loud enough to drown out the sounds outside the window. They listened to the Beatles, the Rolling Stones, and the Doors. Most of it was just plain noise to Theckla, but Noël seemed to love the song "Light My Fire," and so Theckla replayed it for her four times in a row. The awful lyrics about setting the night in flames didn't seem to remind Noël one bit of what was going on down the street.

Sometime during the last "Light My Fire" replay, Freddie came up to assure them that Adam was sound asleep downstairs in his easy chair. "The phones went dead," he muttered to Theckla under his breath as she stopped the record player. "The wires must've got burnt." He slipped her a bottle of his favorite whiskey, his Seagram's, the one he saved for the best and worst occasions, and nodded toward Noël.

She followed his lead. "Baby, would you like a little nip?" She held up the bottle. Noël stared at it.

Snatching the Seagram's, Freddie moved into the kitchen.

"Where you keep your glasses, girl?" Eventually finding the right cupboard, he poured a shot of the amber liquid into two glasses and downed his own portion quickly. He handed Noël the other glass. "You sip this potion, and it'll settle you right down." Before retreating back downstairs, he pecked Theckla on the cheek. "It's gonna be okay," he told her.

Without flinching, Noël gulped down the shot of whiskey like an old sailor. Heading back to the kitchen for more—the wavering flames casting shadows as she moved past them—she poured herself a little less than twice as much as the one before and sat back down on the sofa.

Theckla wracked her brain for another distraction. Afraid to risk turning the TV back on, she settled for the radio, tuning in Freddie's usual channel where they were replaying Dr. King's speech from earlier in the day.

As his distinctive voice filled the room, Theckla saw Noël's shoulders beginning to relax, the tautness in her body visibly diminishing. The sirens from more emergency vehicles shrieked down the street, their red lights reflecting through the window as they sped by, and Theckla turned up the volume. Dr. King was warning about the immorality of war, the poison of hatred.

It was a lengthy, impassioned speech, a condemnation of America's presence in Vietnam, so powerful that Theckla feared Freddie was right about Dr. King putting himself in further jeopardy. He spoke of our moral, spiritual obligation to care for neighbors and nations beyond our own borders, invoking Christ's appeal for unconditional love as epitomized in the Gospel of St. John; exalting love, not as weak or sentimental, but as the supreme, fundamental force of life.

Noël stirred. She crossed her arms around herself and pressed them against her belly, her shoulders slumping. Dr. King went on to quote someone named Arnold Toynbee: "'Therefore the first hope in our inventory must be the hope that love is going to have the last word.'"

"Make him stop!" Noël cried.

"What in God's name is the matter?"

"Make him stop!" Noël sprang up. "They're going to kill him!"

"No one's gonna hurt him." Theckla scrambled to shut off the dial with fumbling fingers. "Dr. King will be okay."

"I'm not talking about Dr. King!"

"Then who are you talking about?"

The dim room was stone silent. For now, the sirens had stopped. Noël paced back and forth for several seconds before sitting down again. She seemed to want to speak, but couldn't or wouldn't—almost like she was fighting the urge to throw up.

"It's okay, you can tell me," Theckla coaxed.

Her face in the candlelight was as pale as a dead woman's. "Dr. King talks just like he did."

"Like who did?"

She tore through her hair again. "Everything about this night reminds me of him. And the night we left Hyssop."

"Of who?"

"Pastor Raymond Roberts."

"And who's Pastor Raymond Roberts?"

Noël shifted in her seat.

"Tell me—who's Pastor Raymond Roberts?"

"He was—" Noël paused, tried again. "He was a Baptist pastor back in Hyssop. … And my mother was in love with him."

The vomit had finally spewed.

She looked amazed. So was Theckla. "A Baptist pastor?" She tried not to show her alarm. "Surely you don't mean that he was a black man?"

Noël nodded.

Theckla tried to gather her wits as she watched Noël get up from the sofa and head straight for the uncapped Seagram's on the kitchen counter. "Go easy on that stuff. You're gonna be out cold if you're not careful." Noël seemed to absorb her words, stopping momentarily before pouring a relatively small amount into the glass.

"Come back, sit down here with me." She patted the sofa cushions. "Tell me more about this Pastor Raymond Roberts."

Noël did as she asked, sat down again.

"Your mama most certainly didn't go to the black church, did she?"

She shook her head emphatically.

"Then how on earth did she ever get to know Pastor Raymond?"

"At the tent revivals. We went there to hear him."

Ah, the tent revivals. Theckla nodded. She knew full well that curious white people often sat or stood on the sidelines of the big Negro revivals, gawking and pointing as if they were a circus act. Noël's mother must have been among the rare ones who understood the source of their divine passion. "So, your mama listened to his sermons and fell in love with him?"

Her eyebrows knotted. "It was more than that."

"What do you mean?"

"He counseled her. At his church."

"Counseled her?" Theckla couldn't fathom such a situation—a white woman reaching out to a black pastor for that kind of help. "You mean, she met with one of his staff, not him directly."

"No, I mean she met with *him*. Alone." Noël took a gulp of her drink. "Except for me. She always took me along after school, in case someone saw her, while Bo looked after the boys."

As Theckla tried to absorb the implications of what she was saying, she could see that Noël was tottering on the edges of some internal abyss. "So, your mama went to get some counseling." She took a long, strong look at Noël. "And she took *you* along?"

She nodded.

"How old were you?"

"I'd just turned seven. It was the same birthday I got Amelia Rosalie."

"Only seven." Theckla shook her head, her eyes intensifying with an assortment of strong emotions.

"Pastor Ray was waiting for her behind the church doors, locking them as soon as we came in." Noël's gaze got stuck on something on the far side of the room, maybe a candle flame; whatever it was, the eerie light seemed to be stoking her recollections, descending her further backward in time, back inside that Baptist church.

"Go on."

"He'd read scripture to her. Play piano. Just talk to her for what seemed like hours. He was so gentle with her, so kind. They'd sit together on the pew as I played with Amelia Rosalie." Noël breathed easier for half a second, a blink of happiness. "I watched my mama open up to him like one or her roses."

The story of young Emmett Till and that pretty white woman raced through Theckla's thoughts. A sinking, sickly feeling gripped her.

"Later—and I mean many Monday afternoons later," Noël said, "we didn't meet him at the church."

"You mean, you stopped going?"

"No. I mean we met him at his house."

Every ounce of her being was telling her to bolt from the room, to stop Noël's unfolding story here and now, to head back down-stairs to Freddie. This was forbidden territory they were entering, dangerous territory; how well she knew. But, for Noël's sake, she forced herself to stay put. "Go on. Get this thing out of you before it kills you."

Noël took one more sip for strength, staring straight ahead as the scene played out in her memory, her pupils dilating to black coals. "Mama put on her favorite red dress that day. But she was afraid. She looked around every few seconds as we walked to his house. When we got there, he opened the back door and shut it fast."

Sirens were bleating again outside, but Theckla was too lost in the unwinding tale to be distracted. Noël set her glass down with a thud, almost missing the coffee table. "Mama told me she was going upstairs with him for a little while. She made me promise two times, three times, to stay downstairs. I did what she said. I waited and waited. I didn't mean to disobey!" As she relived the scene, she seemed nearly a child again.

"I know you didn't. She's not mad at you. Nobody's mad at you."

"But they were gone so long, I got really scared. … So, I tiptoed up the stairs. When I got to the top, there was a long, dark hallway with lots of doors." Her head moved from left to right as she examined the doorways in her mind. "They were all open, except one. I heard sounds behind it. I pushed it open. And I saw them together … in his bed."

Theckla's fingertips rose against her lips.

"I didn't know what they were doing. But I knew he wasn't hurting her." Her eyes glistened with a peculiar wonder. "My mama was looking at him like she was seeing something miraculous."

Theckla swallowed hard; it felt as if she was swallowing her own heart. She feared the ending of this story; more than feared it. What she'd already heard was unthinkable—a black man was a fool to even look at a white woman, let alone take her into his bed, let alone a black preacher, and let alone in the deep south. That poor, deluded man must have harbored an almighty love for her mama to take such a reckless, ludicrous, perilous risk.

Her own nightmare images of Mobile, Alabama, were whirling through her head, including the day Freddie lost his teeth, his smile, and God knows how much else they lost that monstrous day. She felt the Goliath fires of hatred raging outside the windows, against the never-ending shrillness of the sirens.

"Somehow—someone found out about them," Noël said. "I swear it wasn't *me* who told!"

"I know, baby. I know it wasn't you."

"Do you think my mama thought it was me?" Her eyes seared into Theckla's.

"No. She knew it wasn't you."

Reassured, but only slightly, Noël eventually picked up where she'd left off. "Daddy came home from work late that night. He told us, 'There's a bad story going around about Pastor Ray being alone in his church with some white woman, and a group of men are on their way to his house to settle the score.' Mama rushed to the door, but he grabbed her tight, held her there for all he was worth. She kept hollering for him to let her go. My brothers were on the verge of tears. They knew there was something bigger, more complicated, going on, but they didn't understand what it was. But I did."

The liquor was making the words flow freely now. Theckla shut her lids.

"And then ... And then, the men did it." Noël fell silent.

Theckla opened up her eyes. And she shuddered. She recognized the expression on Noël's face, that grievous look of living through trauma too horrific to have survived it. "And then, the men did what?" she asked. Her throat felt like sand. "Tell me what they did."

It was Mr. Walston's truck," Noël whimpered, "—he was

Daddy's foreman. And he and the others … they… they chained him up. They chained Pastor Ray to the back of Mr. Walston's pick-up truck."

"Oh, my almighty God!"

"And they dragged him through the streets, right past our house," she cried. "Bo opened the door—and me and the boys saw it! We heard his screams!" She pressed her fists tight against her ears. "Mama was screaming too, the two of them together … And then his howls stopped. Suddenly."

Noël's hands fell limp into her lap. She seemed emotionless now; gone to that safe place that Theckla knew firsthand mercifully holds us in our anguish.

"Daddy kept yelling at Mama to shut up and pack," she continued, her voice becoming monotone. "The boys were running all over the house throwing their things into a big pile in the middle of the room. Mama was shrieking, louder and louder. She was out of control. Daddy yelled at her that her place was there with him, with all of us. And she thrashed at him, punched and kicked like a wild woman in his arms. I ran to her, but Daddy pushed me away. And he hit her with a terrible whack. He hit her so hard that she fell against the table." Noël paused, regaining her emotion. She looked at Theckla, forlorn. "And he broke her, Mrs. Chavis. My mama never said another sentence in her life."

Her body began to tremor again, same as when they were heading up the stairs, as if there was more to tell. What else could there possibly be?

"As we drove out of Hyssop," she said, "past the Baptist church, Daddy slowed the car for a second. We saw something hanging from the tree. Something dark and mangled, maybe three feet long, shredded and unrecognizable. A spotlight was shining on it, as it dangled from a rope. And then I realized—it was him, what was left of him. They just hung him there like that, proud of what they'd done."

A flood of grief streamed down Theckla's cheeks; Noël's body finally went still. At long last, her vile secret was all out.

"Please, don't cry, Mrs. Chavis," Noël said as innocently, imploringly, as that little girl she'd been. "Pastor Ray had the last word. I know he did. His spirit was swaying there in the moonlight as peaceful as my swing."

Only a child would've seen it that way. To compare such an abominable sight with the restful, forgiving motion of a backyard swing. Though she could barely hold herself upright, Theckla managed to put her arms around her and set her head against the pillow. "Rest now, sweet girl. It can't hurt you anymore."

As Theckla tried to absorb the horror of the story just revealed, she became aware again of the sound of the sirens. Hate was a tangible presence, not only there inside that dim room with the candle flames casting their grotesque shadows all over the walls and ceiling, but outside the window too, and down the street. It felt like apocalypse to her.

Not knowing what else to do or say, she began singing one of the old church hymns. "'*Precious Lord, take my hand, lead me on, let me stand …*'" She sang, and she sang, and she kept on singing long after Noël had drifted to sleep.

She sang for their decimated neighborhood, for their splintered country, for her Freddie and their lost dreams, and she sang for her—sweet, fractured Noël Trudeau. And long before she stopped singing, she sensed a much greater presence in the room. Just like Dr. King had spoken of, and Toynbee's first hope, and maybe—as Noël had imagined—just like Pastor Raymond's spirit too. There was something mightier than hatred that held us all together, something woven deeply into our souls. And it always had the last word.

≈≈

An hour or so later, still sitting on the sofa beside Noël, Theckla heard a knock on the door and wondered why Freddie wasn't using his key.

"Are you in there?" The stranger's voice sounded out of breath. "Are you okay?"

Noël was still out cold. Carefully, Theckla moved Noël's wilted body aside and repositioned her head on the pillow. When she opened up the door, a man was standing there dressed in National Guard fatigues. Looking closer, she recognized him: It was that Ziemny boy, Rick's older brother. He pushed past her and over to the couch, huffing and puffing as if he'd run all the way over from the riot scene and up the staircase. "Is she alright?"

"She had a pretty rough night."

He picked up the empty whiskey glass, sniffed it, then looked at the uncapped Seagram's on the counter. "Yeah, well, I don't know what the hell she's doing in this neighborhood anyway." His eyes narrowed; he wouldn't look at her.

Theckla ignored the insinuation; it was always best to do that. "They had to call in the National Guard? Is it that bad out there?"

"It's a fucking zoo! I don't know what these people—" He stopped himself.

She wondered why he was here, though pretty certain she already knew. "Nice of you to leave your post to come check on her. Won't your platoon, or whatever you call it, be missing you?"

Just then, Noël moaned. For a second, she opened her eyes, saw him standing over her, blinked a few times as if making sure he wasn't a mirage. Smiling, she drifted back into her stupor.

Tenderness engulfed him.

"You're really relieved to know she's okay," Theckla said.

"What?" Snapping out of it, he made eye contact for a brief second, unmasked.

"I meant to say, your brother will be relieved."

"Yeah, well … there's no point mentioning to him that I was here tonight."

"No. Of course not."

He left without another word.

ALL YOU NEED IS LOVE

TEN

MAY 1967
LEON

HERE we go again, Leon thought, as the bleak scene at Saturday's breakfast table played itself out—a perfect replay of yesterday, the day before, and the day before that: Mom, blubbering into her scrambled eggs because Ricky insisted on dating a married woman; Ricky, long-faced and battle-scarred, too anxious to eat a bite; and him, taking on their mother all by himself until she got so worked up that she stormed out of the kitchen. Through it all, Dad sat without a word, too divided to take sides.

The only difference was that this particular morning after Mom and Dad had left the kitchen, Ricky broke down and wept, sparking another brutal nerve attack. "Noël thinks we should stop seeing each other too," he said. "She's been pushing me away for weeks now."

Consumed with guilt, Leon watched him splash cold water from the kitchen faucet over his bumpy face. Ricky blotted at the welts with a damp kitchen towel, his top lip puffed out like a pillow. "I think she's afraid I'll get caught in the crossfire if her husband finds her."

Leon couldn't stand it anymore. Today was the day.

≈≈

The map of Ohio spread out on his bed, Leon traced the

letter-number correlates until he located the tiny little dot with the name Willow beside it, east of the Indiana border and several miles south. Recently, Ricky happened to drop the name of the town she came from, as well as her husband's last name, and—*voila!*—Leon had the information he needed to do a little research at the library until he found him: David Eugene Ketchfield, living at 35460 Locust Road in Willow, Ohio, a plumber who owned a business called The Pipe Cleaner.

Leon calculated his route, a two-hour drive in his estimation, give or take. Before he left, he called Stella to inform her that he had some errands to run. "The whole day?" Her voice rose in disappointment. When he promised to take her out for a candlelight dinner at her favorite restaurant later on, she perked right up again. "I'll wear the new dress I bought downtown," she said. "It's short enough to look like something Twiggy would wear."

Even as he got into his car, Leon wondered what he was doing and why he was doing it. He told himself it was all for Ricky. As long as there was a husband lurking in the shadows, both Ricky and Noël would be stuck in this indeterminate state, like the dreaded Purgatory the old nuns used to scare them with in Catechism class.

It was a warm spring morning, the weekend before Memorial Day, a pleasant day for a long drive as the world sprang back to life after another long, harsh Langston winter.

When he switched on the car radio, the Turtles were singing "Happy Together." Hopeful lyrics, melancholy tune. The poor singer couldn't fathom himself loving any other except one unforgettable woman for the rest of his natural-born life. *Crazy fool.* The sea was full of starfish.

Leon sang along softly, until Noël's image exploded into his thoughts. Quickly, he shut it off.

Sure, she was on his mind, but only because her situation was so troubling. Not only the abuse she'd suffered at her husband's hands, but the fact that she was alone in the world, in that apartment, in that lousy part of town. The way she was trying to raise her kid on a waitress' salary. Not to mention her old beat-up car out front with the cracked windshield on the passenger side and the rusting tailpipe. If her situation was eating away at him, it had to be devouring Ricky.

Alright, so it wasn't his fight; it was his brother's. He had his own life, spinning out of control, to worry about. Stella's bridal shower was two months away, and half the neighborhood would be there. In six months, she'd be his lawfully wedded wife and his future would be sealed like a casket. Why the hell was he trying to fix Ricky's life instead of his own?

He started to chicken out. Only inertia propelled him forward; it was easier to keep on driving than to make the effort to turn the car around. He practiced what he'd say to Ketchfield once he got there.

How bad could this guy be? What if he turned out to be a decent fellow, and everything she'd told him was a crock of shit? Maybe Ketchfield would be relieved to divorce her, itching to move on. But what if he wasn't? What if he did intend to take her son away from her out of spite, and Leon was abetting him? What if he was some crazy yahoo who pulled out a shotgun or something?

Leon glanced at his reflection in the rearview mirror. It wasn't like him to do something like this. Not even remotely. This was a ballsy, brazen thing to do, way out of bounds, beyond meddling. But he was doing it for Ricky—better for him to risk Ketchfield's shotgun now, than Ricky later on. He was doing it for his mother too. Otherwise, there'd be no peace for either of them.

Leon kept reminding himself of his heroism all the way to Willow. This was a good deed. An over-and-beyond good deed. He was taking this bullet for the family. He was definitely not taking it for Noël Trudeau.

He turned the radio back on and heard "Something Stupid" by Frank and Nancy Sinatra. His thoughts drifted. He was back in the dark stairwell with Noël, staring at her beautiful face. In his mind's eye, he saw her eyes in front of him again, the vulnerability, the sadness ... their shared desire. The wheel in his hands swerved, and he jerked it back in place.

She was his brother's girl. He was doing this for Ricky.

Willow, as it turned out, was a two-bit little burg with a blink of a downtown, modest homes, and weeping willow trees everywhere he turned, too many to be believable, as if a blissful Johnny Appleseed had skipped through here while wigged out on LSD. Leon wondered what it was like to grow up in a shoebox like this. Pretty as Noël was, she was a petunia in an onion patch, ripe for the picking by local yokels like Ketchfield.

It took him a long time to find Locust Road, but eventually he did. It was way out in the sticks—nothing near it except the railroad tracks—a gray-shingled house with an old stone wishing well out front. A white van with "The Pipe Cleaner" stenciled on the sides sat on the gravel driveway, along with a pickup truck, parked crooked. The curtains were closed up tight.

Leon glanced at his watch; it was almost two p.m. As he got out of the car, the utter silence of the country was shattered by an approaching freight train—the track was less than forty yards away. He covered his ears until the roaring sound passed. Who buys a house beside the railroad tracks in the middle of nowhere? What a helluva place to live.

He knocked on the door. Nothing. No sound except some

chirping sparrows bathing in a water spout. After a few seconds, he knocked again.

A girl appeared, maybe twenty, maybe less than that, her long chestnut hair disheveled, her sweater buttoned over the wrong holes, as if she'd dressed hurriedly.

"You didn't open the door, did you, Marybelle?" Leon heard a man's voice behind her, then saw a burly blonde guy coming out of a back room, bare-chested, unshaven, his eyes heavy with sleep or hangover. "Now's not a good time, buddy," he said to Leon. "We had a really late party last night, and I'm in no mood to buy anything."

"I'm not a salesman."

"Then who are you?" He tented his hand over his eyes to see Leon better against the sunlight.

"I'm here about Noël Trudeau."

"Noël Trudeau?" A mishmash of emotions overtook Ketchfield's face, among them, what appeared to be anxiety. "What about her? Are you some kind of cop?"

"Nope."

He leaned against the doorframe, visibly calmer. "I mean, I thought maybe you were here to tell me she's dead or something." He seemed to be trying to justify his relief. "So, who are you, and what are you here for? And what's your name?"

"My name is—Ricky."

"Ricky who?" He stretched a bare foot across the threshold, his second toe longer than the big one.

"I'm here to offer you a pretty sweet deal," Leon said.

"Oh, yeah? And what might that be?"

"Noël and I want to get married. The problem is she's still married to you."

He swung the door open, and Leon took it as his invitation to enter. He stepped into a room cluttered with plumbing supplies, tool kits, and empty Chinese food cartoons littering the coffee table. "I'll make this quick and painless," he said. "File for divorce, and sue her for desertion. She doesn't want anything from you but her freedom. No child support. No alimony. Nothing. Just a clean break." He'd rehearsed these lines so often in his head that it felt like he was dreaming.

Marybelle's eyes lit up. "If you get divorced, babe, we can get married as soon as I graduate. We can take over my uncle's shop in Kentucky, just like we talked about." She turned to Leon. "I graduate in June."

"Congratulations," Leon said, his eyes fastened on Ketchfield.

"Now, wait just a cotton-pickin' minute, Ricky. Slow down, here." Ketchfield glanced at Marybelle. "This guy and I have business to settle. Go and wait in the other room."

As instructed, the girl disappeared down the hall.

"Okay, let's talk about Noël." Ketchfield's blue eyes sharpened. By now, he was waking up, and he looked more respectable, especially after he finger-combed his thick golden hair. He reminded Leon of some 1950s matinee idol, only bulkier, built large, square, like a tank. "I'll admit I was pretty pissed off after she ran off and left me like that. The whole town was talking behind my back. Where is she nowadays?"

"That must've been rough for you." Leon glanced toward the hallway, where the girl had vanished. "But it looks like you've moved on. And so has she." He handed him a lawyer's business card, Hank Maternowski, a cousin of one of Leon's best friends from high school. He'd made a little arrangement with Hank: He would secretly pay for the divorce, and Hank would tell Noël that he was doing it pro bono. "Serve her papers, and send them to her lawyer at this address."

Ketchfield looked down at the card. "This lawyer's in Valparaiso. Is that where she ran off to? What's in Valparaiso—besides you?"

"We'd like to get this divorce going. We want to get married right away."

"I told you to slow down, bub. What's your hurry? Sounds like you knocked her up … Oh, wait I forgot. She can't have any more kids. Guess you're out of luck in that department." He studied Leon's reaction as if the disclosure might be a game changer.

It was, if wanting to wring his neck counted. "You took care of that, didn't you?"

"What's that supposed to mean?" His jaw went slack, his eyes clouding over with something that seemed to Leon like regret, or possibly denial to cover his culpability. "I don't know what she told you, but I'm not the villain she makes me out to be. I really tried to do right by her. I married her before I even graduated. There aren't a lot of guys who would've done that, the honorable thing, you know?, after she drops the bomb that she's pregnant."

"You're a real prince."

"Damn right, I am! It was a huge sacrifice." He looked down at the card, bent it in his palm. "And what if I don't want to contact your lawyer? What if I want her back here beside me, 'til death do us part?"

Leon loathed the thought of Noël being anywhere near him. "It's been nearly a year since she left. You probably want to get on with your life."

"Don't tell me what I want!" Ketchfield folded his arms. "I said I'll think about it." His eyes narrowed. "But it's obvious what you want. You want her bad, don't you?"

Leon broke eye contact for an instant. When he looked at Ketchfield again, he was surprised to find him staring at some object on the wall. "I used to want her too," Ketchfield said. "A long time ago." Snapping out of whatever kind of memory he'd drifted into, he appeared newly bitter, his knuckles pressed against his hips. "But let me tell you something—she ain't worth it. Maybe you don't know the half of it. Did she tell you that her mother is nutty as a fruitcake? Her old lady hasn't spoken a word since they moved here; just stares at you with crazy, weird eyes. Did you know that her aunt blew out her own brains a few years back?"

"I know all of that." Leon struggled to appear as if none of it was coming as a shock.

Ketchfield tapped his fingers against his mouth, and Leon noticed that his nails were bitten down to the point that his fingertips were puffy and red; a guy with issues. "She ruined my life." Ketchfield's voice dropped in volume. "There my friends were, having the time of their lives the last year of school, and there I was, stuck in my parents' basement with a frigid wife and a bawling brat." As his eyes shifted to the back hallway, the lawyer's card in his hand fell to the floor. "Janie Sutton. She's the one I really wanted—she was a real lady, not a cheap tease like Noël. But after Noël trapped me, Janie never took a second look at me." He bit at his thumbnail. "Noël is an ingrate. She didn't appreciate my sacrifices. None of them."

"She made some sacrifices too."

"Oh, yeah? Name one. Did she tell you that she went ahead and named my own kid after her brothers instead of me?" His anger and revulsion heightening, Leon listened as Ketchfield's resentment toward Noël unraveled like a ball of string. "Truth is, she's looney-tunes. Did she tell you she cut off all her hair once—just chopped it off zig-zagged, on purpose—trying to make herself look like a freak? Who does that? If you ask me, she's one blip away from being as psycho as her old lady."

"She'd have to be, to marry a jackass like you." Leon glared at him.

"Is that so? Maybe you're the jackass for coming here and doing her bidding. You want to settle this thing outside?" Ketchfield raised his fists; an empty threat, probably, meant to scare Leon off. Ketchfield was at least four inches taller and a good thirty pounds heavier.

Out of nowhere, for reasons he didn't fully understand, Leon came at him with all he had, and they both went plummeting against an end table. Ketchfield seemed to want just one good whack at him, but Leon was geared up for a full-scale fight. He rammed a left hook into Ketchfield's jaw; he'd learned the best spot for a knockout while in the National Guard. Marybelle sprang out from her hiding place, yelping.

The two of them went at it, banging into furniture and lamps, while Marybelle squealed after each thing hurtled to the carpet. The pain felt cathartic to Leon. He'd never actually fought a guy before, not even close, but some kind of rage—against Ketchfield and anything in his own nature even remotely similar to his; against his troubled, confused state of mind; against, God help him, his reprehensible feelings for his own brother's girlfriend—was giving him a supernatural edge. They pounded each other long enough to make Leon question every single thing he used to believe about himself and his world.

"Stop it, already!" Ketchfield said, his lip bleeding. "You're a fucking lunatic, you know that? You make a perfect pair. Take her."

ELEVEN

JULY 1967
NOËL

O N the second to the last Saturday in July, another letter from Cynthia arrived in Noël's mailbox, along with a manila envelope from a law office in Valparaiso. Assuming the big envelope was some kind of solicitation, Noël opened Cynthia's letter as soon as she stepped back inside. A quick read revealed that Cynthia had decided to transfer to Berkeley in the fall. "San Francisco is the hub of it all," she wrote. "Me and my friends are heading out there in a big caravan so we don't miss one more minute of the Summer of Love."

Refolding the letter, Noël leaned against the wall at the bottom of the stairwell, trying to imagine what it felt like to be so carefree, to be able to flit to the hot spots of the country the way the moths had flocked to the overhead porchlight ... where they'd ended up trapped. Something about Cynthia's new adventure made her uneasy, but she couldn't quite put her finger on it. Envy? Anger that Cynthia was *finding herself*, as they put it now, while her brother lost himself in Vietnam?

The Summer of Love—a questionable title. It could just as well be called the Summer of Hate. San Francisco hippies might be floating in a love haze, but race riots were erupting everywhere else—not just in Langston, but in over a hundred cities, stoked by the sizzling summer heat. Last weekend, Newark was a war zone, triggering another disturbance in some city in Illinois. And before that, it was Buffalo and Cincinnati.

What a pessimist she'd become. It was the Summer of Love; she should leave it at that, believe in its promise the way Cynthia did.

She opened the manila envelope and pulled out an official-looking letterhead. There, in black and white, was a letter from someone named Hank Maternowski informing her that he was enclosing divorce papers filed by David E. Ketchfield. She fumbled through the papers until she found the clause about what mattered most to her: David's requests with regards to their son. Thank God!

Her heart was beating so fast that she had to stop twice just to catch her breath before she reached the top of the staircase. She could hear the phone ringing inside her apartment.

"Noël, it's me," said Rick when she picked up the handset. "Are we still on for later?"

She didn't tell him what she was holding in her hand; saying it out loud might jinx it.

After she hung up, she tried to digest the news, combing through every paragraph, word by word. It was real. He didn't want a thing to do with Adam: not paternal visits, no offer of child support, nothing.

Not one single cord of connection to David Ketchfield ever again. It was too good to be true.

And yet, the complete lack of funds, now that it was soon to be permanent, worried her. How could she even pay for a divorce? She scanned down further and saw that Maternowski was willing to represent her as part of his pro bono community service. How did he know she couldn't afford it? She read one of the final pages in the thick packet, the one that said David intended to move to Kentucky.

All of it seemed unbelievable. But she couldn't help feeling sad for her little boy. A child deserved two loving parents who wanted him. She could hear him playing in the back bedroom with a balsa wood airplane that Freddie had assembled for him that morning during breakfast. After setting the papers down on the coffee table, she headed for his room.

He was sitting on the floor, making *zoom-zoom* noises as he flew his little plane back and forth through the air, higher and lower over the clouds of the creamy bedspread. Kneeling down beside him, she grabbed one of his small plastic red men, deepening her own voice to pretend he was roaring in awe about the wondrous airplane, as Adam kept exclaiming, "I'm Sky King!" Eventually, she gathered a whole crowd of little red men to watch it take off and land.

They played together like that for the next hour, her thoughts wandering. She wanted him to have the freedom of being a child, to live in a world of toy airplanes and tiny red men and little princes. She wanted him to grow up with the parental love and nurturing that she and her brothers had to live without.

After their game, she baked a batch of his favorite cookies, Adam chattering at the card table, while she rolled out the dough. What did life hold for the two of them now? How could they make it on her salary? How could she afford to send him to college?

And then there was that other nagging question she was trying not to think about. How had this miracle happened? Leon had offered to go to David and finagle a divorce. Was it really him who had freed them?

When Rick arrived two hours later, she stuck the lawyer's letter under his nose. "Holy mackerel!" His crooked grin appeared. "What made him finally do this?"

What, indeed. She searched his face for a clue, but there was none. "It doesn't make any sense," she said. "I don't understand why David's lawyer sent these papers to some attorney in Valparaiso, who's offered to represent me for free. Or how this Maternowski guy knew where to find me." Still no reaction. "When I saw the lawyer's Polish name, I thought maybe he was a friend of— yours."

"Nope, I had nothing to do with it. I wish I did." He studied the letterhead. "The only *Maternowski* I know is a kid named Greg that my brother went to school with, but he lost track of him years ago. I don't know a soul in Valparaiso or anyone named Hank."

Her suspicions confirmed, a swarm of butterflies launched in her stomach. She sunk into the sofa.

"But who cares how it happened?" Rick dropped down beside her. "The important thing is that it *did* happen. This is the best news I've heard in a long time." He kissed her cheek. "Finally, you and I can move forward. This is our beginning!"

The butterflies churned to acid. Cynthia had written that the hippies were wearing buttons that said, "Reality is a nice place to visit, but I wouldn't want to live there." After this divorce went through, reality was exactly where Noël would be, and reality wouldn't allow her to hold her feelings in suspension, to keep living, as Leon had phrased it, in limbo.

"Let's celebrate," he said. "I'll be back at six to take you and Adam out for a special dinner."

After he left, she stared at the manila envelope on the coffee table. Rick wanted to go full-throttle now; there were no more barriers to hold him at a distance. She couldn't let this drag on. It had to be done tonight. Like tearing off a bandage, she would tear him out of her life, let the pain sting for a while and be done with it.

Tonight, come what may, she had to end her relationship, imaginary and otherwise, with both Ziemny brothers.

≈≈

After a late lasagna dinner at Antonio's, Noël tucked Adam into bed while Rick waited for her in the living room. She stalled around, pausing in the hallway, trying to muster up the courage as she rehearsed opening lines. *Rick, this is one of the most difficult things I ever had to say. Rick, there's something we need to talk about.*

It was no use. There was no good way, no kind way, to break someone's heart. When she entered the living room, he was standing by the easel, paintbrush in hand.

"Come here," he said. "I have a surprise."

Slowly, she walked to his side and took a weary glance. The portrait was finished.

It jarred her. There she was, painted in white lace, sitting in a dark room filled with burning candles, one side of her face hidden in shadows, only one visible eye. An amazing likeness, though nothing like her. It was too exquisite. "I don't know what to say."

"Do you like it?"

"It's wonderful."

One thing was certain: the finished portrait was her confirmation that she had to do this tonight. Oh, how she hated goodbyes. Each time you said goodbye to someone you loved, you lost another chunk of yourself, until, eventually, there was nothing left but empty spaces.

"You're an amazingly talented artist."

"I had an amazingly beautiful model." He put his arm around her waist, pulled her closer, kissed her cheek gently.

She tried not to go rigid, but the harder she faked it, the stiffer she became. "The portrait is finished now," she said. 'I guess that means—"

"This is chiaroscuro," he interrupted, "the technique I told you about a while ago. Light and dark together in the same package." His voice was soft. "Just like you."

"And you too."

"Me?"

"The first time I met you, Rick Ziemny, this is what I thought." She moved away, toward the sofa. "I thought, 'such a gifted, sad boy. How can he be so loving and so sad at the same time?' But now I know how—a big, loving heart runs out of space eventually, doesn't it? It breaks to make more room."

"I think that's the connection between us. Like the first night we met. Remember? That was a fateful night."

A bolt of pain ripped through her, swift and piercing. He wasn't going to make this easy. She had to regroup, reassemble her thoughts. She fled into the kitchen, pausing in front of the refrigerator, her back toward him. *You can do this, Noël. You have to do this.* Grabbing two cold bottles of Coke, she rejoined him in the living room and started lighting her candles. When she was finished, she switched off the lamp, the flame shadows doing a spirited ballet on the walls.

"You and your candles." He patted the cushion beside him.

Sitting down, she turned her head away from him, praying for the strength to get the words out. "Rick, there's something we need to talk about."

"There sure is."

When she faced him again, she saw him down on one knee, popping open a velvet box with a diamond ring in it. "Noël Trudeau, please make me the happiest man in the world and marry me."

She suppressed a gasp. She hadn't seen this coming, not at all. She felt blindsided, totally derailed. Here she was about to cut him out of her life at the precise moment he was asking her to give it to him.

"You have to know that I'm madly in love with you."

"I'm not even divorced." She clung to limbo, that old, worn-out excuse.

"But you will be soon."

Her thoughts scrambled. "You don't know me well enough."

"Of course, I do! We've known each other for six months already. And what we don't know, we'll learn as we go along. That's one of the best parts."

No, he had it all wrong; that was the worst part. He didn't know the first thing about her. Not about Hyssop, her mother, Pastor Ray. Nothing about her life with David. Or the way Aunt Clarry had died. He knew none of it. He saw her through an artist's prism, as a fantasy woman in white, sitting in a shadowy world. That's who he loved. Not the real person underneath. "You have no idea about my past."

"Then tell me. Trust me enough. Nothing could make me stop loving you."

Why was he so kind to her? Tears welled up. If she could get through only one day without weeping, but she couldn't remember a day like that. Freddie Chavis teased her about it; he called her a river machine ("Go ahead, girl, cry me another river").

"I'll tell you what," Rick said. "Let's tell each other all of our secrets tonight."

Her head started spinning; the nausea was overwhelming.

"Here's mine. I drink too much. It started because of my nerve problem, but then I got to like the taste too much and couldn't stop. I used to drink nearly a half a bottle of vodka every night, give or take. Whenever you hand me a pop, I wish it was vodka." The words came out too quickly for her to absorb. "But since I met you, I don't need to drink anywhere near as much. You make me so happy, and I—"

"Stop!" Was he trying to tell her he was an alcoholic? She stood up.

He snapped the little box shut, shoved it back inside his pocket without the slightest sign of anger or reproach, no emotion, except that aching bittersweetness that had drawn her to him from the start. "I was going to wait 'til Christmas to ask you, but I got swept up in your news today." He forced a smile. "But it's too soon. I can wait. I can wait as long as it takes."

"I might never be ready to marry again."

"Then I'll wait until never."

His patience was salt on an open cut. She glanced at the easel. She wished she could hold one of her candles to the edges of the canvas, set it on fire until that fantasy woman shriveled away into smoke.

"Let's stop this conversation for now," he said. "I won't mention it again. Not until you're ready."

"But we need to talk this through."

"Shh. Not tonight. It's not the right time." He got up, turned on the TV, ignored her imploring expression. "Oh, look, Marshal Dillon and his old sidekick, Chester. I love this show."

She knew what he was doing. He was stuffing his hurt feelings down deep. Alcoholics did that, didn't they? That was the reason they drank in the first place—to stay afloat, to stay sane. Only it ended up pulling them down in the undertow. Though Noël wasn't an addict, she understood the process. He hid in a bottle; she hid in an imaginary room, safe and dark. But it was all the same.

He stared at the TV and, truthfully, she was glad for the reprieve. What a pair they made. "You want some potato chips to go with *Gunsmoke*?" Her voice was weary with surrender.

"Sure, why not?"

She retrieved a brand-new bag from the kitchen cupboard and

ripped it open. He grabbed a generous handful as they settled back against the cushions, still acting as if he was really watching the TV screen, while his mind was probably whirling as fast as hers was. Would she ever have the guts to tell him goodbye?

"Oh, by the way. I almost forgot." He leaned forward, pulled out a small card from the same pocket where the engagement ring lurked. "I told Ma about the packet from Maternowski that you got today, and guess what? She wants to invite you now."

"Invite me where?" Noël looked down at the invitation in his hand, embossed with white wedding bells and silver ribbons.

"To my brother's bridal shower next Sunday. Well, his fiancée's, I mean. Afterward, we're having a big dinner at the house."

"I can't go. It's out of the question."

"You have to go! Ma is extending an olive branch. Please don't disappoint her, and me, by throwing it back in her face. I already told her you'd come."

His hazel eyes were beseeching. Her mind wouldn't work anymore.

She watched Miss Kitty descend the long staircase, feathers in her hair, that well-placed black beauty mark on her cheek, and she wished she could jump on Marshal Dillon's horse and gallop away, get out of Dodge, as they said. All the while, Rick gazed at her with his puppy-dog eyes.

Eventually, she relented. *I'll go to that party, and it'll be my swan song.* She wasn't certain whether she spoke it or just thought it, but she must have said the first part because he kissed her forehead in relief.

The rest of it, she didn't say out loud. She didn't tell him that this wedding shower would be the woman in white's final performance. She would meet his mother. She would, one last time, see Leon, the man who had purged David from her life. She would watch his flesh-and-blood fiancée open each and every bridal gift, the penance she deserved for harboring such hopelessly prohibited feelings for the wrong brother. And then, when Rick drove her home, the woman in white would dissolve in front of his eyes, and she would be left standing there, the real, unlovable Noël. He'd have his portrait—she'd make sure he took it home with him tonight—to remind him of that make-believe girl who could never break his heart.

And then it would be over and their ever-after would begin. No happily in sight for either one of them.

TWELVE

JULY 30, 1967
RICKY

THE Sunday of Leon and Stella's party felt as sticky as a rainforest, hot and humid with temperatures soaring into the nineties by midmorning. During mass at St. Stan's, Ricky watched the women delicately raise their embroidered hankies to their sopping foreheads. In the pew ahead of him, Mr. Golubski had sweat rings under his armpits as big as basketballs.

As soon as Father Chet gave the final blessing, a posse of aunts and cousins hightailed it out of church, straight over to the Pulaski Legion Hall to help set up for the two p.m. party where more than two hundred guests were expected. Slowly, the enormous room was covered in giant pink tissue bells and white crepe-paper streamers. Mr. Minczewski had rented a helium tank for the day, and he was inflating dozens of balloons, which the ladies tied and hung in between the streamers. Each of the small card tables set up around the room was covered with a pink linen tablecloth, a touch of elegance Ma insisted upon, protected, of course, by the customary paper placemats. The crowning touch was a long white banner reading, "Congratulations, Leon and Stella" in fancy gold calligraphy, strung across a makeshift stage at the front of the room.

When it was done, Ricky didn't have the heart to tell Ma that the room looked vandalized more than decorated.

He had his own problem to worry about. Things had nearly come to a halt a few days ago when he and the other men had received strict orders from Ma to disappear from the hall until it was time to haul out the gifts. "You mean you won't even be there?" Noël had groaned after he shared the news. "Now I won't know a soul." It took over an hour of persuasion to convince her to attend the buffet afterward instead of the shower. "But just for a little while," she said.

Even if she came to their home for only ten minutes, Ricky knew her appearance would be a watershed moment in his life, the first time he'd ever walk into a party with a date on his arm. Not just a date, the love of his life. He was more nervous than the groom-to-be.

Ricky was still helping set up at around one when Leon and Stella arrived at the hall. Leon was wearing the new black suit he'd purchased from a men's store downtown, not their usual neighborhood shop, with an olive silk tie to match his eyes. As their aunts gushed over how handsome he looked, Leon seemed to Ricky about as happy as a captured felon, the same defeated expression that darkened his face when Stella gave him polka lessons in their basement, and yet Leon endured those lessons anyway so as not to look foolish at his own reception. This whole wedding process seemed to be taking its toll on him. Sometimes Ricky heard the sound of his footsteps roaming the house in the middle of the night. Pre-wedding jitters, he presumed.

By one-thirty, Ma was already trying to push Ricky and the other guys out of the hall while poor Leon remained the last man standing. As a stream of women in brightly colored dresses and flowery hats began entering the double doors one right after the next, Ricky and his dad headed home to set up for the evening.

Compared to the shower, a relatively small group had been invited to the after-party; sixty or so, and most of the food had been cooked the night before. After expanding the dining room table with two extra leaves, Ricky and his father spread out Ma's best handmade embroidered lace tablecloth and set out the chafing dishes, stacks of clean plates, and silverware. The kitchen radio played as they worked; right now, Sammy Davis Jr. was wondering what kind of fool he was.

His father slipped into the den to polish up his pride and joy, a new Wurlitzer he'd purchased earlier in the year, one of those fancy organs with a double keyboard and dozens of colored keys that sounded like different instruments. The organ had become the focal point of their parties, especially when Leon took over the bench.

It took more than an hour for Ricky and Stella's brothers to pack up all the shower gifts from the Pulaski Hall and store them in the Minczewskis' basement. By the time Ricky got back to his house, Noël was sitting in her car waiting for him. She rolled down her window in obvious relief.

"You didn't have to wait out here for me," Ricky said. "You should've just gone inside."

"Walk into a roomful of strangers by myself?"

"Don't worry." He grinned. "I'm here now."

The party well underway, Ricky felt cheated about the grand entrance he'd hoped for. As Noël planted herself on the living room sofa, he took a quick survey of the rest of the house. Most of the guests, including Leon and Stella, were downstairs in their newly paneled basement, a remodeling project that he, Leon, and their father had labored over for weeks, including the installation of a fully stocked bar on one end of the room. He didn't need to search for his dad; the organ groaned from the den. "*Ojeny!*" Mrs. Lipinski said as Ricky passed by. "Does your father have to play so loud?"

Ma was in the kitchen, wiping her dripping brow with the back of her hand when Ricky entered. She was standing over a hot pan sizzling on the front of the stove, the other burners simmering with boiling pots. "Well, is she here yet?" she asked.

"Yup, she's here."

Turning down the dials, she untied her apron and tossed it on the chair. "Let's go meet this girlfriend of yours."

Noël rose from the couch as they entered the living room, a tentative expression on her face. "Finally," Ricky said, savoring the moment, "I get to introduce the two most important women in my life."

With restrained smiles, they eyed each other. "It's so nice to meet you after hearing Ricky go on about you for so many months now," Ma said. "My, my. You're even prettier than his portraits of you." Cringing at the word *portraits*, Ricky hoped Noël didn't catch the plurality.

Leon and Stella emerged from the basement, his suit coat discarded, his tie hanging loosely around his neck. "You must be Noël." Stella rushed over. "We've been hoping to meet you for so long. Haven't we?" She turned to Leon. His face taut, he glanced quickly at Noël. "Oh, that's right," Stella said to him. "You already met her, didn't you?"

"I gotta hand it to you, you lucky dog." Leon's best friend since junior high, Ted Budzinski, slapped Ricky on the back as he surveyed Noël from head to toe. "You got yourself a real beauty here."

Though the comment turned Noël bright pink, it filled Ricky with pride. He thought it charming that she blushed so easily, even though he knew she considered it a betrayal of her own body, a softer version, maybe, of his welts.

"Please grab yourself a plate," Ma said. "I'm just finishing up with a couple more things in the kitchen, but I'll be back to spend time with you kids later."

Her blonde curls wilted by the heat, Stella sat down on the sofa, surveying Noël with that discriminating inspection a pretty woman gives an even prettier one. After Leon's long line of beauties, Ricky couldn't believe that he'd ended up with a girlfriend more beautiful than his. "Sit here with me, Noël," Stella said. "Let's get acquainted. Who knows? Maybe we'll end up being sisters-in-law someday." Ricky's heart galloped.

Stella looked up at Leon. "Come join us, sweetie."

Without a word, he disappeared into the den.

"Oh, him and that organ," she said. "Nothing can keep him away from that music of his—whether it's his record player, the radio, or that Wurlitzer in there."

"When are you going to be married?" Noël asked her.

"New Year's Eve day." Stella's face lit up. "The church and reception hall are going to look like a snowy dream—white roses and white orchids everywhere. My dress has pearls and white sequins all over it. And I'm hoping Leon will wear white too."

"Leon, the virgin groom!" Ted got up from his chair. "Even on Halloween, he couldn't pull that one off."

Stella's throaty laughter filled the room. "You'll be wearing white too, you know. You're the best man."

"Lord, have mercy." He left for the den.

Ricky tried to catch Noël's eyes without success. After a few minutes, he could hear the sound of the song "96 Tears" coming from the den, as true-to-form as Question Mark and the Mysterians' version on the radio.

"That sounds like my honey." Stella sprang up from her seat, along with a few others, to go get a closer listen, just as Ricky's dad entered the room with a pile of sausages stacked on his plate.

"That kid of mine," he said to Mr. Grembowicz. "I take the goddamn lessons, and he's the one who plays that thing like Liberace."

Ricky waited until he got settled down in his chair before capturing his attention. "Hey, Dad … This is Noël."

His father's face was deadpan as usual. Like Leon, he seldom smiled, but his eyes warmed in a way that was just as good. "Noël, huh? Just like Christmas."

She beamed at him, the first genuine grin Ricky had seen from her all day. "It's nice to meet you, Mr. Ziemny."

Gazing at her for a minute, Dad's eyes dimmed. "Do you know who you remind me of? You remind me of my mother, may God rest her soul. She had a big, beautiful smile, just like yours."

A lump formed in Ricky's throat. Dad seldom mentioned his beloved, long-lost mother. Ricky didn't know what moved him more—his father's touching compliment or Noël's tender expression after hearing it.

"It looked like Marshall Field's in that hall today, didn't it?" Aunt Gertie burst into the room like a rocket. "Oh, my gosh, I can't wait for that wedding. Don't they just make the sweetest couple?"

Noël stirred restlessly in her seat, and Ricky feared she was getting antsy to leave. "Let's try a change of scenery." He grabbed her hand and led her into the den.

Leon was straddling the organ bench, smoking, engrossed in a conversation with Ted and Mr. Orlowski, when they entered the room. An idea occurred to Ricky; a way he might dispel some of his coldness toward Noël. "Hey, brother, I have a song request."

Leon looked up.

"Can you play 'Light My Fire'? It's Noël's favorite song."

"I'm not a jukebox," Leon said. "Besides, I don't know it that well."

Ricky couldn't fathom why he was being such a grouch. Surely he'd gotten over that wacky theory about her being a hooker by now. "C'mon," he urged. "Give it a try."

"Yeah, come on, Leon." Ted joined in. "Play this exquisite woman her favorite song, or I'll sing it for her myself."

"Oh, spare us." Leon moaned. Resting his cigarette on the lip of the glass ashtray on top of the organ, he swung his other leg around the bench.

"I shouldn't have come," Noël murmured in Ricky's ear.

"Don't be ridiculous." Taking her hand again, he guided her over to the organ where everyone else in the room had gathered around and positioned right in front, dead center.

Leon paused a few seconds, his head bowed as if collecting his thoughts. When he touched his fingers down on the keys, instantly, the vibrant sound shook the small room.

"Wo, ho!" Ted said. "You've been holding out on us, buddy. That's the way to play it."

Leon seemed to be concentrating hard on his fingers as they skated over the double keyboard. Though he never had one lesson, he played by flawless ear. When he finally glanced up, he looked straight at Noël.

It's working, Ricky thought. His brother was finally coming around, trying to be hospitable. But then it changed. Leon was staring at her too long—long enough to give Ricky's heart an almighty twist.

Her face flushing, Noël's eyes darted away.

Ricky tried to calm himself. Knowing how bashful she was, he had to assume that Leon's laser attention was making her self-conscious. Maybe Leon was trying to unnerve her on purpose. But when she looked at his brother again, this time, her eyes illuminated—shockingly so. Having studied her face for hours while painting her portrait, Ricky thought he'd seen all of her expressions by now, but not that one; never *that* one. His soul ripped.

Leon played on. As the intricate chords escalated in fervor, the glances between them, more than glances, grew in frequency and intensity. But they weren't quite in sync—as soon as Leon gazed at her, she turned away; when she looked back, he lowered his eyes to the keyboard. Ricky noticed her hands gripping the top of the organ for support; that crazy, throbbing muscle in Leon's cheek. He could feel the tension between them, the crackling of flame. Was that why Leon had been so ill-mannered, because he was fighting his own feelings?

Ricky took a peek at Stella, standing behind his brother. Since Leon's face was obscured from her, she focused on his dancing fingers in complete oblivion. Beside her, Ted bobbed his head to the music. Mr. Orlowski nibbled from his plate. No one else seemed to be picking up on it, on them.

Once more, Leon looked up at Noël. She turned away, her cheeks rosy again. The electricity between the two of them seemed unmistakable to Ricky, like live power lines, loose and snapping, fighting against the jolting moment of connection. And in the closing chords, that moment finally came—their eyes met without flinching, without apology. The shooting sparks were enough to electrocute Ricky.

The song was over, and the little group applauded.

"Bravo!" said Ted. Stella slipped her arms around Leon's shoulders from behind, whispering some sweet nothing into his eardrum. Why didn't anyone else see it? Ricky felt like a madman.

For the rest of the party, Ricky stayed downstairs, sipping one vodka after the next, trying to block out his fears. He didn't speak to Noël. He sat there, ruminating.

"What's wrong with you?" she finally asked.

"Nothing." He nodded toward Mr. Bartkowiak, who was tending bar, to freshen his drink.

Noël leaned close. "I really think you've had enough."

Ricky seldom got mad, and certainly never before at her, but this comment made him angry. It was perfectly okay for her to moon into his brother's eyes at the organ, but she wouldn't allow him to sit in his own house and have another drink? What gave her that right? Why were the rules of their relationship always hers to make, and break? He loved her, that was for damned sure, but until she loved him back, she had no rights. He slugged down the recharged vodka in two big gulps.

"What's wrong with you?" she asked again.

It was a valid question, bringing him to his senses. What *was* wrong with him?

He mulled the incident over again in his addled brain, trying to get some perspective. Leon and Stella had remained upstairs since the organ serenade. The song request had been his own lamebrained idea; not Leon's, not Noël's. Leon was playing her favorite song at Ricky's own request, a wildly passionate song at that, and Ricky had put her right in front of him. As the liquor accumulated in his bloodstream, he began to feel better, like a big dope who'd allowed his own insecurities to drop him off the deep end.

He felt better, but Noël obviously didn't. She looked like a stretched rubber band about to snap, scanning the room every few seconds, every time a new pair of footsteps sounded on the stairs. Was she hoping they were Leon's?

Knock it off, Ricky. She was reacting to the music, that was all. It was the song she loved, not the player, and he was acting like a jealous asshole. He put both of his arms around her and pulled her toward him. "You look gorgeous in that dress. You know that?"

She pushed him away. "You're drunk."

"So, what if I am? This is a party."

Her turquoise eyes seared into his, but they didn't brighten; not the way they'd lit up for his brother. They had never brightened up for Ricky like that. And now, they looked reprimanding, repulsed even. "You're not acting like yourself," she said.

"And how am I supposed to be acting?"

"Don't do this, Rick. Please, stop drinking. I want to go home."

"Barkeep!" He held his glass up to Mr. Bartkowiak. "Hit me again."

Before Mr. Bartkowiak could reach him, Noël got up and bolted up the stairs. Even drunk as he was, Ricky instantly felt like a heel. Still, he sat glued to the stool as Mr. Bartkowiak poured.

After taking a few more swallows, he decided to go after her. When he stood up, the room was spinning. The stairs were floating. It'd been a while since he'd had this much to drink, this fast, and he guessed he was out of practice, especially on a nearly empty stomach. Grasping the rail, he met Stella coming down. "Have you seen Leon?" she asked.

Without answering, Ricky rushed up the stairs and looked out the window. Noël's car was still parked outside.

He searched from room to room. The living room was over-flowing with guests, their animated features exaggerated in his drunkenness, like cartoon caricatures. A group of men was playing poker at a card table set up in the garage. Where had she gone? Ricky leaned against the counter in the quiet kitchen, the only deserted room in the house, trying to clear the fog in his brain.

And that was when he heard them. Muffled voices. Coming from the most unlikely of places, from behind the door, slightly ajar, of the walk-in pantry, a tiny room off the kitchen. Tiptoeing over, he listened.

"So, this is it?" Leon's voice sounded frosty, strained.

"Yes, but I have to know the truth before I go," Noël replied. "It was you who got David to file for divorce, wasn't it?"

"Maybe," he said.

Stunned, Ricky was about to pull the door open and expose them, but for some reason he hesitated. "But even if I did do it," Leon continued, "I did it for Ricky, not for you."

"I know. You're your brother's keeper."

Relief, like sweet molasses, poured thick through Ricky's veins, soothing and sobering him.

"But, just the same, I wanted to thank you," she said. The door opened a couple inches. Ricky glimpsed her fingers clasped around the glass doorknob on the other side; she was about to exit. He crouched in the shadows.

"For what?"

"For saving us," she said. "For saving me."

There was a pause.

"And now I wish to God that you could save me too." The tone of his brother's voice had changed, not a trace of coldness left. He saw Leon's fingers push the door shut; their conversation stopped there. So did time. Ricky waited. He hoped for some sound, but not the one he heard. Noël moaned softly. The earth crumbled beneath his feet.

A second later, she bolted from the pantry, unaware of Ricky's presence, a dismayed, incandescent expression on her face, her fingers against her lips, where his mouth must have been. She rushed toward the back door.

"Oh, there you are. I was wondering where you disappeared." Stella entered the kitchen as Leon emerged. "Whatever were you doing in the pantry?"

"I'll tell you what he was doing," Ricky said.

Leon twisted around at the sound of his voice, startled to see him there. Noël, almost out the door, stopped dead in her tracks.

"Oh, my God!" Stella cried. "Look at Ricky!"

By now, the welts had exploded all over his body. His skin was on fire. His legs were rubber. His heart in shreds.

"Tell Stella the truth!" Ricky screamed at his brother. "Go ahead and tell her what you were doing in the pantry!" By now, a group of people had flocked into the kitchen, including Ma. The room was whirling around and around; Ricky felt like he might keel over. "Tell them how you couldn't keep your paws off of Noël."

"What?" Stella went ashen. Leon froze against the refrigerator.

"Ricky, sit down. You're drunk." Ma hurried over to him with a chair. The kitchen was revolving, twirling in a slow-motion vortex. She touched his bumpy forehead. "Your face is burning up!" She glared at Noël. "Get. Out. Of. My. House." Her voice was a slow growl.

Ricky looked up in time to see the last look Noël gave him—one last repentant, lovely look—before closing the door behind her.

Sick and ruined as he was, it felt to him that the only light had just left the house, like the moment a dead body loses its soul. Only her absence remained.

THIRTEEN

JULY 31, 1967
THECKLA

H E was still sitting on the steps when Theckla peered out the door. She couldn't see his face, only his back, but she recognized him just the same. Though they were out of butter and needed a bottle of milk for supper, the trip to the Food Stop would have to wait. She closed the door and let him be.

"He still out there?" Freddie asked.

"Um-hm." She glanced at the wall clock. "Going on two hours now."

"Two hours?" He shook his head. "What's he fixing to do? Sit there 'til she comes out?"

Theckla knew an appearance by Noël any time today was unlikely. After coming home from that party last evening in a state of hysterics, she'd gotten ill, throwing up all night long, so Freddie took the boy down to their place while Theckla remained behind, cleaning up after her and trying to calm her down. Around seven a.m., Noël called in sick and went dead to the world. Theckla hoped she was still knocked out, but she couldn't get upstairs to check on her because of him. He'd shown up at around two that afternoon. Just sitting there in the same position, lighting up a cigarette every now and then.

Little Adam was watching the *Match Game* on TV. "Name a kind of fruit," Gene Rayburn said to the panel.

"Satsuma," Freddie blurted out.

Theckla turned to look at him. Satsuma trees had once been plentiful in Mobile, but it remained an unspoken word since the day they'd left there.

His eyes darkened. "I mean, apple."

Just then, a news alert flashed over the screen. Now it was the city of Milwaukee's turn to be on round-the-clock curfew. Racial riots were raging out of control, and the governor was calling in the National Guard.

Theckla couldn't stand to watch the latest round of violent street images. Where was all this going to end? You could only push people so far, for so long, before they snapped. And Freddie's sudden mention of the word *satsuma* had clinched it. She felt like she was suffocating, in need of open space like the Mobile grass fields she used to roam as a little girl. But here she was, trapped inside this apartment without butter and milk. She cracked the door ajar again and peeked out.

"He still there?" Freddie unwrapped two candies from his pocket and slipped one to Adam. Sliding it on to his tongue, he smacked his lips as if tasting ambrosia. Adam studied him, imitating the process, even smacking his own lips at the end of it, content as a kitten.

But not Theckla. There came a time when letting things be was playing into the devil's hands. The people of Milwaukee knew that, and so did he, sitting out there on the stairs. Sometimes you had to rise up and make your voice heard. But there was a right way and a wrong way to do it. If her mama was here, she'd be quoting the good book, reminding her that *speaking the truth in love* was nearly always the right way.

"This has gone on long enough." Theckla headed for the door.

"Don't you go getting yourself involved." Freddie wagged a bent finger. "This ain't none of your business."

"How else are we gonna fix anything? Somebody's got to get involved."

"Well, your name ain't Somebody."

"Better that, than Nobody."

He shook his head again. "When your Aunt Theckla gets that righteous indignation," he mumbled to Adam, "ain't a wild horse that can stop her."

Theckla headed down the staircase at a snail's pace, waiting for him to turn around, but he didn't. Carefully, she maneuvered around him before she stopped.

He glanced up, expressionless.

"Mind if I join you?" she asked.

A neglected cigarette smoldered between his fingertips, a long ashy tip about to break off. His eyes rolled downward.

Despite his silence, she sat down anyway, three stairs below him. "Look, I know what happened yesterday. Noël told us all about it. She's filled up with enough guilt and shame to make her sick all night. She couldn't even drag herself into work today. Looks like you didn't go either."

"I had things to take care of." His voice was clipped, sullen.

She wasn't certain what to say next. "I'm not in the habit of telling people their business, and I don't know you from a hill of beans. But I know that girl. And when I first heard you two arguing in this stairwell that night, I sensed something else was really going on underneath all that bravado. Then when I came up there and saw your faces, saw the way you were looking at each other, well, you know what they say, there's a thin line between hate and love. And that night, it looked to me as if the two of you crossed over it."

He didn't respond, but his face enlivened in a way that let her know she was on the right track. "You don't have to say anything. I know what I saw. Any fool could've seen it."

He raised his head, took a puff of his cigarette.

"She told me that you're the one who got her husband to file for divorce. That was the best thing you could've done for her, that anyone could've done. But she thought you did it for your brother, not for her."

"I *did* do it for my brother." He glanced at her angrily, then his eyes darted away, the way a liar's do. He stroked his mustache anxiously with the thumb and forefinger of his left hand.

"Okay, then. You did it for your brother." Theckla nodded. "My husband told her to stick with your brother, you know. He thinks she needs a man like him. But not me. One-sided love is no good for anyone."

He took another slow drag on his cigarette.

"Trouble is, she doesn't think she's worth love. I keep telling her, 'don't you ever settle for anything less,' but she's got it locked inside her head that she doesn't deserve even a glimmer of happiness. I don't know. Maybe you're thinking you don't deserve it either."

For the first time, he made extended eye contact with her.

She kept on going. "Lord knows, she's been hurt enough in her young life. She's lived through things you can't even imagine. I care about that girl. I'm thinking you do too. Otherwise you wouldn't be sitting down here in the dark, hour after hour in the middle of the day, trying to work up the courage to go knock on her door and tell her that. Am I right?"

"Truthfully, I don't know what I'm doing here," he said. "I guess I don't have anywhere else to go."

"Your mama throw you out of the house?"

"Oh, yeah." He smiled at her bleakly.

The day Theckla had first met him, he eyed her like a wad of gum stuck to his shoe. But not now. Suffering eyes always seemed to see deeper than skin, and, at that moment anyway, her skin color was the least of his worries. "What about your fiancée?"

"I threw myself out of there."

"So, where you gonna be staying now?"

"I rented a room, not far from the mills. I moved in this morning."

Theckla tried not to react. Now that he'd finally started to open up, she didn't want to break the flow. She watched him crush his cigarette out on the step.

"In the beginning, I *was* doing it for Ricky," he said, maybe more to himself than to her. "I swear to God, I really was. I'm not that much of a creep. But it changed somehow, got all mixed-up—after I had a chance to talk to her, see her situation. After I met that son-of-a-bitch she married. After—" He stopped. "Ah, hell, maybe I never did do it for my brother. You're right."

"It's not about being right. It's about listening to your heart. The heart makes its own rules."

"Well, the heart's a selfish bastard then, isn't it?" Agony filled his eyes; he rubbed his forehead. "I destroyed my own brother."

Theckla struggled again for the right words. "Oh, I'm not saying that it won't sting for a while, but your brother will be okay, most likely. He'll eventually get on with his life, won't he?"

"I don't think he will."

"So, why are you here? What is it that you came to do?"

"I don't know." His brows furrowed. "I guess I just wanted to make sure she's okay. It was pretty brutal yesterday."

They sat quietly with their own thoughts for a few seconds. She could hear a firm, muffled male voice coming from the TV in their apartment; it sounded like another news bulletin. "Let me ask you something. Are you in love with her?"

He shook his head no, said yes at the same time. "Who am I kidding?" He nodded. "Oh, God, I *am* a monster, aren't I?"

"You're no monster, baby. You just had some really bad luck, that's all. Falling in love like this, under these circumstances."

"I fought it, and I fought it," he said. "But she just got to me somehow, and I couldn't fight it anymore."

The scenes from the Milwaukee streets played through Theckla's head as she watched him smack his palm against his agonized heart, the site where his own rebellion raged. "Revolutions aren't easy," she said. "People get hurt. Buildings get burned."

"Huh?"

"When all is said and done, only love and justice matter."

"Love and justice." He laughed, unsmiling. "Whose love and justice? Not Ricky's, that's for sure."

"All I'm trying to say is that your love for that girl is like a healing to her. Something she didn't think was possible. She didn't have the first clue how to love a man before you came along. That's a lot to throw away."

The sharp angles of his face softened.

"Over time, your brother will probably come to understand that love is love, and ain't nobody can change that. I hope that happens for him anyway. But it's already out in the open now; the damage has already been done. So, as for the two of you, you could keep away from each other to punish yourselves. Stay miserable, marry other people, let the wrong babies be born. Or you could …" She wasn't quite sure how to finish the thought. That was up to them.

"It's a hell of a way to start, isn't it?" he said.

"You gotta start somewhere. It's your decision. The doors in this stairway go in both directions."

He gave her a long, hard look, without a blink.

Theckla stayed put as she watched him pick himself up, as she listened to his footsteps ascending the stairs, as she heard the thump of his knuckles rapping against Noël's door, as the hard-fought words finally came out of his mouth.

"Noël, it's Leon," he said. "We've got to talk."

FOURTEEN

JULY 31, 1967
NOËL

THE sound of his voice startled her. Leon was standing there outside her door, but he shouldn't have been. And she shouldn't have opened it. But she did. Now they were face to face.

She told him no. *No!* They couldn't possibly be together. Not like this. Not this way. Not knowing the damage they'd done. Even when her mouth spoke the words as he stepped inside, her body swayed to a rhythm of its own. Not its own; it oscillated in tempo with his. It seemed natural, innate, to have him there. She wrestled with herself to figure out why. Who knew why? It remained a mystery why one certain person could implant themselves in another's DNA. Or maybe they were encrypted there all along.

He agreed with her. It was dead wrong of them to even consider being a couple. They had broken his brother's heart, the man they both loved. If they got together, they couldn't live with themselves; they wouldn't have one day of peace. "It's settled, then." He paced back and forth on the braided carpet. "We go our separate ways."

"Okay, then." She shattered inside.

He put his hands in his pockets. "What now?"

"I guess we say goodbye."

"Is that what you really want?" He dropped down on the sofa where she'd been napping, and shoved aside the blanket.

"It's not what I want. But it's what we have to do … isn't it?"

They sat in silence.

"You told me in the pantry that you were breaking up with Ricky as soon as he sobered up," he said. "I only risked kissing you right there and then because I thought it was my last chance, that I'd never see you again."

"I know," she said. "That's why I risked kissing you back."

"And now, look what we've done. And for what? Just to say goodbye all over again?" He exhaled a long breath. "I was crazy to come here."

"You weren't crazy to come." Tossing the blanket on the floor, she sat down beside him, inhaling the scent of his Old Spice for as long as she could. "You were just crazy to believe we had any kind of future. We both were."

"Both?"

As they sat together, side by side, their eyes locked the same way they had locked in the stairwell that night, only this time there was nothing, no one, to stop them. Their bodies were speaking a secret language that was undoing their words as if they were knots in the air. She felt gravity peeling away. When his lips found hers, the tsunami rolled in without restraint.

She let it wash over her, a whirlwind of new, bewildering sensations exploding from somewhere deep inside of her body, with no chance to reason in between. One kiss, one touch, led to another and another; she was powerless against the force of nature that propelled them. How had it been so horribly different with David? Images popped through her brain like flashbulbs. She saw Leon's snow-damp hair on the first night she'd met him. She saw his fingertips on the keyboard playing "Light My Fire," the same fingertips now awakening every fiber, every filament of her being. She let the memories plunder her mind unshackled as he urgently reached for the tie of her robe.

Abruptly, he hesitated. She had told him enough of her history.

"No, don't stop!" she said.

"Are you sure?"

They couldn't leave this unfinished; of that she was certain. This was her one and only chance to prove her love to him, and to herself. Reaching down, she felt her own hands untethering the sash.

Emboldened, he pulled her to the braided carpet, and there he unveiled her, not a shadowy figure in a portrait, but her, in all her stark, unvarnished nakedness. And when, at last, he moved on top of her, and the miracle was hers, she saw her mother's face under Pastor Ray. The tears seeped from her eyes like holy water.

Afterward, he covered her with the blanket. "We've got to be together after that." He wiped away her tears. "Don't we?"

Now she saw the other images—Rick's devastating nerve attack in the kitchen, her mother's lifeless face, Pastor Ray being dragged to his death; the cost they would have to pay. She felt dizzy. Illusion and reality were thundering against one another, and she couldn't tell which was which. But it didn't matter. Right now, Leon Ziemny was both.

She leaned into him like the shade of a mighty tree.

FIFTEEN

JULY–AUGUST 1967
RICKY

FROM the window seat of his upstairs bedroom the day after the shower party, Ricky was watching a single leaf in one of the high branches of the old oak out back. He'd been focused on the leaf for hours—the way it jiggled back and forth in the breeze like a waving hand, the way its shape resembled a tiny Christmas tree, the way one thing revealed all things if you stared at it long enough. When the seasons changed in a few months, that leaf would drop to the ground and disintegrate to ash. But sometimes a leaf fell prematurely, without warning. The way he did last night.

He was a wreck, hollow as a bomb-blasted building. He kept rehashing the events from the day before—not just the obvious one in the pantry, but the sight of their family and friends scurrying away afterward like barn rats. Stella's mascara-streaked face when Leon told her, "It's over." The sound of Stella slamming their front door, going home to the mountain of bridal gifts in her basement. And, finally, his mother's edict to Leon: "Pack up and get out."

As the oak leaf flapped back and forth, he thought about the final scene. Before Leon had left for good, he at least had the decency (or maybe the audacity) to try to talk to Ricky, but it was way too late for that. As Leon had pounded on his bedroom door, the absurdity struck Ricky. The brother who'd had his back since he was a kid had become his ultimate betrayer.

Ricky had drunk himself to sleep.

As he called in sick that morning from the phone by his bed, he could hear Ma and Leon going at it again downstairs through the floorboards. Apparently, Leon had returned to pick up a few more of his belongings. The next thing he heard was another knock on his door. "Let me in, Ricky. Let's talk about this."

Fat chance. Leon could stand out there 'til the cows came home, 'til his hair turned gray, 'til his teeth fell out of his double-crossing head. As far as Ricky was concerned, his brother was dead.

After his father's shift at the mill was over for the day, Ricky could hear him head straight up the stairs to his room. He hammered at the door without cessation. "It's been long enough. I'm not going until you open up." Knowing his father and that tone of voice, Ricky sensed he was getting ready to jimmy the lock, so he got up to unlock the door.

His father's eyes seemed pained at the sight of him. Ricky knew he looked a disaster; he'd caught his reflection in the bathroom mirror the last time he went to pee. The welts were gone, but his skin was discolored from the lengthy attack, his flesh alternately pink and red in patches. The excess of alcohol he'd consumed hadn't helped much either. An open bottle of Stoli stood on the nightstand, about one-quarter full.

His father sat down on the window seat. "Okay, so tell me about this girl," he said. "What makes you love her so much?"

The odd question surprised Ricky. He opened the closet door, hauling out the large canvas and holding it up to his father. "Who wouldn't love a face like hers?" Ricky set the painting down, his eyes glued to it as he backed toward the bed and sat down on top of it. He swigged from the bottle on the nightstand.

"She's a looker all right," his father said. "But there's got to be more to her than that."

"Leon has his hands full," Ricky said. "She's afraid of every-thing—of storms, of sirens, of intimacy. She lights up her living room with candles every night; candles everywhere. It took me a long time to realize she did that because she was afraid of the dark. She's terrified to open up about what made her that way. You think Leon will put up with all that? He's incapable."

"Sounds to me like she's a helluva lot of trouble. And you haven't answered my question yet. Why do you love her?"

As Ricky considered the question, he gazed at her portrait—the "ruse" painting, he called it, the one he had used to prolong his time with her. She made him take it away the night it was finished, told him she couldn't look at herself as some kind of an angel. He thought she was being modest; now he knew she was right. Still, he couldn't bring himself to hate her.

"She's been injured," Ricky said. "I don't know what all she's been through; I gathered it was pretty bad. But she found a way to not get hard and bitter the way most people do. Like lighting candles until it looks like church so she's no longer afraid of the dark. That's her way. She takes ugly things and transforms them." There was a long pause before he added, almost inaudibly, "Like me."

His father got up and kissed him hard on the top of his head. "You're the most beautiful boy in the world." He sat beside Ricky on the bed. "And don't you ever forget it."

"But I'm no match for your other son, Mr. Handsome, am I?"

"Listen to me. I'm gonna tell you something. You and Leon are different as night and day. But I love each of you for who you are. Your brother? He's always been steady as a rock."

"Oh, yeah, old Leon is perfect, isn't he?" Ricky sighed. "But rocks are cold and hard. And she needs warmth; someone to make her feel safe. As steady as Leon might be, he's not the one to do it. She's got a son, and tell me, what does Leon know about little kids? Or being in love? He doesn't even know what love is; he told me that. All he knows about is sex. And he's going to destroy her. The same way he destroyed Stella. And Adele Laskowski. And Loretta Szymanski before that."

"You didn't let me finish." His father scratched his head. "I said, Leon has been steady as a rock, up 'til now. But I never said he was perfect. The fact is, I always worried more about him than I did about you. You wanna know why?"

Now he had Ricky's full attention.

"Because you care about people, and you know what's important. You manage to end up with your heart wide open, no matter what life throws at you. Sounds to me like you and this woman have a lot in common that way. But Leon? He's steady all right, but only because he's hiding from himself. Hiding from life. And, up until now, he's been hiding from love. That's why your mother felt like she had to push him into this thing with Stella. But you're right. Your brother's still got a helluva lot to learn."

Ricky let his words sink in for a moment. "Well, I sure don't want him to learn his life lessons at her expense."

"See what I mean? As much as this girl has hurt you—already, you've forgiven her." His father kissed him again, this time on the forehead. "And you'll forgive your brother someday too. That's the kind of man you are. If you ask me, you're the perfect one."

"But I'm not perfect enough for her, am I?" As tears rolled down Ricky's cheeks, his father embraced him. "Cry it out, my boy. Cry it out."

≈≈

A week later, an envelope arrived in the mail with Ricky's name on it. Immediately he recognized her distinctive, slanted handwriting. At the sight of it, his heart turned over like a dying engine.

He didn't mention it to his parents. He was afraid to open it. When he did, he knew her loss would be real, authenticated, confirmed in writing. He waited until he was upstairs in his room before he slit the envelope and pulled out the frilly notepaper. It smelled like her, like lilac powder. Or maybe it was his imagination. He read each word slowly:

Dear Rick:

Do you remember the day you brought over the book from the Chicago Art Institute and you told me about the paintings? I especially remember the one called The Coast of Labrador, *with that lonely little boat waiting on the shore under a hazy sky, because it made me feel so sad. And you told me that was exactly what the artist wanted me to feel, that he used the power of light to create mood and emotion. It was an amazing concept to me, to be able to paint what "sad" looks like.*

I think it's a powerful and sacred thing to be an artist, like you are. I think God chooses artists by giving them a greater sensitivity, like you have. Cherish that gift, and never stop painting.

I'll always choose to love you; we can choose our friends. But we can't choose the one we end up falling in love with--maybe that's why they call it "falling". And I'm sorry, so very sorry.

I hope you can forgive me, forgive your brother. But I know you'll be okay, because not only do you have the beautiful soul of an artist, but you have that indestructible Polish spirit that can never be wiped off the map.

Love,

Noël

PART THREE

LOVING TOO MUCH

SIXTEEN

OCTOBER 1967
ADAM

IN one catastrophic whirlwind, the Freedom Bird had hoisted him from the hellfields of Vietnam, whisking him off to Los Angeles and dumping him into a filthy hole that seemed more like a nursing home than a veteran's hospital. And, there he was, just like that, back in the World again. Today they signed his honorable discharge papers and told him he was a free man. What a joke. Adam Trudeau knew he'd never be free again.

Was it him or had the world changed so much? For starters, Los Angeles was unrelentingly bright. That was the first thing he noticed when he stepped outside the hospital—blinding sunshine, bright enough to bleed through his squinting eyelids. Slowly, his focus adjusted, and when it did, he saw lush palm trees, airy shops, adults dressed in happy colors in the dead of autumn. For a moment, he wondered if he'd died and this was what heaven looked like. If so, he had arrived with the same baggage.

About ten blocks from the VA hospital, he ran into a large group of war protesters in front of city hall, most of them so-called hippies. When Adam had first left for Nam, the country was divided. Now all of his peers seemed to detest the war and, worse than that, the boys who were shipped there too, as if they'd become the enemy.

The hippies were blowing bubbles, and he stopped and stared

because one of them reminded him of Cynthia. After dissecting every word of her letters, he could picture her here, doing something kooky like this, waving a wand of bubbles at a war protest. Some freak with scraggly red hair down to his mid-back pointed straight at him. "Hey!" The guy yelled to his friends. "Looks like we've got a war monger over there." Pretty soon they were all shouting at him. "Baby killer!"

Adam ducked into a coffee shop across the street. He grabbed a seat at the counter, buried his head in a discarded newspaper, waiting for his breathing to become normal again. As soon as it did, he scanned the paper. Today was Sunday; for some reason, that surprised him. Long years seemed to have passed without one Sunday among them.

The main story on the front page was about Stop the Draft Week. Yesterday the March on the Pentagon had culminated in a gigantic sit-in in the parking lot. Adam read on. Tens of thousands of protesters had descended on Washington, DC—not just hippies but civil rights activists, middle-class liberals, religious leaders, and Vietnam vets too. The eclectic band of peaceniks sang, chanted, meditated, stuck flowers into the rifle barrels of patrolling armed forces, even tried to levitate the Pentagon to rid it of its evils. Though the *LA Times* didn't phrase it quite that way, the demonstration had blown up in their faces around midnight when the paratroopers of the 82nd Division moved in, clubbing and cracking their peace-loving skulls for all the world to see.

A black man, probably around thirty years old, slid onto the stool beside him. "You a vet?" he asked.

"No! Hell, no. I was in an accident." Adam guzzled the coffee and tossed some change on the counter, not bothering to wait for the waitress to take his order. The sudden need for air trumped his growling stomach.

As Adam took off in the opposite direction from the protesters, the streetlight changed to green. A couple of pink-clad girls seemed to be whispering about him as he passed. An old man flashed him a pity look. Adam turned away, pretending to window-shop in a storefront display of Gucci products, where a well-dressed clerk grinned at him from the inside of the store. Adam's heart amped up. He knew this man. He had the exact same face as the gook who'd gunned down Adam's best buddy and fellow medic, Scott Mason.

Adam blinked, stared harder, the man's features changing before his eyes, becoming dark, Italian-looking; not a trace of Viet Cong. Adam rushed away from the window as fast as he could.

The plan was to catch a flight out to Chicago later that night, then take a train back to the station nearest to Willow. Passing a pay phone on Hollywood Boulevard, he thought about calling Cynthia— presumably she was back at school for the fall semester—but he couldn't call her if he didn't know where she was. The last time he'd heard from her, months ago, she mentioned the possibility of trans- ferring to Berkeley. Since then, not a single letter had found its way to him. An ominous feeling had been dogging him ever since.

Sitting down on a bench in front of the garishly purple Frederick's of Hollywood building, he pulled her final letter out from his pocket, reread it.

"I don't know why we fell for this crap," she wrote. "The Establishment, as our parents know it, is fundamentally wrong— selfish and capitalistic, built on the backs of prejudice and war. War is no way to solve our problems. We've got to look inside and find a better way." His eyes jumped down to the sentences near the bottom of the page where the mention of the name "Nathan Bond" never failed to rattle him, no matter how many times he read it. "Nathan Bond, a boy in my philosophy class, is really brilliant. He's trying to talk a group of us into moving to Berkeley in the fall."

After all of that, she told Adam, finally, that she loved him, not in nearly every other sentence as her previous letters, but squeezed in between her last sentence and her signature, an afterthought with its own caret.

The relentless sun beamed overhead. Adam blinked his watering eyes, stuffed her letter back inside his pocket. He didn't belong in this sunshiny place, he was damned well sure of that, but where did he belong? He had to get back to his own gray-tinged world and figure it out, back to tired little Willow, with no machine guns or wild-eyed hippies. He picked himself up from the bench and tried to play the tourist. The longer he stared at the movie stars' footprints, they more they blurred into mud prints of lost comrades in Nam.

A pay phone snagged his interest more than any sights Hollywood had to offer. He had to talk to someone. Anyone. He dug Noël's number out of his pocket, resting the little piece of paper on the small ledge inside the phone booth before tucking the receiver under his chin and fumbling to dial. The receiver slipped away from his chin, dangling from its steel cord. When he bent to retrieve it, the phone number fell to the ground. *Damn it all to hell!* What a freak he was now. With only one arm left, even dialing a fucking phone number had become an acrobatic act.

Repeating the process all over again, he heard the phone ringing. "Hello?"

"Noël?" Adam's voice came out strange, like someone had shoved a cotton ball into his throat.

"Adam! Where are you? Have they released you yet?"

His family already knew about his disfigurement; they were informed he'd lost a limb when the Army sent him off to rehab. "I'm still in L.A., but I got out today. I'm taking a red-eye tonight and a train in tomorrow." He told her exactly when.

"Thank God, you're almost home! Me and Adam will be waiting at the station."

Little Adam, his nephew, his namesake. Would he even recognize him? Maybe he'd be afraid of his uncle now, the one-armed troll.

"But I've got something to tell you," she said.

The way her voice changed, it sounded like bad news. She must've heard from Cynthia. Steadying his body against the ledge of the phone booth, he waited.

"A few weeks ago, some officers came to Dad's house—" Her voice broke.

He knew what was coming next; he just didn't know which brother.

"—to tell him that Bo was killed."

It felt like a car had slammed through the phone booth.

So, it was Bo who'd met his fate, the oldest brother he'd worshipped as a kid, all muscle and brawn. The one who taught them how to swim, fish, catch fireflies in their hands; to dream when life seemed undreamable. The one who'd leapt off the highest grassy mound behind Hyssop Elementary and landed like a bird. The one who always told them, "Let me go first, to make sure it's safe." Gone. Gone. Gone. Beads of sweat formed on Adam's forehead. His lips went parched.

"Adam, are you still there?"

"Yup." He propped himself up against the glass.

She told him the rest of the story between spasms of tears. Bo's body had been ripped apart by an explosion in the middle of a minefield somewhere near Cambodia, she explained. They'd managed to salvage what was left of him and sent him home. The funeral was scheduled for Tuesday.

As she talked, Adam flashed back to the moment when his own

arm was grenaded from his body, torn off like a mannequin's limb into the mud beside him.

Having witnessed it so many times, he could easily picture Bo's remains being zipped into one of those familiar heavy-duty black body bags. The image blurred into the face of Scott Mason dying in his arms, the shock in his eyes outliving him. By now, the perspiration was soaking Adam's neck.

"Are you still there?" she asked again.

He tried to block out that ruthless, indifferent California sun. "Yeah." Though dead with fatigue, he fought to summon his last shred of hope. "Hey, kiddo." The pet name sounded stupid, asinine, completely out of place the second it came out of his mouth. "Have you heard from Cynthia?"

Her pause was heart-stopping. "We kind of lost touch," she said. "You know her family moved away to New Junction, don't you?"

"Yeah, I know that."

"And she's at Berkeley now, but she hasn't answered my letters since then."

Adam's body ached. Cynthia was gone now, too. Not dead like Bo, but gone; gone to Berkeley. Salty sweat dripped into his mouth. The operator broke in, demanding more change. He didn't have enough, so they ended the call right there.

Six hours later Adam was seated by the window on a United flight. People were still filing in, stuffing their cargo into the overhead bins when he heard a hubbub of sorts, some exclamations, a flurry of excitement. And then he saw the reason for it—Senator Robert Kennedy was boarding the plane, standing in a long line along with the others, like a regular Joe Q. Public. There must've been some mix-up in first-class and Kennedy had deferred his seat, or maybe he really did travel like a peasant sometimes, who knew?

He was punier than Adam had imagined, sad-eyed and stoop-shouldered. As Kennedy waited to find his place, a couple of women stuck their boarding passes in front of his face, asking for his autograph. He looked embarrassed, a little repelled by their adoration, but he scribbled quickly. "I loved your brother!" one of them gushed.

"So did I," Kennedy said softly. After glancing down at his own boarding pass, he slid into the vacant seat beside Adam, on the aisle, and clicked himself in.

What a distraction. For a moment, Adam forgot about Bo, Cynthia, his arm. The engines geared up. The lights flashed on the wing outside his window. Slowly, the plane taxied down the runway, waiting for takeoff.

Adam looked at Kennedy, and he glanced at Adam. Kennedy's eyes were a penetrating deep blue. Even in the dim cabin, his tanned skin seemed lined beyond his years. One of his lids was droopier than the other. His gaze moved to Adam's empty sleeve.

"Yup," Adam told him before he could ask. "I'm a vet. I'm on my way home from Vietnam, as a matter of fact."

If it was possible, Kennedy's face clouded further; he already looked more weighted down than Atlas. The plane began to speed up, faster, faster—until they lifted into the air. Slowly, the wings leveled. The "No smoking" signs blinked off.

"I recently visited Southeast Asia," Kennedy said.

"Then you know it's nuts over there."

"Yes, it is. We live here in abundance, and we're sending our young men, like you, to die over there on the other side of the world. I gave a speech in the Senate about it when I got back. I told them that, to the Vietnamese, and to our young soldiers too, this war must seem the fulfillment of Revelation: 'And I looked and beheld a pale horse; and his name that sat upon him was Death, and Hell followed with him.'"

Adam let the prophetic, poetic words sink into his skull. For some reason, they soothed like butter on seared skin, maybe just because Kennedy had pegged it, the atrocity of it all. He looked down at the place where his arm had been.

Adam hadn't told the story of his injury to anyone before, but he felt like telling it now. "I was sent there as a combat medic, and I made up my mind that I was going to be the best one ever," he began. "But it was just like you say, it was nonstop death and hell. I was treating this guy named Mike Weber. He had a chest wound, and I'd just inserted the syrette into his skin and was squeezing the morphine tube when the explosion came. It lifted the two of us into the air, dumping me right on top of him. And Mike said, 'Hey, man, that arm just saved my life.' By the time they medevacked him out, his bleeding was under control. When they got around to me, I wouldn't leave without my arm. I made them take it along. Stupid, huh?"

"Hope is never stupid."

"Maybe not stupid, but dangerous."

Deeper lines creased the skin around Kennedy's eyes.

"You going to run for president next year?"

"Oh, no, no. No." He looked like he was going to elaborate but didn't. "No," he said again.

The stewardess wheeled over her little cart. "Would you like a drink, Senator Kennedy?"

"I'll have a Heineken, thank you."

"And you?" She looked at Adam's sleeve, then his eyes.

"Jack Daniel's. Make it a double."

The stewardess handed Adam two tiny screw-capped bottles, which he put on his open tray before accepting the plastic cup. She popped open the Senator's beer. Adam watched her roll her cart to the next row before he worked up the courage to ask. "Do you mind doing the honors?" He handed him the two bottles.

Kennedy bowed his head in deference as he twisted them open for him.

"Thanks." Adam took a long sip, trying to drown the shame of his newfound helplessness. "So, why aren't you going to run?" Against the roar of the engines, he strained to hear the answer.

"It's President Johnson's election," the Senator said.

Challenging an incumbent was always risky business, Adam supposed, but the way he'd said it and the expression on his face didn't match up; his razor focus on his Heineken bottle was anything but tranquil. It seemed like a well-rehearsed reply, given umpteen times throughout the day to curious nobodies like him who had the audacity to ask. Adam sized him up as he sat in silence; he sensed Kennedy was a conflicted man, at odds with himself. Maybe his conscience was telling him to run, while everything else, maybe everyone else, said otherwise.

"This country really changed while I was in Nam." Adam leaned his head back against the seat. "Even my wife became a hippie. What do you think about the hippies?"

"I think they feel cut off, powerless to change what's happening in this country, and they're trying to pull the curtain down." He took a swig of beer. "They can't get off the earth, so they're leaving it as much as they can."

His Boston accent made "can" sound like "con."

Adam looked out the window, the reflection of his own face staring back at him in the pitch-black night. Was Cynthia trying to pull the curtain down?

Abetted by the double shot, Adam's thinking did a one-eighty-degree turn. Maybe her anti-war zeal, including her pilgrimage to

Berkeley, was in fact an outgrowth of her love for him—a chance to do something tangible about the war. And speaking of one-eighty-degree turns, Adam read enough to know that Kennedy had switched his position on Vietnam, even after his own brother's administration had been a staunch advocate of the domino theory. After a while, Adam decided to ask him flat out. "You didn't used to be against the war. Why are you now?"

Kennedy rested the Heineken on his tray, his hand shaking slightly. "Freedom sometimes has to be paid for in blood." His shoulders sagged. "But it may be that this effort was doomed from the start. I accept my personal responsibility for the decision to be there. But past error is no excuse to perpetuate it."

"I absolve you, Senator." Adam waved his hand over him. "But, with all due respect, that's little comfort to us soldiers. I wanted to be a surgeon more than anything. And now look." He picked up his left sleeve with his right hand, empty from four inches above the elbow on down, and let it drop. "While LBJ sits in the Oval Office and keeps escalating, this is what I'm left with. No arm. No chance to be a doctor. And no oldest brother. I'll get home just in time for his funeral."

Kennedy's deep blue eyes, like bottomless vessels, seemed to collect Adam's sorrow and hold it. Another woman approached with a book in hand, asking for his autograph—apparently, it was a book he'd written, newly published. Adam glimpsed the title: *To Seek a Newer World.* "Not now, please," Kennedy told her.

"A newer world, huh?" Adam said, as the woman walked away. "So, what exactly does that mean to you?"

Kennedy leaned forward in his seat. "To me, it means that each of us can change a small portion of events—stand up for an ideal, strike out against injustice, take the difficult or unfamiliar path for love's sake. It doesn't have to be a sweeping undertaking; it can be the small, everyday acts of compassion and kindness we do in our own neighborhoods, in our own homes. And together those single acts can build a current that reshapes our destiny."

Adam nodded, nostalgic for the noble memory. Though he'd never phrased it that loftily, he used to believe that too.

Once they touched ground in Chicago, Kennedy reached into his pocket and pulled out a gold-toned PT-109 tie bar. "My brother used to pass these out to his best supporters," he said. "And I'd like you to have one, Adam. If you want it, that is."

Accepting it into his open palm, Adam stared at it. World War II was another war, his father's war, a champion's war. He remembered the story. When PT-109 was torpedoed by a Japanese destroyer, President Kennedy had jumped into the Pacific waters to save his crew from drowning. "Your brother was a real hero."

"You know what he said about being a hero?"

Adam shook his head.

"He said, 'It was involuntary; they sank my boat.'" Kennedy got up from his seat, smiling in a way that had no involvement with his eyes. He moved into the aisle toward the exit.

"Hey, Senator!" Adam said.

Kennedy spun around.

"We've been hit by a destroyer, and our country's boat is sinking. I think it's involuntary for you too. I'm betting you're going to jump in—into the race."

Kennedy's gaze intensified.

Noël was waiting for him at the train station, her puffy, swollen eyes trying hard to ignore his disfigurement. "You don't have an arm," little Adam said.

"I don't?" Adam checked his sleeve. "Holy cow, you're right! I wonder what I did with it."

"That's okay." He offered his clumsy little fingers. "You can have mine."

All the way back to Willow from the train station, Adam was dreading the reunion with his father. He could only imagine his resentment over his homecoming, when Bo, his favorite son, never would.

When Adam walked through the back door of his parents' house, he saw his mother first, sitting blank-eyed at the kitchen table without glancing up. His father was standing in the doorway, looking as if he'd aged twenty years, with long gray streaks running through his black hair. Choking back tears, he charged toward Adam, embracing him without restraint. "You've come back to me."

It was that unexpected greeting that finally broke him; Adam crumpled in his father's arms.

Early the next morning, Noël dressed their mother up in her best black dress, white pearls, and makeup, the way Aunt Clarry used to do it, and led her to the funeral parlor, and later on, to the Garden of Resurrection, where the fresh grave was already dug beside Monroe's. The cemetery was jam-packed. Even strangers from surrounding towns came to honor Bo, the war hero they'd read about in the newspaper. A swarm of old VFW veterans from both world wars gathered to provide military honors, including a round of "Taps."

There were no protestors here; Willowites still believed in the valor of Vietnam.

Doc Wharton looked old to Adam too, his cheeks flecked with age spots, only a few wisps of baby-fine silvery hair dotting his head.

Under the green tent, Doc rested his hand on Adam's shoulder—the lighter one—from his seat directly behind him. His surgeon dreams had been as much Doc's as his own. Adam kept his eyes fastened on Bo's coffin, draped with the American flag.

"Bo was a man of faith," Pastor Martin eulogized.

He was right about that. Back when they were kids in Hyssop, Bo used to boast that he had enough faith to move a mountain, and none of them doubted that he could do it. But the mountains proved too many in Vietnam.

The autumn winds were blowing cold, the threat of winter heavy in the air. As the old veterans lifted the flag from Bo's casket and ceremoniously folded it, Adam's thoughts turned macabre. He wondered which parts of Bo actually made it into the coffin. His arms? His legs? Those faithful teal eyes of his? Only Dad, who had motioned them all away at the funeral parlor, had insisted on looking inside the casket.

Now, as his sobbing father stepped closer to receive the triangle-folded flag, he tripped on the tarp and fell to his knees. Who was this broken man? He tried to stand up again, fell back down, this time on his rear. If it wasn't in this place and it wasn't Jack Trudeau, it might have been the kind of slapstick tumble people snickered at. As it was, it was gut-wrenching.

Just as he had rushed to Adam at his homecoming, so Adam rushed to him now. Throwing his only arm around him, he raised his father from the tarp and steadied him against his ribs.

Pastor Martin resumed his remarks. "Bo Trudeau has gone home," he said, "and the angels are welcoming him with jubilation."

Adam looked around. There were no angels here, just sagging, defeated, aging faces in a naïve, ignorant town. He glanced down at his missing arm. He craved Cynthia's presence.

Welcome home—to both Bo and himself. The gulf between heaven and earth never seemed wider.

SEVENTEEN

OCTOBER 1967
NOËL

ALREADY, *it's starting—the terrible cost.* The day after Bo's funeral, it was Noël's first thought when she woke up, the same fear that had been dogging her every morning since she and Leon began their relationship.

Only they weren't the ones who were paying.

Rick was sliding into a drunken pit, Leon had told her, missing days of work and showing up afterward looking like one of the refugees in his concentration camp paintings. And now her own brothers were paying too—one of them dead, the other home from war but still gone, distant and shell-shocked. As the lives of their siblings crumbled around them, she and Leon sailed on through their secret, selfish bliss. He wasn't living with her exactly, his things remained in his own rented space, but he might as well have been.

She ran her fingers over the empty side of the bed, craving him. God, how was it even possible to feel such joy over another person's existence in this world? It wasn't possible. It couldn't be real. Leon was the make-believe conqueror she'd dreamed up during her lonely adolescence, but she was too far beyond rescue now, the damage too deep. Any day, their stolen magic would come to a crashing halt.

≈≈

Her arm locked through Adam's only elbow, Noël strolled through the Garden of Resurrection, while her little boy skipped ahead of them. "I must admit," Adam said, "it's very strange to have a part of your own body missing."

She flexed her fingers, trying to imagine them gone.

"Sometimes it feels like it didn't happen. And then I look down and—fuck, it's really gone. In my dreams, my arm is like a person, talking and walking around all by itself. I chase it through the streets. Usually it outruns me, but sometimes I catch it and pop it right back into the socket. Funny, huh?"

She held back tears; his darkness was infectious. "Do you think you'll stay in Willow?"

"That all depends on Cynthia, I guess. Maybe I'll head on out to San Francisco, who knows? I finally got her parents' number. I'm going to call them today to find out where I can reach her."

Noël remained silent. The fact that Cynthia hadn't somehow, someway, made it to Bo's funeral seemed another ominous sign. Ten feet away, little Adam stood in front of an enormous angel engraved on a tombstone, his little mouth agape. She smiled at him. "She's beautiful, isn't she, baby?"

"Ever since he was a toddler, he's had an affinity with angels," she told her brother. "Sometimes I think he sees them." He shot her a cynical look; her brother wasn't one for celestial notions, so she dropped it there. "You know, you can still go to college," she said.

"Not without cash I can't."

"I promise, I'll pay you back every single dime of the money you gave me before you left. And you can have your car back too. I don't need it. I walk to work."

"Give me a break, Noël. You can't afford to pay me back. You've got a kid to raise. I don't even know how you manage on your salary. Besides, it'll take a lot more than three-hundred dollars to pay for

four years of college. And keep that old beater too. Dad gave me
Bo's car—he sure as hell won't need it anymore."

"What about the G.I. Bill?"

He shrugged.

"You're young enough to start all over again. You can still be a
doctor."

"I couldn't even put on a blood pressure cuff by myself. And
a one-armed surgeon? Yeah, sure. Tell me you'd let me operate on
your child."

Noël paused in sorrow. "There are other areas of medicine,
aren't there?"

"Like a lab tech, you mean?" He shook his head. "You need
two arms for that too. The medical field is a precise art. Besides, I
wanted to be in that operating room more than anything. It's what I
was born to do. Or thought I was."

They reached their family plot. The dirt over Bo was covered
under a heap of flowers, still fresh as a florist's showcase. Little
Adam came over and plucked a rose from the pile, then looked up at
Noël to make sure it was allowed.

She nodded. "You picked the best one."

Grinning, he held it up to his uncle to inspect, but he was staring
down at the ground. At first, Noël thought her brother might be
praying, but then she realized he was only deep in thought. She took
the opportunity to study him after more than a year's absence. He
was lean, straight, tall, not an ounce of fat on his wiry body. His
raven hair, no longer a soldier's neat haircut, was windswept. Of all
of them, he looked the most like their father. She and Bo took after
their mother. Steve resembled neither parent, yet carried that indefinable similarity that most families do.

"You heard from Steve lately?" he asked, as if reading her mind.

"Nope. I've only gotten one letter from him. Really, it was more like a postcard. He said he loves the Navy."

"Doesn't surprise me." There was an edge to his laugh. "Steve's biggest influence is wherever he is at the moment." He scanned the family tombstones while Noël kept an eye on little Adam who'd scampered away again. "And then there's our littlest brother. *Budded on earth to bloom in heaven.*" He read Monroe's epitaph out loud, the way he always did, a skepticism in his voice. "Poor little guy didn't have a chance to be anything, did he? Not even disillusioned."

"His life had more meaning than the rest of us put together."

He squinted at her, incredulous. "He was stillborn, Noël! What possible meaning did his life have?"

Off in the distance, little Adam was talking to the angel statue. She welcomed the soothing distraction. "Look at him." She smiled.

"That kid of yours is something else. Nothing like that asshole you married. I'm so glad he's out of your lives."

"Thanks to you. I couldn't have run away from David without your help."

He ignored her gratitude. "He's in Kentucky now, you say?"

"Apparently so. And I guess his parents followed him there."

"So, Willow is safe territory again. What made him finally file for divorce?"

Noël felt her body tensing. Her Eden, her sin, was off-limits, another of her secrets but the closest to her heart. She had to keep Leon separate from the rest of her life. "It's a long story."

"When's it final?"

"Any day now."

His eyes returned to Bo's grave. Squatting down, he pulled out a red carnation, suspending it between his fingers. "Good old Bo. G.I. Joe to the end. I got some letters from him. This war brought him back to life. He really bought into it, hook, line, and sinker."

Her eyes grazed the hazy sky. "Where do you think he is now?"

"In pieces. Rotting away under a shitload of carnations and roses."

"You don't believe in heaven?"

"I used to." His eyes iced to a grayish color. "I don't know what I believe in anymore. But one thing's for sure—I don't believe in *that*." He pointed to Aunt Clarry's epitaph. "Loving too much kills you. Remember that, sis. Don't ever fall in love."

≈≈

The next morning, as she was packing to return to Langston, Adam received a call from Cynthia. When he picked up the phone and heard her voice, Noël watched the blood rush back into his cheeks. After he hung up, he shared the news: Cynthia was coming for a visit. She asked him to meet her next Tuesday at Pinky's, New Junction's swankiest restaurant.

"What else did she say?" Noël asked.

"Not much." The initial flush of joy gone, the curtain of angst closed over him again.

≈≈

When Noël arrived home, Leon surprised her and Adam with a Saturday trip to a carnival in a nearby city, part of an October Harvest Moon event, complete with hay rides, apple cider, and an amusement park.

Leon was trying hard to win over her son, too hard sometimes, and with the self-consciousness of a man who seldom interacted with children. Adam sensed his discomfort. But the prospect of going to a carnival was not lost on him, and he was all over Leon now, asking question after question as they headed for the car.

Leon drove a shiny black Dodge Charger. As Noël climbed into the black bucket seat beside him, she felt like she was sitting in a cocoon, safe and cozy. All the way to the fair, she snuck glances at him as he drove, even as the dusk turned to black night, and his profile became a silhouette. Every once in a while, he stroked his mustache with his thumb and forefinger; the latest of his mannerisms that she'd noticed. She was still in that delicious learning phase where each new discovery about him was a thrill.

This was their first big outing as a family. As the open road thumped beneath their tires, she pretended that Adam was his child. All the way to the fair, she reinvented her history. They'd met in high school. There had never been a David or a Rick. She was a high school graduate, and Leon had been her escort to the senior prom. And Aunt Clarry sewed her dress; she had never committed suicide.

Off in the distance, she spotted the gargantuan double Ferris wheel, rotating in the black night like a skyscraper. Adam pointed through the back window, giddy with excitement. "Can we ride that one?"

"Of course," Leon said.

Entering the main gate, an exotic cacophony of sounds, sights, smells flooded Noël's senses. A raucous throng of teenagers in tie-dyed T-shirts was boarding the Hurricane while riders on the spinning Flying Bob across the midway screamed bloody murder. The carousel kept repeating "Daisy Bell" in *oom-pah-pah* rhythm. Far ahead of them at the end of the crowded aisle, loomed the double Ferris wheel in all its neon splendor. Her pulse soared when Leon reached for her hand, their first public display of affection.

After a round of corn dogs and cotton candy, and a flurry of rides, including the Flying Bob, Adam pointed to a purple frog sitting on the top shelf of prizes at Billy's Bulls-Eye Parlor. Though it took three turns to do it, Leon managed to win the coveted prize for her ecstatic little boy.

At long last, it was time for the final attraction, the colossal double Ferris wheel that blocked the horizon in front of them like a tower of light. Noël regretted the decision to mount it as soon as the carnival man, reeking of gin, pulled the thin bar down over them with his muscular, tattooed arm. She fretted over the thought that he was probably the one who assembled this thing.

As they began the choppy ascent into the air, the center spokes grinding and creaking all the while, their seat tilted forward, and it seemed as if they were going to go tumbling down, face-first, into the gravel below. Closing her eyes, she clutched Adam—happily nestled in between them with his purple frog—with as firm a hand as she could manage.

Slowly, they climbed higher and higher, until the ride fell into its stride. As it picked up speed, the bumpiness stopped. The wind caressed them as they floated—up, up, up, up—and then a sharp downnnnnnn. They were soaring away from earth, backward first, then forward, with only that flimsy little bar of metal to hold them in place. Up, up, and up they went again, before another sharp descent. Noël's stomach was doing flip-flops.

Just as she was getting used to the cadenced, circular flow in the top wheel position, the ride came to a sudden halt as new riders boarded below. Their seat rocking, the three of them were stopped at the very top, the apex.

She looked around. They were too high in the night sky to hear a single sound. The stars winked above them, a sea of neon blinked below. The moon seemed close enough to touch. As she tried to assimilate the surreal beauty of the moment, she saw it—a little velvet box that Leon was holding in front of her—and her heart lurched. Flashing back to Rick's proposal, she forced the thought away as he flicked it open. The diamond looked like a lassoed star.

"Marry me." It was a statement, not a question.

Speechless, she gave him a look of a thousand yesses. As he slid the ring on her finger, he leaned over Adam, who was happily distracted by the scenery, and sealed it with a kiss, the seat swinging back and forth. The motion no longer frightened her; this was paradise, here and now, the closest she would get, and no harm would dare reach them here.

With a sudden jerk, the descent began. Again came the creaking and the grinding of the inner mechanisms and assorted earthbound noises from the frenzied midway below.

At the bottom, the tattooed man unbarred them.

As they walked back to the car through the maze of the fair, Leon's arm encircling her waist, she felt an aura of radiance illuminating them like a spotlight. Old couples smiled as they passed, and young girls gazed at them, dreamy-eyed.

Back inside the cocoon of his Charger, she let herself dream too. For now, she could block out the rest.

EIGHTEEN

NOVEMBER 1967
ADAM

PINKY'S was aptly named. A pink stucco building with rose-colored pavers framing the entranceway, it had a carefree, Mediterranean feel, diametrically opposed to Adam's mounting anxiety. When he walked into the restaurant and saw Cynthia sitting in front of the half-shuttered window, he felt lightheaded. Except for maybe a more determined, less breezy expression, she was lovelier than the day they'd parted.

He hurried toward her between rows of linen-clothed tables, but the moment her eyes caught his, he saw them go dim; his chest tightened. She rose from her seat and glanced down at his empty sleeve before surrendering to his embrace. The kiss fizzled, a near miss on her cheek. She smiled at him, not the enamored grin he'd imagined all the way over to New Junction, but a forced one with her bottom teeth showing.

It was over.

Adam wanted to get out right then—this lunch was his "dear John" letter delivered live and in-person—but he forced himself to sit down, see it through. He noticed she wasn't wearing her wedding band, and he twisted his own, round and round, with his thumb. He wished he could pull it off, but with one hand that would take some ingenuity, even though it was looser now. What was that word people used when they saw him now? *Gaunt.* He was gaunt as hell; maybe that was the problem.

"I'm so relieved you're back home." Her voice sounded genuine enough, but her eyes brushed past his, toward the empty table in front of them. "It seems like you've been gone for years. And I'm so very sorry about Bo."

The waitress brought over two thick, cardboard menus, passing one over to Cynthia and hesitating a second before offering the other to Adam's only available hand, flustered by his stump like the rest of them. She turned back to Cynthia quickly. "Would you like something to drink?"

"Coffee, please."

"And you?" She asked without looking at him.

"Double scotch on-the-rocks."

Jotting down the order, she moved to the next table.

"Adam, really." Cynthia shook her head. It's only twelve-thirty in the afternoon."

For that moment, she was the wifely girl he remembered, not this polite, deliberate stranger. Slowly, they began to converse, growing more comfortable in making eye contact for longer periods. Maybe it was just time that had come between them, the sudden reunion of intimates, that was making this meeting so devilishly awkward. She told him all about Berkeley, the Haight-Ashbury district, the love movement, the flower-power movement, every kind of movement except a bowel movement. His eyes glazed over until she mentioned the anti-war movement. She stopped suddenly as if she'd made a faux pas.

"That's okay," Adam said. "It's not *my* war."

"I know, but—" She looked at his sleeve again.

"So, are you personally joining these war protests?"

She cupped her hand over his to stop his drumming fingers on the tabletop. "I had to, Adam. Mankind has to find a better way of dealing with ideological differences. We need to try to understand our enemies. This war is pointless. A travesty."

Stung by her words, he sat back in his seat. "That's quite a speech. Forgive me for not applauding."

A tiny tear formed in the corner of her eye. "I'm sorry. I'm *so* sorry! I keep putting my foot in my mouth, don't I?"

The waitress returned with their drinks along with a wire basket brimming with plump, warm rolls. "Are you ready to order, or are you waiting for your other guest?"

Cynthia frowned at the waitress, then grinned at Adam as if being maimed had also made him deaf and blind. "Please give us more time," she said. "We have a lot of catching up to do." The waitress disappeared.

"Other guest? Who are you expecting—Allen Ginsberg?"

"There's something I need to tell you. Since there'll never be a good time, I might as well just say it now." She rested her hand upon his again, this time full force.

He flipped it off, ostensibly to grab a roll. Setting the doughy bun down on the small bread plate, he picked up a knife, buttered it profusely.

"Adam, please. Listen to me. I've met someone … his name is Nathan Bond."

Nathan Bond, that ugly name again. "Brother of 007?" The room was getting warmer, hot even. The roll became a tasteless glob inside his dehydrating mouth.

"I didn't mean for it to happen." Her eyes were filled with raw emotion. "Please believe me! But you and I were so young when we met. We didn't even know who we were yet, and—"

"I hear you—people move on," he interrupted, hoping she would stop talking. "Vows don't matter anymore."

"It wasn't a real wedding. We were just kids!" The tear rolled down her cheek.

Adam's pain intensified, becoming nearly unbearable, then dissipated suddenly. The rest of her words, and there were a lot of them, sailed by in a haze. He felt as if someone had slapped an anesthesia mask over his nose, and she was drifting away. He vaguely heard her telling him that Nathan had driven her here, that he was giving them time to be alone together first, but that he'd be joining them later.

"You mean he came to protect you in case I flip out?"

"No, that's not it at all. It's important to me that you meet him. I don't want you to hate either one of us."

The next thing he knew, a tall guy with long brown hair had appeared at the table. "Nathan's a political science major, and he plans to be a journalist." She turned to Nathan with that captivated look Adam so desperately missed.

"My heart goes out to you, man; it really does." Nathan reached for the basket of bread. "It's a real bummer that you, and all the other guys there, were forced to be pawns in LBJ's bogus war."

Adam knew he should have gotten up from the table the second he'd heard Nathan was due for an appearance. Any self-respecting fool would have done as much. But his legs felt plastered to the floor, the energy zapped from his cells, his dreams floating in front of him like swamp muck. He was retreating into that weird mental place, half Pinky's restaurant, half Vietnam. In between apprehensive glances between the two of them, Adam saw Scott Mason dying all over again at the table on the far side of the room; heard him calling out his name. "Don't let him get to you," Scotty whimpered. "You're better than this."

"Yeah, I'm better than this," Adam caught himself agreeing out loud. He raised his shoulders, ran his fingers over his tie.

Nathan hurriedly ordered the most expensive dish on the menu for the three of them, something called Bistecca Alla Siciliana that Adam went along with after Nathan insisted the dinner was on him. When the waitress set Adam's food down in front of him, a one-inch thick, T-bone steak dipped in some fancy breadcrumb coating, it was impossible to cut with only one hand.

"Sorry, man," Nathan said. "I didn't stop to think."

Flashing Adam the royal crown of pity looks, Cynthia offered to cut his meat.

≈≈

He didn't dare share the gory details with anyone. He told his father and Noël only that it was over between him and Cynthia and let it go at that, refusing to elaborate, even when Noël prodded him for more. Then she made her own confession, albeit sheepishly: She was engaged to some steel mill worker and was planning to bring him to Willow to meet them that coming weekend. "Do you want me to postpone it?"

"Nope. Bring him on. And stop acting as if misery loves company."

≈≈

It was a warm, breezy Saturday, the trees ablaze in color. For Adam, it evoked memories of bygone autumns spent raking leaves and jumping into crackling piles, then scooping them into cardboard boxes before Aunt Clarry burned them in a huge bonfire that lit up the night. He could still hear Auntie's laughter, the kind that made you laugh along.

Lately, she'd been his muse. He'd been dreaming about her—on those rare nights that the Vietnam reruns left him alone. Too many times he'd wake in a sweat, having come out of another endless horror show where he was crawling through heavy mortar ambushes to apply tourniquets and bandages and whatever else to one bloody, mutilated comrade after the next. In his dreams, the dead came back to life only to die all over again—in his arms, as he worked on them, or all alone, before he had the chance to reach them. If only he'd moved faster …

He woke up early that day to clean the house while his mother sat out back, staring vacuously at the lawn where Auntie's flower garden used to bloom. Adam put a radio by her side, cranked it up so she could listen to the Strawberry Alarm Clock sing "Incense and Peppermints."

Back inside, he found his father dusting the living room, the tack cloth filled with grime.

"How long has it been since you dusted?"

"There's a first time for everything," Dad said with a grunt.

Leon Ziemny wasn't what Adam was expecting. Since Noël was so taken with him, Adam had pictured him resembling James Dean, edgy and heart-throbby. Instead, he was common, like a steel mill worker ought to look, with no outstanding features and nothing much to say. Adam guessed him to be around five-foot-ten or so.

Straightening himself up to his full, towering height, his father extended his hand.

Noël made introductions. Afterward they stood around awkwardly. Young Adam saved the day, clamoring for his uncle to scoop him up, which he did as best as he could with one limb. Grateful for the kid's incessant chatter, they took their seats—Adam and his dad on the sofa, Leon and Noël occupying the chairs on either side, the little one bouncing in between. They made small talk about the long drive from Langston and the brilliant autumn colors.

Though Adam hoped to be less obvious about it than his dad, both were scrutinizing Leon, waiting and watching for a reason to like him, but so far he'd given them none. He reminded Adam of one of the guys in his platoon—Alf, the one no one could get close to and, consequently, the one none of them trusted. Leon Ziemny had the same mysterious self-containment.

Once little Adam quieted down, his father started in on Leon. "I hear you're a steel mill worker?"

"Leon is a supervisor there." Noël beamed.

"Working in an assembly line doesn't take much supervision, does it?" His father stared at the ceiling as he said the words. "Sounds like one of those bureaucratic jobs to keep your nails clean."

Leon lit a cigarette. "And what is it that you do for a living?"

Adam watched his dad's haughtiness wane. He was assuming Noël had filled Leon in about how demeaning it was for him to give up his traveling career. "I was in sales for a long time," his father said. "I covered the east coast when the kids were younger, but now, because of my wife, I stay here in Willow. I work in personnel at the Luffkin factory."

The tension between the two men was thick, like jungle weeds in Nam, and the longer the conversation continued, the more entangled it became.

When Noël decided to take Leon outside to meet her mom, both Adams jumped at the chance to escape the room along with them.

Mom was positioned in a large fanback wicker chair, wearing a straw hat, seeming peaceful more than vacuous. "Hi, Mama." Noël stooped down to kiss her. No response, as usual. Noël dropped her voice to almost a whisper. "I want you to meet the man I'm going to marry. This is Leon Ziemny."

Mom's eyes remained stuck on the lost garden.

"I fell in love, Mama!" She leaned closer to her ear. "Just like you did."

Given Noël and their father's strained relationship, not to mention their parents' void of a marriage, it struck Adam as a very odd thing to say. But it worked some kind of miracle—there was a flicker of light in Mom's eyes as she gazed at Noël, then up at Leon. Slow as spreading syrup, the trace of a smile broadened her lips.

She was still alive in there!

Even the kid was shocked. "Look—Grandma's smiling!" he said.

When Leon reached down to take Mom's hand, her fingers grasped it, her eyes glued to his face as if he was a memory she was trying to recall.

All of a sudden their father swept in, ruining the moment as he unpeeled his wife's clamped fingers. "You haven't been yourself all day today, have you?" he said. Her face snapped back into stupor. "Let's get you out of this sun."

The walls were closing in with every moment that Leon and their father were in the same house together. It felt like they were sitting in the waiting area of an emergency room.

Noël wanted to take Leon on a tour of the town, and Adam and the little one, once again, were only too glad to tag along. She showed him the high spots, like the Seashell Supper House, Kolby's Market, and the place she loved the most, the Garden of Resurrection, where they walked for more than an hour among the tombstones while she pointed out her favorite inscriptions. She also showed Leon the exact spot where she hoped to be buried one day, under the weeping willow trees on the far end of the cemetery. To some men it might have been wacky, but Leon seemed to get her.

His relationship with little Adam was more iffy. Leon appeared to be trying his best to be a father figure, but he was wooden, and the kid could spot a faker a mile away. As a result, the two of them had settled into a kind of nonrelationship, reminding Adam of their neighbor's cats back in Hyssop—resigned to each other, yet distant. After his nephew was tucked into bed, Adam suggested that the three of them head over to the Turning Point Tavern for a nightcap. If his father wasn't going to do the honors of assuring his daughter's intended was suitable, Adam figured it was up to him.

Even though it was Saturday night, it was pretty dead in the bar, only a few plaid-shirted old farts in suspenders sitting around a back table playing rummy, slowly getting plastered. Sitting across from him on the other side of the booth, Leon and Noël could hardly unlock their eyeballs from one another.

Silver-haired Mrs. Mossy, the grocer's wife and Willow's best stab at a cocktail waitress, brought their drinks. Adam raised his gin and tonic. "To the two of you." They clinked glasses. "When's the big event?"

"Well, there's not really going to be a big event." Noël's face clouded. "We can't be married in Leon's church."

"Vows are vows," Leon said. "God will hear us wherever we say them."

As Adam guzzled his drink, he flashed back to his own throw-away wedding vows on the altar of the First Methodist Church. He took another sip. "So, how did you meet?"

There was a pause, a flurry of evasive expressions between

them. "I stole her away from my brother." Leon downed a swallow of booze. Noël lowered her eyes.

Taken aback, Adam took another quick taste of his gin. "Well, then … I guess the important thing is that you found each other, right?"

A small portable television, the volume turned off, sat on the mammoth mahogany bar. The eleven o'clock news was showing another anti-war march somewhere out west—a band of young men marching in unison with locked arms, their long hair flowing. Without any sound, it looked almost artsy. As usual, Adam scanned the crowd for Cynthia. Half the women there resembled her. "I think I'll join one of those protests." Adam pointed to the screen.

"Really?" Noël's eyes widened. "What on earth for?"

"Because this war is bullshit, that's why! I lost my arm for no goddamned reason. Screwed up my whole life to do LBJ's bidding." What the hell?, he sounded just like Nathan.

Leon set down his whiskey, eyeing him closely. "This country is messed up right now, that's for sure."

"Messed up? It's anarchy!" The liquor was heading straight to Adam's brain, fueling his bitterness. "Riots, protests, sit-ins, love-ins, the sexual revolution—you name it. You two living together?"

"Not yet." Noel flushed hot-pink. "We're not married."

"So what? That's not stopping anyone else. This is the swinging sixties." Adam drained his glass while Noël played with the little green umbrella sticking out of her sloe gin fizz. She hadn't taken one sip yet. "Move in together and be happy. While you still can."

Now his sister was red as an apple. Had she always blushed so much?

"What about you?" Leon said. "What are you hoping to do now?"

"Hope?" Adam shrugged. "I don't hope anymore. Hope is a

savage wolf. Besides, I have the perfect life right here in Willow. Plenty of time to read and think. Beautiful waitresses …" He glanced at Mrs. Mossy, adjusting her bifocals at the far end of the bar. "The existentialists, Sartre and Camus, they know where it's at. Life is meaningless, indifferent." He wagged a finger at Leon. "Have you ever read Nietzsche?"

Leon shook his head. Noël brushed away tears she thought Adam didn't see.

Undaunted, he continued. "Nietzsche said, 'What doesn't kill us makes us stronger.' But the dumb bastard got it all wrong. What doesn't kill us outwardly, kills us on the inside—it doesn't make us strong; it makes us numb." He held his empty glass up high, so that Mrs. Mossy might hobble off her stool to drown him in more gin.

"Adam is feeling pretty lost right now," Noël said, obviously trying to atone for his bad behavior. "He wanted to be a surgeon."

"Yeah, I know, you've told me that." Leon looked at Adam. "That must be tough. I'm sorry."

"Hey, don't be, man. Opportunity knocks. Dad is trying to hook me up with a big job at the Luffkin factory. Invoicing. A real dream job." He glanced at his sister's face; she was a mirror, and he hated his reflection.

When Mrs. Mossy finally brought him another drink, Noël excused herself to the ladies' room, no doubt having herself a good cry over him in there.

For a few uncomfortable seconds, Leon and Adam were silent. "It's funny," Leon said. "You always knew exactly what you wanted from life. And I never had a clue. And then I met your sister. And I realized she was the missing piece."

Adam smiled at him; it'd been so long since he smiled that it felt like his face was cracking in new places. "That's nice, Leon. I mean it. I really appreciate you saying that."

"You're an intelligent guy, and you'll find your missing piece too. Don't piss your life away just because you lost an arm. Go to college. Become a PhD instead of an MD. You'll still have the same title."

"Good point." Adam's voice was soft. The liquor was already wearing off, the anger thawing into that awful numbness. "Trouble is, it never was the title I was after."

≈≈

The next day, a sunny Sunday morning, Noël cooked an elaborate country breakfast. There was plenty of food but little conversation. Eventually, the three of them piled back into Leon's car, while Adam and his father stood in the driveway, waving goodbye.

"Well?" Adam said. "What did you think of him?"

"He reminds me of that old Polish joke: What's the difference between a smart Polack and a unicorn? Nothing, they're both fictional characters."

"Whoa. Tell me how you *really* feel."

"You mean to say you like him?"

"Yeah," Adam said. "I kinda do. In case you haven't noticed, he's turned your melancholy daughter into a blushing rose. Either he's some kind of magician, or he's the best thing that's ever happened to her."

NINETEEN

NOVEMBER 1967
NOËL

AN hour before closing, a crusty old man appeared in Roy's Diner, wearing a short gray jacket, a sports cap, and bulky gloves. Plopping himself down on one of the counter stools, he demanded a cup of Sanka and a piece of pie. Noël tried to avoid his fixed stare while she gathered the items—the coffee mug from the overhead cabinet behind the counter, the cherry pie from the revolving showcase. As she sliced a big chunk for him, then poured the steaming liquid into his cup, his eyes remained fastened on her the entire time. He looked familiar, but she couldn't quite place him. She slid the plate in front of him.

"You're Noël, aren't you?" He pulled his right glove off with his teeth before stuffing both of them into his jacket pocket.

Though surprised he knew her name, something about the way he asked the question prevented her from being alarmed. She nodded. And then it came to her in a flash. "Oh, sure," she said softly. "You're Leon's father."

"Yup." He took off his cap. "In the flesh."

She didn't know how to react because she wasn't certain why he'd come. She and Leon had wasted no time after her divorce became final. In a week, they planned to be married by Orville P. Mooreland, a justice of the peace who lived on the outer edge of Langston, far away from Leon's neighborhood. Was he here to ruin their plans?

"Geez, don't look so scared." Picking up his fork, he stabbed at the cherry pie. "I just wanted to talk with you a little bit, that's all."

When she'd met him before, at that awful party, she'd been too apprehensive to notice. But now she could see it, remnants of Leon in the color and shape of his eyes. That's where the resemblance stopped. The skin of Mr. Ziemny's face was creased with a menagerie of deeply-embedded lines and wrinkles, most of them going downward, with just a few bending upward. She recalled Rick's portrait of him; he had captured his father to perfection.

"Look, I know you're getting married next Friday." He continued spearing large pieces of the pie with his fork, talking as he chewed. "I haven't said anything about it to her, you know, to the missus. She already thinks you're the Bride of Frankenstein."

Her heart cinched. Of course, she hated her. What mother wouldn't? "But you don't?"

"Nah." He waved his hand. "I keep telling myself—and her too—if both our sons love this gal so much, how bad can she be?"

Noël smiled at the backhanded compliment. "How about a refill?"

He nodded, and she freshened the Sanka. "Yeah, Leon said you're kind of shy." He took a sip. "And that's okay; there's nothing wrong with that. But what I like best about you is your smile. You light up this whole joint when you smile. My mother had a smile like that."

The compliment resonated. He'd told her that before.

Rick had been right—his father's face encapsulated the permanent tragedy of being separated from his parents at a young age and losing his mother later in the Holocaust. But it was also a strong, wonderful face, etched with a range and complexity of deeply-felt emotions, not unlike Mrs. Chavis'. Instinctively, Noël loved him, not only for being the father of two brothers that she loved, but for the honor of sharing his martyred mother's smile.

As he cut the hard end of the piecrust with his fork, she moved around the counter and sat beside him. "How's Rick doing?" She didn't have the courage to look him in the eyes.

"Lousy. But he'll get over it. Life isn't a bowl of cherries." Glancing at the cherry stains on his plate, she wondered if he was making a joke, but he didn't seem to be. "Life is full of hard knocks," he said. "Learning to keep going in spite of them is the whole point. Like trees, y'know? They need winter to get strong. People need winter too. The more winters we get through, the more we appreciate spring."

For her it was reversed. It was the hot summers she feared most.

"Once you're married, everyone will get used to you, after a while."

"I sure hope so. Does Leon know you're here?"

"I told him I might show up one day this week."

"Would you like another piece of pie?"

"Hell, no," he replied quickly. "I'm not supposed to be eating this late as it is. My stomach's gonna be burning like crazy tonight." He pulled his gloves out of his pocket, planted his cap back on top of his head. "So, where you going for your honeymoon?"

"Chicago."

"Chicago? What for? There's nothing there but big buildings and a lake."

When he stood up, she started gushing a million things at once. She thanked him for coming, she told him how much his visit meant, she invited him to return to the diner anytime he wanted, promised him a piece of pie on the house, just like tonight's.

His yellow teeth were visible beneath the dim light as he grinned at her for the first time, new lines crisscrossing his face like a meteor shower. "For what it's worth, I just wanted you to know that you have my blessing."

"It's worth everything," she said.

"Then go get yourself hitched with my boy. The rest will take care of itself."

≈≈

There was no moon the night before their wedding, none that she could see anyway, making her bedroom seem darker than usual, accentuating her foreboding. The flashbacks were after her again. She kept trying to push them out of her brain, but nothing helped.

The empty apartment made her easy prey. Leon was spending his last night in his own apartment, and yesterday her brother had come to pick up Adam and take him to Willow for the week. Noël wandered into his bedroom, squatted down on the carpet, and grasped his stuffed purple frog against her chest.

In little more than twelve hours, Leon Ziemny would be her husband.

She rose from the hardwood floor and sat on Adam's bed, glancing at her reflection in the dressing-table mirror. A mad woman with frenzied hair and frantic eyes stared back at her. How could she marry Leon? How could she marry anyone?

The next thing she knew, she was charging down the hallway, but she didn't make it in time and vomited all over the bathroom. Even as her insides spilled into the toilet, she couldn't stop the memories from playing out in lurid detail. No matter how hard she tried to stuff them down, deep down, they flew out without warning, reminding her that she was poison, worthless.

Her fists tight against her closed sockets, she let out a silent scream. She didn't want to believe them anymore—not when there was a Leon Ziemny in this world.

Curling up against the tiled wall, she tried her final trick, the one that almost always worked; she tried to make herself small enough to disappear. She pretended she was in her secret, imaginary, windowless room where it was safe and warm, with a huge, stone fireplace; a private door that no one knew about.

But it didn't help. This time, nothing would work—except the truth.

Leon was dressed in his black suit and olive tie when he arrived at her door. She was wearing a white lace mini dress she'd made on Aunt Clarry's old sewing machine. After laboring over it for more than a month, it felt old to her already. She should have done more. He deserved better than a homemade dress from a Butterick pattern.

"You look absolutely beautiful," he said. "Ready?"

When he tried to kiss her, she turned away and sat on the sofa, her heart pulsing like a jackhammer.

"What's the matter?"

"I have something to tell you first."

"Now? Mooreland is waiting."

"There are things you have to know about me."

He looked alarmed. "And we can't talk in the car?"

She took in a deep breath, closed her eyes for strength. "All my life I've been hiding a string of secrets, one right after the next. If we're going to be married, you have to know the truth."

"*If* we're going to be married?"

When she opened her eyes, she couldn't tell whether he was panicked or angry. He perched on the edge of the chair opposite the couch and glanced at his watch. "Now's a fine time for this conversation. We're going to be late."

She fought back tears; she couldn't allow them to fall before this was over and done. "You have to know what you're getting into. You have to know who I really am."

He pulled out a cigarette from his pocket, fumbled to light it. "If this is about Ketchfield, I already know. What you didn't tell me, that son of a bitch did. Your first marriage must have been a living hell for you."

"There's more."

"More?" He arched his back as if bracing himself. "Go on."

She wanted to stop. She hated the expression on his face, but she had no other choice. "A long time ago, when I was just a child … my mother fell in love with … a black man."

His head snapped back slightly; he took a deep puff.

She gave him the short version. "He was a pastor back in Hyssop. She used to take me to his church with her when she went to see him, secretly, for counseling. But, once, only once, we met him at his house, and she went upstairs to his bedroom. My father didn't know it had gone that far between them. He still doesn't. No one did. Meeting him alone in church was taboo enough." She paused, forced herself to continue. "I don't know how the men in town found out about the counseling—but they did. And they murdered Pastor Ray because of it. Brutally."

He half-shrugged, not from indifference—at least, she was hoping to God it wasn't—but from what she presumed was indignation. "I guess you can't really blame them, can you?" he said. "I mean, really, to sleep with a married white woman?"

His words cut her. "I told you, they didn't know about that part. At least, I don't think they did."

"So, is that it?"

"No, that's not it." She clawed through her hair. "The night he was murdered, we left Hyssop. After that—" She didn't think she could say it out loud, the secret she and Dr. Wharton had kept for so long, the part she hadn't even revealed to Mrs. Chavis.

"After that, what?"

She tried again. "After that … my mother had a baby, but it was stillborn. My father never knew it wasn't his."

"You mean she had a black baby?" Leon's face went ashen. "How did *you* know?"

"I snuck into the room when he was born."

"How come your father didn't know?"

"Dr. Wharton made sure to cover the baby in a blanket before he carried him to the funeral home. I think he told my father he was deformed or something and that it was better not to look. And then, Monroe was cremated."

Leon extinguished his cigarette. "Well, thank God, it was stillborn. For all your sakes." She felt another thrust, hoping it wasn't meant as heartless as it sounded. "That's a bad story alright, but what does it have to do with you? It's your mother's sin."

"It wasn't a sin! Not hers anyway. But it was mine."

"Yours? How do you figure that? It wasn't your job to protect your mother—it was her job to protect you."

"It *was* my job!—I was the one who was there with her. I'm toxic, don't you see? You should walk away from me while you still can."

He stood up, started pacing. His hands clenched, unclenched. The muscle in his cheek was pumping hard. "Who gave you the crazy idea that you're to blame? Ketchfield?"

"No. He never knew any of this."

"Then, let it go. You were just a child."

"A terrible child."

"There's no such thing."

"You don't understand. Their lives were ruined because of me."

"Whose lives? Why did you think you're responsible? Who made you think that? Someone must have put that crazy idea into your head. Who was it?"

"My father!"

"Your father?" He sat down on the sofa beside her.

She tried not to hyperventilate, took another deep breath. "My father always hated me. As a little girl, I never knew exactly why."

"You've told me that before."

"But it was because he blamed me."

"For what?"

She was too ashamed to look him in the eyes. "One night when Aunt Clarry and the boys were gone somewhere, I heard Mama crying in her bedroom. The door was closed, but I rushed in anyway, and my father was there on top of her. She was flailing her arms and sobbing. When he heard me come in, he stopped. Then he screamed at me. 'Get out of here! This is all *your* fault! None of this would've happened if you had told me she was going to that church of his— but you kept your mouth shut and let him turn her into trash. You're just like her!'"

"Baby, my God, it wasn't your fault!" Leon dropped to his knees in front of her. "No child should have been put through that."

"But there's more." She refused his consolation. "I told Aunt Clarry about it when she got home. After that, she offered herself up to him, like a lamb to slaughter, so that he'd leave Mama alone. Auntie's bedroom was in the attic—the boys never suspected. But I'd hear him creeping up the stairs the nights he wasn't traveling." The sobs engulfed her. "Less than a year later, she killed herself!"

He took her into his arms. "God in heaven, what has he done to you? None of that was your fault! It was him. And your mother.

And Ketchfield, after that. God, Jesus, how much have you been through?" His eyes brimmed with tears, his embrace tightened. "I'll break your father's fucking neck!"

"No, you can't let him know I told you! Or my brothers. I had to protect them. I've kept these secrets my whole life. Look what happened when I told Aunt Clarry. Promise me you'll never tell!" She wept inconsolably.

"You have me now," he said softly. "I won't let anyone hurt you ever again."

She couldn't process his comfort; it wasn't possible. She expected him to walk out on her. But not this. All the secrets were out, and still he was holding her. He knew every horrific thing she'd ever done, and still he remained. At last, at long last, she'd revealed exactly who she was: unlovable.

And still he loved her.

She sobbed until her makeup ran all over his clean white shirt, until she was paralyzed with fatigue, with relief, with gratitude beyond comprehension. A lifelong weight was expunged.

For the next half-hour, there was no sound in the apartment except the muted hum of the refrigerator. She clutched him without moving. Orville Mooreland had probably given up on them by now. "I wish to God I never told Aunt Clarry," she said.

"Everyone has things they wish they could do over. But it doesn't work that way."

She gazed at him. "What kind of things are they for you?"

His brows arched, his eyes glazing on the window. "Once I gave my brother a Bit-O-Honey bar, and he got sicker than a dog. My mother nearly executed me for it."

Noël had heard that story before, from Rick's side. She absorbed the weight of his simple confession. "But what about all those other times?" She stroked his cheek. "You saved him from Billy

Maciejewski on the playground. You told Billy he had a nose like an anteater."

She watched his eyes soften, go hard again. "But then I did the unthinkable, didn't I? I took you away from him."

Her heart stabbed. "You didn't take me away. I gave myself to you."

The pain in his eyes was intolerable. He had absolved her of her burdens, every single one of them, but she couldn't remove his. *She* was his burden. "Is it wrong for us to marry?" Her voice was a hollow sound. "We don't have to go through with it, you know."

He stood up, took her hand, and led her to the door. The question hung between them.

At the end of the walkway was a sign with black lettering that read: O.P. MOORELAND, JUSTICE OF THE PEACE AND NOTARY PUBLIC. A curving walkway led up to a gray-shingled house with red shutters.

Mr. Mooreland picked up his little black book and opened it to the page where the satin marker hung. Noël's whole body trembled. The Moorelands' pimply teenage son stood beside Leon, presumably his best man, while Orville's wife sufficed as her matron-of-honor.

"We are gathered here today to join this man and this woman in holy matrimony." Mooreland adjusted his half-glasses, gazing over them at her and Leon. "'Marriage is not something to be entered into lightly,'" he read.

The short ceremony went by in a blur.

"With the power vested in me, I now pronounce you man and wife."

≈≈

They approached the city from Lake Shore Drive. The night was closing in, and it was too dark to clearly see Lake Michigan just off to the right. As Leon's car wound along the curving drive, past McCormick Place, past the museums, past Soldier Field, Noël caught her first glimpse of the Chicago skyline, a breathtaking, geometric range of white lights, steel, and glass. She felt as if they were heading straight toward a giant diamond with a million gleaming facets.

Eventually they got near enough for the jewel to swallow them. They were in the heart of the city now as they headed north on Michigan Avenue.

"What's that?" She pointed to a large stately building with two mammoth lion statues out front.

"The Art Institute."

She thought of Rick, flinched.

A menagerie of buildings and signs swirled by as they turned and made their way back south: Chicago Theater. Marshall Field's. Restaurants galore. Taxi horns were honking. Scents of bus fumes and food aromas of all kinds wafted through her nostrils. The "L" train rumbled overhead; the raised steel tracks vibrating as they wended their way through narrower, denser streets in search of their hotel. Chicago was an enticing stranger, a world away from the simplicity of Willow or the dinginess of Langston. It throbbed with life.

It was dark when they finally found the hotel, her eyes fixating on the sign of the adjacent parking garage—yellow neon letters flashing: "Park, Park, Park."

Checking in at the front desk happened in both fast-speed and slow motion. She stared at the clerk the entire time, but she couldn't recall whether it was a man or a woman. All she saw was the key being transferred into Leon's palm, hearing the number 1811, and then searching for the elevator.

On the ride to the eighteenth floor, the heavy gold doors opened and closed, and guests with no faces got on and off. Finally the golden doors parted for them, and he led her through a dim, carpeted hallway that twisted and turned until she found herself standing in front of room 1811.

Leon pushed the door open, and she stepped inside. She heard the sound of his fingers fastening the deadbolt, sliding the chain to lock them inside. They were here; beyond the point of no return.

Why should this be different? They'd been intimate many times before.

On the deep sea of the king-sized mattress, their yearning bodies and besieged minds wordlessly plunged each other's depths with the electrifying entitlement of matrimony. He had to be feeling it too—shared ecstasy inextricable from shared culpability.

Could their paradoxes be any greater? They were man and wife, yet his brother's ghost hovered in between. Their guilt bound them as tightly together as it divided them. Confession might be good for the soul, but it couldn't undo a lifetime of ruin. It couldn't fill the voids of their brokenness.

Yet, they were tethered to one another now, legally and otherwise, every gaping crevice, every damaged inch, forever and ever.

The sheets fell to the floor, and time stopped.

There in the eternity of room 1811, as they melded into that sacred, mysterious, combustible place where two people became one flesh, her heart galloped with a sudden, newfound joy, a certainty. It *was* possible after all. It had been consummated, cemented, completed, consecrated. She could feel the difference. Their cavernous holes were filled; their sins charred to ash.

≈≈

After he'd fallen asleep, she lie there, listening to the sound of his breath. Other lovers might have collapsed under the paradoxes, but not them. They loved with Pascal's love; they loved *too much*. And that was what would save them.

TWENTY

DECEMBER 1967
ADAM

AS the year 1968 lurked just around the corner, *Newsweek* magazine was reporting a "sharp sense of crisis in the American
air." *Time* called it a "noxious atmosphere." Adam needed neither
Time nor *Newsweek* to warn him of the mood of the nation. He
recognized the symptoms. The country was a ticking time bomb.

And so was he.

Two weeks before Christmas, the call came that Dr. Wharton
was dying. Informing Adam that it was heart failure, Mrs. Wharton
summoned him over to the hospital in Bedlington. Doc was asking
to see him.

As Adam walked through the wide, sterile hallways in search of
Doc's room, he was reminded of the day Noël had her baby there,
and the second trip back a week later, when she'd nearly died from
loss of blood. In both of those situations, Doc Wharton had been
their backbone. And before that too, including the first day they'd
driven into Willow and on that cold, Christmas Eve when he'd
carried Monroe's dead body to Green's Funeral Parlor. For years,
Doc had been the real protector of their family—from itself.

≈≈

He looked withered in his bed, cranked up to a sitting position, as Mrs. Wharton read the morning paper to him through half-rimmed glasses. When they noticed Adam, they both lit up.

"Sit, Adam." She surrendered her vinyl chair. "I think I'll head down to the cafeteria for a cup of coffee while the two of you chat."

Chat? The word sounded out of place, given the circumstances. *Yeah, Doc, let's have a final chat before you pop off this planet.* After she left, he sat in her place, still warm.

"Thanks for coming." Doc's voice was gravelly, not his normal one. His gray mustache was down to a few scraggly hairs, his head totally bald, his skin the pasty pallor of imminent death. Back in Nam, Adam had seen hundreds of people die in front of his eyes, so why wasn't he used to it yet?

He didn't know what to say or do. Should he shake Doc's hand? Hold it? Tell him he'd be okay? Tell him how God-awful-much he'd miss him? Tell him how his dying felt like the moon was crumbling? Without the moon, the black night would lose its compass. He caught himself fighting tears. Who knew he still had some in him?

"Listen to me, boy," Doc said. "I want you to know how important you are to me."

God, I can't do this! Adam stood up, moved toward the window, his back toward him. The venetian blind was rolled high enough to reveal the parking lot. It was a gray winter day; hazy sky, hazy ground, blurring into one gray blob.

"I know this is hard for you," Doc continued. "Coming home from Vietnam, I mean. But here's what I want to tell you: don't give up. You've got to keep believing that life has a plan for you."

How like Doc—he was the one dying and he was giving Adam comfort.

Adam turned around to face him. He could do this after all. Be strong for him one last time, the way Doc had been strong for them their entire lives. He sat back down in the vinyl chair. "You're the most decent man I've ever known. I'm sorry I can't be the doctor you taught me how to be."

"Well, that's the kicker, isn't it?" Doc smiled sadly. "Even doctors have to get wounded. And die. So, what the hell use are we?" He managed a chuckle that choked in his throat.

Adam wished he could do something—lay his hand on him, pump blood into his failing heart—but he was a eunuch, helpless. "Doc, there's a stinger in my brain. I'm not the same boy you used to know. I can't shake the images of what I saw in Nam—their faces, the things I had to do—I relive it all the time, whether I'm sleeping or awake. It's one thing to live it as it happens, over there in Vietnam. It's another thing to live with it later, over here. I don't think I can. I think I'm going as mad as my mother."

Doc's lips cinched. "And I imagine you saved a lot of lives over there too?"

"Yeah. Yeah, I did. Medics are supposed to save lives. But I wanted to save them all."

"That's not humanly possible. Life and death are conjoined. War and peace too. And courage and fear. A good medic embodies them all, and you tried the best you could. That's what makes you a hero."

"There's nothing heroic about me or this war. We aren't solving a damn thing by being over there! We're killing and being killed for no reason at all."

"You've got a bad case of homecoming depression, the soldier's malady." The way Doc said it seemed more like an observation than a weakness. "And understandably so. Helping others comes naturally to you. Helping yourself, not so much."

Adam leaned over and rested his chin against Doc's frail, chalky hand. Eventually, Doc's other hand—his touch as faint as a sparrow landing—found its way to the top of Adam's head. "Think long and hard about the way you want to use your life now," Doc said. "There are a lot of professions you can still do. Maybe you could become a medical researcher, the one who finds the cure for cancer, who knows?"

Adam raised his head. "Trouble is, there's no money for that."

"Have you looked into the G.I. Bill?"

"Not yet. But I will."

"Give yourself a chance to figure things out, that's all I'm asking. I believe in you, Adam. You've got a brilliant mind. Even more important, you've got a brilliant heart. Cynthia will help you."

"Not likely. She's engaged to another guy."

"Oh … I hadn't heard … I'm sorry." He paused long enough for Adam to raise his head to make certain he was still breathing. "But there a lot of other people who love you. And who need you."

"Such as?"

"Your sister, of course." Doc's voice lowered. "How that girl has suffered. And her boy needs you. Your father too."

"My father?"

He nodded. "I don't think I've ever known a lonelier man."

Adam let his words sink in. He and his family were a messed-up pile of humanity alright. "You know who I miss? I miss my auntie. I think about her a lot. I'll never understand why she killed herself. I still hope and pray it was nothing I did."

Curling his index finger, Doc bid him to come closer to his face, right up to his lips. "Physicians have to carry boulders of secrets around," Doc whispered. "And it gets heavy. That's why our hearts give out. But I'm going to break my Hippocratic oath to tell you something about your auntie. She carried things around too. I'd been prescribing birth control for her, at her request, for the last year or so of her life. I didn't ask any questions about who or why, of course; that was her business."

"Holy crap, Doc." Adam's mind was swimming. As far as they'd known, Auntie had no boyfriends. For a time way back when she first came to Willow, she had a thing for Bob Rose and they went out a few times, but he ended up marrying Betty Jane Brown. Maybe they'd been seeing each other again on the sly.

"But she came to see me a week before she died," Doc continued, "begging me to give her something strong to settle her nerves. I tried to get her to open up about why, and she finally confessed that she'd gotten herself in over her head with some married man. 'Pills won't fix that,' I told her. 'Let me try to help you get out of it'. I prescribed her enough for just a couple days and scheduled a follow-up appointment after that, for when she was calmer. But she said she'd handle it herself, and walked out."

Adam was stunned. "She probably wanted to take the pills instead, not the way she ended up doing it, and you foiled her plan."

Doc nodded sadly. "But talk about guilt over not being able to save everyone," he said. "I still carry that guilt for not doing more to help her, so you're not alone in that regard. The sorrow over losing a life, any life, comes with a physician's territory. We don't have crystal balls. We're not God."

"Yeah, great point. So, where the hell *is* God in all of this?"

"Ah, the big question." Doc paused. "I'm no spiritual scholar, but I've always found my answer in this Bible verse." He cleared his throat. "'Then a great and powerful wind tore the mountains apart and shattered the rocks, but the Lord was not in the wind. And after the wind an earthquake, but the Lord was not in the earthquake. And after the earthquake a fire, but the Lord was not in the fire. And after the fire, a still, small voice.'"

Adam fell silent.

"Maybe I was wrong to tell you about your aunt."

"No—thanks. It helps me better understand things."

Adam stared into his beloved mentor's ashen face. Dipping a tissue into a glass of water on the nightstand, he dabbed tenderly at Doc's parched lips before squirting a small amount of balm on the fissured corners of his mouth.

Doc's eyes fluttered in relief. "See there, kid—you're still one hell of a healer. So, do me one last favor." He beckoned Adam to come closer again. "Physician," he whispered, "heal thyself."

With Adam and his father both working at the Luffkin factory, their shared life was becoming one predictable routine. After losing his arm, Bo, Cynthia—and now, Doc Wharton—within a two-month span, Adam found a modicum of comfort in stale predictability.

As they walked to work each day, their numbness soldered them together like two pieces of the same machine gun. Decked in their polyester suits, they pushed papers around the Luffkin factory administrative offices, silent at the watercooler, where others shared intimate details of their personal lives. Dad still paid Mrs. Neal, the neighbor lady, to check on Mom several times a day. When they got back home, she was always in the same chair they'd left her in, her soiled diaper the only sign of life.

From time to time, while tallying up invoices for ball bearings and parts, Adam's mind would wander. He'd look across the office toward the only window, his thoughts drifting back to the days when he was Dr. Wharton's apprentice and Cynthia was on his arm, that old feeling of happiness zinging through his veins like the old stimulant-opioid double whammy in Vietnam. The U.S. military plied soldiers with plenty of pharmaceutical medications to aid their endurance over there, and Adam had helped himself to his share of them. If drugs were easier to get a hold of in Willow, he'd be an addict now for sure.

"What did you find out about the G.I. Bill?" His father asked as they finished up the dinner dishes. He put the last pan down on the counter to make it easier for Adam to dry it off with the towel; by now, he'd learned all the tricks to assist a one-handed dish wiper.

"I found out I'm entitled to a hundred bucks a month." Encouraging as Doc's pep talk might have been about the possibility of doing groundbreaking research, the G.I. Bill would barely pay for a basic health class at a community college, let alone, finding a cure for cancer.

"A hundred shitty dollars?" His father shook his head. "Things sure are different from when I left the service."

They drifted into the living room.

"Screw the government," Dad said. "We don't need them. Keep living at home for a couple years, and you and I will sock enough money away for a decent medical school. I just paid off the mortgage, so we're in good shape. Together, the two of us will think of something."

The warmth from his father's hand on his shoulder made Adam feel nearly human again.

TWENTY-ONE

DECEMBER 1967
NOËL

NOËL had tucked her candles away on the upper shelf of their closet. With Leon living there now, the apartment had become much too cluttered to even consider lighting them.

Leon's father was a frequent visitor. Each time he came—on the sly from the rest of his family—he snuck in a few more of Leon's belongings until the rooms were full to bursting. Leon had a larger apartment all picked out for them on the fringes of the suburbs, with a little balcony that overlooked a church parking lot, but Noël wouldn't even consider leaving the Chavises. "Tell you what," she told him. "Let's stay here a little longer, and you can use the money to buy that Mustang you've been wanting."

Walt had been the one who shouldered the unenviable challenge of breaking the news of their marriage to Rick and Mrs. Ziemny, and he wasn't one to sugarcoat things either. "The deed is done," he said he'd told them, "So, get over it."

Usually Walt visited in midafternoon, right after both he and Leon got off work for the day. But sometimes when Walt pulled a later shift, he stopped by to visit Noël in the morning. She'd quit her job at the diner—Leon didn't trust the clientele, and her meager wages weren't much of a sacrifice. Both of them thought it more important she remain home with Adam.

Noël kept plenty of beer stocked for Walt. He liked his Drewrys, liked it ice-cold, right from the bottle. As he took a swig during one of his daytime visits in early December, she shared her desire to make the upcoming Christmas holiday extra-special for Leon. "Tell me about your Polish customs," she said. "I want him to feel like he's home."

"There's too many of 'em! I wouldn't know where to begin." Ignoring her eager expression, Walt watched *The Price Is Right* playing softly on the TV. "Okay, okay," he sighed after a few seconds. "Go get a pencil and paper." By the time she located both, he was already starting. "Christmas Eve supper is called Wigilia."

"V-a-g—"

"Nah, there's no V. In Polish, Ws are pronounced like Vs. Wigilia is when each family member shares a special wafer called the *oplatek* with every other member of the family."

"A what?"

"*Oplatek*. O-pwa-tech." She scribbled it down phonetically. "One by one, we wish them something good, or else we forgive them or ask forgiveness, for whatever we did wrong during the year."

She played it out in her mind—breaking the wafer with Rick; his forgiveness. Leon would get his brother back again, and they'd be a real family. She tried to imagine the relief of it, the elation.

"Don't go getting wild ideas," Walt said. "I know what you're thinking, that we're gonna break the *oplatki* and everything will be hunky-dory, but it doesn't work that way."

"It's supposed to work that way, isn't it?"

"Yeah, yeah, it's supposed to work that way." As he took another guzzle of Drewrys, Adam climbed onto his lap. "You trying to work me over too?"

Adam giggled.

"It's gonna take a helluva lot more than a wafer to fix things."

His face creased with a flurry of downward lines. "Lemme just think about it, okay?"

"How much time do you think they'll need?"

"Hell, I don't know! They still don't know I come here to see you two. I tell the missus that I just talk to Leon at the mills. But who knows? Maybe if I keep bringing up your marriage and reminding them that the die has already been cast, we can give the *oplatki* a try."

≈≈

Three days before Christmas, Walt gave her the green light. "I didn't say nothin' about the *oplatek*." He handed her a flat white envelope as discreetly as a pusher of some exotic substance. "I just told them that you might show up on Christmas Eve."

"And?"

"And neither of them went berserky."

Taking the envelope from his hand, she peeked inside. The wafers were paper-thin sheets that felt fragile to the touch, but Walt assured her they were tougher than they looked. Still, she was taking no chances. Standing on her tiptoes, she slipped the envelope into one of the top cabinets in the kitchen, far too high for Adam to reach or for Leon to stumble upon by accident.

Walt gave her one final piece of advice. "Now, don't go expecting miracles."

"Why not? It's Christmas."

≈≈

The *oplatek* wasn't the only thing Walt taught her about. She was a rapt student as he schooled her on the many other Polish Christmas customs, like leaving an empty place at the dinner table for Christ or loved ones who had died, the first star before Wigilia, the hay.

By the time Christmas rolled around, Noël was all set to give Leon a traditional Polish Christmas.

Walt told her that hay was tucked under the Wigilia tablecloth, symbolic of the manger where Jesus was born, covered by a white tablecloth that represented Mary's veil, spread out to form Christ's first bed. These simple traditions, he said, transformed an ordinary dining room table, in their case, a card table, into the sacred birth space.

On Christmas Eve day, Leon was scheduled to work a full shift, and Noël was secretly thrilled since there was so much to prepare.

Walt also had been sneaking in Leon's favorite recipes from Mrs. Ziemny's treasure trove. Five minutes after Leon left for work that morning, he brought five pounds of Polish kielbasa from their neighborhood meat market. Afterward, she and Adam took a drive out to the country in search of a farmer who was willing to part with a few strands of hay. Adam loved the winter treasure hunt. The rest of the day was reserved for cooking.

In her own kitchen one floor below, Mrs. Chavis helped out by cooking the sauerkraut, the mushroom soup, the poppy-seed rolls, and by frying up a batch of her delectable Southern fried chicken—her late mother's mouth-watering recipe from back in Alabama—while Noël prepared the kielbasa, pierogi, *kluski* noodles, fruit compote, and the delicate *chrusciki* for dessert, by far the most challenging. She let Adam help, even though he made each task more difficult. Watching his little fingers try to roll and press and stir was part of the fun. While they worked, they cranked up Christmas carols on the radio, loud enough to assure that the Chavises could hear them through the floorboards.

By the time Noël was finished, the kitchen was a complete disaster, and so was she. Powdered sugar and flour were caked every- where. A clutter of pots and pans, crusted with something or other, was scattered on every available surface. She cleaned it all up, down to the last sifter and rolling pin, until the kitchen shined.

There was only one final task. The most important one. She opened the closet door and pulled out the fourth folding chair. After moving the card table back from the wall, she set an extra place at the table.

"Who's coming?" Adam wondered.

"Very special guests, all the way from heaven."

It was already five-thirty p.m., dark outside. After helping Adam with his bath, she took the time to pretty herself up, slip into Leon's favorite dress, and douse herself with perfume. Next, she turned off the lights and plugged in the Christmas tree, the one that Leon and Adam had dragged up the stairs last weekend. And if things weren't perfect enough, it was beginning to snow.

≈≈

Leon arrived home an hour later, dropping his car keys on the table beside the door, his usual habit. Sniffing the aromas, he looked up in confusion, as if expecting his mother to emerge from the kitchen.

Noël told him to close his eyes. Taking his hand, she led him into the small space. "Now—open."

He blinked at the array of foods spread out on the counter. "Did you do all this? For *me*?"

"Who else?"

Pulling her into his arms, he held her there long enough for Adam to get antsy. He was clamoring to start eating, but Noël informed him that they had to wait until the first star came out. "It's the Polish tradition, isn't it?"

Leon nodded. And so the three of them bundled into their winter coats, rushed down the stairs and out into the street, where the snowflakes were falling fast and dense. Adam stared straight up at the sky; his eyelashes dusting white, wondering aloud which direction Santa's sleigh would be coming from. But the sky, including the north, was too pink to see either the stars or Santa. As they headed back inside, Leon teased her in the stairwell. "I think you're more Polish than I am."

Before allowing them to start eating, she told them that there was one more tradition. Sliding the envelope out of the top kitchen cupboard, she handed one wafer sheet to each of them. "This is called an o-pwa-tech," she said to Adam, pronouncing the word just as Walt had instructed. "It means wafer."

"What is it?" Adam wondered.

"Why don't you let Daddy tell you?"

Leon pulled out his chair, sat down beside him. "Well, it's kind of like a magic cracker."

Adam's eyes enlarged.

"Here's how it works. You break off a little piece of my cracker and eat it. And then I break off a little piece of yours and eat it."

"Why can't we just eat our own?"

"That would wreck the magic."

"Why?"

"Because after I take a piece of your cracker, I make a special wish, just for you, or I apologize to you for something I did to make you mad. Then I eat it. And it's the power of the *oplatek* that my wish for you will come true. And then you do the same for me."

"Like blowing out birthday candles?"

"Sort of." As Leon broke off the wafer, Adam's face glowed with wonder. "Let me think about this for a minute." Leon wrinkled his brows in mock contemplation. "Okay, I got it. I hope that Santa brings you that new dump truck you've been wanting."

"The red one?"

Leon nodded.

"Now it's your turn." Noël coaxed Adam. "Now you wish Leon something nice."

With some difficulty, he managed to tear Leon's pulpy wafer. "I wish you get a new car."

"You mean the red one?"

Noël broke into laughter, while Adam dashed over to the trash can to spit out his *oplatek*. "Adam Stephen Beauregard!" she admonished.

"It tastes yucky, Mommy!"

"He's right." Leon said. "It tastes like a paper plate."

Squatting down on the floor in front of her son, Noël broke off a piece of the discarded wafer he'd left on the table. "We've been through an awful lot together, haven't we, little man? May you become a doctor someday like you dream about." She handed him his first Christmas present and watched as he opened it with glee—the toy doctor's bag he'd been wanting. Pulling out the bendable thermometer, he took her temperature.

"Okay," she said to him, "you don't have to eat it, but break a piece of my *oplatek* so that you can share a wish with Mommy."

He did as she said. "I wish you don't cry anymore." Enfolding him against her, she closed her eyes, fighting hard to keep his wish. "Can I go downstairs now and wish Uncle Freddie and Aunt Theckla something nice?" he asked.

"Later. I promise."

Satisfied, he scrambled back into his seat, some of the hay falling to the floor in the process.

Leon eyed her strangely before bending down to pick up the wayward strands. "Hay too?" The look on his face made all the effort worthwhile. After breaking her wafer, he held her in his arms again and whispered against her ear, "I don't want you to cry anymore either, and I'm going to chase away everything that's hurt you."

It was time for the last wish. "I'm sorry for all the things you had to give up for me," she said to her husband. "And I hope you get them all back again—starting tonight."

Adam was anxious to unwrap his presents. After storing the leftovers in the refrigerator, they allowed him to open one more before they left for the Ziemnys' house, saving the rest of them for Christmas morning. He took that gift, a fiery red dump truck, and three wafer sheets along with him to the Chavises, who were only too glad to spend Christmas Eve with him. Asking Adam to pretend he'd never met Walt was neither possible nor fair, so they felt it best to leave him behind. She and Leon also delivered a laundry basket full of gifts to the Chavises, small items that Noël had been stashing away for months.

Sometime in between the moment they'd gone outside to look for the first star and got into the Charger, the snow had stopped. The night sky had lost its pinkness and blackened; now the stars were everywhere to be seen. As they drove through town, the jitters were getting the better of Noël, the reality that they would soon be seeing Rick, and Mrs. Ziemny, face to face. "Just take a deep breath," Leon suggested, though she hadn't said a word. His eyes were fastened on the street, his jaw set tight, the muscle in his cheek twitching.

By the time they entered his old neighborhood, the snow was falling again. The streets were narrow, cars parked solidly on both sides, with room for only a single car to drive in between. The homes were built closely together, almost every one of them decorated with

Christmas lights; a few displaying elaborate manger scenes, complete with wise men, camels, and sheep that glowed in the dark.

The car rolled up to the curb in front of the Ziemny's two-story brown-brick house, where a plump Christmas tree with big colored bulbs shimmered in the picture window. They headed up the short walk to the front porch. Reaching the door, Leon didn't bother to knock; he pulled it wide open.

Noël was surprised to find a roomful of strangers, the small space humming with the muffled roar of numerous conversations. Mrs. Ziemny was sitting by the Christmas tree, laughing and gesturing as she conversed with some woman. When her eyes met Noël's, she froze.

"Well, look who's here." Noël heard Walt's voice behind her. His back toward his wife, he gave her a big wink.

Mrs. Ziemny rose from her chair and approached them as if they were radioactive. She extended both hands toward Leon. "You look so thin."

"I do?" His fingers lingered in her double grasp. "I don't know why. Noël made all the traditional Polish food for me tonight, and I had three helpings."

The sound of her name, the reminder that she existed, seemed to offend her. "Hello, Noël," she said. Her spine stiffening, she offered no other gesture of welcome.

A handful of other people, none of them Rick, began flowing toward Leon one by one, hugging him and telling him how good it was to see him again. A few of them congratulated him on his marriage, some avoided the topic; the rest were not so generous— ignoring him and looking Noël over, their eyes darting away whenever they met hers. Leon sat down on the far side of the room, while Walt led her over to the chair beside his own.

It was a big relief to sit down. Entering the room had been the hardest part. Now that the general roar of the group was resuming, Noël could fade into the background, compose herself. But she still had to face Rick. Where was he? She looked around again to make sure she hadn't somehow overlooked him, but he was nowhere to be found.

She hadn't paid much attention to this room the only time she'd seen it, back at Leon's after-shower party, when there was so much else to distract her. Now she studied it carefully—the dark antique furniture, the large mirror on the wall over the sofa, the hardwood floor, the yellowing white lace curtains, the framed picture of the Virgin Mary. Hanging over one of the tables in the corner of the room was a bronze plaque that read, *God bless America, our home sweet home.*

Eventually she had the courage to look at Mary Ziemny herself, at first quick glances, then for longer periods of time—her hair was still brown, not one hint of gray. She listened to the things she was saying to her friends, the sound of her easy laughter. Reaching inside her purse, Noël fingered the *oplatek* envelope, awaiting the right moment.

Leon was absorbed in conversation with two men. He was holding a drink, but Noël had no clue how it got there. By then, he'd lit up a cigarette and was nestling it there between the fingers of his other hand, taking a quick puff every once in a while, then a sip from his glass. Someone planted a drink in her hand, and she was glad for it. She took a gulp, startled by its strength. Within minutes, her cheeks were warm, her body beginning to relax.

Suddenly Rick burst through the front door, and her heart sank—he looked ravaged, unshaven, puffy. Halting near the stairs, he scanned the room. His eyes met hers, his expression unrecognizable in its coldness.

Somewhat unsteadily, he walked toward her. Even before he

pulled her up from her chair, she smelled the liquor on his breath. Planting a kiss on her mouth, rough enough to burn her lips, he howled, "Sister! Is that what I should call you now?"

Conversations stopped; every eye in the room was focused on them. Noël wanted to disappear, but there was nowhere to run. Leon remained on the other side of the room. She was trapped.

A protective arm slipped across her shoulders from behind. "Well, what the hell else can you call her?" Walt's voice boomed. "She *is* your sister."

Heading for the uncapped vodka bottle on the sideboard, Rick poured himself a drink. From the other end of the room, Mary glared at her.

Noël snapped her purse shut. Coming here tonight had been a mistake. This was no time for forgiveness. She wondered if it ever would be.

≈≈

"It's called the Pasterka," Walt explained as they opened the doors of the massive St. Stan's church. "You know what that means?" He answered his own question. "It means 'Shepherd's Mass.' We have an old Polish tale. The way the story goes is that Jesus was born at midnight, and the whole creation was transformed in that hour—water became wine, stones moved, animals started talking like humans—but only the people who were pure in heart could understand them."

Her arm tucked under his, Noël smiled at the imagery.

"I bet *you* could've understood them," he said.

Even after the scene with Ricky, Walt had insisted she come with them to Midnight Mass. As they inched up the long aisle together, their pace was halted by the size of the crowd. Mrs. Ziemny's earlier warmth toward Leon had chilled to ice; she craned her neck in the opposite direction as they walked ahead of them, side-by-side.

Noël skimmed the enormous sanctuary for Rick, thankful not to find him, then guilty for her gratitude. Her eyes soaked up the splendor of the magnificent church—the carved ivory altar, countless statues, the mosaic images of the saints watching them from the ceiling. As she got closer to the altar, she became conscious of human scrutiny. Some people whispered; others pointed as she passed.

Mrs. Ziemny selected their seats, entering a pew a little more than halfway up the aisle, on the right-hand side. It was impossible not to notice Stella sitting in the row just ahead. The scent of her Shalimar cologne—doused with too heavy a hand, the same as the day of her shower party—made Noël's nostrils twitch. Shooting Noël a hateful glance, Stella fastened her ardent eyes on Leon. Mrs. Ziemny patted Stella's shoulder affectionately as she scooted past her.

Gut instinct gripped Noël. Was it fear? Insecurity? Protecting what she most cherished? She didn't know what it was, but she pressed her body close enough to Leon's to cause his arm to wrap around her, then met Stella's eyes with proprietary defiance. Finally, Stella turned her head around, away from her husband.

It was a mean thing to do, especially when it dawned on Noël that one week from then, New Year's Eve, would have been Stella and Leon's pure-white wedding day, but she didn't feel as guilty about it as she should have. She was too busy feeling guilty about everyone else. About Mrs. Ziemny. About leaving her son and the Chavises on Christmas Eve. And Rick, of course. Always about Rick.

Her cruel gesture toward Stella hadn't gone unnoticed by Mrs. Ziemny. From the other side of Leon, she leaned forward slightly, catching Noël's eyes with a tacit look of disapproval.

Noël looked away, up toward the stern, mosaic faces on the

ceiling. Slowly her eyes roamed the church. The intricate details of the stations of the cross on both sides of the sanctuary. The enormous stained-glass windows with their brilliant scarlets, blues, and purples. Her gaze drifted to the other side of the congregation, where Rick sat amid a group of strangers, his switchblade eyes again meeting hers. How had she done that? Turned such a gentle soul so hard?

Her gaze shifted toward a white statue of Jesus with outstretched arms. His marble eyes stared at her too. Only they weren't stern, hard, or disapproving, but kind. Forgiving. She allowed herself to sink into them.

Father Chet appeared from a side entrance, a tall man with a red stole draped over his white alb, taking his rightful place on the altar against a sea of poinsettias, the same color as his stole. "Rejoice!" He lifted his hands toward the ceiling. "Christ is born!"

He climbed a spiral staircase to the alabaster podium and opened a huge white Bible. Reading from the book of Matthew, he described the night the holy child was born, the appearance of the strange new star in the sky, the wise men bearing gifts.

As Noël listened, a feeling of overwhelming joy was enveloping her. She thought about Walt's enchanting version of the first Christmas and their little kitchen back home, transformed into the sacred birth space. When Leon slipped his arm across her shoulders, she felt euphoric. Here she was, sitting in this awe-inspiring church, nestled between Leon and Walt, feeling safer and more loved than she had a right to feel. Tears blurred her vision, diffusing the colors of the cathedral. Leon offered his handkerchief.

From the balcony of the cathedral, a lone female vocalist sang:

O Holy Night, the stars are brightly shining; it is the night of our dear savior's birth. Long lay the world in sin and error pining, till He appeared and the soul felt its worth.

When the time came for communion, she remained seated, understanding that she was barred from participation, ostensibly because she was not a Catholic, but she knew her own reasons all too well. Leon hung back too.

"Get up." Walt whispered as he moved past her toward the aisle, clutching her hand too tightly to disobey. "This night is for everyone."

As she waited in the long line, chin tilted downward, her fear, her shame, her guilt mounted. She imagined the indignant stares beaming at her from all directions. Buttressed between Leon and Walt, she was physically unable to turn back, despite her mounting urgency to do so.

But when her turn came to ingest the holy wafer, so similar to the *oplatek*, she was overcome by an unexpected swell of certainty, a visceral sense of belonging in the exact place where she stood. *Everyone*, as Walt had whispered, was part of this same body, no exceptions, no exclusions. That she was undeserving didn't matter.

The bloodred wine she sipped from the golden chalice washed through her.

This was it. This was salvation.

On the way out of church after the service, an older man ambushed Leon in the vestibule, pulling him aside and wagging his index finger in front of his face. He was lambasting Leon in Polish, but Noël didn't need a translator. The man pointed at her, then at Stella, and she realized he had to be Stella's father. A woman beside him—Stella's mother?—egged him on in a thick Polish accent. "You geef it to him! Poor Stah-la! Poor Reeky!" A crowd started to gather.

As the group enlarged around him, Leon stood there

uncomprehending. Stella remained on the sidelines, a strange mixture of horror and satisfaction, in equal measure, on her face.

Noël was paralyzed. When she finally saw Rick enter, she caught his eyes. "Help him," she mouthed, silently pleading. Rather than interceding, he leaned back against the wall and smiled at the scene, as if he relishing Leon's debasement.

"Hold it," Leon said finally to Mr. Minczewski. "This is my wife now." He stepped away from the group, over to Noël. "And I'm not going to let anyone"—he scanned the angry faces in the tight space, faltering at the sight of Rick for a second, then continued—"make me apologize for loving my own wife."

Mr. Minczewski stared at him, dumbfounded. Stella looked demolished. Rick ebbed into the mahogany wall. Leon came for her and grabbed her hand. Just before they escaped from the vestibule, she saw him dip the fingers of his other hand into the basin of holy water and cross himself.

Outside, the snow, muffling all other sounds, was falling in thick, glistening flakes that covered their coats and hair, making the world feel clean and new again.

TWENTY-TWO

FEBRUARY 1968
LEON

"I'M not Ketchfield!" Leon flicked on the lamp. "See? It's me."

I'm sorry," she cried. "I just got confused all of a sudden."

This was the second time she'd stopped him at the moment of consummation because something—who knew what it was this time?—triggered another flashback. "I'm okay now," Noël said, clutching the white sheet against her chest as if he was Godzilla.

Well, goody for her, but I'm done. He turned off the light. Sitting up against the headboard, he rummaged to find a cigarette in the dark.

"I'm sorry," she said again.

He knew he should tell her it was okay, comfort her like he'd done the other times, but he was too tired to go through that rigmarole again tonight. There was no smooth path for them. Whenever he thought they'd found it, it slipped away. He let her sniffle into her pillow until she fell asleep.

He stepped into the living room to smoke some more, to pour himself a drink, and to think. Outside the big front window, the snow was falling. There was nothing on television except the test pattern, so he put the radio on softly.

"Nights in White Satin" was playing; a song that got to him in a big way. Closing his eyes, he let the Moody Blues sing his soul to him about a love that cut so deep that it sucked up everything else.

Noël Trudeau had become his whole world, his reason to get up in the morning and to crawl into bed when the day was done. Even on nights like this, when the white satin became a bed of nails. He exhaled a long stream of smoke.

Ah, hell, he'd been feeling down in the dumps all day. Today he'd cornered Ricky in the break room at the mills and told him, "I miss you. You're my brother."

"There must be some mistake," Ricky had responded. "I don't have a brother." And he walked right out of the break room, a hit-and-run, leaving Leon half-dead by the soda pop machines.

Torn, that's what he was. Leon was torn, like a sheet of paper, right down the middle. Ricky, his parents, and his old neighborhood on one side; Noël, Adam, and this makeshift Motown on the other. And he was stuck between the two. Sometimes he didn't know who he was anymore.

Maybe the dilemma was all in his head, the choices already made. To his brother and extended family, he was some kind of pariah who couldn't expect to see their welcome mat unfurling any time soon. The oddest part was that he no longer detested living in this neighborhood. He'd actually grown to like the Chavises, more than like them. Freddie was a man of few, yet choice, words, worth listening for, and Theckla was a wise, old Buddha who could read Leon like an X-ray.

After he'd first moved in, he used to drive for miles just to shop in a white drug store, a white grocery store, breathe in white air again. And then one day he was in a hurry and stopped to buy ciga-rettes down the street. When he walked into the shop, Freddie was standing there with a group of colored men, and he pretended not to know him. Later, he apologized. Though he didn't say it that way, Leon's whiteness had polluted his airspace. The realization hit Leon hard. He and Freddie were the dark and light of the same photographic image.

Leon took a long sip. His mother would butcher him if she knew how he was changing.

Adam padded into the room in his bare feet and stopped in front of him, rubbing his eyes as if Leon was an apparition. When Noël was awake, he competed with Leon on purpose to steal her attention, but when she wasn't around, or Freddie, whom the kid worshipped, he gave Leon half a chance. "What's a matter?" Leon asked. "Can't sleep?"

Adam shook his Beatles hair.

"Me neither. Must be one of those nights. How about a drink?"

Following Leon into the kitchen, he accepted a glass of juice. They came back to the living room and sat together on the sofa, Adam's legs swinging. He reminded Leon a little of Ricky at that age, the way he sometimes watched him and mimicked what he did. Leon took a long sip of his drink, the warmth of the whiskey sliding down his throat. Adam sipped his juice exactly the same way.

"Taste good?" Leon asked.

Adam nodded, wiping his mouth. He wanted to hear a story to make him sleepy, so Leon picked up the *Reader's Digest* on the table and read some jokes, but Adam stared at him as if he was reading in Japanese. Flipping through the magazine, Leon found an article about how people act like their dogs, and Adam liked that one better. After that, they listened to a few songs on the radio until Adam's eyes got heavy. Leon tucked him back into bed. Within seconds, his little arms were curled contentedly around his purple frog. *God, he's so innocent.*

As Leon walked back to the living room, he felt his own weighty responsibility to protect him. It was his job to protect him, and Noël, too, but sometimes it scared the living hell out of him because it was the same way he should have protected his own brother, and look how he'd screwed that one up.

Before he and Noël married, he was able to shut Ricky out of his brain when he was with her. Now, he was always with her, and she and Ricky cohabitated his thoughts, smashing together like asteroids at certain insufferable moments like the one in their bedroom a few hours ago. He'd been thinking about his earlier encounter with Ricky, the scars he'd left on his brother, and he'd gotten angry with himself all over again. He guessed he'd inadvertently translated that anger into something that had sparked another flashback for her. Once more, it was his own damned fault.

The hourly news break came on the radio. Leon heard Walter's Cronkite's voice, only he wasn't giving the news; this time, he *was* the news.

"To say that we are mired in stalemate seems the only realistic, if unsatisfactory, conclusion."

They were replaying Cronkite's diatribe from his program last night when he'd brazenly declared the Vietnam War was unwinnable. Unwinnable! For crying out loud, this was the United States of America.

Leon clicked off the radio, lit another cigarette. Last month, there'd been a surprise attack against the South Vietnamese called the Tet Offensive, and it had shaken up the pro-war world, including a big kahuna like Cronkite, including Leon. Now the whole country was torn, just like him. Mired in stalemate.

If Noël was able to have his child, maybe this stalemate with Ricky and his mother would end. But thanks to Ketchfield, that solution could never be.

"Do you mind if I join you?" He heard her voice from behind.

"Not at all." He tried to sound as if he meant it, but he ached to be left alone. If he was, he could turn the radio back on, get lost in music and nicotine, a splash more of whiskey, but now she was here, and he couldn't go adrift.

She slid beside him on the sofa. "I'm sorry."

How many times could she say it? "It was my fault, not yours."

Picking up on his mood, she stood up to leave.

"No, stay." This time he really meant it.

When she sat down again, he crossed his arms over her, her back against his torso. Together, they watched the falling snow outside the window.

"Snow covers up ugly things," she said.

"Like what?"

"Oh … cracked streets, dried grass, dead leaves …"

He knew it was none of those things she was really thinking about.

When she turned around, the sight of her face up close staggered him the same as the first time. She tightened her arms around him in a way that let him know he was Leon again. Ketchfield had vanished for the night. Ricky too.

The ghosts gone, they could breathe again. They were back at the carnival, stopped at the top of the Ferris wheel, suspended in time for however long it lasted.

He moved on top of her, wiser now. He was as crazy as the hippies to believe that they could remain here in this sublime, unspoiled place. This was the most they were going to get. Patches of perfection. Slivers of Shangri-La.

After they pulled apart, he heard the grinding motors of the snowplows outside, their dirty tires rampaging through the snow like Army tanks.

TWENTY-THREE

MARCH 1968
THECKLA

ON a Saturday evening in mid-March, Noël invited Theckla and Freddie up for hot dogs, pork and beans, and potato salad. The cold spell of the last couple weeks had snapped, and picnic food seemed less out of place. As they entered their apartment, little Adam dashed over to Freddie. "Can we pitch tomorrow?"

"Ain't Leon teaching you that now?"

She and Freddie had seen Leon taking the boy out back to that dinky little patch of grass in the courtyard to practice baseball on Sunday afternoons, where he'd also planted a rosebush for Noël.

Adam smiled up at Freddie. "Yeah, but I want to play with *you!*"

Catching Leon's brief, yet wounded, pout, Theckla grasped for a distraction. "Did you hear Bobby Kennedy's running for president?"

"No kidding." Leon switched on their set. After a series of commercials, the top story on the six o'clock news showed clips from earlier that morning in the caucus room of the Old Senate Office Building where Kennedy was announcing his candidacy. "I do not lightly dismiss the dangers and the difficulties of challenging an incumbent president," he said at the podium, a gaggle of his children sitting behind him. "But these are not ordinary times, and this is not an ordinary election."

"That's a thumb in the eye to LBJ," Leon said.

"LBJ deserves a thumb." Noël came out from the kitchen, taking a seat on the arm of the sofa beside her husband. "Bobby is the only one who can end the war."

"What about McCarthy?" asked Leon. "If you ask me, Bobby's an opportunist to jump into the race and steal his thunder."

"McCarthy ain't got no chance of becoming president," Freddie muttered under his breath.

Theckla eyed her husband; though he had plenty of them, he rarely expressed strong opinions in the presence of white people, not even Noël and Leon. She shifted her gaze to Leon who seemed tense, distracted. No doubt about it, something was up with him, beyond slighted feelings. Maybe she could steal a moment alone with him.

A few hours later, after *The Hollywood Palace* began and Noël shuttled Adam off to the bathroom to ready him for bed, she seized the opportunity, especially after Freddie stood up to leave. "It's time for me to hit the sheets too." He yawned. "It's true what the Scriptures say: 'Once a man, twice a child.' Coming, Theckla?"

"In a minute."

After he left, Leon sat back down on the sofa, glancing toward the hallway every now and then with agitated eyes. They could hear Adam chattering from the back room. The child was taking up more and more of his mama's time now that he was older, and Leon probably felt a little squeezed out. Maybe that was it. All of a sudden, Theckla burst out laughing.

"What's so funny?"

"You're drinking whiskey out of a Flintstones cup."

Leon didn't laugh with her. Instead, he held the silly little glass straight out in front of him, staring at it.

"What's going on with you tonight?" she asked gently.

Glancing toward the back room again, he lowered his voice.

"Don't tell her a word of this. Ketchfield called here last night. Just before dinner."

"Her ex? What in the world did he want?"

"I don't know, and I don't know how he found out where we live either. He said he was coming this way for a visit and he wanted to see Adam. But I think it's her that he really wants to see. He seemed taken aback that I answered the phone. Either way, it's no damned good."

"What did you tell him?"

"I told him to stay the hell away. I told him I'd slap a restraining order on him if he sets one foot near them."

"You think you scared him off?"

He took a sip of his drink, looked back toward the room off the hallway. "He raped her, you know. That's how she got pregnant in the first place."

Theckla knew it alright, but she said nothing. A confidence shared was a sealed vault in her book.

"And it'll be over my dead body before he sees her again." He ran his fingers anxiously through his dark hair. "I wish she never had a kid with him."

The look on his face troubled Theckla almost as much as what he was saying. "Adam came into this world in a bad way alright. But it's not his fault."

"I know, I know." He emptied his glass. "But it drives me nuts what Ketchfield did to her. He stole our chance to have our own child. And I know what that son of a bitch looks like, and Adam looks more like him every day. Sometimes it just gets to me."

She studied his face in the dimly lit room. Since the day she'd met Leon, she'd summed him up to be a complicated man, a work in progress. Every human being, of course, had a good angel and a bad one sitting on their shoulders. She just couldn't quite figure out which side he would end up landing on. But he had heart—oh, she knew that to be a fact—a malleable heart, and that made all the difference. When hearts were changeable, that's where hope came in. Besides that, she felt a kinship with him. She knew a thing or two about contradictory feelings.

"Listen, I'm going to tell you something." She leaned in closer, her voice firm. "Noël's had a whale of a past, you're right about that, and she can be a handful sometimes. That's not gonna change, no matter how much you wish it so. But she loves you—lock, stock, and barrel. And as for that little boy, *you're* his daddy now."

"I know, and I'm trying. I really am. I wish they gave father lessons." He laughed sarcastically. "Maybe Freddie can teach me in his spare time."

The comment, whether wry or regretful, was an injury she could not pardon. Though anger was an indulgence she could rarely afford, it seethed through her bones. "Look here!" she said. "I'm gonna tell you something else. Something no one knows north of the Mason-Dixon Line."

Seemingly startled, maybe by the rise of emotion in her voice, he gave her his full attention.

"Back in Alabama," she said, "we had a sweet, tender fruit called the Satsuma orange, seedless and thin-skinned, plentiful in Mobile County. On my Freddie's chest and lower torso, he bears the slash-marks of a knife blade. He got them when he was eighteen years old, the year I married him, after four white farmers beat him sense-less for stealing a Satsuma orange from one of their trees. His body healed over, but his scars never did: the missing teeth, the distrust, and—" Her voice broke. "Those men came close to castrating him … close enough that he couldn't father a child."

Leon's face flashed with alarm. "My God, Theckla!"

"Freddie used to be fearless and full of pride. They took that from him too. So, don't you go joking with me about father lessons. My Freddie would've made a giant of a father."

"I'm really sorry. I had no idea."

He pressed his hand over hers, the consoling touch surprising her. No white man had ever dared to touch her like that. Her ire subsided like a passing windstorm. When they made eye contact, he withdrew his hand, cleared his throat.

"Noël doesn't know any of this?"

"No." She lowered her eyes. "I tell her how beautiful Mobile was back in the early nineteen hundreds, but I leave that part out. I know she told you about her, uh—her Pastor Raymond—and the story's too much the same. I didn't want to go picking those scabs open. But here's why I tell you this tonight. When you've witnessed hatred first-hand, the way she has, the way Freddie has, the way I have, it's something you don't get over. It changes you, rewires you. Me and Freddie had no choice but to get used to those evils. But Noël remains as tender and thin-skinned as the Satsuma."

The next day, Sunday, with temperatures soaring into the eighties, Noël told her that the three of them were going out for ice cream; Leon's idea.

Later, Theckla and Freddie could hear commotion coming through the ceiling, the sound of them arguing. "Are they ever gonna stop that racket?" Freddie shoved the sofa pillow over his ears. "Lord, if she wasn't so dang pretty, she'd have a hard time hanging on to him."

"What do you mean by that?"

"C'mon, Theckla. How many times a day does that girl cry? Poor Leon must be plumb wore out by now."

Theckla left him to go to that spot in their kitchen where she could hear particularly well, through the vent near the ceiling, and she managed to catch enough to piece the source of their disagreement together. Somehow Adam managed to get his sundae with hot fudge, caramel, and pecans all over the backseat of Leon's sporty car, and the gooey mess was smeared all over the seats, door handles, everywhere.

"He should be punished!" Leon shouted.

"Don't you dare! He's just a little boy."

"God forbid I should get a share in parenting. You're spoiling him."

"I'm not spoiling him! That's what little boys do. It's just a silly old car."

"It's a brand-new car! I'm not going to have some kid ruin it before it's even six months old."

"Some kid? He's *your* kid."

"We both know better than that."

Theckla recoiled at the sound of his words.

"I didn't mean it like that," Leon said quickly. "I'm sorry."

Though he was trying to atone, it was too late.

Noël's reply didn't come for a long time, and when it did, Theckla could have sworn it was the voice of another woman. "It's a good thing the seats are vinyl."

TWENTY-FOUR

APRIL 4, 1968
NOËL

THE commotion at breakfast that morning could've been a comedy skit if it wasn't so frustrating. As Leon seated himself at the toy-strewn table, he ended up spilling coffee all over Adam's stuffed purple frog, and Adam wailed like a banshee. When Noël jumped up to clean the mess and Leon moved his chair aside, he nicked a chunk of the cupboard in the process.

Later, as Adam sat in the living room watching cartoons, Leon restated the inevitable. "We've got to get a bigger place. You know that."

"No." She refused to reopen the familiar conversation. Leaving the Chavises was out of the question. "I'll make it work. I'll clean it up."

"How? You gonna put this stuff on the roof?"

"I'll find room somewhere."

"Come on, Noël." He sighed. "You know Adam needs a yard. He's too big for that crummy courtyard."

Thankfully, she found the perfect diversion. After spying the headline on the local section, she snatched the morning newspaper away from his stack. "Oh, look—Bobby Kennedy is coming to Langston."

He picked up the sports page, buried his head in it. "Who cares? You're just trying to change the subject."

She read on. "To your old neighborhood."

Now, she'd piqued his interest. He looked up. "To *my* neighborhood? Really?"

"Really." She scanned the article quickly. Now that President Johnson had dropped his bombshell about not seeking re-election, Kennedy had a real shot at the nomination, but he had to make up for lost time. Indiana just happened to be the first primary in Kennedy's presidential campaign, and Leon's neighborhood, of all places, one of his first stops.

"I'll have to call my brother," she said. "Bobby sat right next to Adam on his flight home last year, and Bobby gave him a PT-109 tie clip. Maybe he'll want to take a day off to come see him. It might help get him out of his funk."

The Thursday that Bobby Kennedy was coming to town turned into a real family outing. As it turned out, Adam *was* interested in seeing Kennedy and made the trip from Willow the day before, spending the night on their living room sofa. Leon and his father, who would join them later, were winding up a week of vacation and planned to attend the rally too.

As *The Today Show* played in the background, Leon was loading up the Kodak Instamatic while Noël baked a pan of hot cinnamon rolls to serve the group for breakfast, including the Chavises. "Won't you come along?" she asked them.

"Why not?" Mrs. Chavis said. "How about it, Freddie?"

He didn't respond. He was preoccupied by the sight on the TV screen—an endless line of black sanitation workers on strike in

Memphis marching silently, each one holding an identical sign: "I am a man." Hugh Downs reported that Martin Luther King Jr. had come to town to help their crusade.

The six of them piled into the car to set out for Leon's church with the double steeples. Noël was the first to spot Walt. He waved to them from the top of the church steps as he stood between two gigantic speakers blasting "Lady Madonna" from a portable sound system. The narrow street in front of the church was already jampacked with mostly retirees, women, and children, the majority of working-age men already gone to their jobs.

Noël was buoyed by the vitality of the crowd; it felt like a parade was about to start. A black-frocked nun lorded over a group of uniformed Catholic-school students, sprung from their classes for the historic event, and the little boys were practicing their whistles for when Bobby's car came into view. A hoard of old veterans wearing Army caps from both world wars, some of them friends of Walt's, twirled small American flags on wooden sticks. Instamatic cameras were clicking. Hundreds of homemade signs swayed to and fro: "God bless you, Bobby." "Langston welcomes RFK." "Cut your hair!" "*Kocham Cię.*"

Pointing to the last sign, Noël asked Leon what it meant.

His pea-green eyes focused on her. "I love you."

She was confused by his sudden passion in such a public place. "I love you, too."

"No," he smiled, "that's what the sign says."

"Oh." She blushed in embarrassment.

"But I do love you." He leaned over and kissed her right there on the street, in front of his old neighbors, yet everyone was too whipped-up to pay them mind. Little Adam was hopping up and down, clutching Freddie's hand on one side, Walt's on the other, not one judgmental glare at them, as Leon had privately feared, for being mixed company. In addition to the Poles, there were plenty of other black people besides the Chavises. And in that sea of excited, happy humanity, no one seemed to care much who belonged to who.

Noël's brother squinted against the sun before slipping on a pair of sunglasses that made him look like he belonged in Paris more than Indiana, missing arm or not. The PT-109 clasp held his tie in place. He was filling out a little since he came back home, killer handsome in his aloof way, and Noël noticed the way some pretty girls were trying to catch his eye. As "Scarborough Fair" played on the loud speakers, one of the old veterans thanked him for his sacrifice. Adam saluted in mutual respect; a sacred brotherhood.

A murmur went through the crowd. *Bobby was coming!* All bodies stirred into chaotic motion—signs began waving, people pressed forward, and the surrounding sounds of laughter, shouting, and screaming charged the air. Simon & Garfunkel were cut off in mid-song. As the limousine rounded the corner, a rumble of mismatched voices called out his name.

And there he was—Bobby Kennedy, brother of a fallen president—sitting alive and well on the back of an open yellow convertible, his wife, Ethel, by his side; a *Look* magazine cover sprung to life in front of Noël's eyes.

Within seconds, the car stopped, and Kennedy got out and moved into the mob. They rushed toward him, tugged at his clothes, tousled his hair. His aides unsnarled him from the frenzy and led him back over to the car, where he climbed on top of the trunk. He stood less than sixty feet away from them.

Finally, Noël got her first unobstructed view. He was a surprisingly small man, an unlikely figure for his Herculean destiny. His shirttail was already pulled out, his sleeves flapping from missing cufflinks swiped as souvenirs, his sandy hair in disarray. Bodyguards clutched him around the waist, struggling to steady him as he bent to shake as many hands as possible. He reminded Noël of the *Little Prince* that Rick had read to them about, fragile and wistful, as if he could fall to the ground without making a sound.

Someone handed Kennedy a microphone, and his first order of business was to point to the person holding the unfriendly sign. "I *did* cut my hair this morning." He pushed back a clump that had fallen near his eyes, his toothy grin flashing. "Can't you tell?"

The audience laughed, cheered. Impromptu, they burst into song. "*Sto lat, sto lat, Niech żyje, żyje nam…*" Noël saw her son's mouth drop open in awe at the sound, his eyes staring up at the groundswell of emotion on the faces surrounding him.

"It's a traditional Polish song," Walt explained. "They're wishing him to live one hundred years."

Kennedy's eyes softened. "I am, uh, pleased to be here in Langston, Indiana. I feel in my own heart that we have something important to do here today."

The applause forced him to pause. "This is the most dangerous time that you and I could live in," he continued, "but that also makes it the most interesting time. Our future may lie beyond our vision, but it is not beyond our control. Tennyson once wrote: 'The lights begin to twinkle from the rocks; the long day wanes; the slow moon climbs; the deep moans round with many voices. Come, my friends, 'tis not too late to seek a newer world."

The words reverberated in Noël's brain.

Kennedy jumped down, waded into the crowd again, shaking hands all along the way. As he headed straight toward their direction, the excitement around them magnified to fever pitch, the masses merging into one giant organism as they flung out their outstretched hands.

Everything suddenly went surreal for Noël; it was one of those moments when life stood still, long enough to nearly catch it in her hand. As "La-La Means I Love You" flowed through the loudspeakers, she watched it happening in slow motion: Leon hoisting a giggling Adam high on his shoulders. Freddie's jubilant shouts as he pumped his fist in the air. Walt, waving a small American flag that his buddies had handed him. Mrs. Chavis' face, lit up like a schoolgirl. Her soldier brother come back to life again, his eyes teeming with purpose. A field of arms surrounded them—black ones, white ones, male and female, old and young—tangling together like braided hair.

Grabbing the camera from Leon's pocket, she clicked, clicked, clicked.

She'd done it; seized the astounding moment, captured it from every angle, frozen it on Kodak film.

Later that same day, after Adam returned to Willow, they turned on the TV, and the news bulletin brought them to a halt: Martin Luther King Jr. was dead. Shortly after six p.m., he'd been gunned down in cold blood on a motel balcony in Memphis.

CBS replayed the clip over and over again—his final public speech from only the night before foreshadowing his own death, his prophetic promise of reaching the Promised Land one day.

But for now, the promise, the dream, had been crushed. Noël looked around the room.

Leon sat with arms folded as Adam played in a corner by himself; Mrs. Chavis' face twisted in sorrow; Freddie retreated into that silent space he inhabited; riots were breaking out in cities all across the country. And the arms untwined.

TWENTY-FIVE

MAY 1968
ADAM

WHEN Adam went to rouse his mother for breakfast, he found her cold and stiff in her bed, her eyes wide-open. He knew she was dead, but he checked her pulse anyway, waiting in futility for the tremble of a beat. Her face was frozen in a vivid expression, as if she had been asking some kind of profound question as she drew her last breath, or maybe seen the answer. At any rate, she looked more alive in death than life. He called out to his father to come quick.

Dad stopped in the doorway. "We need to call the doctor."

"She's dead. There's nothing the doctor can do."

He appeared to look through Adam. "We need to call the doctor," he repeated. He began tidying the room—hanging up a blouse that had been slung over a chair, dumping an untouched glass of water into the plant by the window. He wouldn't allow Adam to pull the sheet over her face or open the drapes. He especially wouldn't let him close her eyes. He seemed unable to grasp the situation until the men came with the gurney to take her body away to Green's Funeral Parlor.

Covering her with a blanket, not in a body bag, the undertakers rolled her down the hallway and into the living room. As they approached the front door, Dad blocked their way. "Lily! Lily! Lily!"

he cried out to her like she was Lazarus. The men looked to Adam for assistance.

"She's gone, Dad." He put his arm around him. "You can't bring her back." Guiding him into a chair, he freed up the pathway.

As soon as her body left the house, it felt empty, eerily still and silent. Only then did Adam realize how much of a presence Mom had been in her nonpresence. His father remained in the chair Adam had deposited him into, barely moving for the rest of the morning. "I didn't think she'd die before me," Dad finally said. After that, he fell into a trancelike silence.

Adam made use of the time to call Noël and break the news. To his surprise, she didn't shed one tear, saying simply, "Now, she's finally whole again," as if certain of that. She told him that she'd come to Willow first thing the next morning.

After that, he called Steve, now stationed in San Diego. Though Steve had had his opportunities, he didn't bother to visit home once after returning from the littoral areas of Nam a few months ago, shaking his family off of him like dust from his boots. He had no reaction, other than expressing doubts about being able to get leave to come for the funeral. Adam knew it was a line of bullshit.

By early afternoon, Dad was talking nonstop, a cross between spewing and rambling. He told Adam about the day he'd met their mother, about their wedding day, about Tiki, the kitten they bought the first year they were married, about Bo's difficult birth. He reminisced about her laugh, her fondness for old Charlie Chaplin films, her emerald eyes. The bottled-up memories came tumbling out.

His stroll down memory lane unhinged Adam. Now, while her dead body was lying on a slab, was a fine time to discover how passionately he had loved their mother. At one point, maybe just to put a cork in the reminiscing, Adam asked him how he did it—how did he bear being apart from her all those years he spent traveling to the East Coast? But he continued his detailed recollections as if Adam hadn't said a word.

As Dad droned on, Adam struggled to come up with his own recollections of his mother. At one of the tent revivals in Hyssop, she had cuddled him close as he'd unclasped a pearl bracelet from her wrist and made believe it was a cowboy's rope, swirling it around her index finger, the fencepost. And, smiling down at him, she had galloped two fingers of her other hand across his lap like a horse. That was the best memory he could think of.

His dad was in no shape to make funeral arrangements, so later that afternoon, Adam dragged himself over to Green's Funeral Parlor. Ben Green, an old classmate of Noël's and the son of the owner, was just back from embalming school or whatever it was they called it, waiting eagerly for him in the vestibule. Back in high school, Ben had harbored an unrelenting crush on Noël, and he'd reminded Adam of Porky Pig. He still did.

Ben led him to the back, a showroom of coffins, where Adam selected a silver one, the "Eternal Rest" model, the second-least-expensive option available. Though money was definitely an object, he felt guilty choosing the cheapest. But trying to make the other arrangements, the more personal ones—like what color and style of garment she should be buried in, her favorite flowers, or what verse should go on her memorial card—was excruciating. "How can I possibly know what dress color she'd like, when I don't even know who the fuck my mother was?" He screamed at Ben. "I might as well put on a fucking blindfold and choose everything at fucking random!"

Ben glared at him like the raving lunatic he was.

Adam fumed. Why was all of this *his* responsibility anyway?

Using Ben's phone, he dialed up Noël. She told him she would take care of everything when she came the next morning—the dress, the flowers, the music, every single detail. Ben seemed more relieved by her offer than Adam. Maybe *relieved* wasn't the right word—he was so excited that Adam thought he was going to pee in his pants.

≈≈

As promised, Noël and Adam arrived in Willow at nine-thirty the next morning. "Where's that husband of yours?" Dad asked. Leon had to work, she said, and would be joining her on Thursday night.

"Like the steel mills will come to a standstill without him," he mumbled.

When the four of them sat down in the kitchen, their father slipped back into his brooding reverie, weeping at one point as he recalled a road trip they took to Montana early in their marriage. "Lily made me stop in the middle of nowhere just to listen to the quiet."

Adam kept waiting for Noël to comfort him, but she didn't make the slightest effort.

They left little Adam with their father while the two of them returned to Green's Funeral Parlor. As Adam had no doubt she'd be able to do, Noël smoothed over his earlier rudeness, while Ben dabbed at the unending drops of perspiration pouring from his non-neck with his silk handkerchief, his beady little eyes shining like the dusty lights of the creepy chandelier. For "old times' sake", he even knocked off the cost to open the grave.

It seemed to Adam that Noël was relishing the task of making these funeral arrangements, sharing some kind of clandestine fellow-ship with their departed mother. She insisted that she wear a red dress in the coffin because it was Mom's favorite color. "How the hell do you know what her favorite color was?" Adam asked.

She didn't answer.

Though Ben Green's small collection of clothing in the back room had no red dress, it did have a pinkish rose one. Adam strongly suggested that pinkish rose was fucking close enough to red. But Noël would have no part of pinkish rose. Smiling sweetly at Ben, she thanked him for his time and told him she would bring him the dress later on. She ended up going to three different department stores, in three different towns, until she found just the right shade of red.

After she came home from the dress excursion, she rushed around doing this and that. It appeared to Adam that she was performing the useless duties to avoid sitting with their dad. By then, he'd dropped the sentimental banter, withdrawing inside himself.

As evening came on, Noël was on another mission, digging around in their mother's old belongings, even venturing up to the filthy, unfinished side of the attic, where none of them had gone for years, to continue her rummaging. "What the hell is she looking for?" Dad asked.

When she finally stopped searching later that night, Adam assumed she'd found whatever it was she'd gone up there to find. Or maybe she'd simply given up.

Having the funeral at the First Methodist Church was their father's idea, the one detail he insisted on. Adam and Noël preferred the Baptist church in Bedlington, but he was more than adamant. Unfortunately, so was Noël. Adam had to resort to taking her out to the back porch. "Cut it out! It's the only thing he's asking to have his own way."

"But it's such a *big* thing."

"Drop it, Noël. She's his wife."

She finally relented.

The next morning, Dad donned his most expensive suit, looking almost like Adam remembered him as a child when he used to strut down Center Street in his wingtip shoes. The body was laid out in the largest room of Green's Funeral Parlor, another special surprise from Ben.

As they approached the coffin slowly, red vigil lights flickering on either side, they were startled—Mom made a stunning corpse. Against the satin pillow, her snowy skin had almost a rosy glow, her black hair styled with a decorative ruby comb, her red lips set with a slight upturn. Her old pearl bracelet was the only jewelry she wore, but she needed no adornment.

Sobbing, their father sunk to his knees.

Once again, Adam gestured to Noël to give the man some long overdue comfort, but she raised her chin and walked away. And so, it was up to him. He kneeled down beside him.

The viewing took place from two in the afternoon until eight in the evening. The day seemed endless, especially with so few visitors, accentuated by the huge room with row upon row of empty chairs. As expected, Steve didn't show up from California. Their mother had no friends. The few people who did bother to pay their respects were coworkers from the Luffkin factory or neighbors who'd never had one single conversation with their mother.

As no one, except Dad, knew who Lily Trudeau really was, making conversation was more than difficult. About all that could be said was, "She sure looks beautiful." And everyone said it. Over and over again.

Only two flower arrangements arrived: one from the Luffkin

factory and one from Dr. Wharton's widow. Considering their mother's passion for flowers in her earlier life, the lack of them, even more than lack of mourners, crushed Noël. She took it upon herself to order half a dozen arrangements, an extravagance that Leon would be paying for, Adam presumed, for quite some time.

By late afternoon, the coffin was surrounded by flowers.

Later in the evening, Doc Wharton's grandson, a few years older than Adam and back in Willow on spring break from medical school, made an appearance. Adam was sitting in the back when he entered the funeral parlor, eyeing him with both envy and esteem. He made a point of seeking Adam out.

"I wanted to become a doctor because of you," he said.

"Because of me?"

"Yup. I was green-eyed jealous of you. My grandfather used to talk nonstop about what a great surgeon you were going to be—" He stopped himself abruptly, his eyes darting from Adam's sleeve. "I'm sorry. That was a thoughtless thing to say."

"Not at all. At least your grandfather got one doctor out of this."

When they arrived back home, Leon was waiting by his car. Noël threw her arms around him. "Why are you hiding out here instead of coming to the funeral home?" Dad snapped.

Leon's eyes flashed in anger, not one word of condolence. His seething antagonism toward their father didn't let up throughout the evening. He challenged him on nearly every word that came out of his mouth, no matter how inconsequential—if Dad said the time was ten-fifteen, Leon corrected that it was ten-seventeen.

Adam couldn't figure out why he was being such a butthole at a time like this. Noël was no help there either; she stuck to her husband like gauze on dried blood.

≈≈

The next day dawned, their mother's final day above ground. Before leaving for church, they stared into her face for the last time, trying to memorize it.

"I love you." Dad bent over to kiss her lips. "I always will."

Noël requested to remain alone with the body for a few minutes. Before Adam closed the door to give her privacy, he heard her say, "Mama?" like she was beginning a real conversation. He saw her unclasp the pearl bracelet from around Mom's wrist and slide it into her pocket. And then she pulled out an object from her big black purse, an old Bible.

Adam recognized it immediately. It was Pastor Ray's Bible.

There was no mistaking it; the front cover was nearly torn off, right under the gold lettering that read, *Holy Bible*. He'd never forget it because Bo and Steve used to point it out and laugh about it. Even as little kids, it had looked odd to them for a pastor to be toting around a torn-up Bible like that.

As he left the funeral parlor and walked toward the awaiting hearse, Adam couldn't fathom how Noël had gotten her hands on it. Then it dawned on him that it must have been what she was searching so hard to find in the attic. How on earth did Pastor Ray's Bible ever get mixed up among their mother's old things?

It was reassuring to Adam to observe the way Leon took good care of Noël the whole day—supporting her, holding her hand, or kissing her temple whenever she cried, which was a lot. His tenderness toward his sister exacerbated his own sense of isolation, his loneliness over not having someone of his own to comfort him, especially while gazing at the altar of the First Methodist Church, the site of his secret wedding to Cynthia a lifetime ago. Secretly, he'd been hoping that she might have grown tired of chasing nirvana by now, sick of Nathan, the self-righteous bore, and found her way to the funeral. But it wasn't to be.

After the service, the motorcade made the slow trek through Willow to the archway of the final destination, the Garden of Resurrection, where another open hole awaited beside the graves of Monroe, Bo, and Aunt Clarissa. The remaining Trudeaus were nearly outnumbered.

Later, after little Adam was in bed and it was over and done, they were sitting around the kitchen table, not saying much of anything. Leon made no secret that he wasn't keen on spending another night in their father's house, but Noël was exhausted, and so they'd decided to get a night's rest before heading back to Langston first thing the next morning.

Dad got up from the table and leaned against the counter, asking Noël which of their mother's things she might want to take for herself.

She looked up at him with a kind expression, the first one she'd graced him with all week. "Can I have her painting of the rose on fire?"

"I don't even know where it is." He sat down on a chair on the other side of the kitchen.

"I do. I found it up in the attic the other day."

"So, that's what you were looking for." He seemed relieved. "Sure. Take it, if you want it." His face relaxed, a faraway look in his eyes. "I remember the day your mother did that painting. It was a beautiful summer afternoon, and Lily was sitting out on the back porch looking at her rose garden. Her hair was tied back with a red ribbon. She stuck the paintbrush between her teeth while she thought about just the right colors to use. As she turned her head, her hair fell loose from its ribbon on one side. She looked so pretty that I thought someone should be painting her instead."

Noël's lips quivered. She buried her face in her hands.

In one fluid movement, their father rushed to her side and caressed her hair. Adam thought it touching, a long overdue breakthrough. But Noël must have thought that it was Leon, because when she opened her eyes and saw it was him, she flinched, went rigid.

"Get your fucking hands off of her!" Leon lunged toward Noël as if rescuing her from a predator. "What kind of man are you, anyway?"

Dad looked stunned. "A better man that you are, you dirty, Polack!"

"Not as dirty as your little secrets," Leon said. "And you conned her into believing they were all *her* fault, didn't you?"

"Leon, no!" Noël gasped.

He was too worked up to stop. "What kind of man forces himself on an insane wife? What kind of man drives her sister to suicide? No wonder your wife had to turn to a nigger for love."

"No!" Noël cried out.

"Are you some kind of a lunatic?" Adam shouted at Leon. Even as he said the words, the sight of Pastor Ray's torn Bible flashed through his brain. The connection, though blurred and contorted, was made. But how could their father possibly be responsible for Auntie's death? Auntie killed *herself*—because of a married man.

As he watched his father getting red, the deep scarlet red of a condemned man, Adam's head started to spin.

"And I made damned sure that the black bastard was crushed to road kill like the animal he was!" His father's face was nearly purple with rage.

"*You* made sure?" Noël clapped her hand over her mouth. "Oh, my God—it was *you!*"

By this time, Adam was too weak to move. His legs were Jell-O.

Dad was charging toward Leon with clenched fists, bobbing like a boxer, ready to strike. "And I'll do the same to you, if you don't shut your mouth!"

"Are you threatening me?" Leon said. "Go ahead. Punch me. You think you're such a goddamned big man, but that won't change the fact that *he* made your wife pregnant."

An injured sound, beyond a wail, came out of Noël.

"What?" Their father stopped dead, his arms dropping limp at his sides. "You mean *Monroe* … was …?" He started stumbling backward into the refrigerator. "No, no, no—it couldn't be. Oh, my God in heaven, no! It never went *that* far, did it?" He looked desperately at Noël. Slowly the color drained out of his face, the purple disappearing, the red, until there was nothing but an awful, pasty whiteness about him. His eyes lost their anger, their intensity, any emotion at all, becoming two pools of hollowness, as if he was shriveling up and disintegrating right there in the kitchen, in front of their eyes.

In one savage moment, Leon Ziemny had torn their family to shreds.

TWENTY-SIX

MAY–AUGUST 1968
NOËL

NOËL watched her father teeter from the kitchen and retreat to his room. As soon as he left, Leon began packing, throwing their overnight items into a duffle bag and shouting at her to wake the child for the long drive back to Langston. "We can come back and get your car later on," he said, heading for his own with their belongings. "Let's just get out of here."

Once Leon was outside, Adam hissed at her from across the kitchen table, "Tell me how much of this you knew all along."

Noël found she was unable to do what either of them commanded; she couldn't move or speak.

"Was all of that true?"

Her silence verified it.

He pressed a clenched fist into his forehead. "My whole life is nothing but a pack of lies. My father is a murderer, and my mother is a whore."

"That's not true about Mama."

"It's not? Hmph. I guess I don't recognize the truth even when it bites me in the ass. Then again, why should I believe you when you've kept things from me my entire life."

"I did it to protect you!"

"Protect me? Ha! Who do you think I am? Some kind of fragile lunatic, like our dear, departed mother? What a selfish bitch she was! She did the most dangerous thing imaginable, no matter what it cost. She tore Dad apart, and us—and Monroe—my God, what would have become of Monroe if he didn't die? How could she expect Dad to raise her black bastard love child?"

Leon came back into the house. "Didn't you wake Adam yet? What are you waiting for?"

At the sight of him, Adam rose from the table. "It stinks in here all of a sudden." Shoving past him, he stormed out into the night.

"What's he blaming *me* for?" Leon mumbled.

Noël could hear the screeching sound of Adam's tires careening down the street. It seemed like miles before the distressing sound faded away. "Come on, get the kid up," he said.

"I can't leave Willow like this." She couldn't bring herself to meet his eyes.

"What?"

"I said I can't leave like this! How can I leave my brother like this?"

"And what about me?"

"What about you?" Betraying her family secrets was unforgiveable. And so was using that ugly word to describe Pastor Ray as if it was always somewhere close on his tongue, even after the Chavises.

"So, now it's all my fault for trying to slay your dragons?"

"They were *my* dragons! I told you those things in private. How could you just blurt them out and shatter Adam that way?"

His hands shook slightly; he looked like a train wreck. "You mean like I shattered my own brother by marrying you?"

His words injured her to the core; the straw that broke her. Splintering into uncontrollable sobs, she laid her forehead against the tabletop.

"Here come the waterworks again." He stood there motionless.

"I was only trying to save you. The same thing I've been trying to do since we met."

If this was his best stab at an apology, there was no conceivable response.

"You know what? I give up. I'm going back to Langston tonight. With or without you."

She heard his footsteps walking away, the screen door swaying on its hinges, the car engine revving in the driveway. How could he leave her like this? He wouldn't; he couldn't. She listened as the car moved down the street. He would come back. He would get down to the end of the block, turn around.

She waited.

But he didn't come back.

Leon was gone; he'd left her and Adam all alone with her father. She looked around the kitchen, a frightening, alien place. As if from a distance, she felt herself rising from the table, tiptoeing past her father's closed door to gently wake her son. "Mommy and you are going for a ride."

"In the middle of the night?"

"Yes," she said. "A midnight ride, like Paul Revere."

Once they were inside the car, she wasn't certain where to go. She only knew she couldn't remain in that house, go back to Langston, or leave Willow until she and her brother had a chance to talk things through.

The late spring night was warm, no breeze at all, with a low, full moon. For a second, it reminded her of the night they'd left Hyssop, only now it was her own son in the back seat, sound asleep in the bed she'd prepared for him. There was only one safe place she could think of to flee.

≈≈

The gates to the Garden of Resurrection were wide open. Navigating through the winding roads in the darkness, she was struck by the reminder that her mother was here. With Adam asleep and locked serenely inside the car, she stumbled toward the familiar tombstones, collapsing in front of the fresh grave, buried under a heap of earth and scattered flower arrangements. All at once she was consumed with terror—*Mama is suffocating!* After tossing the flowers aside, she clawed into the dirt, digging a hole nearly a foot deep before she finally returned to her senses.

She sat there, helpless. How long she remained stuck in that same position was anyone's guess. Her body shivered and her limbs went numb. Stretching out her legs until the tingling stopped, she looked from grave to grave, lit by the light of a bright, full moon, her thoughts racing. Her eyes fastened on Aunt Clarry's headstone:

When one does not love too much, one does not love enough.

The scene in the kitchen whirled around and around like a cyclone inside her head. Tonight she had found out that her father was the cold-blooded mastermind who'd orchestrated Pastor Ray's murder. Beyond even that, what stunned her the most was that he had committed the heinous act, not because he didn't love their mother enough, as she'd always believed, but because he loved her *too much*. It was a truth beyond her grasp.

She longed for a touch of human warmth. Pulling a red rose from the mass of flowers, she brushed its soft petals against her cheek, pretending it was her mother's hand. "I'm the only one in this world who understands your love for Pastor Ray," she told her. Mrs. Chavis couldn't fathom it. Her father was driven to murder because of it. And now that he finally knew, Adam was crucifying Mama for it.

But not Noël.

So what if her father loved Mama with every ounce of his being?

It was an obsessive, controlling love that left her mother feeling trapped and tormented. Noël had seen for herself how Pastor Ray's love had resurrected her mother, reviving the life and love in her eyes, enough even to notice her own children again. The only thing that wasn't right about Mama's love for Pastor Ray was everyone else: the wrong husband and a racist world.

Had she not witnessed, first-hand, her mother's love for Pastor Ray, she wouldn't have believed that such a thing existed. Her concept of marriage would have been her father and mother, herself and David, a trial to be endured, a vow into slavery. Letting Noël in on her clandestine love was the most important legacy her mother could have given her; a hope that had kept her close to her mother her entire life, a hope that had sustained her, enabled her, ultimately, to open her heart to Leon.

She gazed at the teddy bear silhouette of Monroe's tombstone. Sweet, unsullied Monroe. "Adam was right about one thing," she said to him. "If you lived, you wouldn't have stood a chance. They would've driven you out of Hyssop and Willow and every other town in between. Or worse."

She allowed her memories to slip back to their first long winter in Willow. All those months, she'd wondered whose baby was it going to be?—her father's or Pastor Ray's? Whose seed was stronger, the chosen one?

Her mother must have been wondering too. And on Christmas Eve, they got their answer. Monroe was their answer. Noël had ounce found a poem to describe it:

An angel in the book of life wrote down your baby's birth. Then whispered as she closed the book, "too beautiful for earth."

Too beautiful for earth. Noël's own son was beautiful too, and she longed to shield him from the venom of a cruel, unloving earth. Yet, how could she, when its sorrows bled through her own pores?

Lying down on a pillow of roses, her thoughts drifted to a concept Rick had taught her about. Chiaroscuro, the juxtaposition of light and darkness together. Diametric opposites, inextricably entwined. Like love and hate. Day and night. The sun and the moon. Unable to be separate, unable to be one. Like Mama and Pastor Ray.

Like … her and Leon?

All at once, the foundation of her life shifted beneath her. *What if loving too much is worse than hate?*

The thought ravaged her, a consuming fire incinerating her most sacred beliefs. Her father had loved her mother too much and had done the unthinkable. Her mother had gone ahead and kept loving Pastor Ray too much until it ended up ruining every last one of them, including her father, especially her father. What if her Mama was as much a murderer as he was? More so? And what if she was just the same? She fought to drown out the sound of her father's voice inside her head—*"You're trash! Just like your mother."*

She sat up, gasping for breath.

Just like Mama's love for Pastor Ray was selfish and destructive, so was her own love for Leon, doomed because it was stolen. She'd torn apart Rick to have him. And Stella. She had destroyed her own brother by keeping so many secrets, and now that he knew them, she ruined his only chance to start over again with their father. And before that, Aunt Clarissa had committed suicide because of what she had told her. Noël loved them all too much, and look at what she'd done to them.

The sobs riveted her body, convulsing her over and over again.

Completely drained, she lay prostrate on the cold, hard ground. It was all she could do to open her eyes. Overhead, the sky was deep purple, preparing itself for dawn in that fleeting, chiaroscuro moment when the moon and the sun were changing guard until the one eradicated the other.

When one does not love too much, one does not love enough.

The inscription she'd built her entire life upon had crumbled. It was vile, obscene. She wished she could rub it away, make it vanish from the tombstone, from the face of the earth. And herself along with it.

The next day, her brother quit his job at the Luffkin factory. Desperate enough for assistance, he allowed her to help him move his belongings past their father and out of his house, into a third-floor apartment in an old Victorian home a block down from Center Street. The new place provided the privacy to have long, overdue talks on the back porch while their neighbors were away at their jobs and her son frolicked in the fenced backyard. Together, they sifted through every single family secret.

"Just one more thing," Adam said. "How the hell did Mom ever get a hold of Pastor Ray's Bible?"

"He gave it to her the day before he was murdered," she said. The painful memory had been clearly revived during her long search in the attic. "I saw him slip it into her bag at the last revival. He must have had some kind of premonition. Anyway, the night we left Hyssop, I made Dad stop the car so I could run back into the house to get Amelia Rosalie, and—"

"I remember that." He interrupted. "He got mad as hell and kept honking the horn. I was terrified he was going to drive off without you."

"Me too. But when I got inside, I remembered about the Bible and where Mama stashed it. It seemed more important to me to grab that instead."

After two more days together, Adam asked her to leave, to go back to Langston where she belonged. "Don't be hurt," he said. "I just need time to be by myself. I'm taking all my savings and going on a long vacation."

"Where will you go?"

"It doesn't matter. What I'm running away from is inside of me. I'll be in touch when I get back. I promise." He smiled wearily. "And don't be so hard on Leon. He only shot off his big mouth because he loves you, you know."

Did he still?

What Noël needed was the same thing Adam did: time alone. Time to sort out her complicated feelings. Time to forgive Leon. Time, like her brother, to find a way to live with herself. But with a child and husband, she had no choice but to get back to living.

When she returned to the apartment, Leon was at work and the Chavises were still in Chicago visiting relatives. Walt stopped by later that afternoon. "It took her a while to get to this point." He started out. "But the missus is throwing you and Leon a wedding party this Saturday. She just felt like it was time."

A wedding party? *Good God, why now?*

As he drank a cup of Sanka, not beer, in deference to her mother's loss, he slowly shared things about his own mother and father. He told her about the pilgrimage he made to Poland after World War II to look for them. Though he never found a trace of his Dad, he discovered that his mother had perished in the Treblinka concentration camp. "I know what those camps were like," he said. "I was with the troops who liberated Buchenwald."

"How awful for you."

"It wasn't about me." His face contorted in grief. "Over twenty thousand were still alive—living skeletons inching toward us from all directions—starving, battered, walking corpses, most of them in striped uniforms. There was stack after stack of naked dead bodies piled on top of each other as if they were garbage, their eyes still open. Holy God, the smell was unimaginable! It's a horror I'll take to my deathbed. Not only what I saw with my own eyes, but knowing the hell my own mother went through."

Afraid to probe any further, Noël waited for him to say more, but he ended it there. "Let's go to your church and light some candles. For your parents and my mother."

Walt drove her and Adam over to St. Stan's. Because it was a weekday afternoon, they were the only people in the massive sanctuary. Together they knelt in the back where dozens of votive lights twinkled, picking up the long matchsticks and igniting two more wicks; Noël helped Adam light a third. Then they stepped back, watching them get lost against an entire wall of flames.

Adam dashed off to give a statue a closer look. Sitting down in one of the pews near the back, Walt pointed to an image of the Virgin Mary. "See that? That's the Black Madonna of Częstochowa. Right before I boarded the boat for America, my mother put an icon that looked just like that into my palm, bent my fingers over it and kissed them. As tears poured down her cheeks, she told me, 'God's mother will watch over you for me.' I still have it." He pulled the oval, lacquered image out of his pocket and handed it to her. "I've carried it every day of my life."

Noël held it, squeezed it.

"My mother was a saint. It broke her heart to put me on that ship. But she did it anyway. You know why?"

Her eyes were glued to his.

"Because she loved me, that's why. I was her whole world, her only child, and she loved me more than anything. She loved me enough to give me a better life, before it was too late. She sacrificed her own happiness for mine. That's what real love is."

Noël's heart wrenched, pounded. She gazed at him, her face reddening.

"What's the matter?"

Like Walt's mother, tears clouded her own eyes as she returned the icon. "You just gave me the answer to something I've been struggling with."

"Oh, yeah? Like what?"

"Like what it really means to love 'too much.'"

'Huh?"

"You reminded me that it's a good thing."

He nodded. "It's the best thing."

She wiped her eyes. "So, why is it called the Black Madonna?"

"Because she's black," he replied in his characteristic plain-spokenness. "Some say she got that way because the smoke from centuries of votive candles charred her face."

It was a sobering thought. Noël turned to look again at the wall of candles behind them, a flickering sea of human suffering, petitions, and pleas, and she tried to imagine century after century of countless tiny flames, just like theirs, slowly becoming a bonfire large enough to blacken the face of the Mother of God.

When Leon got home that night, they reunited as strangers, his eyes going cold at the sight of her reticence, her distrust. She also saw the weariness in him, a resignation. And because neither one of them made the first move, they allowed something irreparable to happen: They let the chasm between them crack wide open.

Noël's nerves were jangled. The meat she served for dinner was overdone, the potatoes nearly raw. He forced down the supper. Even Adam noticed the change. He picked at the awful food with his little head bowed, retreating to the soft animals in his room as quickly as he could.

She and Leon watched television for a while, their silence growing barbed wire. They stared at Walter Cronkite on the screen—he was announcing that Robert Kennedy had just won the California primary, virtually guaranteeing his presidential nomination. Noël smiled at Leon, but he didn't notice.

They stayed up late enough to see Kennedy's acceptance speech in the Ambassador Hotel ballroom in Los Angeles. Maybe it was the thrill of winning, but Bobby looked radiantly handsome to Noël, lighter somehow, fully at peace in his own skin. He joked about his dog before recapping his bold vision for an unselfish, united America, no longer at war. The last thing he said was, "And now it's on to Chicago, and let's win there."

Leon shut off the TV, and they went to bed.

Lying there wide-eyed, Noël was thinking that maybe Kennedy's victory was a rainbow of sorts—not just for the country, but for them too. Hope was hope, and she needed a dose of it. She reached out for Leon.

They ended up making love, but it wasn't the same. The weariness had spread to every nuance of his touch. She moved closer to him, closer. Despair gripped her. As close as two people could get to one another, they could never get close enough, could they?—and when they pulled apart again, they were more alone than before. Unable to be separate, unable to be one.

After Leon fell asleep, she returned to the living room and turned on the television to a chaotic scene in the ballroom of the Ambassador Hotel. Panic-eyed young people in Kennedy campaign hats were wailing, embracing, screaming, pleading for a doctor. What in the world had happened?

Within the jerking black-and-white camera frames, she saw the pandemonium taking place in a dark kitchen pantry behind the ballroom. She caught a glimpse of Bobby Kennedy lying on the floor … of two men cradling his bloody head … she heard a reporter say, "The happiness has now turned to tragedy." And there was Walter Cronkite again, sitting at his desk in the newsroom, the same way he'd been there to announce the other brother's murder, though Bobby still clung to life.

Noël sobbed into her hands.

A day later, Kennedy's campaign manager read a short statement with vacuous, uncomprehending eyes. "Senator Robert Francis Kennedy died at one forty-four a.m. today, June 6, 1968. He was forty-two years old."

≈≈

"Party, party, party," Leon's Aunt Sophie, Mary Ziemny's sister, handed Noël a large gift as she approached them in the reception line. "That's all we do lately—go to parties." She embraced Leon. "We were all looking forward to a big Polish wedding for you, you know. But, oh, well. This is a nice party."

The next woman in line smiled at Noël. "Remember me? I'm Aunt Gertie. Well, my real name is Gertrude, but everyone calls me Aunt Gertie. So, where did the two of you end up getting married?"

"Orville Mooreland, a justice of the peace," Leon replied, his posture shifting from one foot to the other as he unconsciously touched his suit coat pocket. Noël knew he was dying for a cigarette.

The first sister turned around. "A justice of the peace? *Ojeny!*

That's not a real wedding. Since you had to go to a justice of the peace, you should have at least gone to Harry Szymanski, a countryman."

"Harry Szymanski isn't a justice of the peace. He's a plumber." Aunt Gertie laughed. "You think they should have been married by a plumber?"

Sophie shook her head in confusion. "Oh, well, I guess it doesn't matter now. What's done is done. No use crying over spilt milk."

It seemed like the reception line took hours. One person came through the line, and the next one, and the next, all of them unknown to Noël; a part of Leon. She didn't realize how fixed and unchanging her own smile was until the muscles in her face began to ache. The guests pumped her hand with generic handshakes, then shared affectionate embraces with Leon or snippets from his past life of which she had no knowledge, including a best friend, Ted Something-Or-Other, whom she'd seen only once or twice before.

One of the strangers asked her where her parents were, and the innocent question struck her as confrontational. That simple inquiry clearly delineated Leon's world from her own. Leon came from *somewhere*—he'd grown up with these people, shared the same churches, schools, shops, traditions; the same faith. He belonged to this rich tapestry of intersecting lives. The Trudeaus, on the other hand, came from nothing, nowhere, and any history they had was to be blotted out, left unspoken.

She still hadn't seen Rick, but she'd heard an uncle say he was tending bar in the basement. Some of the men set up card tables in the garage and began an impromptu game of poker, puffing on cigars, while many of the women gathered in the living room, sharing stories of their children and grandchildren without the need to pass around photographs because everyone had known everyone since the day they were born.

Noël hopelessly tried to think of something she might contribute to the conversation. As they bantered about the church bazaar, the bake sale last week, and the fish fry this coming Friday, she gave up. She slipped out of the room and into the den with the neglected organ. The television played softly in the corner of the room.

Bobby Kennedy's flag-draped coffin was being taken from New York to Washington, DC on a slow-moving train. Tens of thousands of mourners had turned out to line the tracks all along the way— Boy Scouts saluting, veterans somberly carrying flags, women in hair curlers, everyday families holding homemade signs—blacks on one side of the track, whites on the other. All of America, except them it seemed, had turned out to say goodbye.

Noël went outside to play with the children. They were chattering as if members of the same family, these children who were altar boys together and made their first communions side by side. Like her, her little boy stood longingly on the sidelines. When she reached for his hand, he moved nearer to them.

She returned inside. Some of the older people were sitting in the corner of the living room, speaking Polish. Another group was discussing the exhibition of Polish art that was currently on display at the neighborhood cultural museum, specifically the paintings of the winged horsemen. The striking image seemed perfect. If Poland had remained "wiped off the map", as Rick had told her the night they'd met, none of them would have been here. But they were here. Poland had survived, and the winged horsemen surrounded her.

Even she, in some small way, was testimony to their resiliency. She had been a thunderbolt who'd stormed into their lives, and yet, less than a year later, they were fêting the marriage that had outraged them. How could she possibly ask for more from Mary Ziemny? Noël had broken her heart in two, and she was throwing her a party.

Walt was too busy to play the organ or spend time with Noël— he was freshening up drinks, setting up extra chairs, doing whatever hosts did at any given moment. She kept looking around for Leon, standing by his side whenever she located him, but he had no inclination to spend time with her. She couldn't blame him. The air got thin when she was around; awkward questions or strained silences. As long as she wasn't with him, he fit perfectly into the group, snug and safe in his spot, with so much to say to them and nothing to say to her.

Eventually, he joined the men in the garage, including Ted, for a couple rounds of poker. He was back in his element, a fish returned to sea. This wasn't their wedding party; this was his homecoming.

Finally, she retreated to the basement.

Every once in a while, Rick's gaze caught hers, and she turned away, though she didn't want to—he was the warmest presence in the room. Somehow over these many months, he'd found a way to forgive her; she could see it in his eyes.

As he served drinks from behind the bar, he helped himself to several glasses in between. Later, when the merriment in the room was loud and plentiful, she tried not to notice him making his way over to her.

He pulled up a chair. "You just tell me," he leaned toward her, "—if my brother is hurting you, and I swear to God, I'll kick his ass."

"He's not." She diverted her gaze.

"Then why do you look so sad?"

"My mother died."

"I know," he said. "My dad told me, and I'm really sorry. Are you sure that's all that's wrong?"

"Isn't that enough?" Noël sensed that people were noticing the intimate tone of their conversation, but she was too afraid to look around.

"Then tell me, how *is* life with Leon?" He searched her face for a hidden meaning in whatever she might reply.

"I love him." She said it both earnestly and apologetically.

"I know you do." His eyes saddened in a way that made it obvious that her answer still stung. "You only look around for him every two seconds. But tell me, where the hell is he? Why isn't he sitting here beside you instead of me?"

"You've got to forgive him, Rick."

"Never. Not as long as you're around." He put his lips against her ear. "If you ever need me, I'm here for you."

She rushed back upstairs, back to the lonely den where Bobby's funeral train was still chugging its way to Washington. Later that night, he would be lowered into his grave at Arlington National Cemetery, not far from his brother. And that would be that. No more Kennedys. No more King. The country had been ceded back to the amoral status quo, with blacks on one side of the tracks and whites on the other. The quest for a newer world was over.

Noël remained alone in the den until Mary Ziemny came looking for her. It was time to slice the beautiful three-tiered wedding cake with white buttercream frosting and decorative red roses. "I heard you like roses." She smiled at Noël.

Finally, she and Leon were side-by-side, holding the same knife over the cake that spelled, in yellow candy lettering, "Happy Marriage."

≈≈

The fourth Saturday morning in August, Leon left the apartment to go visit his old neighborhood, presumably for a haircut, but he didn't ask Noël to go along. She was used to it by now. Ever since his homecoming party, he made regular trips back there on Saturday mornings, bringing home bags of Polish bread and *paczki* from the Polonia Bakery, but never any stories of who he ran into or what they'd said.

Finally deciding on an epitaph, she used the time on that Saturday to order the headstone for her mother, choosing a verse from *Four Quartets*, by T. S. Eliot, a poetry book that Adam let her borrow from his bookcase. Noël gave them her instructions—under her mother's name and dates—to inscribe the following:

To make an end is to make a beginning …
And the fire and the rose are one.

Leon was later than usual. When he finally came home, it was nearly three in the afternoon. The second he walked through the door, slightly disheveled, a jolt went through her. The smell of death was all over him—Stella's Shalimar perfume.

Noël fought the urge to scream, to weep. Instead, she recoiled into that fractured place when the world separates to an island of grief. She knew this moment was coming, but he'd forced her hand sooner than she'd hoped. And now it was here.

The pain pulsed in every cell of her body, the unbearable agony that Walt's mother must have felt the moment she raised her eyes to the horizon and saw that approaching ship.

TWENTY-SEVEN

AUGUST 1968
LEON

LEON was a compulsive reader. Not of lofty books, like his brother-in-law, but of everyday things, like cereal boxes, instruction manuals, and the newspaper, of course. As he sat on the porch swing in the fenced-in courtyard out back staring up at the moon, he thought about the quote he'd read on a calendar at work: *You can hide from everything except the moon, the sun, and the truth.* Was it Buddha who said it? He couldn't remember. He lit his final cigarette for the night.

In the oppressive heat, sweat ran down his temples. Still in the high eighties at quarter to midnight, the dog days of summer were in full swing. He took a long puff, his mind wandering again, the crazy way that minds do during idle moments. He'd read in today's paper that the term "dog days" had nothing to do with overheated canines but with the Dog Star, Sirius, and its position in the universe this time of year, a star the ancient Greeks associated with catastrophe. Maybe they were right. The Democrats had started their convention in Chicago earlier tht day, and it promised to be a colossal mess.

He was distracted by a noise behind him. When he turned around, Noël was standing in the back doorway dressed only in her flimsy nightgown, framed by a halo of light streaming in behind her from the ceiling lamp. Half of him wanted to sprint to her; the other half wanted to flee. He stared upward, wondering why she'd decided to join him when she hadn't bothered to come out to the courtyard with him for weeks.

She traced his gaze at the moon. "Sometimes I wish you and I were all alone up there," she said.

Pitching his cigarette to the ground, he stood up, unwilling to begin a conversation at this hour, particularly one that would inevitably end with her in tears. "But we're not on the moon, are we?"

"Don't leave."

He sat down again, rocking the bench. The apartment was sweltering, especially their bedroom where the useless fan blew the same steamy air around, but he longed to head back inside anyway. He had a bad feeling that something irrevocable might happen if he remained. Maybe it was his guilt gnawing away at him.

Last Saturday when he'd gone back to the neighborhood, he'd run into Stella outside the bakery, and she was more than sympathetic about how unhappy he looked. Like a fool, he'd taken her up on her suggestion to take a drive in her car to talk about it without the whole neighborhood watching. A mile or so out of town, she'd stopped on a deserted road, slid closer to him. "She's not like us," she cooed. "She doesn't understand you the way I do." One thing led to another, and before he knew it, they were going at it like teenagers in the backseat.

After it was over, Stella's face looked triumphant in the bald sunlight, confident that she was the one he wanted, when all he'd really wanted was to stop wanting Noël. He hated himself, and Stella too. "Call me," she said as they parted, but it'd be a cold day in hell before he did. And hell was where he belonged.

Now it was Noël's face he was staring at, a face that never stopped stunning him, no matter how familiar. She looked away, toward the rosebush he'd planted for her in the spring—still barren sticks that never produced flowers or shown any other sign of life. "Why do you think our rosebush didn't bloom?" she asked.

"Maybe we planted it too soon," he said. "Or too late."

"Kind of like us?"

He got up from the swing, determined to leave this time.

"Please, Leon, don't go. Don't you love me at all anymore?"

"Of course I love you! But you're like the wind or something, one mood one minute, and completely different the next." The words flowed in spite of him. "I don't understand what you want from me. When I went head-on with your father, you acted like I committed a mortal sin."

Tears, more than predictable, welled in her eyes. "I'm sorry I'm so hard to figure out. But you know exactly what Stella wants from you, don't you?"

He knew he should've gone inside when he'd had the chance. He tried to recalibrate. Should he walk away? Deny it? Why bother? Like old Buddha said, you can't hide from the sun, the moon, or the truth. "That was a huge mistake."

She shrugged, an odd reaction, as if resigned to his infidelity.

"How did you know?"

"Stella always marks her territory with her trademark perfume."

The fact that Stella always wore the same perfume was news to him. "Just for the record, I'm not her territory. I never was. It meant nothing. Absolutely nothing."

"Oh, Leon, don't you realize that sex never means nothing? If it's not giving something, everything, then it's taking it away."

His chest was on fire, an attack of heartburn that flared up when he got worked up late at night, an unfortunate idiosyncrasy he'd inherited from his old man.

"Anyway, I don't want you to tell me you're sorry. I want you to vow it to me." She reached inside the folds of her lavender nightgown and produced an envelope. The moonlight illuminating her pale hand, she carefully unwrapped an *oplatek* wafer, broke it, and handed half to him. Surprisingly, she managed a smile.

His father had told him that her smile reminded him of the sun coming up, a line he stole from an old movie, *The Misfits*. But it was an accurate description. Even in the darkness, Leon absorbed its warmth.

"I shared an *oplatek* with your dad today," she said.

"Why? Why would he need to forgive you?"

Her smile faded.

He cracked off a piece of her wafer. "I'm so damned sorry about Stella. You've got to believe me. It's you I love. It's always been you." Slipping the tasteless *oplatek* into his mouth, he let it dissolve on his tongue, his shame and frustration giving way to melancholy.

She tore off a small corner from his wafer. "I forgive you. And I'm hoping you'll forgive me for the pain I cause you. I promise you that I love you with my whole heart. Remember that promise, no matter what."

As she put the piece of *oplatek* in her mouth, he waited for the sadness to leave her face, but it only magnified. Taking his hand, she pressed her remaining wafer into his palm and folded his fingers over it, kissing them. "Think of this as the Madonna of Częstochowa."

"What's that supposed to mean?"

She didn't reply.

In the boiling-hot bedroom, he made love to her into the dawn. The alarm clock shrieked just before five a.m.

As he sat alone in the kitchen drinking his coffee, he was thankful she didn't get up with him. If she did, they would've had to talk. And then they'd be back to reality, off of their "moon", as she had phrased it. Last night they'd admitted that they still loved each other, but that was never the problem.

So, what was the problem?

Spoken or unspoken, their shared remorse over Ricky had doomed them from the start. The only difference was that all those other things had piled in on top of it now. Like his stupidity with Stella. And her past, always her past. They were *her* dragons, she'd said to him that night, not his. Meaning, he was helpless to slay them. Meaning, he couldn't set her free.

Having drained his coffee, he put the cup in the sink.

By quitting time, he was dreading going home. Stalling around, he did little jobs that could've easily been done the next day by one of his men, lingering an extra hour. He thought about calling her to tell her he'd be late, but he didn't. Maybe if she was worried, she would feel relief, not tension, when he walked through the door.

Parking on the street in front of their apartment building, he saw the light in their living room window. The rest of the building was dark. The Chavises had gone back to Chicago to tend to a sick aunt. Climbing the stairs he'd ascended hundreds of times before, he paused when he reached the top. Noël sometimes waited for him, opening the door before he had a chance to use his key, but not tonight.

He fumbled to find the lock in the dark. She probably wasn't opening the door because she was pissed off that he was late and hadn't bothered to call. Swinging the door open, he was greeted only by the sight of an eerily uncluttered apartment. Where had she managed to hide the junk?

"Noël?" He walked through the living room, then into the kitchen. No supper simmered on the stove. He went down the hallway. When he entered Adam's room, it hit him like a freight train. Except for the bed and dresser, which came with the place like the rest of the furniture, the room was stripped down to the bone. All his toys were gone—his baseball, the purple frog, the red dump truck. Frantically, he pulled open the closet—his clothes were gone.

Leon raced into their bedroom and flung open their own closet door. Her side was empty, just empty hangers.

Staggering backward onto the bed, he called out her name in a daze, this time knowing there'd be no answer. He fought to conjure up a logical explanation as he looked around the room. The terrycloth slippers beside the bed were gone, the cosmetics on the nightstand were gone, the lavender nightgown on the bed was gone.

There was no other explanation. Noël had left him.

For the first time in his life, Leon wept. He buried his face in the scent of her pillow and sobbed. His nose ran; his eyes stung. He got up from the bed, walked purposefully into the kitchen, and opened the cupboard where his liquor bottles were kept. *Thank God, they're still here.* He poured himself a tall drink, wishing the Flintstones glasses remained in the cupboard, but they were gone too. He ached for the ever-present sound of Adam's innocent little noises.

Gulping the whiskey, he awaited its numbing effects. "What do I do now?" The sound of his voice echoed hollow. Maybe they'd be back.

That was it. Feeling the liquor slightly, he fished for a cigarette in his pocket and lit it. That was her strategy. She was doing this to teach him a lesson, exactly like he'd worked late to teach her a lesson. She figured that if she left him, it'd give him a scare, bring him back to his senses. Well, it did. When he found her, everything would be fine. The things that had wedged in between them paled in comparison. "You win." He lifted his arms in surrender. "I admit it. I can't live without you."

Only the silence answered.

As he turned around toward the kitchen cupboard, he noticed a single dinner plate sitting out on the countertop. It was obvious she'd placed it there for him to find. As he approached, he saw a small paper slipped underneath. It was official now. She had left him a note.

He didn't want to read it, but he had to, and he might as well just do it quick and get it over with.

LEON

You and I shared more magical moments together than most do in a lifetime. I'll carry every single one of them in my heart forever and ever. But as long as I'm with you, neither you or Rick will find peace.

I love you. Only you. I love you too much.

And so, my love, that's why I want you to set sail for a better life.

NOEL

P.S. Your favorite dinner is in the refrigerator.

She really thought he'd be able to eat? He scoffed at the irony, absentmindedly opening the refrigerator, where the kielbasa and potatoes and green beans were wrapped, and he flashed back to Christmas Eve.

Scraping the meal into the garbage can, he returned to his drink and cigarette.

He reread the simple note until he could hear her speaking it. He studied every single word, trying to decipher hidden meanings in all of them. *Forever and ever*, a phrase a child would use, typical of her. *Set sail for a better life.* A pretty way, he guessed, to say she was dumping him. *I love you too much.* What the hell did that mean?

He sat down at the kitchen table, finished his cigarette, sipped his drink, read the note over and over. There was something odd about the way she'd spaced their names. He looked at it again. *Leon*, in reverse, spelled *Noël*. Maybe he was dense, but he'd never realized that before. From now on, he couldn't even see his own goddamned name without thinking of her.

She had her chance to say goodbye, but where was his? He poured himself another drink, trying to envision her smile, her eyes; the images were already losing clarity.

His father would be devastated. What would he tell the guys at work? He'd been married for only nine months. What would the people in his old neighborhood think? *I told you so*, that's what his mother would say. If anyone could understand, it would be Ricky— they even had their twin goodbye notes—but chances were zilch that he'd care to commiserate with a traitor like him.

The ashtray by then overflowing, he flicked his latest ashes onto the tabletop. That was what brought him back to his senses—a small flame charring a paper napkin. He pounded it out, glancing at his watch in the process. Eleven p.m. Somehow he'd lost four hours sitting there in the dark, and though he'd consumed over half of the bottle, he couldn't get himself drunk enough to stop the pain. Eventually, he passed out at the kitchen table.

He awoke the next day, Wednesday, stiff as a corpse, the realization hitting him all over again. He called in sick. The whiskey was his breakfast, along with a few more cigarettes. He kept trying to convince himself that she'd be back. And since she'd be back, there was no point in telling anyone she'd left in the first place.

He drank until he was dead again. And when he resurrected, he drank some more.

By evening, he was lost in time. His head was pounding. His

stomach burned. He needed a dose of diversion to ground him. He turned on the television.

Chicago was a combat zone. Right there on the TV screen, hordes of police were beating up thousands of bloody protesters in front of the Hilton Hotel, teargassing them, clubbing them, spraying even innocent bystanders with mace. "The whole world is watching!" the demonstrators chanted. A split-screen shot showed the pandemonium inside the Democratic convention. Senator Ribicoff stood at the podium accusing Mayor Daley of using "gestapo tactics" on the streets of Chicago. Daley mouthed the words "fuck you!" from the riotous floor.

The whole country had gone stark-raving mad. Leon pulled the plug out of the wall.

Wednesday rolled indistinguishably into Thursday except for another call to work to tell them he'd be off until Monday. The liquor was starting to take its toll. He was throwing up greenish slime. The back of his head felt like it'd been whacked with a shovel. He drank some more.

Later, he was roused from his stupor by urgent knocking. He staggered from the sofa in his stocking feet thinking maybe Noël had come home at last. When he opened the door, Theckla was standing there.

Theckla! He felt such intense comfort at the sight of her that he fought to control his emotions. She was the only person in the universe who could possibly share his sorrow over the magnitude of Noël's loss.

"Sweet Jesus, what's happened to you?"

He had no idea how bad he looked until he saw the expression on her face. "Noël left me." Confessing it was excruciating.

She gasped; her dark eyes clouding with distress. He sat down on the sofa, and she landed beside him, taking both of his cheeks into her hands. "Listen to me, baby. We'll figure this out." Her fingers felt warm, a lifeline.

It dawned on him right then, how much he'd grown to care about this woman. Not so long ago, he'd been ignorant and blind, ashamed to be her neighbor. But he was a different man now, a man with a wound in his soul, and his eyes wide open. This woman had saved him from himself more times than he could count, despite her own unfathomable wounds. She was saving him again now.

"I should have caught on," she said. "She came to me Monday morning, but she didn't say one word about leaving. She gave me a pretty pearl bracelet and told me I was more like a mama than her own. And she cried when she handed Freddie a drawing the little one had done of him and Freddie pitching balls. I had a funny feeling she was saying goodbye to us, not just before our trip to Chicago—a final one. But Freddie said, 'Nah, you know how she is.'" Her eyes scanned the living room. "Oh, my dear God … What are we going to do without them?"

As she broke down into sobs, Leon wrapped his arms around her, surrendering his last bit of strength to hold her there. Closing his eyes against her face, he let her tears sink into the pores of his sinful, dead body, like a burial anointing.

TWENTY-EIGHT

SEPTEMBER–DECEMBER 1968
RICKY

THE call came over dinner on the Sunday of Labor Day weekend. While Ricky and his mother continued eating their meal, Dad answered the phone. After he said "hello," he grimaced and went pale, and Ricky feared he was having a stroke. But within seconds, he realized the problem wasn't medical.

"My God, what's the matter?" Ma dropped her butter knife.

"It'll be okay, son," Dad rasped into the receiver. "We'll be there first thing tomorrow." Hanging up the phone, he refused to look at either one of them. "Noël left Leon last week," he announced. "He's moving back home."

Ricky was speechless, stupefied.

"We should go over there right now," his mother said.

"He doesn't want us to do that."

"Why not?" she asked. "What else did he say?"

"Not much. We'll find out tomorrow."

Dad came back to the table and sat down. Lost in their own thoughts as they processed the news, not one of them uttered a word.

A tempest was bubbling inside of Ricky—shock, outrage, relief, concern, anger—nearly every emotion a human being was capable of, was surging through his body. From the start he'd known his brother would end up chasing her away, crushing her.

"So, he wasn't sick after all?" his mother asked. Leon had called off from work last week telling them, and the personnel office, that he'd had a bad case of stomach flu.

"I guess not." Dad jabbed a fork aimlessly at the roast beef on his plate.

"Well, thank God for that." She crossed herself. "Sick bodies wither away. But spirits heal." Ricky looked up at her, thinking it was the other way around. "We'll get up bright and early tomorrow and bring him home," she said.

"Mayb you will, but not me." Ricky threw down his napkin. "I don't want him here. And I don't want to set foot in that apartment."

Ma gave him an icy stare. The day Leon ran off with Noël, Ricky had seen his mother go rigid, the same way a blown-out candle turned to cold, hard wax. "This anger between you and your brother has to stop right now," she said. "The cause of it just left him. Left all of us. He needs you now—both you and your pickup truck."

His *pickup truck*?

When Ricky didn't reply, the softer Ma made a sudden comeback. "I know how much this hurts you, honey." She got up from the table and hugged him. "But this too shall pass."

The next day, all the way across town, the welts stayed on Ricky's face, new ones erupting over old scars, all of them bleeding together to form large areas that the doctor called plaques. He'd had frequent attacks over the last year and knew the drill like clockwork. By the time they pulled up in front of the apartment, he was a swollen, rutted mess.

Ma was so appalled by her first look at the shabby building in the midst of a colored neighborhood that she didn't even notice.

Ricky waited until his parents went in with an armload of empty boxes before pulling his trusty flask out of the glove box and drinking it dry. He climbed out of the cab of the truck and mounted the familiar staircase, the distinct odors rushing in—fried grease, the scents of meals long gone by, mingling with that peculiar smell that permeated old buildings. Pierced by memories, he stumbled on the wobbly step near the top, same as the first time. The door to the apartment stood wide open.

Leon was sitting on the sofa looking like a feral animal, unshaven and unkempt, his legs straight out on the coffee table, his posture slumped. Ricky was glad he was a shipwreck, especially when he didn't bother to give him as much as a glance when he entered the room. Ma was already picking up odds and ends, tossing them into boxes. His father sat sunken in the chair opposite Leon. "What a great loss, son."

"How can you say that?" Ma stopped her packing, her penciled eyebrows arching in disbelief. "Ever since the day that girl descended on our family, we've known nothing but heartache. Getting rid of her is the best kind of loss I can imagine."

Ricky took a seat near the kitchen door, the one he used to occupy when he'd waited for Noël to finish tucking in Adam at night, rousing another flurry of warm, excruciating memories, some recalled often, others half-forgotten. He could picture Noël coming out of the kitchen, a pop in her hand, an army of burning candles flickering as she passed.

"Why didn't you tell us last week?" Ma asked.

"I thought she'd come back." Leon's eyes were rimmed with heavy shadows, his body gaunt, his complexion tinged with a strange, dehydrated cast. Ricky recognized the symptoms; he reminded him of the man he saw daily in the mirror.

"I'll sure as hell miss that smile," his father said. "That girl's smile was like the sun coming up."

"Stop it!" Ma screamed. "Leon doesn't need to hear things like that." Picking up the ashtray on the coffee table, she dumped the mountain of ashes into the wastebasket.

While she was out of the room, Leon pulled out the last cigarette from the cellophane package in his shirt pocket and lit it. Package crumpling in his hand, he tossed it on the coffee table and looked straight at Dad. "I don't even know where to start looking for her."

"Looking for her?" Ma reemerged from the kitchen. "For heaven's sake, why would you do that? How much more humiliation can you take? Hasn't she done enough already? Look what she's done to your brother. And now to you." None of them had the strength to protest as her outburst continued. "This woman has torn my family apart, over and over again, destroyed both of my sons. And still, you can't let her go?" She glared at her husband. "Even you can't stop reminiscing about her smile. What's the matter with all of you?"

Leon was the first to get up from his seat. "You know what?" he said to her. "You're absolutely right." His father glanced at him quickly, looked away.

For the next couple hours or so, they silently packed up Leon's belongings, he and Ricky careful to dodge one another at every turn. "What kind of woman has purple drapes?" Ma asked as she walked through the small rooms for the first and last time of her life.

At last, the back of the truck was loaded, ready to go.

Leon left the apartment without looking back, Ma following close behind. Ricky watched his forlorn father turn around just once before exiting into the stairwell. As for him, the gravitational pull to remain in that space was stronger than his legs. Ricky stumbled through each of the small rooms one final time, touching the stucco walls, glancing at the sofa where they used to watch TV, even opening the empty Frigidaire where she kept the colas, unable to bring himself to walk out the door.

Noël and little Adam's presence was still palpable. He wanted to savor it, memorize it. It took every muscle he had to close the wooden door behind him and head down the staircase.

Outside again, he felt the heat of the September sun on his skin as he secured the last load of boxes in the bed of the truck. "It feels like we crawled out of the catacombs," Ma said.

The three of them squeezed into the cab, while Leon revved up his apple-red car. "Too bad that hot-rod was more important to him than moving his family away from the catacombs," Ricky said.

Leon took off from the curb first, and they trailed behind.

Halfway home, Leon signaled to them to stop, and they pulled off on the side of the road. He changed his mind, he told them. He suddenly decided he didn't want to move back home after all, adding that he was certain that the little apartment in the back of Michalek's Dry Goods Store must be available since it was always for rent.

"You can't live in a place like that!" Ma said.

"Follow me there." He got back in his car.

Ricky halted the truck in front of the brick building, the year 1910 chiseled over the top of the second story in large, block digits. Two or three rambling additions stretched into the back alley. Though the rest of the rented apartments didn't look too bad from the outside, the smallest one remained unoccupied, and soon they discovered why. It was a godforsaken little space, pungent with water damage and decay, only one grimy window looking out into the alley by the Dumpster. In Ricky's estimation, this was the perfect sty for his pig of a brother.

≈≈

By the time Leon dragged himself over for a visit back home a week later, Ricky had enough time to absorb their separation, and he'd formulated a plan. He would go looking for Noël to make certain she was all right. After a time, maybe, he could take up with her again. Nothing romantic, but she needed a friend, a companion, to help with her son. How in the world was she managing anyway?

When Leon entered the kitchen through the back door, Ricky was ready for him. "So, what are you going to do—divorce her?"

"Yup." Leon was stony. "As soon as I find out where she is."

The answer threw Ricky. It didn't occur to him that she would run anywhere else except to the brother who had returned from Vietnam, but surely Leon had thought of that. He said it anyway. "She's probably with Adam."

"Nope. She's not." He grabbed a cooling cookie from the baking sheet on top of the counter and took a bite. "Adam's on some extended trip somewhere."

Leon's arrogance infuriated him. "What did you do to her?" He strained to keep his voice low. Ma was upstairs ironing, and he wanted her to stay put up there. "Why did she run away?"

"Her decision, not mine." Leon shoved past him.

Ricky followed him into the living room. "You know what? You're a cold-hearted SOB. For some reason, she loved the crap out of you, but I knew it would end up like this."

"Here comes the 'I told you so'. What took you so long?"

"You're damned right here it comes! She's all alone somewhere. And probably scared as hell. She has a child to raise, for God's sake."

"Not *my* child."

"You *are* a cold-hearted bastard!"

By now, Ma was charging down the stairs. "When is this going to end?" she cried.

At last, Leon looked Ricky square in the eyes. "Let's get this straight, once and for all. My marriage is none of your business, and it's not up for discussion. Mom's right; she tore us apart. So, let's do ourselves a favor and not mention her name again."

His cruelty offended Ricky more than stealing her away in the first place.

One month and several dead-ends later, Leon's attorney finally located Noël through Adam after he returned to Willow, and he served her with divorce papers, which she didn't contest. It all went quickly, without a hitch.

A week before Christmas, a manila envelope from the law firm was delivered to their address, rather than to Leon's dive in the back of Michalek's Dry Goods Store. It sat on the table by the stairs gathering dust until Dad could bring himself to deliver it to Leon in person.

Ma was the only one who perceived their divorce to be the best Christmas present imaginable. Up to that point, she'd remained low-key about the holidays, but now she pulled out all the stops, decorating the house from top to bottom.

That weekend, Ricky made his planned trip to Willow.

He discovered her brother no longer lived there. The closest he came to picking up Noël's trail was a brief conversation with her father at his front door, who informed Ricky that he had no clue where she lived now. He didn't even know that she and Leon were separated, let alone divorced. But he seemed pretty glad to hear the news.

There was nowhere left to look. Noël had vanished into thin air.

≈≈

By three o'clock on Christmas Eve, their kitchen was filled with mouthwatering scents of all kinds, from kielbasa to *chrusciki* to poppy-seed noodles to sauerkraut. Ma had invited more than thirty people for Wigilia supper, including Stella and her parents, hoping to reignite some old sparks.

Later that evening, well past nine p.m., Leon arrived, dressed in his black suit, looking nearly like his former self. Stella lit up when he walked into the room, and he acknowledged her with a simple nod of the head, nothing more. For now, even Ma would have to be content with that.

By that time, vodka aplenty was flowing through Ricky's bloodstream and, to his own surprise, he was feeling pretty damned okay for the first time in a long while. Aunt Gertie plopped a Santa hat on his head. Ma sliced him a hulking piece of her Dutch apple pie. Later, Stella caught him under the mistletoe, planting a red-lipsticked smack on his cheek. The truth be told, it felt great to be able to enjoy the holidays again without the trauma of running into the love of his life, his brother's wife, in every doorway.

Maybe it was all the animated people surrounding them, or maybe it was just his own spirits lifting, but Leon's gloominess suddenly stood out like a storm cloud. As a small group plunked out "Jingle Bells" on the organ, Ricky surveyed his brother as he sat on a folding chair near the front door, his downcast eyes attached to the hardwood floor, immune to the merriment. He'd barely said a word all night. Their friends and relatives had been trying to rally around him all evening long, asking for his help with as many festive activities they could think of, but Leon had declined each invitation with a slight shake of his head.

Ricky sat down in the chair near the stairs, still staring at him. There was no denying it. Ricky could see it now, the permanent strain that was making his brother's face look a lot more like their father's. When Ricky was growing up, Leon had padded the sharp edges to soften nearly all of his falls. But who softened Leon's?

"It's time for *oplatki*!" Ma came out of the kitchen, carrying a silver tray of wafers. Leon fled outside to the front porch.

She shot their father a worried expression. "Just let him be," he said softly.

While everyone else in the room was hugging and breaking wafers, Ricky glanced at the closed front door, fighting with himself. *Should I go to him, or shouldn't I?* His soul-searching reminded him of King Arthur's monologue in the movie *Camelot* he'd seen last weekend. As Arthur struggled with forgiving his best friend and his wife for falling in love with each other—("What about *their* pain and *their* torment? Could it possibly be civilized to love myself above all?")—Ricky had remained in that theater transfixed, until all the credits rolled and every seat was empty.

He yanked the Santa hat off his head and flung it on the finial of the banister. He grabbed his coat and two wafers from the tray. It was time, past time, for him to be a king.

Leon was standing in front of the porch light, smoking, the other hand holding the rail, a faraway look in his eyes as he gazed across the street.

"Can I join you?" Ricky asked.

He didn't reply. He didn't even turn around.

Even though it was frigid outside, barely twenty degrees, Ricky sat down on the stoop, wrapping his scarf two times around his neck. Leon remained standing, the smoke from his cigarette blowing off the porch in a long stream, drifting across the front yard before evaporating into the night air. There were no sounds except distant barking from a neighbor's dog down the street.

"Remember our Dalmatian when we were kids?" Ricky said. "You named him that goofy name."

Leon squinted at the memory. "I haven't thought about Tommy Dorsey for years. Man, did I love that dog."

"I know you did. You and him were inseparable. When the day came to put him down, I think part of you was put to sleep too. You never wanted another dog after that."

"Why are we talking about this?" Leon snapped. He took a final puff before discarding the butt.

"You can't stop living, Leon. Pain and loss are a part of life."

"Yeah, well, they're a pretty lousy part, if you ask me." He pulled out another cigarette, but didn't light it. "Stop trying to be there for me. I sure as hell wasn't there for you, was I?"

"Maybe not." Ricky paused for a moment. "But we need to do this."

"Do what?"

When Ricky stood up to retrieve the *oplatki* from his pocket, Leon's eyes enlarged at the sight of them. "No, I can't."

"Well, then, just forget it!" Ricky threw the wafers to the floor of the porch. "You think this is so easy for me?" Heading for the front door, he felt Leon's grasp on the sleeve of his coat.

"It's not you," Leon said. "It's me, all me. You're my kid brother, and I let you down. More than let you down. And I'm sorry. I'm so goddamned sorry for every stupid thing I ever did."

Despite the lump in his throat, Ricky managed a laugh. "And you've done an awful lot of them."

Leon smiled.

"But just for the record," Ricky said, "loving her wasn't one of them."

≈≈

By midnight, their family was ensconced in their usual pew inside St. Stan's, waiting for the Shepherd's Mass to begin. Father Chet approached the altar and raised his arms, exhorting all to rise. "Let us join together in glorious song."

The congregation stood as the magnificent pipe organ heralded the grand entrance of the full choir, bursting down the middle and side aisles two by two, singing the familiar Christmas carol at the top of their voices and starting it, of all places, at the chorus. "Noël, Noël, Noël, Noël—"

The sound of her name reverberated throughout every corner of the church.

Ricky's head jerked back. His father, beside him, sagged in his seat. Ma winced, as if a blinding sun was streaming from the altar. But the expression on Leon's face was beyond words—he looked as if the choir was twisting a butcher knife slowly through his heart.

And that's when it hit Ricky. Noël Trudeau wasn't just someone they loved; she was something that happened to them. A seismic wave, a turning point, a rare event. She fell from the sky and hurled through each of them like a comet.

But which hole was bigger, he couldn't say—the hole she filled or the hole she left.

NOVEMBER 1972
ADAM

AFTER months of dreaded anticipation, Adam was really doing it. He stared down at his own index finger stuck into the slots of the rotary dial, spinning out the right combination of numbers that triggered the lost connection. He'd already chickened out and hung up twice. This time, he let it ring.

When his father answered and heard his voice, there was a long pause. Adam kept talking to fill the void. "Sure, sure, come down and see me," his father finally said. They made a date for the next day.

Tomorrow would be the first time they would lay eyes on each other in more than four years.

He was standing in the doorway when Adam's car pulled up. If it wasn't their old house with the same digits over the front door, Adam might not have recognized him. Only in his mid-fifties, Dad's hair had already turned solid gray, his upper back misshapen with a hump that bent him slightly at the waist, his periwinkle-blue eyes caved into his skull. Maybe his father was thinking the same thing about him, how much he'd deteriorated in such a short time.

They didn't embrace. Instead, they bobbed around each other, nodding awkwardly, reminding Adam of some weird animal ritual.

"Let's sit." Dad slapped his palm on the top of one of the old chairs, the dust flying from years of vacancy.

"Still not so good at dusting, huh?" Adam's lame joke fell flat. The whole house seemed eerily untouched since the day they had left him behind. "So … how've you been?"

"Oh, you know." Dad's voice trailed off, his eyes blunting with something that looked like pain—physical or somewhere deeper?

Adam gazed at the empty mantel where dozens of family photographs used to rest—their school pictures, Auntie Clarry's high school graduation portrait, the largest one in an ornate gold frame: his parents on their wedding day. He could still see the missing photo in his mind—his angelic, mother dressed in flowing white lace; his father in his Army uniform, bursting with charisma. He struggled for a conversation starter. "I went to visit Steve in California last year."

"Oh, yeah?" Dad's long fingers drummed on his knees. "And how's he doing?"

"Fine. Just fine. You know Steve, he always lands on his feet. He's got a baby now and everything."

Adam watched his father's face sag under the latest load of rejection as he took in the news of a grandchild he'd likely never know. He stopped himself from elaborating. Why belabor the point that Steve was the only one who had successfully survived their childhood?

"Where you living now?" Dad asked.

"I moved to Langston three years ago. I got a job in one of the big factories over there."

"You don't say. Doing what?"

"Invoicing."

"Oh." He looked genuinely disappointed. "What about college?"

"I still think about going sometimes. To I.U., but—" Again, he stopped himself. Who was he kidding? His college aspirations, like all the others, had pretty much drifted off the radar screen. The silence seemed deafening. He glanced up at the barren mantle. "Still working at Luffkin?"

"Yup, yup." Dad nodded.

As Adam stared into his pasty face against the flowered wing chair, he caught a glimpse of himself a few years down the road. Just like him, Dad had bigger-than-life dreams that had imploded to debris, and this was what was left of them. Two broken men with empty mantels.

It had taken Adam a while to get to this place, but he was there now. His father had committed unforgiveable wrongs, to be sure, but Adam had come to realize that everyone did, and usually to the people they loved the most. Who was he to be the judge and jury? Unforgiveness was an unbearable weight.

"Hey, Dad. I just wanted you to know, for what it's worth, that I, uh … I love you."

In that instant, his father's face was like a cactus suddenly blooming. The most amazing thing. There it was, a shoot of life.

On the long drive back to Langston, "Moon River" popped into Adam's head; Aunt Clarry's favorite song. Andy Williams' version had gotten popular a year before she died, and she used to sing along with it on the radio.

Adam dreamed of her off and on. They were always good dreams, a respite from the Vietnam night terrors. In his dreams,

Auntie knew just the right things to say and do, and he'd wake up smiling, then drift peacefully back to sleep like a tucked-in child.

Maybe dreams were part of the grand design to help people work things out. Or divine visitations. Who knew?

Back at his apartment, Adam watched the presidential election returns on TV without bothering to turn on a lamp or the sound. He poured himself a Jack Daniel's. Nixon was winning—a landslide victory over George McGovern—no surprise. The newscasters were saying that Nixon was certain to end the Vietnam War during his second term; a promise he'd been breaking for years. His face filled the television screen—fleshy jowls jiggling back and forth as his raised arms flashed the peace sign, his darting little black eyes growing smaller whenever his grin expanded. *Happy man.*

Adam took a sip, his own little stab at happiness. It tasted like water, dead and flat. Even Jack Daniel's had lost its *raison d'être*, as his old friend Sartre might put it.

The phone rang, and he glanced at the clock. Nine p.m. Noël called the same time every night. Sometimes he picked the receiver up, sometimes not. Tonight, he wouldn't. He didn't feel like talking about his reunion with their father.

Noël was as adrift as he was. After she'd left Ziemny, her son became her lone mission. It wasn't easy for her, a single mom with no real work skills. If it wasn't for food stamps, church pantries, and subsidized housing, he wasn't sure how she would've survived. Living in Bedlington for the past few years, she waitressed at some lace-curtained, folksy diner called Best of Cluck, owned by a silver-haired widower with diamond rings on his fingers, thirty years her senior, who maintained a chain of chicken-themed joints across Ohio. For being candy on his arm when required, she got job security and daytime hours.

After meeting him once, Adam was pretty certain that the only action inside the old rooster's pants was his over-stuffed wallet. He hated the degrading arrangement his sister was cornered into, but she was the sole breadwinner, bound and determined to send her son to medical school one day and numbing herself for duty's sake. She refused to even consider marrying again after Ziemny. "The Trudeaus are like mourning doves," she said. "We mate for life."

The tune from "Moon River" still drifting through Adam's head, he took another sip. Seeing his father today had been his last act of unfinished business. He was glad, for Dad's sake, that he'd made the trip. To die unloved was to die before death.

Now what? There was nothing left on Adam's list.

He didn't know exactly when the idea infiltrated his brain like a fever coming on. Maybe it was right then while he was watching Julie Nixon kiss her happy daddy.

It wasn't exactly a brainstorm. He'd been gravitating toward it for years now, since Vietnam. But the time was never right; there was always something left to do. So, he'd just kept it there, simmering on the back burner like a pot of stew. Now that the idea was out in front, out there in the open, he couldn't let it go.

He toyed with it the rest of the night.

He could drown himself, but that seemed too harsh, to throw himself in frigid water and die frozen to the bone. He kept a pistol in his bureau drawer, but suppose he fired a bad shot? Besides, shooting your brains out was so needlessly messy.

Actually, the method of choice was never in doubt. He'd learned about a lethal combination back in Nam—just the right mixture of pills and booze so that death came slow and sure. Over the last few years, he'd been stockpiling pills. Doctors were easy to manipulate when you knew which buttons to push.

He watched Tricky Dicky take his bows.

≈≈

The Spanish moss blowing in an otherworldly wind, Adam was sitting on a blanket under the cypress tree with his brothers and Noël, while Pastor Ray preached at the revival. Beside Adam, Bo batted his paddleball, a streak of a hundred in a row.

In the big tent, less than ten feet away, his mother and Auntie listened with all the others.

*"Each of us has a piece of God inside of us—a different aspect, a different nuance, a purposeful and unique expression of his love." Pastor Ray clutched his torn-up Bible as he spoke. "And God is the sum of these pieces, the sum of us. So, when we hate a piece, harm a piece, disregard a piece, we break the chain, we break the very body of God. Because God **is** Love." Each word poured from his mouth slow as honey, forceful as fire. "Only love grieves. Only love saves. Only love sacrifices. Only love forgives. Only love dares. Only love lasts. In love we are born, and to love we return. Don't you see, my friends? When we don't love too much, then we don't love enough."*

Adam's eyes cracked open.

He was back in his rented room again, no longer a starry-eyed boy. Even as he stared at the blank white walls, he could still smell the scent of the cypress tree, feel the wind on his face.

He stumbled into the bathroom, started shaving. The vivid dream fading, his bold idea from the night before resurfaced, sizzling in his mind as he gazed at his own reflection in the mirror of the medicine chest. By the time he headed for work, he was on an unstoppable course.

He couldn't concentrate on anything else. The papers in front of him blurred into unreadable lines. The clock hands pointed to some meaningless numbers. The only real thing was the urgency he felt. He got up from his desk and walked out of his cubicle. Past the clacking typewriters. Past the smoky breakroom. Past the sound of flushing urinals in the men's room. Never again would he have to spend another minute in that dreary office. Outside, on the way to his truck, he inhaled the stench of the Langston air.

Noël and his little nephew, his namesake, were his only regrets. And, now, his father too. Because of them, he would not die unloved. Still, even the thought of them couldn't keep him from his appointed task.

His next stop was the bank. Withdrawing all his money, he opened two interest accounts in the savings and loan across the street, one in Noël's name and the other in Adam's. He'd been able to save up quite a bit over the last few years in anticipation of his own college plans. But giving it all away felt even better. Little Adam would be a proper doctor one day with two arms, and Noël, at least for a while, wouldn't have to sell herself to any more sugar daddies just to get by.

He waited until it got dark. He wanted to see the stars. He wasn't sure why.

It was a balmy night. Night had an honesty all its own, much more so than a sunny blue sky. A bright moon loomed overhead. A row of stars blinked. In his smallness, he felt connected to them. He, too, was a tiny speck of light that must matter somewhere in the scheme of things.

Tomorrow night at this time, he would be dead; the world would be going on without him. His place in it would close over, and a new life would be born somewhere else, bloody and bawling. And the cars would still be rolling along the highways. And Tricky Dick would still be flashing his *V*-signs. And war would go on ad infinitum. And new visionaries would come along who dared to change this fallen, broken world, only to find out the hard way that no one person could. Unless we all change, nothing changed.

How did this world get so broken? What did *fallen* really mean? Did it mean fallen as if from a high place, the way their mother had fallen and shattered like a tea cup? Could we ever get back to that high place? or must we be broken to return?

Endless questions ran through his mind: What would become of him afterward? Would he be one of the stars? Would he cease to be anything at all?

Adam didn't have any answers, just questions, perennial questions, and that seemed like enough. The questions were what we came here to find. The answers unknowable.

Maybe he'd go straight to hell. But if a flawed man like him could find his way to forgiving his father, surely God would forgive him too. Adam had seen the face of Jesus Christ during too many tent revivals to believe that the God of Love would send him, or anyone else, to a hell worse than this one.

When he went back inside, he ran a hot bath to smell clean for the undertaker. The fresh lanolin scent of the soap saturated his nostrils. The tiny facets of the bubbles sparkled like miniature crystals under the bathroom light. Slipping down into the warm, bubbly water felt as soothing as sliding back inside the womb. How ironic that doing simple things for the last time was every bit as fascinating as the first; there was an eternal symmetry in that.

Afterward, he dressed himself up in his best white shirt and blue jeans. There were only a couple things left to do. He took it out from his top dresser drawer and slipped it into the same envelope with the bank books, then scribbled Noël's name on it, along with a one-lined note.

Next, he opened the tiny bottles, one by one; it was difficult to uncap some of them with only one hand, but he managed to assemble the optimum dose and emptied the capsules into a full glass of booze. His final, lethal cocktail. He was ready.

He held out his hand, steady as a board. What a damned good surgeon he would have made.

He gulped the Jack Daniel's quickly.

A dizziness seized him, almost immediately. Lying back with his head upon the pillow, he waited.

A surge of unexpected memories swirled out of nowhere, pulling him along in their wave. He saw himself rescuing Arthur Conley from being bullied, handing his car keys over to Noël for her escape, saving countless lives in Vietnam, his father's blooming cactus face, two new bank books. In the mist of remembering, he heard it. His phone ringing, urgent and insistent. Instinctively, he knew it was Cynthia.

But it was too late. He was already floating away. Floating, floating, down Moon River.

THIRTY

NOVEMBER 1972
LEON

A S he sat reading the newspaper in his upstairs apartment, Leon was interrupted every so often by the sound of tires straining for traction on the slick street below. A Saturday night, Stella was asleep in the bedroom, opting to stay over because of the snowstorm, even though the Minczewskis' house was less than a mile away. The first time she'd stayed the whole night, her parents had pitched a fit, but over time they got used to the arrangement. It was a moot point; in two months they'd officially be man and wife, with more than two hundred guests set to witness the nuptials.

His landlady was a different story. From the beginning, she'd warned him that overnight female guests were strictly taboo, so they concealed Stella's extended visits from her. It wasn't difficult to do since the old brick house was built solid and soundproof.

He was almost finished with the local section when he stumbled across a small article. Scanning the headline, "Suicide Suspected in Death of Vietnam Veteran," he read on:

Vietnam veteran Adam Trudeau, 24, was found dead in his home yesterday after an apparent suicide from a drug overdose. An autopsy has been ordered to determine the cause of death, but it is believed that Trudeau ingested a lethal combination of drugs and alcohol. He served as a combat medic in Vietnam and was honorably discharged in 1968 after sustaining an injury.

Dr. Timothy Addams, deputy county coroner, said there was no evidence of foul play. Trudeau was born on May 25, 1948, in Hyssop, Louisiana, and he had lived in Langston for three years. He is survived by his father, Jack Trudeau of Willow, Ohio; a brother, Steve Trudeau, of San Diego, California; a sister, Noël Trudeau, of Bedlington, Ohio; one nephew and one niece. Services for Trudeau will be at 10:00 a.m. on Friday, November 17, at the First Baptist Church in Bedlington, Ohio. Burial will be in the Garden of Resurrection Cemetery in Willow, Ohio. Friends may call at Green's Funeral Parlor in Willow from 6 to 8 p.m. on Thursday.

Leon reread the short article, dissecting every word, reminding himself for a moment of the way he'd read Noël's goodbye note. His pulse accelerated each time he got to her name (*Noël spells Leon in reverse …*). He searched his pocket for a cigarette. One of the main reasons he took this apartment was because his landlady allowed him to smoke inside.

So, Adam really killed himself. It should have been unbelievable, but it wasn't. Since the day he met him, Leon had sensed a day like this was coming.

He read the article again, staring at her name in black and white. (*Noël spells Leon in reverse …*) For the first time in more than four years, he knew exactly where she would be from six to eight p.m. next Thursday, and ten a.m. on Friday.

What if he showed up at the funeral parlor? He played it out in his mind.

Taking the cigarette from between his lips, he rested it against the side of the ashtray. It was a dumb idea. She was no longer using his name; she was *Noël Trudeau* again. But surely she had to be with some other guy by now. He read it again. She was living in Bedlington. What caused her to move there? Probably whatever guy she was with.

It was a dumb idea. She would be standing there weeping over her brother's open coffin—open because he took pills, he didn't blow out his brains—while another man comforted her. When he came traipsing in, she'd give him a look that said, *What do you think you're doing here?* And he'd think the same thing and get torn up all over again.

Stella wrapped her arms around his shoulders from behind, and he nearly jumped out of his skin. "Sorry, sweetie." She said. "I didn't mean to startle you."

Pushing the newspaper out of her sight, he knocked over the ashtray, spilling the sooty contents all over the shag carpet, including his lit cigarette. He stomped it out, leaving a little black hole in the fibers.

She stooped down to help him wipe up the mess.

"I'll clean it up," he said. "I've dropped this thing before."

She nodded, her eyes showing way too much concern for the situation at hand.

"They're only ashes." He struggled to remain calm.

"Maybe so." She searched his face. "But ashes can turn into sparks."

≈≈

By the time Monday morning rolled around, Leon had returned to his senses. The hell with Noël Trudeau. What was the point of messing up his life for the chance to see her again?

The decision to nix the trip to Willow gave him some relief, but not anywhere near enough. Doing his job was mission impossible. "What's the matter with you today, Ziemny?" one of the guys finally asked. "You got your head screwed on backward or something?"

Leon walked outside the plant for a breath of fresh air; as fresh as it got anyway under the churning chimneys of the steel mills. That guy was right—he must have a loose screw.

The next thing he knew, he was marching into his boss's office, informing Buzz that he needed to take Friday off to take care of some pending business. "And this business just came up all of a sudden?" Buzz asked. After reminding him that in only two months, he'd be taking a full week off for his honeymoon, he relented without much of a fuss. "Just take the goddamned day off, Ziemny."

Leon began the long drive to Willow shortly after dawn on Friday. The temperature had been tepid enough to melt Saturday night's snowfall, yet despite the warmth, the sky was pinkish; sailor's warning. The scenery was desolate, the vibrant autumn colors already disintegrated to drab, lifeless brown. Most of the trees stood barren.

He switched on the car radio. "Ain't No Sunshine" was playing, a divinely depressing song from the previous year that had reminded him of Noël from the first time he'd heard it. Most every song did.

He passed the familiar landmarks as he drove—the Union Bank in the center of the small town of Hampton; Buckie's Ice Cream Castle, where he, Noël, and Adam had once stopped for hotdogs, now closed for the season, piles of leaves trapped beneath the abandoned picnic tables. At the intersection of US 127 and the final turn west toward Willow stood the Crossroads Café, an ominous name.

By the time he reached the Garden of Resurrection, a green tent had already been erected. Rolling to a stop, he realized Noël wouldn't recognize this car; long ago he'd traded in the flashy Mustang he bought when they were married. He looked down at his watch. He'd miscalculated. The funeral service was starting in Bedlington about now. It'd be a couple of hours, give or take, before the entourage arrived.

He got out of the car, walked through the crackling leaves toward Adam's awaiting grave. The once-lush weeping willow trees on the far end of the cemetery looked dead this time of year, their drooping yellow fronds sparse, like the thinning hair of an old crone. Halting at the covered hole awaiting Adam, he crossed himself, recited a short version of Hail Mary. "Sorry it ended for you this way," he said. "But it was a rotten thing to do to her."

He walked a wide circle around the cemetery, reading the inscriptions that Noël loved, until he ended up where he'd started from, pausing at the sight of the Xs scratched on her Aunt Clarissa's headstone. Retrieving an old nail file that Stella kept in his glovebox, he tried as best he could to rub the Xs out.

It was about twelve-thirty when he spied the procession from the confines of his car, a long trail of high beams, like a lighted snake wending through the winding road. His heart raced like a wild man's.

He was parked far enough away to see people leaving their vehicles, but not clearly-defined faces. He spotted her; she was dressed in black from head to toe, a veil covering her face. No one was comforting or supporting her. Little Adam—was it really him?— shuffled through the leaves beside her. He'd grown up, eight years old already; no longer the toddler he remembered.

It felt like a million years since they were his.

He glanced over the others behind them. Her father had turned into an old *dzia-dzia*. An inconsolable girl with long blonde hair sobbed between two people who appeared to be her parents. Adam's old girlfriend?

Slowly, as quietly as he could, he stepped closer until he reached the back row of mourners. A few people turned around to notice him, but not her, not her father, both sitting in the chairs in front of the flag-draped coffin, their backs toward him. In the third chair sat a tall, dark-haired man who resembled Noël and Adam enough to reassure Leon that it was her brother, Steve, the one from California.

"The Lord is my shepherd; I shall not want." The minister prayed. "Surely goodness and mercy shall follow me all the days of my life, and I shall dwell in the house of the Lord forever."

The American flag was lifted from Adam's casket and ceremoniously folded by a few old veterans before being presented to Noël's father. Assembling in a single line, the mourners each deposited a long-stemmed carnation on top of the newly exposed, shiny surface of the coffin. One old woman left a stethoscope in lieu of a carnation. Careful to avoid her father's attention, Leon focused on the back of Noël's head, watching her rise from her seat and, hand in hand with the blonde girl, place the final carnation.

The service was over. How was he going to make his move?

As the mourners dispersed, Noël lingered in her chair, her head bowed. Steve went to her again, whispering in her ear; he seemed to be persuading her to leave with the others as he pointed to the cars. After exchanging a few more words, he returned to the black limo without her, Adam at his side. Leon noticed that a car had been left for her, her dead brother's same old beater.

Now was his chance.

His steps made no sound on the tarp as he approached. When he sat down beside her, her black-gloved fingers sprang to her lips, and she let out a sound—half sigh, half moan. Her head falling against his shoulder, she wept and wept and wept. Leon breathed in her scent; she still smelled like lilacs.

Slowly, he lifted the black veil to reveal her face. "Why did you leave me?" he heard himself asking.

≈≈

He drove her to a coffee shop in town. After the waitress filled their coffee mugs, Noël asked about Ricky. "He's okay." Leon left it at that.

"Has he forgiven you?"

"Yes."

"I knew he would."

After that, she mostly talked about her own brother, shaken beyond grief that she wasn't there to prevent his death.

"You couldn't have stopped him," he told her with more than a twinge of guilt for being the one who'd spilled the family secrets to Adam. "You can't give someone else the will to live."

"It's not fair what life did to him," she said. "Before this war, he had so many plans."

It distressed her when she learned he was going to marry Stella on the third Saturday in January. "So, there's still a Stella?" she asked herself more than him before answering her own question. "Well, of course there is."

Things were blurring for him. Even though she was in front of him, this seemed like a fantasy often imagined before he went to sleep at night. They'd not spoken one word of love, yet their connection was undeniable, unaltered by time. They didn't look at each other as they talked; they penetrated each other.

The other patrons seemed to notice too. Whenever Leon became aware of them, they were staring with knotted eyebrows, not bothering to look elsewhere. The waitress slapped the bill on the table, walked away.

"What's her problem?" Leon asked.

"I guess she thinks I have some nerve being here with you when I just buried my brother," Noël whispered. "That's what living in a small town is like."

"Then let's get the hell out of here." He got up from the table, wondering all the while where on earth they could possibly go. The only thing he could think of was to take her away to the Moonstone Inn and sort out their lives there.

He'd first discovered the Moonstone Inn on a long drive he took alone on a Sunday afternoon shortly after she'd left him, her words echoing in his head—among the last she'd said to him—about wishing they were off by themselves, on the moon. It was nothing fancy, just a small, run-down, old-English-style motel that sat on a narrow two-lane winding road out in the middle of nowhere, nothing around it except for Lake Michigan, right across the street.

When he mentioned the Moonstone Inn to her outside the diner, her eyes lit up. "Can we really get away like that?"

"Of course we can. We can do anything we want."

Without so much as an embrace between them, he drove her back to her car at the cemetery. Adam was with Steve and his family at a motel down the road, she said, the only lodging in town. They were planning to leave the next day for San Diego, where Adam would stay with them a couple days by himself before she joined him. She told him she was remaining behind to tie up some loose ends in Bedlington, including quitting her job. She planned to remain in San Diego through Christmas.

The Moonstone Inn idea sounded far-fetched as soon as he was away from her eyes. He felt disoriented, completely out of place and time, and he had to stop to calculate what day it was. Was this really happening, or was he dreaming? He had to figure things out. Tomorrow was Saturday, a workday; his shift started at seven a.m. sharp. How would he explain wanting the extra time off to Buzz— to Stella?

Stella seemed a distant figure from a past life. What was he doing to her? Already he was considering the ramifications of canceling another wedding. What about Ricky?

Everything was getting foggy, except the one, glaring, God's honest truth: He was in love with Noël Trudeau. He always had been, always would be. He could tell it was the same for her. Maybe love wasn't even a strong enough word to describe the cosmic pull between them.

Whatever it was, they had no choice but to follow wherever it led.

≈≈

He stopped by Rose's Drugstore to buy a carton of cigarettes, some throwaway razors, a toothbrush, toothpaste, a comb, shaving cream, and a few other incidentals to take with him to the Moonstone Inn.

"Just passing through?" the clerk at the counter asked him as he rung up his purchases, eyeing him as if he'd already heard gossip.

"Just passing through." Leon nodded. "Got a pay phone around here?"

"In the back."

At the rear of the store, Leon found a phone booth beside an old-fashioned soda fountain in a room with hardwood floors and ceiling fans. He deposited enough change to call Buzz. Phoning him so late in the evening from this throwback place felt odd, incongruous. Who was this man, this *Buzz* he was calling, and why on earth did he require his permission to abdicate his own life?

When he asked for the days off, Buzz bit his head off. "You could've at least given me more fucking notice, Ziemny! When the hell are you planning to be back?"

"Thursday. I'll be back on Thursday."

"That's Thanksgiving."

"It is?" Another complication. "Then I'll be there Friday."

Once Buzz excused the time off, the rest of his assorted words went unheard. Leon was already contemplating the next call, the one to Stella.

By that time, he was almost certain their wedding would never happen, but he couldn't break the news on a pay phone in the middle of a soda shop. Instead, he stammered around, telling her something similar to what he'd told Buzz, that he had some out-of-town business to attend to before the wedding, something he'd been putting off.

Her voice was so soft that he had to shove the receiver tight against his ear to make out the words. "But I don't understand what you're doing," she said. "Where are you?"

"I'm in Michigan." He lied.

"When will you be home?"

"Sometime on Wednesday. I really have to go now."

"So, you'll be home for Thanksgiving?"

"Of course I will."

"Leon?" Her voice got suddenly louder. "Are you sure you're not in Ohio?"

"Ohio? Why would I be in Ohio?"

It was difficult to get away from her questions without hanging up on her outright. He was grateful when the operator did it for him, demanding two more dollars for a few more minutes of conversation. "I don't have any more change, Stella. I'll see you later." He hung up, pretending she wasn't already on to him. Come Wednesday night, she would hear the whole truth and nothing but.

"You a friend of Noël Trudeau's?" The clerk finally got up the balls to ask him on the way out.

"Nope." Leon looked straight into his meddling face. "I'm her husband."

≈≈

It was a dark night; the sky thick with clouds. Since there was only one motel in town and Noël and her family were in it, Leon drove his car into the Garden of Resurrection, the one place he knew he wouldn't be bothered, and parked on the road beside the Trudeau plot.

He visited Adam's grave. A red satin ribbon, "Beloved brother" rested on top of the heap of flowers.

Stooping down, he stroked the ribbon. "I'm not very good at apologies," he said. "But here goes. I know life didn't turn out the way you hoped. And I'm sorry if I added to whatever made you do this. I'm as sorry as I can be. But I love your sister. God almighty, I love her." He looked up at the moon. "Anyway, I hope you can finally rest in peace. And I hope you don't mind if I keep you company tonight."

Scrunched in the backseat of his car and covered by his coat, Leon had strange dreams—Adam's face was flush against his back window, and he was tapping on the glass. Funny thing was, he had two arms. When Leon lifted the knob to let him in, Adam gave him a nod, one single, approving nod, then backed away and slipped under the pile of flowers.

Leon arrived at the motel around ten the next morning. Noël was packed, ready to go. Since she was going to take a bus directly from Bedlington to O'Hare airport, she asked Leon if he would drive her back to Bedlington after their stay at the Moonstone Inn. She'd made arrangements to leave her car at the motel in Willow, where she'd pick it up when she returned from California.

"No problem." Leon lifted her small suitcase into the trunk.

She opened her purse and pulled out a little box. "Before you start the car, I have something for you."

"What is it?"

"It's something Adam left to me. But I want you to have it."

"You sure?" Leon took off the lid. A gold tie-bar in the shape of a boat gleamed in the sunlight, "Kennedy 60" written across it, the one Robert Kennedy had given to Adam on the plane.

"Remember the day we saw Bobby in your neighborhood?—how he stood on the car and quoted Tennyson? My brother was wearing it that day." Her eyes misted. "Anyway, that was Adam's final note. He put this pin in an envelope with my name on it and wrote: *'Keep seeking a newer world.'*"

Leon leaned over and kissed her cheek. "No more seeking." He fastened the pin to his tie. "That's what the Moonstone Inn will be."

≈≈

It was still there, thank God, and still called the Moonstone Inn. All the way to Michigan, Leon was afraid it might have closed down by then. It was more dilapidated than he'd remembered, but it sat directly across the street from Lake Michigan which more than made up for its shabbiness. Noël sat up straight when she saw it, her eyes flashing a variety of feelings, not unlike her expression the night they found their hotel in Chicago. "Our own little cottage by the sea," she said.

A sign hung on the office door instructing guests to register at the Shell station in town, less than a half-mile away.

Once they found it, Leon went inside and paid the clerk upfront for four nights. The guy gazed down at the bills in his palm as if it was the most money he'd seen in a while. "The motel is empty right now," he said. "Come summertime, we're plenty busy, but not so much this time of year." He handed Leon the room key. "I'll give you the best room in the house, a great view of the lake."

"Are there any restaurants around here?"

"Just down the street, there's a local diner. Nothing fancy, but great food." He shoved a registry book in front of him to sign. "In case you get calls or something." Though Leon knew that was impossible, he didn't feel like pressing the point. Instead, he scribbled "Mr. and Mrs. Ziemny."

Noël was dreamy-eyed when he returned to the car holding the room key. "Room 1811?" she asked, recalling their Chicago hotel room number.

"Not hardly. Looks like we'll be the only guests."

He stopped the car in front of the rustic shingle marked "Room 4," and grabbed her suitcase out of the trunk. Swinging open the door, he inhaled a mixture of must and air freshener, the same scent he bought at the car wash to hang from the rearview mirror. He set her suitcase down beside the bed.

Noël stepped across the threshold slowly, her eyes scanning the room. There were two yellowing vinyl chairs, probably once white, standing in front of the large window overlooking the lake. The double bed was covered with a flowered pink bedspread that reeked of the room.

"It's not exactly room 1811, is it?" He carefully removed the PT-109 clasp before pulling off his tie and tossing his suit coat on the back of the vinyl chair.

"It's even better." She moved toward him. "It's our very own moon." Pressing her open lips against his mouth, she slid them down his neck.

The unexpected gesture unleashed the unbearable yearning he'd been trying to restrain. At last, they were alone together in this deserted place in the middle of nowhere. Far away from Willow, from Langston, from suicide, from divorce.

Melding together on top of the bed, they disappeared into that indescribable somewhere.

≈≈

When she finally awoke twelve hours later, her eyes looked bright and refreshed, the way they used to when they were first married. Stretching out beneath the sheets in contentment, she smiled at him. "I'm starving!"

He sat up against the headboard beside her, dipping into the little stash of food they'd picked up along the way. They spread processed cheese and Canadian bacon on saltine crackers, fed them to each other, and washed them down with root beer, kissing in-between bites just to reassure themselves that the other was flesh-and-blood. "Why in God's name did you ever leave me?" he asked her again as they entwined under the sheets.

He had to keep reminding himself that beyond this room, the real world waited just a few hours away. But it wasn't working. The Moonstone Inn was a parallel realm of existence. All other dimensions were figments of a meaningless reality.

Later, they crossed the road, deserted except for the flurry of gold and crimson leaves blowing in circular movements across the gravel, and headed out to the lake, raising their coat collars to their chins to cut the sting of the November wind. He couldn't figure out why the leaves were still colorful here, not brown and brittle like everywhere else. They stumbled down a stony path toward the water, the waves beating against the large rocks lining the lakefront.

There wasn't really a beach, just some sand littered with sharp stones, broken twigs, and forsaken shells. The sound of the water swooshed in their ears as they climbed to a flat spot on one of the larger rocks and sat down, the waves crashing against its base. As she gazed out at the lake, her eyes became translucent.

"What are you thinking about?" he asked.

"I'm thinking about—right now," she replied. "That's all there is."

≈≈

Afterward, they walked a mile to the greasy spoon, where they ate an early dinner. The other patrons looked like locals who frequented the Chuck Wagon, with sun-ravaged faces gone pale in the off-season, acknowledging one another by first names. The "daily special" was all the fried chicken and clams you could eat. As small as she was, Noël consumed more than he did.

Her mood was one he'd not seen before. She was radiant, glowing, as if she didn't have a care in the world—laughing often, not once mentioning her dead brother, playing with the strands of her hair like she was flirting with him. Unbelievable as it seemed, her sadness had vanished. The only time she got reflective was after she slid a dime in the jukebox, choosing the Association's old song, "Everything That Touches You."

As Leon watched her standing alone, he was overcome with desire to dance with her. Crossing the room, he didn't care what the others thought. He took her hand in his, and they moved together in front of the jukebox; her head against his shoulder.

When they returned to the booth, a woman with dyed orange hair approached. "Are you newlyweds?"

"How did you know?" Noël beamed, then proceeded to go into great detail about their imaginary wedding, much more than the woman could've cared to hear. Noël gushed about their beautiful candlelight ceremony at St. Stan's, how his father had escorted her down the aisle, the single red rose she carried. Listening to her tell it, Leon almost believed it actually happened.

After dinner, they walked leisurely back to the motel, hand in hand.

"A single red rose, huh?" he teased. "But, you know what, that reminds me of something. Theckla told me she planted a rosebush in our honor, and she said it's got the biggest, most beautiful red roses she's ever seen."

"Mrs. Chavis?" She stopped walking, her eyes enlarging. "You still talk to Mrs. Chavis?"

He nodded. "I call her every now and then."

"Oh, my God, Leon!" She grabbed his coat collar. "Where on earth is she? I've tried and tried to find her!"

"She and Freddie moved back to Alabama a month or so after we split. I helped them pack up the place. Freddie passed away last year."

"No! Oh, no. Is she okay?"

"You know Theckla. Somehow, who knows how, she's always okay."

The next night, long after the sun went down, they crossed the road and climbed atop their rock. The lake water was like clear black glass, reflecting a full moon with a hazy yellowish halo.

Leon crossed his arms around her, her back against his chest as they gazed up at the sky, the lake breezes playing with their hair, the lulling sound of the water lapping against the rock. It reminded him of that night in their apartment. They were sitting the same way, in the same position, only then they were on the inside looking out at the falling snow outside their picture window, not assimilated into nature, like now.

Dark and light clouds were rolling over the moon's surface, a dramatic sight, mirrored on the surface of the water. The longer he stared at the moon, the more it seemed it was sailing through the sky, trying to outpace the clouds. The longer he stared, it felt like they were gliding too, as if their rock was floating further and further out to sea, unanchored.

As he kept gazing up at that gigantic moon, the more potent and illusory the feeling became. He felt weightless, bodiless, pulled out of time. This wasn't a Monday; there was no such thing. They were drifting among the stars, the only two people in the universe.

"I wish we could stay like this forever," she said.

Their final full day at the Moonstone Inn turned out to be warmer, though still chilly enough to require coats. They made the short trek to the lake and perched atop their rock. Today was the day they'd reserved for a special purpose—to work out the details of their new life together. As a symbolic gesture, Leon took the PT-109 tie clasp out of his pocket and held it up.

As she gazed at it, he detected a hint of that familiar melancholy of hers returning.

But he was ready for this conversation, more than ready. He'd been thinking about little else for the last few days, and he knew exactly how they should to do it. "I'll break things off with Stella tomorrow night," he said.

"The night before Thanksgiving? Ouch. How brutal for her to have the same thing happen twice."

"I know, but it's got to be done, and it's better to just get it over with. It's my fault, not hers."

"*Our* fault." She corrected.

"It's nobody's fault. It's just the way it is, that's all."

"I'm afraid, Leon."

"Afraid of what?"

"Well, lots of things. About hurting Rick again. I'm afraid that he and your mother and all your relatives and neighbors—and maybe even your father this time around—will hate me, hate us, even more than they did before."

"They won't hate us." He said the words slowly. As he considered what she was saying, he played out their likely reactions in his head—the horror in his mother's face when he broke the news; Stella's hysterical sobs. He'd already imagined Ricky's mournful eyes a million times over. His brother had forgiven him, that was true, but would it stay that that way if she came back into their lives? Despite his best efforts to force them out of his head, the images of their faces had been haunting Leon since he arrived at the Moonstone Inn. "So what if they hate us? This isn't about them. This is about you and me."

Noël gave him an unbelieving look. "Maybe here in this place, it's just about you and me. But we both know it's about them too, and always has been. Worst of all, I'm afraid that *you'll* end up hating me."

" Me? I could never hate you."

"You say that now, but don't you remember how you wouldn't even look at me when we were cutting our wedding cake at your mother's party?"

He abhorred the memory of that day.

"I'm a mess, Leon. I know I am. An even bigger mess than when we met. It'll take me a long time to get over my brother's suicide, if I ever do. And I'm afraid that I won't be able to be the wife you deserve."

"You're more than I deserve."

She smiled sadly.

"I'll get my apartment ready while you're in California," he said. "I'm living upstairs in an old house. We can get married right away, as soon as you get back."

"So, your apartment is in your old neighborhood? Close to everyone who'll hate us for what we're doing?"

He shrugged.

"Does it have a big enough bedroom for Adam?"

"Well, I'm using the extra room as a junk room right now. Cleaning it out won't be a problem, if we end up staying there. It's not a huge room, but I think it'll be big enough."

She looked out at the sea. "Adam is in third grade now, you know. He's not a baby anymore."

He lifted her chin to face him. "I promise you, I'll be a better father this time around. That's one thing I've been thinking about since you left me. I'm ready to be a father now. I know I can be a good one, if you'll both give me another chance. I'll look for another place while you're gone, with the biggest room for Adam that I can afford."

Leaning against him, she wound her arm through his.

The waves lapped against the rock. A few passing seagulls screeched overhead.

"You know what I've been thinking about lately?" she said. "I've been thinking that it might be nice to go somewhere brand-new, like San Diego, where there's sunshine all the time and everything looks different."

"You want to move to California?" Her comment surprised

him, shook him, really. He stared at her without expression, uncertain how to reply.

She nodded. "Steve says they have great schools and state colleges there. It's important to me that Adam goes to medical school when the time comes." She looked up at the sky, then back at him. "Leon, let's do it! Let's go away to California together! We really could start again over there. It'll be a new world, a fresh start for all of us."

Joy exploding on her face, she grabbed his shoulders, accidentally jarring the PT-109 pin loose from his hand and into the rushing water.

She gasped. For a moment he was afraid she was going to jump off the rock after it, and he held her back. "It's gone," he said.

The foamy water churned on, indifferent. They both sensed the irrevocable.

"I'm sorry I suggested California," she said, after a long pause. "I know your life is in Langston."

"Well, I have a job there. A good job. I can retire when I'm forty-eight, with a great pension."

"I know." Another lengthy silence intervened. "Leon, I love you. I loved you from the moment I saw you. You gave me something I didn't think was possible. You gave me the best I can ask from this life. Even the night I found out Adam killed himself, I kept thinking about you so that I wouldn't go crazy. I thought about Wigilia and the Christmas Eve we were together. And your father, your wonderful father. I wished you were here with me, and now you are here. And now I wish we could stay at the Moonstone Inn forever." There was a strange, expectant expression on her face, as if she was waiting for him to tell her that remaining there was an option.

"But I know we can't." Her face dissolved in sorrow.

He stared off into the horizon. He couldn't go through it all again, the tumult of breaking his world apart for her, only to be left alone in the end. He couldn't live through her leaving him a second time, and it felt like she was already starting to.

"Do you love Stella?" she asked.

The unexpected question threw him. For the better part of the last six years, fate had caused him to contemplate, at one stage or another, a lifetime with Stella. For whatever reason, Stella had outlasted the other women. She was easy to be with, subtle, like the drapes she'd picked out for their living room, off-white, going with anything, not a splash of purple like Noël. Life with Noël Trudeau would be an uphill climb; he knew that. Life with Stella Minczewski promised to be an old, soft easy chair.

"Well, sure—I must love her."

"I never loved any man besides you." She started to cry. "You see, everything's worse now, more complicated. You're in love with her now."

"I didn't say I was in love with her! I've never been in love with anyone but you." His eyes glazed on the water. So, what was he trying to say? Maybe that there were two kinds of love—the love you could live with, and the love you couldn't live without.

She bit her lip. "Tell me what you love about her."

"I don't know. I guess the fact that she sticks by me, no matter what."

She threw her head back, as if he'd landed a punch. "Unlike me?"

He didn't reply.

"Well, maybe I did love another man too, besides you." The blood rushed into her cheeks. "I loved your brother." She drew out each word for emphasis, then searched his face as if to assure that she'd reciprocated and wounded him in kind. She had. Her eyes flooded with remorse. "I loved him like a twin soul, like another brother. He's the part of your father who inherited his Holocaust pain. And you, you're the part that's the survivor." She reached out for his hand. "How could I help loving Rick when he's the one who led me straight to you?"

"He never got over you," Leon said. "My brother is a dreamer and a drunk. A bad combination, if you ask me. Maybe an inevitable one."

"Do you blame me for making him an alcoholic?" Her voice was filled with self-recrimination.

"My brother drank long before you came into his life." He didn't say out loud the rest of what he was thinking; he knew she suspected it anyway. That their marriage was the catalyst that had caused Ricky's drinking to spiral out of control. It was a burden they'd both carry to their graves.

A large flock of seagulls cried out on the rocky shore.

"Marry Stella," she said. "I mean it."

Her words stung. More than stung.

"She'll keep you living on more than cigarettes. She loves you, not the way I do, but in a safe, secure, and sane way. I'll be happy knowing you're playing poker in the garage with the other men at all the parties to come."

He looked at her blankly. He felt like he'd been rammed in the stomach by a Mack truck. He didn't expect the conversation to go this way. He expected them to talk about getting back together and discussing the best plan to do it. He knew going through that upheaval all over again would be hell. But he didn't expect this to happen, that they would even consider going their separate ways after the Moonstone Inn. "What about us?"

"I left you for a reason," she said. "I wanted you to find peace. And I still want that. I couldn't bear it if we failed again, and we ruined even the memories."

"So, you'd rather hang on to what was rather than what could be?"

"Maybe."

There was a sudden chill in the wind.

"Where do all the best dreams go?" she asked. "My brother's surgeon dreams? Bobby Kennedy's newer world? Martin Luther King's promised land? They have to go somewhere, don't they?" Her eyes appeared endless blue, like the water. "Wherever they go," she turned around wistfully to look at the motel, "we have a house there."

He didn't understand her; the words were meaningless. It was finally dawning on him that the Moonstone Inn was a stolen time. All along, he was fighting to believe they had a future, but the battle was already lost. He tried to imagine their tenth wedding anniversary. Cheering together at Adam's ballgames. He tried to picture her getting old. He couldn't form any of the images. Not one.

He stared at her, sightless. Who was she? Maybe she was from some parallel world, a dream he'd dreamed up. Maybe this wasn't even happening right now, and there wasn't really a Moonstone Inn, except in his imagination.

He felt her fading away from him. Already, she was a mirage.

Wednesday was excruciating, the most difficult day of his entire life, more painful than the day she'd left him. For years, he wanted his own chance to say goodbye. Now, it was here, and it was a torture worse than death.

They made love one final time. He didn't intend on it, but after they showered and dressed, he got this god-awful feeling that he'd never see her again, and it just happened. Afterward, her weeping was a brutal, incessant sound.

Before she left the car to enter her apartment in Bedlington, the last thing she said to him was, "Thanks for taking me to the moon."

Surprisingly, she didn't cry. Instead, she smiled the smile that was like the sun coming up.

≈≈

She was gone.

Leon glanced at the empty seat beside him, her gentle scent evaporating even before he left Bedlington. The car felt like the inside of a tomb.

Overhead, the sky was black in patches, gray in others, as he passed unfamiliar drugstores, banks, and schools. By instinct, he turned onto a two-lane highway that seemed like the right road out, but the longer he drove, he wasn't so sure.

He was lost. Literally. No longer part of her alien moonstone world or his own familiar one of steel mills and Stella. He was driving down a lonely, deserted highway on the day before Thanksgiving, increasingly uncertain he was on the right road.

Just then, the sky opened up and rain crashed down in windy torrents blowing across the asphalt. The windshield wipers couldn't clear the water fast enough for him to see the road signs. His mind was spinning, a horde of feelings gushing through him, stoking the urgency to find his way back. When the windshield wipers finally surrendered their battle and the rain blinded him, he pulled off the road. Switching on the car radio, he was jolted by the sound of "Nights in White Satin."

"Son of a bitch!"

The recently re-released song took him right back to her, back to those sacred, fleeting nights of their marriage. How could songs do that?—make you relive the same feelings, tear open the old injuries, as if no time had passed? Old and new pain mingling together, indistinguishable, he turned up the volume and allowed the music to drown him, line by line, inch by inch. He wept until there was nothing left in him.

When the last note played out, the cesspool that had been churning inside of him subsided. Every last emotion spun into a funnel and drained away, sucked down into a place too deep to be retrievable. A few seconds later, the downfall ceased. One swipe of the wipers, and the windshield was clear.

He pulled the car back onto the highway.

Another song started to play, one of his all-time favorites by Eric Burdon. But there was no resonance. He put it on louder, louder. No tune, no thrill, no life. It was nothing but noise. He and his music were mercifully dead. He turned off the radio, then the wipers. Everything was quiet.

Eventually, he spotted the marker that told him he was on the right road. He wasn't lost; he never had been. He knew exactly where he was and where he was going. He was in the empty, songless silence of himself, heading straight home.

THIRTY-ONE

January 1973
Noël

NOËL left California earlier than expected, returning to Willow when notified that her father had dropped dead of a heart attack while shoveling snow. Nearly the entire town turned out for his funeral.

Her childhood home was now hers, ghosts and all, and she and her son moved in. She didn't like California. It worked for Steve, but sad and enduring Willow was the place for her. Southern California was Christmas without snow, a desert in disguise, no past and no natural vegetation—just palm trees and flowers trucked in and planted overnight. Like the trees, everyone there seemed rootless, reinventing themselves. But how could they do that, she wondered, when it was our scars that defined us? Deep down, we remained the damaged children we used to be.

She spent long hours walking through the house and the Garden of Resurrection, talking to her dead family, to the photographs of her brothers that her father had left behind on the mantel (not one of her or her mother). She decided that it was the chronology of life that made it so difficult to understand. The timing was always off, out of sync. What if she'd found Leon first? What if Cynthia had phoned Adam just one day before? How wonderful it would be to die at our pinnacle, at the top of the Ferris wheel, instead of all alone in a rented room or shoveling snow, when our best moment had long eroded into the measure of all we'd lost.

≈≈

Though leaving Leon and their marriage had been the worst day of her life, she didn't regret making that ultimate sacrifice because she had done it for him. What she did regret, what she'd never forgive herself for, was leaving the Chavises behind in the process. On New Year's Day, she unrolled the tiny piece of paper with the scribbled phone number on it and dialed the phone.

"My sweet girl—" Mrs. Chavis choked. "I knew I'd hear from you again someday."

"I've been looking for you for years," Noël cried. "I even went back to the apartment once and pounded on your door 'til a glassy-eyed addict opened up."

"So, how on earth did you find me?"

"Leon gave your number to me."

"Leon?"

By then, Adam was tugging at her sleeve, awaiting his turn, so Noël lowered the receiver between them. He told her that he still had the baseball that Uncle Freddie had given him; how he remembered everything he taught him—every pitching trick, how to play Fiddlesticks, how to assemble a balsa wood airplane, how to act brave even when he was shaking inside. "I never want to forget him!"

Noël stroked her little boy's hair. The line crackled as the three of them struggled to contain their emotions.

"You have no idea how much you meant to him. No idea." Mrs. Chavis' strength returned. "So, you keep holding on to that baseball like it's your Uncle Freddie's hand, and he'll always be there with you."

"Promise?"

"I promise. What grade are you in now?"

Adam went on to tell her all about his world. His new room with the cowboy lampshades, his baseball card collection, how his third-grade teacher, Miss Masters, looked like the Quaker Oats man.

"You got my number from Leon, huh?" she said, after Adam was all talked out. "Please tell me that means you're getting back together."

"I'm afraid not." Noël spoke more softly. "He's getting married later this month."

"Yes, he told me that." She paused. "I don't know this Stella woman. But I do know the two of you. And I know what love is. And I keep on praying."

They talked for over an hour, as if no time had passed. They talked about Freddie's death from stomach cancer, how lonely her life was without him. "Come live with us!" Noël urged her. "We've got plenty of room."

"That's a real nice offer, but these old bones aren't up to moving again. Besides, how many black people you got in Willow?"

"None … but that wouldn't make any difference, would it?" Even as she said it, Noël thought about the subtle prejudice that jaundiced the town, the racial slurs she'd heard over the years—from Clive Rose, his brother Bob, and others, even Pastor Martin. Skin color didn't matter a fig in her world, but it always seemed to matter in theirs. "We've got to find a way to be together somehow—I can't lose you again!" Noël started to sob.

"There, there, sweet girl, don't you go crying. You won't lose me. We got our phones … You're too young to know how lasting memories are just yet. When we take our precious photographs off the wall and just the nails are left, we can still see them in our mind's eye, can't we? Well, can't we?"

"Yes." Noël inclined into the receiver and closed her eyes, allowing herself to be rocked from miles away by the sound of her voice.

"It's the same thing with the people we love. They don't leave us, baby, not ever. That's what God put us here on this earth for. To find the ones we love. And, after we do, it's love that stores them in that lasting place where they can never be taken away."

One of the nicer things about small towns was that their doctors were more flexible. And the late Dr. Harley Wharton's grandson, Joshua, was able to squeeze Noël in for a Saturday-morning appointment so that she didn't have to miss work at the Seashell Supper House. Her second appointment in less than a week just happened to be the same day, the same time, as Leon's wedding—the third Saturday morning in January, at eleven a.m.

The harder Noël tried not to think about it, the more the impending nuptials consumed her. Since Leon was marrying Stella in his own church, it dawned on Noël that he must have gotten a Catholic annulment declaring that their marriage had never existed. She wondered if Walt's mother had ever second-guessed her decision to let her son sail into a new life after she found herself walking alone down the Polish streets, yearning for his hand to hold. Of course, she had; how could she not?

Whenever Noël closed her eyes to sleep, the nightmares came. She saw them assembling into the pews of that magnificent church, one by one—Walt, Mrs. Ziemny, Rick, Aunt Gertie—until the jigsaw puzzle of Leon's life was finally complete. Their prodigal son had returned and was marrying the right wife this time. She'd toss and turn until the sheets were soaked with sweat, then wake up the next morning feeling physically ill, throwing up the little she'd eaten the night before.

Dr. Wharton had taken some blood and urine tests. He was going to give her the results today, along with something to help her sleep.

≈≈

His nurse called her into the examining room of the basement office of the old robin's-egg blue shingled house. As she waited, she looked around, marveling how little it had changed over the last ten years. Shutting the door behind him, Dr. Wharton cut straight to the chase. "You're pregnant."

"Pregnant?" She was dumbfounded. "How could that happen?" She tried to absorb the news. "Your grandfather said I could never have another baby. That it was physically impossible after my injury. I never planned on this."

"How does that old Yiddish proverb go?—'We plan, God laughs'? Sometimes life has a plan of its own."

"Are you absolutely certain?"

"One hundred percent. You're eight weeks along."

Eight weeks ago, the Moonstone Inn happened. She glanced at the clock on the wall, both hands straight-up. Twelve noon. Leon was now the husband of another woman.

≈≈

Walking slowly down the street, she was stunned. Being pregnant hadn't even crossed her radar screen. Why would it?

It was an unseasonably spring-like day; no snow and a high,

warm sun. Passing by the familiar storefronts in a fog, she ran her fingers over her stomach. Leon had always been present inside of her, but it was official now, bona fide, even Dr. Wharton could see him with a scientific test. They weren't annulled anymore. Out of a spun dream, lacy as Spanish moss, a life had been created.

How would she tell him? When should she tell him? Should she tell him?

When she reached home, she spotted Adam playing baseball in the empty lot across the street with a group of neighborhood boys, their coats piled in the grass. She watched him through the open curtains; watched him swing the ball round and round tight in his fist, his special, super-duper pitch, the way Freddie had trained him. None of the others boys could bat it. He took off his cap, wiped his brow and replaced it again, contented and proud.

She went to her bedroom and slid an old shoebox out from under the bed. She didn't allow herself the luxury of doing this too often, but she did it now. Carefully, she removed the series of Kodak prints from their plastic sleeve, taken on the day Bobby Kennedy came to Langston.

And there they all were again, their little band of wayfarers— Leon hoisting a giggling Adam high on his shoulders; Freddie shouting jubilantly as he pumped his fist in the air; Walt waving an American flag; Mrs. Chavis' face lit up like a schoolgirl's; her soldier brother, his eyes teeming with purpose.

She had a name for them now: she called them *moonstoners*. They weren't the ones formed by the rays of the sun, but from drops of the moon, their luminance hidden beneath an opaque veil. But when they were cut, they reflected a single streak of light, and there it was, captured forever on film.

Adam's death had brought Leon back, resulting in a new life growing inside of her, and it all seemed a circle, an unbroken circle, their streaks of light, like crossing currents, giving them a gazillion reasons to remember, to forgive, to keep seeking. And to love too much.

A flutter of life stirred within her, though it was much too early. Maybe it was just a ripple of hope.

ACKNOWLEDGEMENTS

SOME novels are so close to an author, the one you can never give up on, and *The Moonstoners* was that one for me. Consequently, it came hard, with many detours and transformations along the way. My heartfelt thanks to two sensitive and gifted editors: Tiffany Yates Martin, who believed in this novel's potential from the get-go and was indispensable in clarifying my vision, and Susan Edwards, whose insights helped me take it to the next level. I learned so much from both of them! Thanks also to Fran Lebowitz and Amber Qureshi who helped fine-tune the manuscript in its later stages.

I also want to thank the unforgettable influences of my tween years that formed the germs for this novel. To the lasting touch of a handshake from Senator Robert F. Kennedy, who came to my city numerous times while running for president, inspiring me and an entire nation to keep seeking a newer world. To the internal soundtrack that played in my brain while writing this story: the extravagantly rich and resonant *The Yard Went On Forever*, written by Jimmy Webb and sung by Richard Harris, an album I received for my fourteenth birthday that became a part of me. And to other moonstoners of my youth, those pilgrims from the Silent and Baby Boom generation who dared to share their light.

And lastly, which is always firstly, I want to thank my blood editor, my sister Judy, who suffered and rejoiced with me through each and every revision, yet somehow never stopped believing.